AGE OF CONSENT

ALSO BY JOANNE GREENBERG

AGE OF CONSENT

Joanne Greenberg

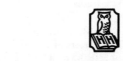

HENRY HOLT AND COMPANY
New York

Library of Congress Cataloging in Publication Data
Greenberg, Joanne.
Age of consent.
I. Title.
PS3557.R3784A7   1987   813'.54   87–11911
ISBN: 0-8050-0542-0

First Edition

Designed by Paula R. Szafranski
Printed in the United States of America
1 3 5 7 9 10 8 6 4 2

ISBN 0-8050-0542-0

TO JOHN WILLIAMS

The author would also like to thank:

Dr. Richard Zallen
Dr. Gerald Wisnicki
Interplast
Ed Myers

AGE OF CONSENT

❧ PROLOGUE ❧

MAY, 1980

They were moving through rivers of heat westward across Algeria. Daniel traveled light, taking only two assistants. They had been in North Africa for almost two years, but he had learned how to break a camp with stunning speed, to travel quickly, to use what help they found, and to destroy and leave behind everything not absolutely necessary. His fame had grown to legend and the legend told of his compassion and panache: the hands of a healer, the spirit of a warrior.

The doctor remade faces, primarily the faces of children born deformed or destroyed by accident, war, or disease. For thirty years he had moved across national boundaries as though they did not exist. He followed wars and the calamities of hurricane and flood. In such ruins and in the ruins of poverty and dislocation, he set up his camps to do his delicate, demanding surgery.

Sometimes there were hospitals, but the pictures taken of him, especially the famous ones, showed him in mountain camps, barrios, villages of stone and wattle-adobe, of thatch and mud, of corrugated tin-roofed sheds, his tall, angular body stooping into the narrow entrances made for smaller people.

At present, his two surgical assistants were Kenneth Sprague and Victoria Jamison, both very young. They had had no day off in almost a year. There were three local assistants also, and interpreters, drawn from local families. Sometimes the camps had one hundred people.

On a morning after one of the rare but total downpours of desert places, two men came into the camp. They looked like locals but they spoke good English and were clever, watchful men. "The Archbishop of Málaga sends greetings," one said. "He heard you were in danger. We are here at his order, to . . ."

"To shepherd us?"

"To shepherd you out. Why not visit Málaga for a time?"

They came out of the wind-haunted spaces of the desert into Oran, world-shocked by the brightness, busyness, movement, crowd, and noise. Sanborn sent a cable to the Archbishop. Kenneth found himself a place to be bathed and barbered. He bought a clean shirt and light cotton pants at a market stall. Victoria saw herself in a glass window and sighed. She went to a shop and got five yards of patterned voile with which she made a sari—her long, dark red hair was in a braid. It made them both look Oriental. Sanborn wore the dark pants and gray cotton fishing tunic that were his trademark.

They crossed the Mediterranean to Málaga overnight. The day was breezy and clear. At the port, the Archbishop's car was waiting for them.

There were eight in the party: the Archbishop; Sanborn and his assistants; Fathers Lactance and Solano, who were medical doctors as well as priests; the Archbishop's secretary; and the driver. They headed along the Costa del Sol and then turned up into the mountains.

To the assistants it seemed like a holiday. Father Solano told stories of the pirates of this coast. When Father Lactance was told that Victoria came from Larned, Kansas, he begged her for stories of the mythic home of John Brown, and Jesse James, and Quantrill's raiders. Kenneth's home had been Snowflake, Arizona. Both of the assistants sang their high school songs for the amusement of the priests.

During the trip, Sanborn sat relaxed, not speaking.

2

They stopped for lunch in a small mountain inn near Vélez-Málaga.

"Now," he said. "Why are we here?"

The Archbishop smiled. "We had it from several sources that there was danger for you. It seemed prudent to send help out to you and then to invite you away. The work you do so well is becoming more difficult with the present political situation."

Sanborn nodded, then said slowly, "It's not time to stop, is it?"

"Perhaps it is time to accept more help."

No one spoke.

They were sitting outside on a patio, looking down over a parapet of red flowers. As they sat, some white birds, a small flock of them, flew up from places in the rock beneath, their wings sounding like a scattering of applause. "Pigeons!" Victoria cried. "No!" Sanborn's voice was exultant. "Doves, white doves!" For a moment he raised his hand as though to catch one. The birds grouped, turned their left wings up in unison, and disappeared as though through a slit in the air.

A waiter came and told the Archbishop that he had a phone call. The Archbishop rose and left, and in a moment was back. "We are urgently needed, all of us."

He explained quickly as they hurried to the car. On the mountain road between this village and one farther on, a schoolbus full of children had gone over the edge. Men with equipment had been dispatched, but since the Archbishop's party was close, it was thought they might give first aid, and if necessary, absolution for the dying. The Archbishop gave the chauffeur a series of orders in rapid Spanish, then the chauffeur opened the doors and shouted curious children away. He turned the car, spraying gravel from the tires. They headed north, into the higher places.

The hills became more rugged, the road more tortuous. No one spoke. The car seemed to crawl around the curves in the road. Coming over a rise, suddenly, there were two men ahead and a quickly made barricade. "Just here—" one man gestured, and the Archbishop began to roll down the window to speak

3

to him when the car, which had been inching forward, suddenly shot ahead, forcing one of the men to jump out of the way and over the lip of the road. The chauffeur shouted something and the Archbishop seemed suddenly to go berserk. He half rose and began to pull at the clothing and arms and heads and even hair of his guests, trying to force them down on the floor of the car. There was a consciousness of time stopping, although they perceived that the car was moving and the world inside the car was filled with sudden light and fire and horrendous noise. Some of the guests of the day were dead before they knew what had happened, dead on the intake of breath in surprise. The chauffeur, streaming blood, gunned the well-made machine past the second barrier and around the turn of the mountain, out of range. There had been so many passengers that the living supported the dead, and so, in a sense, aided their murders because no one could get down quickly enough.

The call came to a newspaper in Madrid. The caller stated that an organization called Bloody Thirteen had "punished" the Archbishop of Málaga for his stand against Basque separatism. If innocent others had been killed, let it be known that those who chose to defy the national will could afford no friendships. Reporters called the episcopal residence and were told that the Archbishop and his party were overdue. The news came from Benegalbon, in the mountains. The Archbishop's car had been ambushed. He had been severely wounded by machine-gun fire. With him were four priests and two visitors from India. One of the priests had been hit in the hand by a bullet and was in psychological shock. Apparently the Archbishop had been spared because he had been shot first and had fallen, and then he had been fallen upon by the bullet-raked bodies of the others. A second priest had been shot so many times that he was barely identifiable. The others, the Indian couple, had been killed instantly. Another priest had been on the floor but had been killed by shots fired through the bodies of the others. The chauffeur, who had also been shot, had steered the car away and taken it

4

almost to the village farther on before loss of blood caused the shock that incapacitated him.

It was not until the next day that the Archbishop, from his hospital bed, issued a statement that was read by an aide: "God rest the souls of good Father Lactance and of Father Perrine, my secretary. Father Solano will recover to serve once more, but what have these killers done in their wrong-headed violence? Our guests were Dr. Daniel Sanborn and his two surgical assistants, people whose deeds made them candidates for universal praise, not for death in so terrible a way. We had come together to plan means by which his great work could be carried on more smoothly. Our meeting would have resulted in help for the very people these arrogant terrorists claim to champion. As for us, we and our nation stand humiliated because it was here on our land that such noble lives were so tragically ended. God rest and bless the souls of all of them."

Had Daniel Sanborn been less famous, news would have gone to the families first. His celebrity made the telling more cruel. Victoria's family learned of their daughter's death on the evening news. A neighbor told the Spragues.

✥ 1 ✥

Vivian had been shopping, which she usually did on Thursdays. She was in a cab; the cab had gone through the park and turned south on Fifth Avenue.

"Something's blocked up there—" the driver had said as they came close. "It's TV; there must be five of them vans there—" and then they had pulled up, or tried to, and Vivian had realized that the group had gathered at her house.

Because of the crowding, she had gotten out at the corner and gone toward her gate. The Sanborn house was one of the few private homes left on Fifth Avenue. There was an apartment building next to it. The TV people must have moved to her gate to keep space open in front of the apartment. Probably a celebrity was visiting. Several months ago there had been a film star—perhaps they were making a movie.

As soon as she approached and turned in, people started shouting at her. The bags made her fumble at the gate. Everyone poured in behind her, passing her and running ahead. Did she have a statement? What were her feelings? Had she ever heard of Bloody Thirteen? None of it made sense. There had obviously been a mistake. Doris was at the door opening it, and the people were pushing, and suddenly there was a hard push

6

from behind and Vivian lost her balance. She thrust a hand out, dropping a package.

"Do you have any bitter feelings against the Archbishop?"

"What?" Now she knew there must be a mistake. She did not know an archbishop.

"The Archbishop," the voice said, "because the bullets that killed your brother were meant for him."

She heard herself say, "I have three brothers. I don't know an archbishop."

The voice answered, "Daniel Sanborn; your brother Daniel."

Suddenly there was a dislocation, a difference in the way her eyes and ears were working, as though poison had been injected . . . The day went white to the lips and icy cold. She kept thinking, "This is silly. This is very silly." Before her was the dim shape of the doorway. Doris had opened the door. At last she got inside. The whiteness had gone red and teeming as though her brain were showing her its own working. The doorbell rang fiercely. From the recesses of the house, the phone began to ring.

As she stood helplessly in the front hall, her brother Steven came. "I thought there might be press here—I had no idea, this—this." He told her the little he knew.

"But Daniel wasn't in Málaga. There must be a mistake. He was in Algeria—why was he with the Archbishop? What was he doing in Spain?"

Steven sighed. She knew the question was meaningless. "I don't know," he said.

Paul came half an hour later bustling and planning, as he did in times of grief. He had been this way at their father's death five years ago, and their mother's last month, a death from which the pain in Vivian had not yet died back into sorrow. Even his speech was oddly clipped and short. Paul was a lawyer; his thoughts were well organized and mostly of legal matters; which were Daniel's papers? Was there a will? Steven put in a call to the Cardinal's office. They told him that a Father Keith and a Father Louis were on their way over. Then he sent for a man from his office to give a statement to the press. They sat and talked about the disposition of Daniel's body. Vivian watched her brothers working and thinking. They seemed satisfied with the plans they were making. She sat on the couch opposite them with her hands in her lap and thought about Daniel.

Had his body been badly disfigured? His face? How terrible it was that he, who had been so passionate about the control of his own life, about independence, autonomy, had had no control at all of his dying. How he would have hated that. She hoped she wouldn't have to see pictures of— She wanted to remember him as he had been when that photographer, yes—Koizumi, took the photographs that were now famous. She had loved those pictures of Daniel's tall, gaunt body, his bony nose and suffering eyes. One saw his anger at injustice, his sternness in protection.

Paul was asking again about Daniel's papers. Vivian was thinking about the calls she had to make. She had a heavy schedule of appointments and the spring shows to cancel, and she desperately wanted to call Abner, who was in Stockholm now and would soon be leaving for Germany. Suddenly he seemed much farther away than Sweden. She needed the comfort of his voice. Steven was still making arrangements. She reached for a piece of paper and began listing the museums and private collectors to whom the now rash promise had been made: "I'll be there."

Steven was talking to her. He and Paul had agreed that Daniel should be buried in Spain in the closest Jewish cemetery. A memorial ceremony here. On and on. Vivian got up from the couch and walked to the kitchen to tell Doris to make tea for the people who would be coming. She passed Paul talking on the phone. He looked more at ease as he spoke about Daniel's death than he ever had in Daniel's presence. Things could have been saved, when they were young, she thought. Years ago, all of them might have learned to love one another, instead of splitting up into two camps—she and Daniel, Paul and Steven. What could she have done then, to heal things? Mother had tried, Father, too, in his way. Too late, now, too much polite defense. She remembered Paul and Steven going off to college, how they smiled and deflected everything with good-mannered ease. She had a picture of herself figuratively running after them, shaking her finger, officiously, demanding that they love Daniel. She had played mother too much when she was a child and had grown up to be no one's mother. Passing Paul's back, she went into the kitchen and told Doris about the tea. Then she went back to the silent room where Steven sat, writing memos about Daniel's funeral.

In a few minutes, Doris came in to ask some questions. These days she wore an ancient and faded taffeta maid's uniform with a yellowed lace collar. Her feet bothered her and she had on a pair of run-over felt slippers. She had been crying. Vivian wondered why. Then suddenly she thought, it's for me, and the tears, which had not come before, began to well in her eyes.

Her brothers didn't notice. She fought the tears away. It struck her again that neither of the men had spoken about Daniel himself, not a word, no hint of reminiscence. They were talking about the funeral, the safe deposit box, and a will. Now and again they sighed as if with satisfaction, checking off things on the list they were making. Daniel had never married—no complications there. Because he had been away for so many years, no one in their families knew Daniel. No one of them would really miss him, and no one would be there to help in the healing by memory that Jewish custom strives to produce. Only she— only she—

When he had come home he came in secret and stayed in the room with a view of the back garden. He rested and read and took baths in which he spent hours napping. That had caused her great anxiety. He would not now, not ever, drown in a bath. She wept a little, quietly.

It was time to get up and go to the phone. The museum first—Blake. He would call the people from Connecticut. Travel agent. The trip to the porcelain exposition in Dresden would have to be canceled. The June show in London—maybe not. She thought she might go upstairs and use the phone in her parents' room, which she had occupied with her mother since her father's death and where she now slept alone. She wanted

9

to watch the westering sun go down over the park and put out the day. As she rose, there was the sound of the bell, a harsh, old-fashioned sound, a sound to summon servants. It would be the priests.

Doris appeared in the wide hall. Paul made the *tch*ing sound with his tongue. "She looks absurd in that uniform."

"I've told her," Vivian murmured. "She thinks it's elegant."

"Those slippers—" Steven said.

Vivian answered a little tartly. "Remember how good she was to Dad and Mother. How kind. I haven't got the heart to tell her— She has bunions and her feet hurt."

"What about your clients?"

"I seldom meet them here. When I do, I answer the door myself and use the library."

"Hmmm," Steven said.

The two priests who came did not have clerical collars. They wore dark suits and had discreet pins in their lapels, crucifixes with crowns. They were vigorous men in their late thirties, with firm handshakes. One was the New York Archbishop's secretary, Father Louis. He took Vivian's hand in both of his, expressed his condolences, and then told her that he had read her careful evaluation of the Sudermann 1810 dinner service. "I have a small cup-and-saucer collection myself."

Vivian was surprised. "Those evaluations are usually confidential—"

"—unless one's friend is a potential buyer—"

She nodded and began to think about Daniel again, which made her know that there had been a ten-second respite, a moment of the old, happier life that had been hers two hours ago.

The other priest, Father Keith, was saying that it would be he who would be traveling to Málaga. He had a good grasp of Jewish funeral practices. The four men began an urbane murmur: burial, memorial—the Archbishop was planning a large public funeral for the two fathers who had died. There were other dispositions to be made. On and on. Vivian sank away again, nodding automatic approval when a question came her way. Shock had been succeeded by lethargy. In a pause, she asked, "Where are his things?"

They were caught slightly off guard. "The things he had with him," she said.

Father Louis understood. "They are being sent. The vans—the surgical camp things were in Oran. They seem to have been moved somehow. We are trying to locate them. Inquiries have already been made."

Paul asked some more questions about international law and how the forms were to be filled out. Then Vivian said, "And were there—were his assistants with him?"

"Yes."

"Were they also—?"

"I'm sorry," Father Keith said, "I thought you knew. Both of them were killed along with the Archbishop's secretary and another priest-physician who was in the party."

"What were their names?" Vivian asked.

Steven and Paul looked at her, and she saw in each his movement of politely restrained impatience. In Steven it was a tightening of the jaw, the barest bite of his front teeth that made the muscle bounce as he trapped and bit down on his annoyance. Paul's two fingers went up and down, up and down; not quite drumming, but admonishing, as though if he could, he would pull her away. These very things, small perhaps, unacknowledged, had been bequeathed long generations ago by fathers and mothers. Father drummed, mother clenched, and the years and the generations bore these fragments along, changed, in new faces, to the faces of children, nieces, nephews, on and on down the years. The Sanborn chin, the Sanborn walk, the quality of the silence between words. Vivian was suddenly weeping quietly. "Excuse me," she said, and got up. "My brothers will make the plans. I'm sure I'll approve of what you decide. Please help yourself to tea and cake. Thank you for all your help."

It was all she could say. A rage of sorrow was blowing away the screens she had hung to keep it genteel and contained. Control was going. She left the room tear-blinded, counting on a lifetime of remembered steps, where one turned, where the hall led past the library and up the stairs to her room. There she could let the torrent loose, to rage and cry, and she was thankful that the house was so heavy and old, so thick with dust and carpet, massive furniture, and habit that she could explode a bomb in that room and not be heard.

But when she got there, the tears stopped abruptly. Across the hall was the room Daniel used when he came to them, exhausted and drawn. The robe and pajamas he used were still hanging there, his bed waiting, a few books—murder mysteries, notebook, pens. In the bathroom were the thick towels he liked, his toothbrushes and hairbrushes and nailbrushes. In her own room, in the closet, were the albums she kept: one of pictures of the family; one, Daniel's. New material would be coming. She would have to set up a table in his room. There could be hours, days to be there, lost in remembering. She looked forward to it with something like yearning. She saw herself sitting in that room serene and busy, eased of this anguish and of the unlooked-for anger that had begun to close her throat almost to strangling.

She moved the dressing-table chair to the closet, got up on it, balancing carefully, and took the albums in her arms. They were bulky, and overbalanced her for a moment. She had not realized that shock and sorrow could make her clumsy. She got down from the chair shakily and took the albums to the bed.

She opened Daniel's album, knowing that the first picture, the single, haunting picture she had stolen to keep years ago, was the one she would look at most carefully this time. It had been taken on the boat by another passenger and sent to the family then, in 1928. It was indistinguishable from a hundred other war pictures—of wars before and after. He stood like any one of a thousand displaced children, pale and alone, wide-eyed with world-shock, in borrowed clothes. Like those others, he had a card wired to the buttonhole of the rough coat he wore. It made her think of a parcel. His legs stuck out stiltlike from under the coat. He was six years old, a refugee child from a family of starving, beleaguered people living in Jerusalem. This shock-muted child, pulled by her parents from Arab raids and famine and the threat of worse, had come to be her adopted brother, had grown into a language, a habit of life like hers, and then had gone beyond that into a worldwide language, worldwide habit, worldwide fame. He had been compared to Albert Schweitzer, to saints of the past. He had chosen his difficult life, consenting to its impossible lacks and discomforts in order to give the total service that such a life demanded. The child waif who had once screamed in terror at being put into his own bed, had for a quarter of a century gone homeless in service to the wretched of the world. His death should be causing sorrow, not anger. She wondered why she felt so much anger.

Paul and Steven were downstairs but were the priests still here? She got off the bed and in her stocking feet went out of the room, taking a sweater with her because, although it was May, it seemed cold to her. She went down. The low voices were murmuring away in the front parlor. When she came to the entrance, they all rose. The anger went red in her. "We're an old family," she announced quietly. "Did you know?" She could see she was shocking her brothers. "Like the Rothschilds, we are old enough to have a coat of arms. People who see it think we were tailors or cloth merchants, because our coat of arms is literally a coat, or rather, a tunic. But it isn't a tunic, it's a special garment. It was called a sanbenito. Our name used to be Sanbenito. We got that name during the Spanish Inquisition. Do you know what a sanbenito was?"

They were all staring at her. "Vivian, really—" Steven said.

"A sanbenito," she continued, "was a garment used by the Inquisition to humiliate forced converts who were found to be insincere in their conversions. They wore that garment to the stake. It was sleeveless, a very simple piece of clothing, mass-produced, I suppose. When we left Spain, it was with that name, Sanbenito. The family went to France and then to Holland . . ."

"Vivian, these men are not interested in family background . . ."

The priests demurred. Vivian went on smoothly, with the gracious smile and gesture she had learned in classes no longer

13

taught. "The Inquisition thought it could force consent. You can see how silly that was, can't you?"

"Vivian, this has been a shock, and—"

"Our branch came to the American colonies in 1640. We were founders of the first synagogue in New York. We kept the name Sanbenito until about 1840 when the American family decided to change it to Sanborn. We kept the old rebus on the seal. Does it not seem ironic to you that one more of us should die in Spain in the company of an archbishop? I understand those burnings were made quite the occasion with the highest prelates in attendance."

"Vivian!" Paul almost shouted. They were all stunned.

"It's family history," she said ingenuously. "You can tell the Archbishop to look it up." And then she stopped.

She had been impolite. She herself was shocked at what she had said. It was because everyone seemed so satisfied with his part in Daniel's obsequies. The Church was going to have a big event; Paul and Steven had been given scope for their competence. The press had something to report; rabbis and ministers the world over would have subjects for sermons on his life. She alone had the sorrow and the secrets, the grief and guilt which had been paved over by the family so deeply year after year that on its spot nothing grew. She said, "Excuse me; the day has been very difficult," and went upstairs to look again at the label-wearing waif in the photograph and the other photographs of the man he had become.

The top part of the old picture was bent. Daniel had found it once and had been in the act of tearing it up when Vivian caught him and took it away and hid it. He hated that picture, and was anxious about it the way one might be of an incriminating letter. "They won't know," Vivian had promised. "No one will ever know." Rash promises. Sanbenito.

14

❧ 2 ❧

Years after Daniel's adoption, Vivian had asked her mother how it had come about. Henrietta Sanborn was a woman of great reserve, even for those times. She had weighed her words carefully. In 1927, she had said, England had Palestine as a protectorate. Its protection was not complete. For generations, roving Arab bands had raided Jewish settlements and the Jewish quarters in the cities and suburbs. There were riots in 1920 and 1921. The Arabs were alarmed by the increase of population caused by World War I's distress, and the Zionist movement was bringing even more people to Jerusalem. There were inevitable clashes.

"A man came and spoke in the synagogue about the problem," Henrietta said. "The man begged us, as people in comfort, to take Jerusalem's orphaned or destitute children into our homes. He had a list of such children, and on that list was a five-year-old boy with the name Sanbenito—Daniel. Your father made inquiries and learned that in the 1820s one of the branches of his family had gone to Cyprus and from there to Jerusalem. He made contact with the family. The parents were dead and the children were being cared for by an aunt. They and she wished to stay where they were, but Daniel was the youngest and most frail, and she wanted to send him to safety. Of course, we made plans to bring Daniel to America.

"Just that name—we could have missed him so easily.

"It was the sixth of February, 1928, a windy, overcast day, I remember. Your father took Steven to the Fifty-ninth Street pier and they met Daniel. The poor boy was clanking with amulets against the evil eye. We brought him home. We were unaware . . . we did not take into account . . . how different his life must have been."

Even then, Vivian had smiled at her mother's reserved understatement. The boy had been a panicky animal, shrieking in a street argot of Yiddish no one could understand. Beds terrified him, and for days he had huddled in a corner beneath a blanket. The etiquette of eating frightened and bewildered him. He was suspicious of bathing alone; the very size of the house and number of rooms caused terror. For three days he woke from nightmares wailing. During the day, his eyes followed the family but he would not move freely through the house.

Vivian had been ten years old, busy with school and friends, but eager for this new excitement at home. She had been annoyed with her brothers, neither of whom seemed eager for another brother. They had resented Daniel from the start. His looks, his muteness, his bewildered manner clashed with their picture of themselves and their family. Raised with gentility and reserve, they used form as a weapon. They slid away. It was easy enough—Steven was getting ready for his bar mitzvah, Paul had his activities, sports, friends. With barely a greeting, they were away to their busyness. "So long, Dan, see you later . . ." They never touched or were touched at any point of their lives longer than form demanded.

Vivian saw them doing it and she ran headlong to Daniel's defense. At ten she was just beginning to outgrow her dolls. She took him on. Soon she became an officious and bossy parody of a mother. She taught him how to eat, how to sleep, how to speak, how to use a handkerchief, take a bath, answer a telephone. The little boy was a stranger to tact, subtlety, and discretion. Instinctively, she felt that his life in Jerusalem had had none of those things. Years later, when she had words for it, she thought he must have been beaten hard and kissed just as hard, screamed at and then forgiven with tears, and mostly ignored without apology. Her parents' well-bred remonstrances and gentle smiles of affection were more foreign to him than the new language, which was spoken without a movement of face or hands.

Daniel learned with stunning rapidity. He ate the strange food with the dozen implements that brought it to his lips, used the beds, the baths, the clothing. In a month he was in school. In another six, he was speaking English well. Paul and Steven's disgust and dislike evolved into a well-modulated indifference which Vivian never forgave. She had thrown herself into the project to instruct her elders and they had merely shrugged her aside. From time to time, Henrietta Sanborn had tried to heal the breach in the family. She spoke to the boys, to Vivian. She arranged summer picnics and canoe trips to include all their friends. She encouraged friends for Daniel at school and among the younger children of her set. Everyone bore her attempts with tact, did what was easy. Paul and Steven slid away from the stiff, remote youngster as silk slides off crystal. Because, although Daniel learned well, his learning seemed to come without spontaneity or joy.

Pictures in the family album: summers at Lenox, Christmas vacations at Lake Placid— Had no one noticed, looking through all those viewfinders, seeing all those prints and putting them into the albums, how much alike the pictures were? Daniel was always standing apart, unsmiling. The two older boys were always aggressively seigneurial with tennis rackets or ice skates; their hands held props like scepters. The parents sat in genteel oblivion. Closer to Daniel, Vivian would be standing angrily, or later, as adolescence claimed her, looking like someone who had wandered in from another picture. As the years went on, the split became even more obvious. Except for the obligatory family shots each summer, Paul and Steven were shown with

17

groups of friends—all in white ducks for tennis, all in plus fours for golfing, a life in the pictures of little but summer sports and winter sports.

Then there was each one's year abroad. Paul was interested in law and spent his year studying European legal systems. Steven was sent to the Orient on jobs for the family's import business. Vivian's year was spent in Europe with relays of chaperoning aunts. Her trip began the interest and study which would become expertise and a specialty in the authentication and evaluation of antique European porcelain. All the album showed were the customary photos of ship departures and arrivals. Vivian turned the pages of what seemed like a golden time. It wasn't, of course. The family was charitable and the Depression awful. They watched the horror building in Europe; Raphael, the father, went on two trips himself to attempt with others an organization of rescue. Many of these pictures were not dated, but suddenly the date was obvious: 1941 and Paul in uniform, then Steven. Vivian, already quite knowledgeable in the properties of ceramics, got work in a small, secret laboratory doing research with porcelain for military applications, particularly in bomb detonators and thermostats. Daniel went to college.

The family had not thought to give him more than a routine medical examination when he had come from Palestine. The doctor then had said he was malnourished but healthy. He had never complained of weakness or pain. Everyone was surprised when the army rejected him for "cardiac abnormalities." Childhood illness, the doctor said. Minimal symptoms but low endurance for stress. Remembering all the flurry that had gone on, the consultations, the specialists, Vivian smiled. Daniel's life had been one of incredible physical stress and endurance. The army doctors had measured the wrong things.

She got up and walked to the window. The day was going down. Already children were coming home from school, walking on the park side, talking and laughing under the trees, their shadows pulling over the stone wall. It was almost five. There were still calls to make, and at last the one to Abner in Stockholm. They were to have met in Dresden at the show next week. At least she wouldn't have to tell him about Daniel's death; the newspapers would have done that and he would be prepared for her not coming.

Their friendship had been a constant surprise and joy to Vivian. They had met at a show in Venice in 1960, and again the next year at one in Geneva. He had been a curator then, in Israel. They saw each other two or three times a year, until Abner moved to New York. His wife had had a stroke during the birth of their second child and their families had wanted them home. Vivian and Abner's friendship had stayed a friendship for years, growing imperceptibly deeper and warmer as time went on. Abner did not want to leave his wife, who had been in a nursing home all these years. Vivian had wanted to take care of her parents and provide a place for Daniel to rest and regain his strength. They saw each other often in New York. They felt freer when they met abroad at shows. They had gone to Russia together and to the exposition in Florence. Abner understood her so well that she wouldn't need to explain herself. He would understand the pain she felt in Daniel's death, and the anger. They had talked about marrying when they were free.

All the freeing had been done on her side. First Raphael had gone, then, last month, Henrietta. Now Daniel. "I feel necessary," she had once told Abner. "Daniel comes for only a few days every three or four months. Sometimes it's only twice a year, but I'm necessary then." At first, Abner had been a little resentful of Vivian's devotion. Three times over the years she had been in Europe at a show or for an evaluation, had gotten a two-word telegram from Daniel, and had sped home to care for him. In Belgium she had gone while Abner was out, leaving a note for him. Later they had argued, a rare, painful argument. "And if your wife had had a crisis—" There had been a time of coolness between them because of it, but in the end it resulted in that special knowledge Abner had of her. They were friends first.

Vivian felt that, helping Daniel, she had played a part in something of profound importance to herself and the world. She had made possible a physical and psychic haven. He would

19

come to her exhausted, sometimes trembling with fatigue and hunger. Sometimes he had to sleep away the miasmas of jungles and the fevers of deserts and the despair of a hundred encampments. Once he had said, "Those people are all the same in one way: their eyes follow you, lines of eyes. Their faces are different colors and shapes. They wait in heavy clothes or in no clothes at all, but their eyes are the same. Their eyes follow you everywhere."

She knew nothing of his medical work or of the politics or economics of the places he visited—he had never told her the details of where he had been or how he worked, or problems, conditions, victories, losses. He sent her postcards telling her where he was, no more, yet she had known herself involved deeply and irreplaceably at the heart of his enterprise. With Henrietta's death, this had not changed; with Daniel's death— For a moment, she saw herself as her brothers seemed to see her, a delicately bred, unworldly woman, whose expertise was in an area far from present realities, who was now to be as protected as the porcelain she studied and who was also a responsibility along with the great old house, and to be handled with some of the same mixture of affection and impatience. She wouldn't be able to stand that, but she had no idea of what to do. Her work was intellectually stimulating but it would never demand the complete self Daniel's needs had demanded of her. The pictures in the album began to blur before her eyes. She closed it and opened Daniel's book.

There was his high school graduation picture, but she saw now what she had not seen before, that even as he stood with the other graduates, he stared straight out of the picture, like someone unconscious of the camera or the group. College—he had gone to Raphael's college. He had done well there, but he never told her, then or afterward, what the experience had been like for him. She thought how he must have been uncomfortable, singled out as odd in looks, in manner, as separate as ever. In that class picture his façade was smoother. It was hard to tell the difference between withdrawal and dignity, but there was still no hint of softness or a smile. Daniel had requested that his year abroad be deferred. The war had just ended and Europe and Asia were in shambles. Could that money not finance his start in medical school? Raphael had been surprised. He had not imagined Daniel as a physician. Vivian had a clear memory of that conversation. They were at Lenox, all down by the lake. Daniel, who was good with his hands, had been fixing the motor on the outboard. He and Raphael spoke with studied casualness because they did not understand each other and knew it. Daniel said that his college grades were best in subjects allied to medicine, and that as a medical researcher he could find the intellectual challenge that most interested him. Raphael accepted the explanation. That fall Daniel entered Harvard Medical School.

It was possible in those days to work one's way through. Daniel tutored in chemistry and took shifts in the hospital lab. Raphael had protested that this was unnecessary. Vivian felt her father's hurt. There seemed to be, in Daniel's refusal, more than self-respect; it was plain to Raphael and Henrietta that Daniel did not consider himself fully a son. Paul had gone to law school and Steven had entered the family business in fine style. The family was proud of Daniel but their pride was careful, and it had a sad edge. They all knew that a certain kind of happiness was lacking in Daniel. He was respectful and never failed to send a note or to be present at family parties or religious holidays. He gave no less, but he gave no more. Each one in his family felt the absence in his own way. No one ever spoke of it.

Vivian was then unable to help. Her work during the war had been highly classified and had transformed her reserve into secrecy. One of the other workers in the lab was Bernard Eitzer. They fell in love and married, but Bernard was obsessed with the war and in 1944 lied his way out of the lab and joined the marines. "I couldn't *fight* in the lab," he wrote to her. He was never to fight anywhere. He was sent to the Pacific and killed in Okinawa on the beach. They had been married for two years. Vivian's work had become part of the technology of the atomic reactor. At the end of the war she left the lab and began to find that her prewar interest in the art of porcelain and her wartime knowledge of its nature gave her a special expertise. She recovered in its beauty. She began to study very seriously.

Daniel had graduated from medical school with honors. Vivian looked at his graduation picture and sighed. Perhaps she was trying to read too much into the expression she saw there. Everyone in that picture was trying for a kind of chilly professional dignity.

It was after medical school and internship that Daniel finally asked for his trip, a trip to England to study the new medicine developed there during the war. Raphael and Henrietta were enthusiastic. The waiting had made sense. Time abroad might make him easier in his surroundings, and they were glad that he was following family tradition. They and Vivian saw him off to London.

And then he disappeared. Their letters to his address in London were returned "Undeliverable." Vivian's came back scrawled "No such person." After a month of silence, there was a single card from Zurich saying that he was safe and well but had changed his plans. There was no return address. Two more months went by without a word.

Three months after he had left for England, Daniel returned, gaunt and silent. To Vivian he had the same look, in an older face, that he had had when he had first come to them. What had happened to him? Where had he been? Why had he not written? He would say only, "Please, don't ask me. I can't answer you now." He rested at home for a week, returning to the pattern of nightmare wakings he had had as a child. At the end of the week, he apologized for the pain he had given them. He had been to places beyond the reach of mail. If he had caused them anxiety, he was sorry. He told them he had changed his mind about going into medical research and had decided on a clinical specialty: plastic surgery, specifically, maxillofacial reconstruction.

They had all been shocked by his physical condition. Now they were amazed by this decision. Vivian remembered her father's confusion. The choice seemed random and disappointing.

22

Plastic surgery—wasn't that face-lifting, nose fixing? So many of Vivian's acquaintances were having that kind of surgery it was possible to tell whether a nose had been done by Miller, Camperman, or Steen. Daniel explained that only part of the specialty was cosmetic in the usual understanding of the term. In any case, he said, he had decided. He would have to learn a good deal of dentistry and much more facial surgery. Dentistry? Vivian smiled as she turned the pages of the book, remembering the confusion of those days. Once again she had come forward to interpret her brother to his adoptive parents. Vivian listened carefully to what Daniel had to say and then went to a friend's brother who was a surgeon and got him to explain the specialty. He recommended some reading. Vivian read and then explained to her parents. They had been worried and then deeply hurt by Daniel's disappearance. His return in pain and silence deepened the hurt. They knew something terrible had happened to him, that he had been spiritually injured in some way on the trip he had taken. It saddened them that he would not speak about where he had been or what had happened. It was Vivian again who suggested that he might have gone to Jerusalem, to try to find his old family. No one had been able to ask him.

It awed Vivian to think how far Daniel had gone from those beginnings. She marveled at his resoluteness, his power and endurance. Her friends said he was a difficult person to know. That was because his work and the path he had chosen gave him no time to cultivate charm or a skill with small talk. In the book, the pictures began of Daniel's surgical camps and articles in praise of his work in India and Korea. Then, Peru, the wonderful pictures in Peru . . . Vivian paused over them for a long look. It had been years since she had studied them; their power remained unchanged. And here were the two pictures by which the world had come to know Daniel Sanborn.

After the earthquake of 1970, a renowned photographer, Kenji Koizumi, had gone to Peru and had photographed Daniel as he worked among the mountain people there. Koizumi had taken many pictures: the doctor, the patients, the villages and the land, but two portraits had won awards and had caught the interest of a public hungry for images of compassion and sacrifice. The more popular one showed the doctor taking a tiny, starved child from a young assistant. The child faces away from the viewer and the camera catches the doctor's hand coming up in an almost maternal gesture as though at once to reach for and to protect the child. The expressions that have been captured are riveting and complex. In the assistant's face, a terrible sorrow; in the doctor's, exhaustion, indignation, and a dogged tenderness. As a poster, the picture had been used for many purposes by many groups. In 1972 it had been used by a Vietnam War protest group, which had run its motto underneath the picture in stark white print: GIVE A DAMN. In the other picture the doctor sits almost asleep in the light of a small kerosene lamp. In his posture one can feel something of what he must have seen; the exhaustion so great that sleep could come even in that twisted and uncomfortable position.

She looked at his strong face. Could *he* have suspected during the growing years when she was defending him how strong his will really was? Her eyes began to water and she realized that it was not with weeping. She was straining to see the pictures in the dying light. The sun, surprisingly, had gone down over the park. The day was over. She had outwitted for two hours the suffering that waited all around her.

As the quality of the light changes in the city, the quality of the sound is transformed. The daytime sounds are composite: morning mixtures of voices and machines that blend into a cataract—noon, afternoon, the cataract rises and falls in force and composition, but after twilight the sounds become discrete—the hiss of air brakes, tires protesting too sudden a stop, distant sirens, nearby sirens, bus doors, even the steps of shod feet, now not all, but each, one by one. The birds had stopped, suddenly, as they do when the light goes, as though they have never been crying all day in the trees and busy in the sky. Here and there a bat was beating the twilight high above the park. Laughter of young people passing was suddenly clear and discernible, separate from all the other sounds in the city. And so it would be all night long.

It was now too dark to read, to see the pictures she had mounted in the album, and read the newspaper print, which over the years seemed to have gotten smaller. She looked at the clock by the bedside. It was eight-thirty. Doris was probably keeping dinner; Paul and Steven and the priests must have left long ago, imagining that she had been weeping and not wishing to disturb her. She was used to being considered by her brothers but not consulted—taken care of, but by their ideas of what that care should be. She would have wished to apologize to the priests, thanking them politely for their visit. In the days to come everyone would want to spare her the details, when the only comfort would be forgetting and the only forgetting would be in attention to details. She went down to relieve Doris of the wait.

❦ 3 ❦

It had been less than a month since Vivian had presided over a house of mourning. Paul and Steven returned for form, their families came, the priest came, and Vivian's friends. Others came who were distantly acquainted because Daniel Sanborn had been so famous.

Vivian sat dry-eyed through the short memorial service and the traditional mourning.

The visitors brought none of the reminiscences, the stories of personal involvement or affection, because none of the callers knew Daniel Sanborn well and some of them not at all. They spoke of what they had read but not experienced. Even Abner's many calls from Sweden did not touch her sorrow. Nothing did. When Steven came, Vivian met him in the hall. He looked into the living room and saw that there were only three people there. He asked Vivian which of his children or grandchildren had come to sit with her. She felt annoyance rising from some unexpected depth. "They don't have to check in. I'm not counting who came and who didn't."

"Vivian, it's a family obligation; I would simply like to know who fulfills that obligation. Did Marjorie come—Jacob? Joseph? Ruth? I called Ruth particularly."

"Then ask her, not me."

"I don't know why you are being difficult about this. I'm asking which of my family has come."

Vivian's anger was out of all proportion to the statement that provoked it. "Let's talk about Daniel. This is *his* shivah. Why did you never take the slightest interest in him or his work? Why, when we learned of his death, did you express not the simplest regret to me?" She was amazed at her own response. Steven's request had been a simple one and typical of Steven, who was a little frightened of the new laxness in the younger members of the family. Vivian had no idea why she had erupted at him again. She could have put off his request in her usual way of dealing with him—vagueness and passivity ("Well, I'm not sure . . ."). These and sudden errands elsewhere were her defenses against her brothers' displeasure and had been for years. Sometimes her passivity angered her. In her work, she was forthright and even courageous. Her recent stand on the Sudermann collection had gone against well-known authorities in the field. Two-thirds of the pieces in the 1810 dinner set were the finest porcelain from a factory in Bavaria that had shut its doors in 1862. The rest she had not authenticated. She was reasonably sure they were excellent imitations. Her detailed analysis was being studied in museums all over the country where there were large, "complete" collections. It amazed and shamed her that this courage did not travel into her brothers' country. When she was with them, she seemed to become a kind of child. Like a child, she was now having a tantrum. For all the sudden self-indulgence, her temper had done nothing to relieve the pain. There was no catharsis in it, only puzzlement.

On the third day, Doris came in while Vivian was sitting with Paul's wife, Mollie. "It's going to be on TV," she said. "They just announced it. They're going to show part of that Spanish funeral." The bell rang and Doris went to get the door. The day was humid, smelling of mustiness, the breath of buses and trucks and standing water, and Doris was limping with her bunion. Mollie looked after her with distaste. "My girl wears a nice apron thing—neat, but not—"

27

"Oh, really?" Vivian said, as much like her usual self as she could manage. "Doris likes taffeta."

"But it's gone green."

"I know."

They sat uncomfortably on the ritually uncomfortable mourners' stools. Doris brought in a box of flowers. "These came," she said. Vivian looked at the card. It was Kenji Koizumi's.

"He was the photographer," Vivian said to Mollie, "the man who took those pictures."

"Yes, I know. He's very famous."

"There's an address here—" It was in the city. Vivian realized that she might call him, that she might even go and see him. Perhaps he might have some memories of Daniel in Peru.

Vivian and Doris sat together on the couch in Raphael's old study and watched TV to see the memorial service in Málaga. The Archbishop was still in the hospital, the commentator said, but people had come to pay tribute to Daniel Sanborn, the assistants, and priests. The cameras moved on lines of people filing past the three caskets and the table displaying pictures of Daniel and his assistants. Vivian stared in amazement. There were people of every color and kind, women in saris, men in long tunics, tall Africans in dashikis, veiled people, and hundreds of others in ordinary street clothes—"a line," the commentator said, "that symbolically stretches around the world."

There was a short biography of Daniel, his college, medical school, some of the countries to which he had gone. There was nothing about his having been adopted, of course; no one knew about that. Vivian recognized the picture of his medical school graduating class as it was shown. There were mentions of the others who had died: the physician priests and then the assistants and their pictures. Victoria's picture showed her proud in her nurse's uniform. Kenneth Sprague looked remarkably young and vulnerable, grinning. The commentator said that he had dreamed all his life of working with Dr. Sanborn, that he had trained for that purpose. Their bodies had been sent to their families in America. The pictures of both of them brought tears.

"I should have gone," Vivian murmured almost to herself. "Someone should have been there to stand among all those mourners." They were showing one of Kenneth's pictures, taken when he had first come out to Algeria. He and Daniel were standing side by side looking like Bedouins, but the boy was grinning in that wide-open way of young Americans.

"You couldn't have gone," Doris said. "You had to be at the service and to keep the house open."

"A form," Vivian answered, "a silly form for no one who really wanted or needed it. I should have been there."

They were showing the mountains, the place where the horror had happened, and then the car. "Don't look," Doris said. The commentator was saying that no one knew anything about Bloody Thirteen. Some of the twenty-five or so assistants that Daniel Sanborn had had over the years were . . .

"Twenty-five assistants?"

"That's what he said."

"I never thought about that—that twenty-five people knew him, shared his work, his discomforts, twenty-five people who could explain . . ."

"What?"

"The things he never explained to me all those years, all the times he came home so desperately tired."

"I remember, and that fever and the diarrhea—"

"They knew him better than we did—better than anyone here . . ."

The scene had returned to the lines in the cathedral courtyard. "Statements are being collected," the commentator said, "from the mourners . . ." There were voices, many at the same time, moving forward and then receding, a tapestry of voices: "He came to our country during the terrible flood . . ." "His caravan crossed our hills. No place was too poor or remote . . ." "All the faces, the deformed faces of our children . . ." "When he stopped at our villages, he sought out those on whom no one wanted to look . . ." "He changed them. No one needed to be hidden in pity." "We in Greece . . ." "To us in Bangladesh . . ." "To us in Peru . . ." "He came to Ethiopia . . ."

The tributes went on and the lines moved and then there was a break in the line as it went past the three caskets and the table. A tiny girl came out of the line. She was in a faded, flowered dress, and she wore a small garland of white blossoms in her dark hair. Alone and without shyness or hesitation, she took the hand of the man who had just passed. The table was too high for her to see over. She was asking to be lifted. The man took her in his arms and as he did, she lifted both hands to her head and took the garland and placed it before Sanborn's picture. Then she said something in her high, childish voice, and the man translated, and the commentator listened and then said in translation, "This is from the children."

❧ 4 ❧

And then the letters began to come. They were a scattering through the mail slot; then, as the weeks went by, more and more. Vivian had gone back to work but had canceled her foreign trips until the fall. She was now very busy at home. The letters and calls had become a flood. She had thought at first to read and respond to each as it came in, but now there were so many that she was forced to take them up to Daniel's room and sort them out in stacks for reading. They came from all over the world in a dozen foreign scripts and in labored English. There were effort-frayed notes from schoolchildren and letters from people who had worked with Daniel in Bangladesh and Peru and Somalia. There were letters from child-patients now grown and from admirers in big cities and small towns and villages who had never known Daniel Sanborn but who had admired him and wanted to honor his work. Paul came once, and Vivian took him up to Daniel's room, and showed him how she had set up a long table on which the stacks of letters were spilling out of their outgrown boxes. She picked up one of them from a smaller pile.

"A woman named Eunice Comber was in Tibet with Daniel back in 1956. She says, 'How wonderful it was to be part of that small caravan that made so steady a way through so dark a forest.' She lives in Westminster, Maryland, now. A person might—one might even go down and visit her to find out . . ."

"To find out what, after all this time?"

"What it was *like*, what they actually *did*; to hear the little things, the little funny, sad details of their lives. I missed that in the shivah. Remember Mother's mourning days? All the old stories, the old memories, the double and treble versions of everything, and laughing about how differently we saw those things—" Paul shrugged. There had been too much unsaid even at that time. Vivian went on, "I've made this list of Daniel's places and the years he was there. I hope to trace the line he took, and here are the people who worked with him in each place. The list is very sketchy because I've had to depend on the accounts that mentioned the names of the assistants, but now, with letters coming in, I'll be able to fill in much more and maybe I can write to people and ask them with whom they worked . . ."

Paul had had no interest in Daniel's work; the very room they stood in, the sunniest in the house, was one he felt had been taken from him and even now demands were being made on a sympathy and concern to which he was not equal. Vivian couldn't help herself. "Listen to this," she said, and read: " 'I was blessed to work with Dr. Sanborn in Africa from 1974 to 1977. His medical work illumined his spiritual gifts to those poor and wretched people. May Christ and His Blessed Mother grant him peace and rest among the blessed in Paradise. Our convent has dedicated a series of novenas to his memory and has offered masses for his intention.' This is from a nun, a Sister Mary Binchois. The convent is downtown, right here in the city."

"That's nice; it's a fine tribute."

"I could see her, perhaps, a visit—"

"Look at the letter again, Vivian. What do you have in common? How could you talk to her at all?"

"Maybe it would be difficult, but here's another letter—

32

It is given to very few of us to see greatness personified. To even fewer is given the privilege of taking part in the enterprise of a great man. I had this privilege because I was with Dr. Sanborn in Vietnam and other places in 1966 until early 1968. His path led from there to other challenges and other dangers and finally to his death to which he went, typically, trying to help others. He was not compromised in this death, forced to be less than he had been, and to very few is this also given. For whatever you did to arm such a soul, the world owes you its thanks.

It's from a Dr. Alston Fletcher and he's here, in the city also—Seventy-third Street at Central Park. I could call him up—I could see him easily."

"But why would you want to? He's been years away. What did he say, 1968? That's twelve years. He didn't ask you to call. These are simple letters of condolence, that's all. A call would be an imposition, really, improper, and you've never done things like that. It worries me, this extreme interest in Daniel's life now that it's past. You served him for years, but it's over—I—we were hoping you would be done with serving, now."

"I loved Daniel; can you understand that?"

"Of course. I also realize that we—Steven and I—never did. I didn't even like Daniel, and that must have hurt you. It divided the family in an unfortunate way. We couldn't feel what we didn't feel, though we might have been more gracious to him, I suppose. You have to remember that he did his part all those last years. I won't go into that. You know it all well enough."

"You never—"

"In any case, it's in the past, and a reasonable person puts the past behind him. It seems morbid to me, the fuss, the letters, the list, tracing the assistants, those books you keep. Of course one mourns a loved one, but all this—you seem to be saying that this—interest of yours, will go on into the future, beyond the time it should. That worries us. You see that."

This time Vivian's resentment was dense with other emotions. Did he really think she could so easily forget work vital to her and to the world? Here was a last chance to see into the reality of Daniel's life. He had always been too tired or ill to talk to her about the places, the people, or the work itself. The moment passed and she stood before Paul, silent, neither confirming nor denying what he had said. The stillness, giving nothing, embarrassed him, and he kissed her on the cheek and got ready to leave. "Think about what I've been saying. Next week we see Sam Bernard—Tuesday morning. We'll pick you up at ten, so we can all go to the office together." He had not asked whether she had the time free. It was typical.

Sam Bernard had taken over the family's legal work when Guttmacher had retired. Daniel had been happy to give the lawyer access to his safety deposit box, for which Vivian paid and had the key. Vivian knew she should read over the copies of things Daniel had given her, but she went instead back to the room where the letters were.

The idea of contacting the nun and the doctor—people who were here in the city and who had known Daniel in a way she had not—had taken hold of her imagination. Would it be an intrusion, as Paul said, to press a claim dead and discharged and perhaps forgotten years ago? Or were those people waiting a chance to be asked, to set a mark on those years, to tell a story, to say *amen* to the words that had been said at a faraway funeral to which she had not gone?

Another letter—from Bangladesh: "How could I have found a husband and made a family, disfigured as I was . . ."

From Angola, through a missionary: "Now my face smiles when I do, is sad and angry when I am. How great a treasure is this common thing."

And another:

I won't sign my name, but I was one of the doctor's assistants. I failed him and myself and I stole money from him to get back home. I have always been ashamed of what I did. I repaid the money long ago, but I was too ashamed to tell the doctor how sorry I was to have left him like

34

that, and that I lacked the strength to keep going. I wish I could tell the person who worked with [words crossed out] that [words crossed out] did all they could, but I was not strong enough. Everyone admires Dr. Daniel Sanborn but those of us who were not equal to his vision admire him most deeply and truly of all.

Of course there must have been those also, people who became ill in the field, or for whom the work was too hard, the hours too long, the isolation too great. She thought she should have known this long ago. Now she was surprised that it had never occurred to her. She looked more carefully at the letter. There was no signature. The letter was typed and she could not tell from the style whether it had been written by a man or a woman. She took up another. It was from Bolivia:

We were with Daniel Sanborn in Peru for two years. We met as his assistants, and married afterward. We wanted to continue in the way he had shown us. We became doctors, came here to Bolivia, and set up the Daniel Sanborn Clinic. It is now a small hospital with trained local associate staff and nurses. We treat everyone who comes to us through financial arrangements with private donors and some help from churches in America. We have been able to fund studies of preventive nutrition. Would you do us the great favor of telling us Daniel Sanborn's birth date? The people here wish to give us a festival day. We feel we would honor their love more deeply if we chose a day more special to us than any private anniversary of our own.

(Signed) Stephanie and Richard Van Zandt

This letter she would answer now, although not with Daniel's birth date, which she did not know. She would tell them what date he had arrived in America, which was February 6, and, setting her wishes above her brothers' admonitions, she would tell them of Daniel's adoption. She was excited and happy to be doing this. Peru. That would mean they had been with Daniel

35

some time between 1970 and 1974. That was the trip when Koizumi had done the picture study. She went to the album and turned the pages until she came to his story: "*Wars and Faces*: Kenji Koizumi captures the life of a dedicated surgeon."

The *Life* photo story showed the two famous pictures, the one with the child and the young assistant, and the one later, with Daniel sitting alone, almost asleep. Was that assistant Richard Van Zandt? She had recently looked at the two pictures and at the others, but for Daniel, not for the assistants or patients, not for the buildings or the people. This time she studied the scenes of camp life, pictures of the vans, the waiting people, the operating room set up in a village building of corrugated metal, the village pump where the people stood around the assistant who was getting water. It was the same young man. There were pictures of the local people cleaning the operating room. Vivian wondered if Koizumi had more of those pictures somewhere, the ones the magazine did not use, pictures she could search for the other assistant and for the visitors who sometimes went out to see Daniel. There were some names in the body of the piece: Cecelia Counselman and Douglas Likens. There was no picture of Cecelia; the man must be Douglas. She had hoped to see the young people who had met and would marry. "Silly romantic," she murmured.

She reached for the chart. If Cecelia Counselman and Douglas Likens were in Peru at the time Koizumi was there, did the Van Zandts come after? She filled in the names under the ones she had already listed in parentheses. Now there was a way to find out. She would write to the Van Zandts in Bolivia and ask them who had served before them and who after, and to all the assistants she could send that question, which was fair, she thought, and not an imposition, and could be easily answered. She sat down to write her letter, but in the back of her mind there was the thought of the other letter she had seen, the unsigned one, and a little shadow of sadness moved across the page. Someone was sitting with her, grieving. Someone was with her whose story she would never know, but who grieved more deeply than any of the mourners who had come to sit ritually in the house.

36

Who was he? Why had he failed? He had taken money and had repaid it, but years and years later, he felt the pain of failure still, the guilt of betrayal.

The day they were to see Sam Bernard, Vivian got dressed in a dove-gray suit and had an early breakfast. She had gotten the papers which Daniel had left in her keeping. The packet was small.

She knew both of her brothers resented Daniel's share of the inheritance, which was substantial. They resented even more his use of it, and of almost all of Vivian's portion as well, to fund his work. When the article and pictures had come from Peru, Vivian had spoken of them with pride. Steven had shrugged and said, "It's a great thing, but it's financed with four generations of money other men made. It's money he never earned and will never pay back." Paul had been a little gentler. "Yes, Vivian, he's doing fine work. Please keep your principal in the bank. Send him the interest. Please don't sell anything for him—" But she had, three times, and there had been a coldness since, and more silence surrounding the mention of Daniel's name.

There was the bell. She got up, ready. Steven was waiting. At the curb was the cab with Paul inside. Almost immediately they began to tell her what to expect.

"Daniel wouldn't show me his will, although I advised him to, simply because taxes can be punitive if the instrument isn't written to protect the funds. I do know that he now has comparatively little. He never reinvested. The income from interest—I think it all went—uh—out there."

"He did wonderful work with that money," Vivian said.

Paul sighed. "We've been through all this before; let's not do it again."

"No, let's not." Steven's voice was very slightly edged under its softness.

"He had no interest in money in itself," Vivian continued.

Steven snorted. "That's a bit grand, isn't it?"

Paul said, "Especially since he had to finance his work. I asked

Father before he died to give Daniel his share in a trust—to let someone—it didn't have to be one of us—invest for him, and give him an allowance out of it, funneling the rest into a good investment plan."

"I think Father knew how little you liked Daniel."

"I won't lie about it, I didn't like him. He was sullen as a child and ungrateful as a man. Vivian, have you forgotten how he disappeared, just disappeared, going God knows where and not letting the family know? Letting Mother and Dad worry and imagine he had been kidnapped or murdered somewhere?"

"That was about thirty years ago. Surely by now we can forgive him for that."

"What changed? Did he come to Father's funeral? Did he come to Mother's? Did he stay one day beyond *his* immediate need?"

"He was in central Africa when Father died, miles from anywhere. He was in Algeria miles from a town when Mother died. I don't even know if he had the news when *he* died."

"Did he ever call or write or make a trip to come and see us? Was there one Passover Seder, one New Year's dinner, one birthday letter?"

"Might he not have felt your coldness?"

"This is ridiculous," Paul said. "Nothing is served by arguing. The people we're discussing are dead and there's nothing more to be done."

"But both of you are angry"—Vivian's voice rose a little—"and you've been angry for years—at Daniel and at me."

"Well, this is not the time—"

"When is? We didn't really sit shivah for him, really talk about him, about our relationship with him." The cab pulled up at Bernard's offices.

"Paul's right," Steven murmured. "It serves no purpose."

They rode up in the elevator without speaking. When Sam Bernard came to guide them back to his office, he said, "I was very sorry to hear about your brother's passing. He was a remarkable man. Remarkable."

"Yes," Paul said, "he was."

38

In the office, Bernard started right away. "I've gone over what Dr. Sanborn gave me. It's not complicated in any way. Your brother made a will ten years ago and this past August he came in and looked over what I had. He wanted his share of the family business to go to his sister, and his remaining shares in the family stocks to be divided equally among the three of you. There is one other beneficiary named. I don't know if you are aware of this, but Dr. Sanborn was the recipient of many prestigious awards. The Dutch government gave him a humanitarian award, which came to thirty thousand dollars, and the king of Sweden in 1978 gave a grant of money. There have also been many awards from private foundations, here and in Europe. Most of the money was used to further his work. Some remains; there is presently a total of one hundred and ten thousand dollars." The three family members looked at one another.

"I didn't know," Vivian said.

"He was," Bernard answered smoothly, "a man of great reticence and modesty. He said that the plaques and certificates, etc., were in the attic at your home. I don't believe he ever added up the *money* from these awards. Alex Guttmacher kept it, and when I came on as your attorney, the doctor sent the checks to me. I've written to the beneficiary of this money. It was difficult to get in touch with him personally because, as you know, he travels a good deal, but I will soon be able to make personal contact."

"Who is the man?" Steven asked.

"Oh, didn't you know? I assumed you all knew."

"It must be someone in the work," Vivian said, "someone who will carry on—"

"No," Bernard said, "it's Jack Ripstein—you know, the nightclub comic, uh—Jack the Ripper."

Vivian was dumbfounded. They all were. Paul and Steven said nothing. She sat in the silence for a moment, then blurted, "But my brother doesn't know any comedians—" She laughed, trying to explain. "He visited New York no more than four times a year, and then he always preferred to stay in. A *comedian*?" She looked at her brothers. Their formal faces had slid down over their eyes, cheeks, lips. Still, Steven's jaw muscle worked its work, Paul's finger rose and fell, tapping out his message: I am annoyed, I am annoyed. "Do you know who he is?"

"I've—I believe I've seen him on TV," the lawyer said, "but I think he does most of his work in nightclubs."

"Pearl and I saw him in Las Vegas two years ago when we were there," Steven said with distaste. "We walked out. It was a filthy act. Filthy."

"But I don't understand—"

"There is nothing to understand." Paul's finger was drumming faster. "He made the bequest, and unless we plan to contest it, which I don't see us doing, all we can do is forget about it."

They sat still. At last Vivian said, "Did he know? Did Daniel know how much there was?"

"He must have—not exactly, because of interest accruing, but last year when he came in, we added the amounts up. I remember the figure then was about ninety-eight thousand. I talked to him then about municipal bonds—he had been putting off making a decision. He seemed to want to keep that money liquid. Of course, at his age, long-term investments began to lose their attractiveness—"

"I don't care about that!" Vivian cried. "Who is this man, why did Daniel do it?"

Paul's drumming stopped. He stared at her, and said, "Why should this action of his be different? He was never clear with us, never open. He kept secrets, he kept himself away—"

"What did you ever do to help him get closer?"

"What did *you* ever do but keep him close, and yet he gave you no more. I hated the way he used you all those years and our house as some kind of comfort station!"

"It's the family home; he was family, too."

"Never, no, never!"

Only then did Vivian know the depth of Paul's anger. Under no circumstances would he have raised his voice or spoken of such personal things in the presence of a stranger if he had not been very, very angry, but her anger overwhelmed it. "You haven't read the letters. You haven't seen the pictures. You don't know what a hero Daniel was. You made him aware whenever you saw him that he was with us on sufferance, that he wasn't family. I think I resent most of all your telling me how long my grief should last and what form it should take. You both believe you can do this; I resent . . ." And suddenly, while she felt the utter validity of what she was saying, the rage in it made her stop. The sound of her voice had bounced off the wall and come back to her, strident and bitter. A wave of nausea came from the ebb of rage. For a moment she was dizzy. Then that passed and she was standing where she had gotten up to stand without realizing it. They were all dead still, shocked, in postures gone strange with keeping. Bernard had one hand held over an ashtray; Paul's drumming finger was raised; Steven, eyes wide, was rising to come to her. The breath went out of all of them. She, too, breathed and breathed again; the sound of her breathing was ragged in the silence of the room. Absurdly, she brushed off her skirt and straightened the bow on her blouse.

The lawyer was the first to recover. "These moments of suffering, of family grief, are very difficult," he said.

"Is there anything else?" Steven asked.

"Yes—your signatures on these papers. There is also a private letter to Mrs. Eitzer." He handed Vivian a letter, making an effort to turn to her as he did. Turning back, he made some remarks about taxes. They were all speaking as quietly as people in a hospital.

"You have the figures for the accountant—"

"Yes, here they are."

"We'll see that he gets them immediately."

"That would be best."

Vivian, like a patient, spoke in a normal voice that sounded unduly loud in their restraint. "Why should Daniel leave his money to a comedian? Who is that man?"

They all stiffened for another blow, but Vivian was only tired, bereft, and confused. She wanted almost desperately to be back in the house, home in Daniel's room with his books, with the letters and articles, or resting from an exhaustion the source of which she could not guess. The lawyer shook hands with all of them, being so careful not to patronize Vivian that his care was patronizing. They left at last.

In the street, Paul tried to hail a cab; Steven said nothing as they waited. Vivian had crossed a line that must never be crossed: she had made a scene before someone who was not family and had violated that border of manners and courtesy at which their self-respect began. Their manner said: you have disappointed us.

All afternoon Vivian lay in her room which still had all the old furniture and many of the sickroom necessities of Henrietta's last days. She was exhausted from her outburst, and it had done her none of the expected good.

Sometimes she cried, ragged sobs for whom she did not know. She realized they were not for Daniel, shamefully, not for him. She knew she had allowed Paul and Steven to make too many financial decisions, to patronize and protect her too much. She had let this happen because silence kept the peace and was easy. They had given her reasons, all good ones, for not calling Daniel's assistants, finding others, making the picture whole. But she wanted to see the people who had worked with Daniel, to meet and talk to some of them, to learn what the life had been like. She would do so. A kind of contentment came with that decision. She fell asleep.

She woke at two in the morning from a toil of dreams. There was a light rain falling. She went to the window and pulled the curtain to look at it. She thought about Jack Ripstein, Jack the Ripper. Why had Daniel given him all the money from his awards? She was puzzled, and though she would never admit it to Paul and Steven, a little hurt. Daniel had undoubtedly been saving the money for later use, but why had he not told her about the bequest? She stood at the open window and let the rain come in on her, fine as scarf silk, and as smooth. She had a memory of a sudden, powerful compulsion in the first days after her father's death. She had opened every drawer and closet in the house, seen the contents, inspected them, touching, looking, turning everything over as though to experience and remember, for the last time, her father's house.

The Archbishop's secretary had contacted Paul about the contents of Daniel's suitcase, and a list was being sent, along with such personal effects as he had had with him in Málaga. So far, however, they had found no other records or papers, none of the medical reports one would have assumed to be part of such an enterprise as Daniel's. No one seemed to have any idea as to where they had gone. An inquiry was being made in Oran.

She remembered the letter Bernard had handed to her. It was still in her purse. She turned on the reading lamp and went to the purse, got the letter out, and opened it. It was typed, neatly. She was disappointed; she had hoped to see Daniel's handwriting, a spiky code that looked like marks on a lie-detector tape. Daniel had never been a demonstrative man—there were no messages of love or farewell.

The money part of my estate has been taken care of by the usual means. My personal possessions are yours. The honors I have received are in a box marked with my name. It is in the attic. There is also a small collection of books and a few gifts from our parents. I want you to have the honors most meaningful to you, but pick out from among them, and the other things, some mementos to give to the assistants who were with me longest. I know you kept records so this should not be too difficult.

"But there were no records!" she cried to him. "I didn't have more than a few of the names! I couldn't get them!" It was so like him to want to do well by others, and then to delegate the good deeds to her, thinking she knew what she could never know. One sheet of paper, no list of names or places at all. She almost groaned. He had been thoughtless to those around him; his eyes, his mind, his life were on another plane: humanity. Sometimes he missed what others needed on simpler levels of daily use and concern.

Yet his command validated what Vivian herself had been

43

moved to do. He had thought it would be an easy matter for her. He knew she had collected articles about him and his work. Perhaps among his honors she would find more clues to the places he had been. There were also the postcards and notes he had sent from the cities through which they passed, but those, she had since learned, were marks of passage only, not destination, which was often a place from which messages were not easily sent.

So it was that at three in the morning Vivian was up on the third floor, in the silent, spider-kingdom darknesses of the trunk room, working quietly so as not to disturb Doris, sleeping in the maid's room across the hall. She had found the marked box in a place by itself behind the ell of the chimney. She had opened it and begun to take out the awards one by one, some not even opened. There were scrolls and plaques, and medals of all kinds. Over the years she knew he had brought them one by one in his suitcase and put them up here. Some of them were in scroll cases or boxes, but many were wrapped in tissue paper which had not been disturbed. She felt tears again, but for the first time since his death, she was weeping simply for Daniel, and for the world which had lost him.

5

She wrote two letters: one was to Sister Mary Binchois at the Convent of the Sisters of Mary; one was to Dr. Alston Fletcher at his office. She said only that she was trying to organize Daniel's papers and would appreciate meeting with them to ask some questions as to the years and places of their work with her brother and about the names of other assistants. She included her phone number for ease in making the appointments. She mailed the letters early, excitedly, and then, with the desire to do more, wrote to the Van Zandts in Bolivia, asking the same questions, and to the other assistants who had written. Then she called her grandniece, Harriet, leaving a message on the answering tape. Harriet called back in an hour. "I'm so sorry, Aunt Vivian, about not coming back when I said I would last Sunday. It was only that I—"

"That's not why I'm calling, dear. I'm calling to get some information. With your knowledge of the theatre, I thought you might know—how would I contact a certain performer?"

"Oh, that's easy. His agent." Harriet was delighted. She was not used to being consulted by her elders.

"And where . . ."

"You'd call *Variety*, or if he has a card, SAG or AFTRA. What's up?"

Vivian lied. "One of the women in our theatre group once saw this man and said he was good. I thought we might use him for a fund-raising evening—"

"Oh? Who is it?"

Vivian took a breath and imitated Steven's sister. "I had the name somewhere—it's on a card in my purse. If you'll wait a moment—"

"Oh, that's all right; I just thought I might know him."

"Well, thank you for the information. How are you, dear, are you working hard?"

Vivian had learned to dither so long ago she had forgotten where. It amazed her still that people never seemed to tumble to it. It was a trick, a little shameful since it was dishonest, but it saved feelings and above all, it saved family peace. And if they had never caught on to the lie in it, it was because they didn't want to. Vivian called *Variety* and was given a number for Seymour Feig, Ripstein's agent. It was as simple as that. She decided to use the same lie again. "Someone in our theatre group . . ."

"He's in Atlantic City now. He's been held over and he'll be there for two more weekends. He's at The Breakers."

"If the group can't make it then, where will he be after that?"

"Vegas."

"Las Vegas?"

A sigh. "Yes, that's right, Las Vegas."

Vivian was cheered. "Do you think he might meet with one or two of us afterward, for a short interview—we have a group newsletter."

"That's up to him."

"What would be the best way to approach Mr. Ripstein?"

There was a long pause. "Well, you could write him a note and tell him the group is there, that you came down specially. Tell him that."

Steven had said that Ripstein's comedy act was vulgar—so vulgar that he and Pearl had walked out. Daniel had had no sense of humor, but he did have a sense of propriety. It seemed out of character for him even to know such a man. All his prize money—then it was suddenly clear. She had heard . . . Didn't Bob Hope and Danny Kaye go to entertain at hospitals in war zones and places where people were isolated and lonely? It was that, it must be: Ripstein supported himself with work, perhaps in questionable taste, and then gave shows for Daniel's children around the world, physical comedy, stunts that wouldn't depend on language or cultural background. And, of course, *then* . . .

Then of course he should have one of the medals or scrolls Daniel had been given. There weren't enough for all the assistants. There would have to be choices made. She jotted a note about listing the awards and their countries of origin so that she could match them with the assistants who had done the longest service. She remembered once having charted the porcelain factories of France and Germany that came and went between 1650 and 1900. On this chart most of the information was missing. When she was finished, she picked up the phone and called the bus line for its Atlantic City timetables.

Doris had put her head in through the open door. "How's it going?"

"I forgot about lunch."

"It's on the table but I didn't want to bother you." Doris stood hesitating and then said, "In all the trouble, I guess I was wondering. About the house. I thought you and your brothers went to the lawyer about getting rid of it, maybe, being so big and only the two of us here—"

"We didn't discuss that. If we do sell the house, you'd go wherever I went."

"Oh." Doris's face relaxed.

"Is that what the problem was?"

"Yeah, that was it."

"I'm sorry—I never realized what you would be thinking."

Doris smiled. "You have troubles of your own."

There was a call from Alston Fletcher's office. When the doctor came on, he said he would be glad to talk to her about his two years with Daniel Sanborn, even though the experience had been so long ago. Would she also be interested in seeing something of the procedures they had used in those days? "Your letter stimulated me to get out some of the older cases, the kinds we worked on then—"

"I would like very much to see them." Vivian was delighted.

"I jog during the lunch hours," Fletcher said. He had a somewhat prissy voice, the syllables enunciated precisely, teacher-perfect. "I thought we might walk in the park. I need to get out and if we walked for half an hour, we would still have time for the office and some pictures of what we did."

"What day and time would be most convenient for you?"

"Perhaps tomorrow about noon?"

"I read your letter more than once," Vivian said to the doctor. "It was very moving." They were walking briskly in a part of the park she had not seen since her childhood. The doctor's pace was daunting. Everyone was out today; the paths were almost as crowded as they were on weekends. There was the smell of sun on asphalt, of young bodies breathing and of some of the rankness of their feet. The doctor jogged for fitness, but even his stroll was, to Vivian, like a forced march.

"I admired what your brother did," Fletcher said, "but I sometimes wondered why he chose the remote corners of the world. He was superb, you know, as a surgeon; quick, sure; he had a wonderful eye. He could have gone anywhere, anywhere at all."

"He did."

He gave her a quick glance. "I mean to any hospital."

"How did you come to work with my brother?"

"After internship I looked for a place where I might work with a variety of cases. The big university hospitals are the only ones that do reconstructive, and they have to apportion the available work among the students—you assist, but you don't see as much in a year as Sanborn dealt with in a month. I had heard about him from a doctor who had visited them in Iran and I thought I might try that. It was risky because residency is the time when one makes the contacts that begin a career, but chances to operate would be ten times greater than in an ordinary setting."

"So you went as a student rather than as a humanitarian . . ."

He smiled at her. "Does that disappoint you?"

"It surprises me. The privations . . ."

"Why should ambition be less a motive than disinterested goodwill? Except for Cecelia, my partner out there, I stayed no less time and did no less work than any of those who signed up to rescue a suffering humanity. I was interested in doing the job right, not simply 'bearing witness' like poor dumb Mary Nell, who assisted after me."

"I suppose that's true."

"I was with Sanborn for two years, learning and working, and when I left him I was as widely experienced as I would have been with five years in an institutionalized program." He had speeded his walk; he was almost trotting. "Oh, there were niceties still to learn; the gulf between what he did and what hospitals do is far wider now, but the skills I got in the field were invaluable. I know you're his sister and I hope this doesn't offend you, but I truly believe he could have done more good in a well-equipped hospital than roaming the landscape the way he did."

"—and yet it was the way he chose . . ."

"Yes. I continued to recommend gifted students to him for six-month stretches, that is, if they would go. Peter Hulme, Jimmy Kim—both were my men. I've recommended others, but they didn't want the experience at that cost."

"What was it like to work with Daniel?"

He paused, considering. "We were in Vietnam, but we did a lot of traveling. We went between the lines and in front of and behind the war all the time. Sometimes there were even hospitals, sometimes even good ones. It wasn't always a tent in the mud."

"Please, Dr. Fletcher—could you slow down—I'm winded and I'm getting a stitch in the side."

He gave her the look the fit give the unfit. "People used to

49

look that way at fallen women," Vivian said. "I'm over sixty and I have no Olympic plans."

"One should never let down," Fletcher said, with a little sanctimony in his tone. "Do you know that there were women your age in the New York Marathon? People who let down become flabby."

"Why is that a sin?" she asked.

He did slow down. Her stitch eased a little but she was still short of breath. Fifteen years ago his behavior to her would have been considered incredibly rude. Now it was she who was holding the outworn idea. Nothing sweeps cleaner than fashion.

"What was it like? How was it to work with Daniel?"

Fletcher paused for a moment. Vivian suddenly realized that some of the people she would be speaking to might hesitate to be frank with her because she was Daniel's sister, but after a moment, Fletcher said, "He was the leader. He had to maintain that, even on a three-man team. He had to be a bit removed, Jovian."

"But how did that affect his assistants in those remote places? In some of them, nobody else spoke the language . . ."

"We adapted. Formality is necessary in a situation like that. Otherwise, you let down."

Let down. Vivian was almost sobbing for breath. "Wasn't that an extra strain?"

"Yes, but the rewards were great. There was tremendous intellectual stimulation in learning, in detail, the art of what we were doing. The body has laws and defenses. One must learn what he can use to his advantage, how to plan."

"You mean how to time the surgeries?"

"We'll go back to the office in a few minutes, and I'll show you what I mean. Sanborn had to be totally single-minded, and because he had a captive population, in a sense, he was free to experiment with techniques until he found what would work and what wouldn't." It sounded cold. He perceived she was feeling this. He stopped. "Look at the results," he said. "Skin is an organ, you know. It varies from person to person and with age and gender. What works on a child of six will not succeed with a man of sixty. There is no other way to learn that, and to learn it in all its specifics, except by trying it out."

"Oh," she said.

"Clinically and coldly."

"And the patient?"

"Is asleep."

"And when the patient awakens?"

"Our patients got the assistants—Cecelia and me, and then Mary Nell. Besides assisting, we were there to supply the bedside manner, if you will, and the explanations through a translator, and the instructions for care." He had speeded up again. Vivian sighed and trotted beside him.

"So the assistants did more than help in the operations; they were doubly vital to Daniel's work."

"I suppose you could say so."

"You mentioned other people."

"My partner was Cecelia Counselman. She was there before I came and after I left. I never think of those days without remembering her. She certainly was an original."

"Do you know where she is now?"

"I have her address somewhere. A homely woman—built like a barn. She smoked constantly. She was a wheezer—not fit at all, but she was a good surgical assistant, except for her weight."

"What difference did that make?"

"The human face presents a small area, especially children's faces. Aesthetic considerations loom large at close quarters. She did, however, have the bedside, or should I say, matside, manner."

"Have you heard from her since?"

He laughed. "Oh, yes, I get a Christmas card every year. You should see them! Frosty the Snowman, Rudolph. My practice is quite an exclusive one—my patients' tastes run to abstracts or museum Nativity scenes. Cecelia's card always glares out like a rhinestone in a diamond tiara."

"Yet you haven't the heart to take it away and hide it in the desk—"

"Well, the secretaries like her cards, and the young patients. The children always like hers the best."

They had begun to race back, two strides by Vivian for every one of Fletcher's. She began to jog. "Take longer strides," he advised.

"And the other assistant—you mentioned a Mary Nell."

He shrugged. "She came to replace me—when my time was over. I heard she didn't work out. Breathe deeply, but not quickly. You're not breathing efficiently."

"My legs are shorter than yours." He slowed down, perhaps realizing that at her age she might collapse on him. "Do any of the others keep in contact with you, or only Cecelia at Christmas?" Vivian was still puffing; the words came out two at a time.

"No, we don't communicate with one another at all. I was trained by Cecelia and a woman named Mariella Marcantonio. Mariella was a beautiful woman. Her reason for being with Sanborn, I heard, was some kind of vow, some promise to God. You see, Sanborn couldn't depend on a supply of doctors—not out there, moving around the way he did, bad food, bad water— the wars and the warring tribes. He got nurses, which he needed for the reasons I said, and he trained them to do procedures far ahead of what they would be allowed to do here or in any conventional setting. He ruined them, in a way, for work anywhere else. I told him that, once."

"And what did he say?"

"I don't remember, but he didn't change. I wonder if the assistants were bitter about that when they got back to the real medical world. I trained Mary Nell Anderson, whom I didn't much like. I wonder if that was why we never wanted to keep in touch with each other. More than once Cecelia suggested that we write—a kind of newsletter, but it never happened. Class differences, maybe, but veterans do, after all—we were certainly that."

They returned, at last, to the office. The doctor was obviously underexerted. His secretary was eating her lunch at her desk, a salad and whole-wheat bread. Vivian sighed, feeling dizzy with the exertion. Food and exercise that had once been the province of faddists was now so popular it came at one from everywhere. She knew, for example, that Fletcher had missed his meal on purpose and would not make it up later. There was a primness about his gestures, a punctiliousness about his body language that was almost feminine. It reminded her of Daniel. She studied him as he moved. Daniel had had that same deliberateness about his gestures. It put people off. Perhaps it was a function of the kind of surgery they did, small, delicate cutting and sewing in the smallest muscles and bones in the face. And which came first, the work that made the man, or the man who chose the work: detailed, patient, even fussy?

Inside his office, Fletcher opened what looked like a closet, but was a small room. There were three chairs and a slide projector. "Show time," he said. Vivian recalled that he was also a teacher. "I put these out so you could see some of what we did in Vietnam and particularly the techniques I learned from your brother."

"I'm very grateful," Vivian said. Fletcher had not perspired much on the walk, but in the closeness of the room Vivian smelled some of the tang of his working body. He would have to shower before he saw the afternoon's patients.

He dimmed the lights. First slide. "This is a burn case."

Vivian had to catch her breath. No face. No nose. No mouth. A black-blotched ball, like the moon. "Lots of edema," he said. He was sitting behind her, "so you can't see where her eyes are. They're here and here." Vivian was riveted to the sight, horrified. He was showing her with a little pointer two puckers in the burned sphere. "Are you going to be sick?"

"No, but . . ."

"Study with me, then," he said smoothly, "and you'll be too interested to be sick. The problem here is making a nose, making lips, and grafting here and here," and he put on another picture. "Now, the swelling's gone down a little and we've debrided the burned area and there are a few landmarks. See the cheekbones?" Vivian looked, wondering what it would be like to be someone whose face had been burned away, who couldn't scratch

53

an itch or touch at all . . . and the pain . . . "This is the next picture." She was trying hard to concentrate on the problem. She wanted to cry. The picture was very similar but lines in different colored pencils had been drawn all over it, curved lines, hooks, concave and convex curves, arrows pointing. She tried hard to look at them. "The arrows are placement instructions, the other lines activity instructions, the colors are flesh levels. The human face, of course, is three-dimensional. Like land features, its planes rise and fall. I use colors for that."

"I see," she said.

"The blood supply has to be taken into account, too." Another slide: "My first grafts here, here. Most men do it *this* way first. Sanborn did it here, here, you see? The first surgeons went for cosmetic effect; Sanborn always preached function. He used to teach that with function comes mobility; with mobility, muscle; with muscle, shape; and with shape a natural look. He was right; everyone teaches that now, but back when I started they thought one should sacrifice function for looks. Remember the old face-lifts?" She didn't, but she nodded. "All right, look at the third stage—the blue pencil, the green. The mouth is back here—lavender. This surgery was eyes. All the expression of the upper face is in these muscles . . ." He went on explaining as the face, slide after slide, became slowly transformed into that of a young woman. "Some loss of function—here, here. We're not God—there's only a little feeling in the nose and upper lip—and there'll be drying of the skin. This graft has no oil glands. She'll need to be careful about windburn, sunburn, all that. There are no surface nerves *here*, but it is a face."

"How long did this take?"

"The whole process took about two years because there was a month or two between surgeries." He put up another slide. "This is a bad cleft palate—a harelip. We used to spend days doing these one after another. It's a surprisingly common deformity in some parts of the world. Some of these babies can't nurse and they die. Some can nurse but solid food gets lost up in the pharynx; here, see?" Second picture. "This is Sanborn's technique again. He *always* marked, and that way he often found things others missed." Fletcher showed more pictures: deformities of birth, accidents, disease. "The patients used to ask for the marked pictures. Sometimes they would steal them."

"What for?"

"They cut them up and sold them for amulets and casting spells."

"He did keep files, then?"

"Oh, yes, we all do—it's the best teacher there is."

"Of every patient?"

"During my time, yes. We went into the countries following calamity or war. We stayed on to do faces. Some of the trauma patients only got one or two pages and we sent the case with the patient, but all of the reconstructions were photographed and filed, at least three times. When the files got too cumbersome, he sent them away somewhere. I was going to ask if he had sent them to you."

"To me—no. I never even thought about there being files until Daniel's death."

"I'd have liked to have seen his development, what changes he made and what he tried and discarded. A lot of what he tried he had to discard because of time constraints and supply. Studying his patient's picture is like reading a surgeon's mind."

"I wish I could help you. I have no idea where they could be."

"He had to send them somewhere; we always traveled light. Even the X-ray machine was specially adapted, and we were a good deal more mobile than anyone thought."

"You mean village to village?"

"I mean country to country. I was with him from March 1966 to April 1968 in Vietnam, supposedly. Actually, he'd do a circuit, a bunch of operations, and then go on to another area and come back for the second phase and then away and then back for the third. We usually stayed two or three weeks and away for six and then back. During those two years, we were in Laos three times, Cambodia twice, Korea six times, North and South, for periods up to three months, and we even took a run up to Sri Lanka."

"How did you manage all that?"

"The assistants were not privy to those decisions. He was a secretive man, your brother, but I suppose you knew that."

"Yes. It's one of the reasons I'm here."

"I never figured out how, but he had papers to get into places closed to everyone else. He'd tell us one day that we were moving, and we never knew where. Sometimes we crossed borders without even knowing we'd done it. National borders seemed not to exist for him."

"Why should they, when he was doing so much good?"

Fletcher laughed. Vivian knew the question was naive. "How—how did he do it?"

Fletcher shrugged. "I don't know, but it was almost as though he had shed allegiance and the idea of nationality years ago." He had been clearing away the pictures as he talked. Now and then he would put up another slide, quick looks at faces, faces with the lines drawn, the changes that were Fletcher's plans for making intelligibility out of ruin, a face out of nothing like a face.

"And when did you decide to leave?"

The doctor's voice became slower and hesitant. "I had told Sanborn at the start that I wanted something like a residency—two years. I think he forgot. Of course, his behavior remained correct, very much so, but I think he was angry when I told him that my time was up. He and Cecelia wrote to find a new assistant. We got two people who didn't stay. Then we got Mary Nell. We trained her, Cecelia and I. I knew she wasn't up to the life there; she was one of those idealistic people who think that if everyone loves his children there won't be any more war, and if we all stopped being greedy, there wouldn't be any poverty in the world, and that if she shared this revelation with people, they would change their lives. I suspected she wouldn't last, but she wasn't my problem. I'd fulfilled my agreement and done it very well. I said good-bye, and was able to get home with some injured GIs, helping a medical team."

"So would you say your experience was all positive?" Vivian noticed she was beginning to sound a little like the doctor.

He hesitated a long time and then said slowly, "I had kept careful notes on my own work with Sanborn and had written them up. He was well known by then. I got good job offers and took the best one. I had lost some contacts but there were still people willing to try me. My experience with those hundreds of cases made me quick at spotting strategies according to Sanborn's special gift of using everything. People who saw me operate said that I had gained greatly in the two years and missed very little."

"That's wonderful."

"If there was a cost—I suppose there always is—it was a psychological one: pressure. It's difficult to be away in places so different from life here and then to come back and fit into this—reintegrate. That was difficult. Part of it had to do with the intensity of the work—getting back to a different rate of living—one can only be in awe of a man like Sanborn, your brother—the focus of his intensity was remarkable: a week or two away every four or five months, and half of that in travel, and he'd be back again into the work. The rain, the heat, the cold, the clouds of gnats, the rot of tropics, the dust of upland villages—nothing bothered him. For me, coming back—well, it was difficult. I suppose I should mention that Mariella—the nurse I replaced—helped me in the process."

Vivian had listened without comment. Something was missing, something she couldn't identify. Hadn't Daniel seen how difficult the work was for his assistants? Alston Fletcher's memories of Daniel had to do with skill and technique. There was nothing of a personal note at all. "The experience, then, seen in perspective—"

"Oh, it was positive, yes, I'd do it again for the medical knowledge I got and the life experience. Unfortunately, I don't have sons to pass that knowledge along to, but I've been thinking lately that even my girls might profit from it, although knowledge like that is less seemly in a woman."

"I'm sure you could tell your daughters about it without much loss of their femininity," Vivian said, keeping her tone level.

"Perhaps so, perhaps so," Fletcher agreed, and then, "Well,

it's time to see patients. I hope I've been helpful. And you might try doing something about your exercise. Jogging, running, swimming—all these are good."

"Yes," Vivian said, "I'm sure they are."

On the way home, walking, Vivian was overwhelmed by the memories of those pictures: the burned people, the disfigured people; jawless, noseless; the harelips, the victims of injuries she could not bear to think of. What had Fletcher said, that the nurses took care of the explanations, the sympathy, the "bedside manner." Oh, those faces, those faces! Then she realized that this inquiry of hers might not be so safe as she had thought, so continuously inspiring. She had begun it to find the sources of Daniel's greatness; she might be in danger of losing the greatness in the shadows of it. The words Fletcher had used to describe Daniel—"removed," and then "objective," "detached." What others: "gifted," "artistic"—he gave no picture of Daniel, no vignette of him, no affectionate or even annoyed recollections of the small human acts and peculiarities that make up a memory of someone. Why not? What was missing? She sighed. Those faces. Hundreds. There must have been hundreds of those faces.

And no one but she—not her brothers or her friends—wanted to know these things about Daniel and his work. There was no one to whom she could go with her puzzlement, her odd feeling of incompleteness. Only someone who had been there would know. Oh, Lord . . . she stopped in the middle of the street. She had wanted to ask him about Jack Ripstein, too, and had forgotten. Some questioner. Some detective.

Doris was waiting for her when she arrived at home. "There was a call for you and the letters are on the table."

"What was the call?"

"From a convent, a Sister Mary Birdbath, sounded like—"

"No, I'm not writing anything; I'm only trying to meet Daniel's—my brother's assistants, to talk with them, to learn about the time they spent with him."

"Oh." There was a pause. "In that case, I would like to see you. Our order does not encourage publicity, but it would be appropriate to meet Dr. Daniel Sanborn's sister, and I know that Mother Antonia would like to meet you also."

"Would tomorrow afternoon be too soon?"

"No." Sister Mary sounded surprised but not unpleasantly so. "At four?"

"We're around the corner from the hospital entrance. Let me give you the address . . ."

Vivian lay on the chaise in her room. She felt drained. She had not realized the time it would take to integrate what she would see and hear. Perhaps her visit to the convent was too soon, not giving her time to think, to understand . . . The images she had seen on the photographs, the burned faces, the deformed faces still hung in her mind. Why was it, she wondered, that the cord-strangled horse she had seen delivered on a street when she was a child had stayed with her long after a hundred daisy-drenched Alpine fields had vanished and a thousand star-hung summer nights moved unremembered away? The faces, the faces.

And Daniel had seen them, all of them, by the thousands, and worse, and the assistants had seen and worked with them, washed them, bandaged and unbandaged them without squeamishness. Vivian realized that she had always thought of Daniel in the desert or in the mountains dealing with people who were in shadow as they had been in Koizumi's pictures—there, but not really shown. It was time to see more, to see it all. She had written to Koizumi and she now had Cecelia Counselman's address and two new names to fill in with her list of dates and places. Something wonderful and noble, all those people, all those lands traversed, all those faces seen head-on without flinching. And touched, altered. She had always been taught to try for beauty and serenity, to encourage those qualities, to value them. It was part of the work she did and the life she led. Somehow, this had come to mean that one turned from ugliness and disorder. Now, she would have to seek out those parts of life, to ask about them, to encourage memories of them in others. She wondered if she could. It was time to face the ugliness in Daniel's work, to seek the details of injury and defect as she had always sought the details of graceful form and delicate color in the porcelain she studied.

The convent. Vivian had had the idea of whitewashed cells, arches, cloisters, chanting from a distance, of light, supernal voices rising and falling like a distant view of mountains. The building, but for the crucifixes over the doors of the rooms, looked like the dorm in a not-very-fashionable girls' school. The upstairs parlor, to which she was directed, had the tacky-forlorn look of any common room—summer camp or college or the recreation room of the ceramics laboratory and factory. Everyone's place is no one's place. The disorder put her at ease: a battered TV set, some unmatched chairs, books, board games. Someone had put up bright curtains to make the place homey, but it only made the rest look the more forlorn. A tiny, slender woman in a blue skirt and jacket and a print blouse was sitting at the window, knitting. When she saw Vivian, she got up and courteously crossed the space between them.

"Miss Sanborn, I'm Sister Mary." The high child's voice couldn't be mistaken. Vivian went over and there was a clumsy handshake, each unsure if it were the proper gesture. "I guess you expected the habit—the veil and long clothes."

"I suppose I did—the black—"

"Gone years ago. Ours were white anyway. Frankly, I miss it."

"Did you wear the habit when you were with Daniel?"

"Yes. We had a modified habit then, and of course they were used to it in Africa; they knew what it meant."

"So you were a sister when you were with him—"

"Yes. There were three of us altogether: Sister Adeline and I, and then another sister when Sister Adeline became ill."

The words were measured, modulated, even in the childish

voice. Vivian smiled to herself. Sister Mary was a generation younger but the same upper-class school and trained both of them: "The power of the voice must be sufficient to be heard without the hearer's straining. It need be no louder." In that perfect modulation of tone and volume, though no allowance is made, pain is held, like water in a cupped hand; though the fingers tighten, it runs through, however finely. "I didn't know that Daniel worked with Catholic sisters," Vivian said.

"It was not generally known and it was not in anyone's interest to advertise it. Ours is a nursing order. For a while our bishop thought—we thought—that we might work with the doctor. It would furnish experience for our surgical nurses and a constant supply of assistants for him. We tried—we all tried to the limits of our—"

Vivian had the sense of an almost shattering anguish. "I got your letter," she said, trying to ease a pain the sources of which she could not identify. It drove her to lie again. "My brothers and I read the letter. We were deeply moved. Thank you for writing it." The little woman's mouth was contracted. Tears. Vivian took a step forward. "Please—"

"We worked with Daniel Sanborn," Sister Mary said, "for three years. They were the most challenging, most gratifying of my life, but Sister Adeline, who came out with me, became ill and then Sister Jennifer, who was untrained, really untrained in the *religious* life . . . it is a sword, you see"—Sister Mary was whispering, trying desperately to overcome the tears—"a sword like martyrdom. There is a writer who calls martyrdom a sword. One grasps it to wield against pride, sloth, despair. We were offered a challenge like that. We were unequal to it."

"But you were there for three years . . ."

"It is not my place to criticize either Bishop O'Kane or Mother General, but I felt—I always felt that we could have succeeded had we given our best—had we sent only those sisters most developed in the *religious* life."

"You mean that the selection of sisters was too much dependent on medical skills?"

"On physical strength! On silly physical strength!" She was almost hissing.

"How arduous was the work, physically?" Vivian asked.

"It was nonsense, nonsense!" Sister Mary said breathlessly. "We were busy, certainly. There were days—assessment days, harelip days, rat-bite days, when the line would be all around the camps. Then the assistants would operate also, but there was always time to sleep. We always . . . there was always time. To a worldly person, the times of leisure, though few, would seem adequate, but to a religious, it meant there might be no time for Mass, for reading the office, for exercises of spiritual recollection."

Vivian was aware that Sister Mary had contradicted herself, but she could not bear to increase the nun's pain by mentioning it. "And the doctor, did he understand these things?" she asked gently.

Sister Mary's whisper, trying still to conquer a breakdown into weeping, rasped with intensity. "Daniel Sanborn was a living saint. He did not need what ordinary people need. He wasn't—aware—I mean he was above the ordinary worldly needs. I used to wonder why the dear Lord made him a Jew."

Vivian fought away her shock and impatience. "Jews can be quite spiritual," she said. "I have known some who were."

"Don't you understand? As a Jew, Daniel Sanborn can never be a candidate for beatification. The Church will not—can never recognize him. It grieves me that the world will lose a magnificent *spiritual* example."

"Can't a Jew provide such an example?"

"I suppose in some small way, but not as it could be—such a shame."

Vivian sighed. "I was his sister and I knew him at home, coming back for his rests. I could not know him as he worked, as he traveled. What was it like with him there in Africa?"

The objective question seemed to calm Sister Mary a little. She took her time to answer. "Sister Adeline and I . . . all the assistants used to have foot trouble—a kind of awful itch, and we'd operate standing in basins of potassium permanganate. The chemical left our feet dyed brown. We looked as though we were wearing socks. Someone began calling us the bobby-soxers. All the assistants in Africa took on that name, and it was a kind of—well—a point of pride to us then."

"And Daniel? Was he a 'bobby-soxer,' too?"

"One would not look at Dr. Sanborn in that way. I never— such a thing isn't suitable for us, but he wasn't—he didn't seem troubled by the mundane things, the itches and the intestinal problems."

"Who were the other bobby-soxers? Have you kept in touch with them?"

"Of course I have. I remember them by name every night and I make a novena for each of them twice a year."

"But contact . . ."

"No. Sister Jennifer left the order eight months after she returned home. Mother has her address; Mother Antonia corresponds with her. Sister Adeline has died. I never thought much of the others. Louise Goldman was the Jewish girl. She was from that Kansas City group. She was not a spiritual person. Her conversation was worldly, very worldly."

"Do you know where she is, Louise Goldman?"

"No. Although we are not a contemplative order, there is, there must be, a spiritual component to our lives. This is why we do not mingle in the ordinary way with the worldly."

"But a letter—"

"Such contact takes time away that is better spent in a religious manner—in prayer and contemplation."

Vivian was surprised. The speech sounded rehearsed. It puzzled her that Sister Mary was so little interested in maintaining contact with women who had shared so intense an experience. Perhaps the religious life forbade or at least discouraged such an interest, yet as Alston Fletcher had remarked, they had been veterans together, veterans by choice in an all-consuming war. She decided not to pursue this and asked instead, "Did the doctor seem happy as he worked?"

The Sister brightened. "Of course, the surgery, the operations were often long and grueling and because of what they were, detail was of the greatest importance. We did trauma surgery, too, but that was out of a sense of duty. Dr. Sanborn's happiness came from reconstructing those children's faces."

"And how did he show that he was happy?"

"Oh, others complained of that, but I knew—I always knew. He was very like a religious, you know. He never moved or spoke unnecessarily. His gestures reflected what we call Holy Modesty; his hands did not wave or gesture overly and they were kept close to the body. Some of our newer sisters here could have learned that from him. He also practiced custody of the eyes, never looking about or staring. But I could tell, just as we know here when someone is having a crisis of life or faith. There are small things the outsider would miss. I knew. I always knew." She was smiling gently.

"Were there special rules," Vivian asked, "special rules of conduct or behavior apart from the work you did? You were, after all, young women in a strange place."

"That was why he didn't want us to mingle with the local people. He never forbade us, but we knew. Sister Jennifer and that Louise Goldman—when I was training her—they always wanted to be visiting the people, the villages, going around, learning the languages and talking to the people, being friendly. Dr. Sanborn didn't like that at all."

"Did he ever tell you why?"

"It endangered the work, and it caused . . ."

"What?"

"It was the Devil," Sister Mary said.

"What?"

"Diabolic temptation."

"I don't understand."

"Worldliness, ridiculous political worldliness. Worldly people cannot resist the desire to perfect man in worldly ways."

"You mean to better his condition?"

"I mean to meddle in governments and laws and worldliness.

The Devil knows this. The Devil must have seen Daniel Sanborn's sanctity, feared the example for men, the holiness. He sent those soldiers, those men—"

"Which men?"

"The government, the squads—I hated those men that came to the camps—I hated them!" Again, the whisper against tears; these, tears of rage.

"What men? Did they threaten you?"

"They dared to interrogate *him*, they bothered him with questions and insinuations. They took looks in our sterilizers. They went into our clothes boxes, into *my things*!" She stopped, caught. She dropped her head. "Some of what happened makes me very angry," she said, "unseemly, although it is a righteous anger."

"So you were quite isolated out there—you had only one another."

"We had the Holy Mother of God," Sister Mary said. "She was never nearer."

"And yet the sisters—the other sisters—were not able to stay with Daniel—Dr. Sanborn."

"No," Sister Mary said, almost bitterly.

"I think you would like to know this," Vivian said, "that I spoke with the Archbishop's secretary, a Father Keith, and he told me that the Archbishop of Málaga had talked with Daniel about supplying the assistants he needed. I assume that meant with some kind of protection—three or four people maybe, so that there could be shifts—I understand Daniel worked seven days a week."

"*I* never gave up," Sister Mary said. "The others asked to return, but I knew, I knew what we were offering and I never gave up."

"I had thought you came back with Sister Jennifer."

"We were ordered back. I came because of Holy Obedience. I had been there for three years. Of course it was right that I come back to attend to my spiritual life—a part long neglected."

"In the years you were working with Dr. Sanborn there must have been many physical hardships: leaky tents, rains, droughts . . . he used to come home desperately tired. I never knew how you surmounted those things."

"The motto of the active orders is '*Ore et Labore.*' Work is a form of prayer for us. We were doing His work, so He was always near."

"And did you feel Daniel was near also, I mean spiritually? Did he ever laugh or joke with you? Did he ever acknowledge the difficulties in some special way?"

"You say he came away tired? *I* never saw Dr. Daniel Sanborn tired or impatient, and I will not bring him or his work down to the ordinary, the mundane. He never made jokes if that's what you mean. To see such a person, one looks *up* or one will not see him at all."

"I meant to ask you also if, when you were in Africa, did you ever have visits from Jack Ripstein, the comedian?"

"Who?"

"Jack Ripstein. He's a comedian. I thought the children—"

"Many people sought out our Dr. Sanborn. Some did it as an act of pilgrimage, others to glorify themselves. The Lord must take some special justice on those who act out of pride and vanity, taking the doctor's precious time—time he should be resting, refreshing himself."

"And Ripstein, was he one of those?"

"Who?"

"Ripstein, Jack Ripstein. In his shows he's called Jack the Ripper."

"There were so many. I don't remember."

A bell rang. They both started, and a look of relief crossed Sister Mary's face, quick as a skater having suddenly regained control. "We must go," she said. She murmured, "Thank you for coming to see me. Mother Antonia has asked to meet you, and there's time to do that before evening prayers." She rose and put out her hand, a gesture that was strangely ambiguous. For a moment Vivian thought she meant the hand to be taken, so that the Sister might lead her. When she went to take the hand, she saw that the palm was toward her as though to forbid something. The Sister turned. "We do not chat in the halls," she said. "Also, we do not peep into rooms as we go by, but we practice custody of the eyes. Mother Antonia's office is at the other end of the building." She led Vivian down the hall past a statue of the Virgin to which she gave a practiced genuflection without breaking stride, a graceful dip. The hall crossed another and another. At the end, they came to a door. Sister Mary stopped. "This is Mother Antonia's office," she whispered, and stood and straightened her blouse like a schoolgirl before seeing the principal. "The younger sisters call her Mother Tony. It is unsuitable, really." She gave two discreet knocks. "Come in," came a voice. "In the name of the Lord," Sister Mary said. They went in.

"Mother Tony" was a suitable name for the woman who sat at the desk. She was round and red and cheerful-looking. Her blue skirt and jacket were the same as Sister Mary's, but the blouse was of a different print. The order was temporizing on the uniform. Mother looked at Vivian with alert eyes. "Mother, this is Miss Sanborn, Dr. Daniel Sanborn's sister. She has come to talk about his work in Africa." Vivian was about to correct Sister Mary, to give her married name, but thought better of it. "Miss Sanborn" was convenient, Sister Mary too easily upset.

Mother Tony came from behind her desk and pumped Vivian's hand strongly. "What an honor to have you visit us!" she cried. "And what a light, what a shining light your brother was in the world!"

Vivian said, "Yes, he was."

Mother Tony motioned Vivian to a chair. "We all heard of his death with pain, and all the worse because your brother was in the Church's care."

"It couldn't have been helped," Vivian said. "The Archbishop here has been very sympathetic and helpful, and they gave my brother a funeral consistent with his faith—our faith. I'm grateful for that."

"It's a comfort to know that," Mother Antonia said. "And have you come here to ask some questions about the years your brother was in Africa?"

Vivian began to explain. The words sounded lame to her but Mother Antonia said, "In the old days, people went on pilgrimages. All that geography. Now the search is inward."

"It is a kind of pilgrimage." Vivian had decided not to mention Daniel's will.

"We're very proud of our sisters who did that work," Mother Tony said. Sister Mary's face reddened under the praise. "Has Sister been helpful?"

"Very helpful, and"—she was careful not to say *but*—"do you think I could talk to Sister Jennifer Keene, who also worked with my brother? I understand the other sister who was there is no longer alive. Sister Jennifer may know some of the later assistants. I'm trying to trace them all—to meet the ones I can and learn about the others."

For a moment Mother Tony looked taken aback and then she said to Sister Mary, "Yes, it's true that you and Jennifer worked with other people, isn't it, Sister? It's easy to forget that. Jennifer's had such a difficult time." She smiled at Sister Mary. "I know we're keeping you. Why don't you go on to recreation and I'll see Miss Sanborn to the door." Sister Mary dipped again. "God be praised," said Mother Tony. "God be praised," answered Sister Mary as quickly, and with another dip was gone. Mother looked after her. "She likes the old ways. So many of those ways were—lovely. '*Deo Gratias*' when you left, '*Benedicte*' and '*Domino*' on either side of a door . . ." She sighed. "All gone now, the forms. For so many of us they were lifeless formalisms—a bar to real feeling. But they were with us for so many years and she misses them."

"Mother Antonia, why did the order stop sending assistants to Dr. Sanborn?" Vivian felt comfortable enough with this nun to ask.

"No one knows what really happened to the sisters who worked with your brother in Africa. I was in Montreal during those years, in our order's hospital there. We heard rumors but there were rumors about all the overseas placements. We were completely unprepared for the condition of the sisters who returned from that placement. I've asked Mary, but she won't or can't open up. If you *are* on a quest, you should see Jennifer Keene, who used to be Sister Jennifer but left the order not long after she came back from Africa. She's at our mother house in Montreal; I know it's a lot to ask, but I think it would be fruitful for both of you. Perhaps she will open to you. I hope she will. See her. She needs to be included, consulted. There are plenty of official documents and papers—where the sisters went and what they requested; their letters to the abbess said almost nothing. It was a weakness of those days that a sister tried to seem more holy then she was. The letters were full of '*Deo Gratias*' and 'All for Jesus' and gave us little but the knowledge, sister-knowledge, that they were in great trouble."

"And you have no more idea than that—was there nothing from Daniel?"

"I don't know that he was aware of trouble. Your brother succeeded brilliantly in his work. His success must have given him great pride and happiness. We don't know why our sisters failed, though they worked as hard and sacrificed as much. Something was missing, and their suffering was compounded with guilt. Jennifer suffers that way; so does Mary."

Vivian remembered the letter she had read, the unsigned letter from one of the assistants who used the words "unequal to the work." Was it Sister Jennifer?

"At the mother house in Montreal you'll also find the records of the order's communications back and forth to your brother. If you decide to go, I'll send a formal letter of permission that you be shown everything. We had great hopes of a permanent relationship between your brother and our order—we seemed uniquely fitted to his needs—he to ours. We sent three of our sisters to him in Africa. Sister Adeline came back to us demoralized and dying; Sister Jennifer was spiritually and physically destroyed; you've seen Sister Mary, felt her suffering. She gives us no hint, no word, but she returned to us so nerve-racked that it was years before she could face hospital work at all. She has only recently been able to go back, and that on a very limited basis. Jennifer never recovered."

"Others did not have that experience . . ."

"Yes, we knew that and it led us to think that the extra responsibilities of being a religious made the job too difficult. We stopped sending our sisters. This is no disrespect to the doctor or our sisters. I believe your brother to have been specially blessed, but Glory can burn as well as warm. Please see Jennifer, if you find you can, and if you do, remember that not all martyrdoms are public."

"I had no idea . . ." Vivian said. "I thought—he used to come home exhausted, but—"

Mother Antonia opened the office door and they walked down the hall. She lowered her head but did not genuflect at the statue of the Virgin as Sister Mary had done.

"Is it difficult to be a leader to women who are older than you and longer in the order?"

"Sometimes. We say difficulty is challenge if it's done for the right reasons. I think you are being challenged about your brother. You never thought his greatness would be so hard on others. Virtue is difficult or everyone would practice it. God bless you on your pilgrimage." They were at the convent door. "May I hug you?" she asked. "It's the new style." She was grinning.

"*Deo Gratias*," Vivian said.

They laughed. The hug was gentle and quick. Vivian was physically reticent and Mother Tony must have known it. "Let me know about Montreal," she said, "so I can send the letter."

It was rush hour in the city. Cars and buses were panting in the streets, immobile. People were pouring thickly from the buildings, roiling at the curbs. Everyone had a look of strain or anger or frustration. Subways roared from the grilles beneath their feet. Vivian had been in this mill many, many times, but never with the consciousness that at the same moment a convent full of nuns were readying themselves for evening prayer. She felt herself fighting her way home through these crowds. Her mind kept going back to Sister Mary, to the impression of fragility and brittleness the nun conveyed. The Sister couldn't be older than forty-five; her manner made her seem old. What had been responsible for the terrible anguish in her? For a moment, Vivian felt a flash of anger at Daniel. He had had the capacity to make others follow him. Did he know what a responsibility that was? Why had three sisters come back shattered from their experience? And there was in the other assistant, Dr. Fletcher, a silence surrounding anything intimate or personal, even after two years with Daniel, two years in the closest contact. The sisters were carrying a double weight of allegiance and conflicting priorities. Dr. Fletcher was somewhat rigid in personality. Still . . . still . . .

And where in all this suffering, his, theirs, the patients', did a *comedian* fit? It was odd that Sister Mary didn't remember him at all. He couldn't have been there when she was. It must have been another place, some other time. Yet the sister so consciously un-heard, un-saw, un-knew so much that Vivian wondered at her perceptions of simpler memories. Sister Mary said that Daniel had never been ill. Vivian had seen him ill many times. In illness he had no pallor; his darker skin browned in the sun. In sickness he went gray, an ashen color, unmistakable. Daniel had come to her fevered, shaking, with nauseas and diarrheas, with parasites, rashes, coughs. Sister Mary saw him as unaffected as one of the saints that made up the ordinary imagery of her life. Yet Sister Mary had done what Daniel had done—those faces, that cutting, piecing, sawing of bone, grafting of skin; work in dust and mud, work in poverty and filth—Vivian felt herself reaching toward something, a reality of both of them from the inside—not as they were seen in the work but as they saw it. The knowledge moved toward her for an eyeblink and was gone. Perhaps there were a dozen reasons why Sister Mary had chosen not to show Daniel as something other than perfect. Daniel was dead. Perhaps she had been trying to spare Vivian's feelings. She was almost certain that Alston Fletcher had been.

Again she looked at the people she was passing, at their faces. At her age, almost everyone on the streets was younger than she, and stared past her without interest. She began to imagine their faces as Daniel might have seen them. How could a doctor cut a face apart from its fastenings to bone, shear into muscle, and cleave it away, and then sew it back again, brace it, wire it, and expect it to put back its parade of expressions, its owner's wardrobe of looks? Fletcher's pictures were still-pictures, still as these homeward bound faces were still-pictures, saving their expressions for the supper table and the hour in the backyard before nightfall. How could such things be possible?

By the time Vivian had walked the forty blocks home, it was dark. It had taken her that time to decide that she would go to Montreal to see Jennifer Keene. This Sunday she would be going to Atlantic City to see Jack Ripstein. And at home, there were letters, hundreds of other mourners waiting to be heard.

7

Vivian had not been to a casino since her trip to Europe in the
1930s. The Breakers was a huge hotel, a garish splendor of red
carpet and gold sconces and chandeliers whose lights were globed
with faceted glass that made them shoot reflected beams through
the foyer, which seemed like Madison Square Garden. And no
windows. Although it was evening, there was a daytime pace
to everything: in the hotel lobby, bellmen and waiters rushed
here and there, people were signing in and out, walking, meeting, talking, moving through to the casino beyond. From the
open arch there was almost a roar of voices and slot machines,
muffled by carpets and drapes, but omnipresent and so steady
that Vivian had at first taken the sound for surf.

And everywhere there were the machines, not only in the
casino but also in the hotel lobby and around every corner. They
looked like cash registers with handles; when they were used,
they gave off a loud machine sound. There was the smell of
their works about them, gears and grease and wheels slick with
oil. It must be part of what you pay for, Vivian thought, because
the action could have been made quiet, surely, the smell changed.
While waiting for her turn in line to register, Vivian put a half-
dollar in one of them and pulled the handle. The thing whirred

and spun and she felt the slight friction communicating itself as excitement all along the gears and wheels of it, running, clicking. Then it stopped, first at one window and then the second and then the third, and it was all over. Silence. Letdown. It was like being rejected in some way.

She thought she should rest before Jack Ripstein's show. She had been too nervous to eat lunch or dinner. Her visit here was different from the other visits. Ripstein's relationship with Daniel was mysterious and he had not invited her inquiry as the others had. It was only eight o'clock. The show didn't begin until eleven. She thought she might lie down and relax and try to plan the way she would introduce herself, and the kinds of questions she would ask.

First, she would have to learn what kind of man Ripstein was. She would tell him that she had visited some of the assistants, and hoped to visit or be in contact with all of them. She would not talk about the money, only about Daniel's work and Ripstein's part in it. Daniel had never been a spontaneous person; all his plans were thought out, reasoned carefully. His relationship to Ripstein must have been an important one.

She set her little traveling clock for ten and put it on the nightstand, lay down on the bed, and let herself relax. What seemed like a moment later, the alarm was ringing. She got up and washed her face, applied a little makeup, took her purse, and went down into the day-and-night mill of people and machines.

The casino was as loud as it had been at six, as full, as busy. To get to "the club" she was directed to walk past the entrance, and since the entrance was so big, she had a full view of everything, and of the ranks of robot slot machines, busy whirring, busy stopping, gear-sound, wheel-sound, click of marbles in roulette wheels, cries of triumph or anguish, sound of money and of chips, a sea without waves.

By now she was very hungry, and when she asked where she might get something to eat a floor man indicated the club. She went on past the casino and around the corner to the place where Jack Ripstein was due to appear.

Here, too, there was action, a feeling of daytime at night. She gave her name and was given a tiny seat at a tiny table, wedged tightly among three other tables of laughing people. She felt singularly out of place, understanding now that people did not come here alone. For the first time in years, her singleness stung a little. Abner was in Dresden by now. There had been the calls and she had written two letters since Daniel's death, but she had not told him about this inquiry, this—what had Mother Tony called it?—pilgrimage. Next week he would be in New York and she could tell him then.

She reminded herself that she did not have an introduction to Jack Ripstein and that as soon as she ordered, she should begin to formulate what she could say in her note to him. When the waiter came she ordered a combination sandwich—no ham, thank you—and tea.

"What to drink?" the waiter asked.

"Tea," she said, thinking he had not heard her. He shot her a look. "I'm writing an article," she said. He shrugged and was gone.

She had just finished eating when the lights went down and a man came out and announced that the show was beginning. Tony Benedetti from Heckshersville, Pennsylvania. Vivian turned to the couple beside her and said, "I thought Jack Ripstein was going to be here."

They laughed comfortably. "Oh, this is his warm-up."

Benedetti was relaxed and amusing. He talked about his family being the only Italians in the town where he grew up. Vivian laughed aloud as he explained how misunderstandings kept happening between his parents and the people of the town. He told of his mother's fear that if he ate school lunches he would turn blond. People all around her were laughing. She had not laughed with other people in a long time.

Then there was a girl singer. She sang a love song and then a funny song about love and then the girl sang a song about Ripstein—"Bring on Jack the Ripper, he'll make you strip your zipper . . ."—and then Ripstein bounded on the stage.

He was big—he seemed to fill the room with his energy and fill the eye with his presence. Neither Benedetti nor the singer had gone to the center of the tiny area, but there was another quality, something larger than life, about Ripstein that made the whole room his, that dominated it. He cried out to them, "Look up! Loosen up! *Give up. The Ripper is here!*" They roared back at him, clapping and stamping. He yelled at them: "I'm gonna give you so much of it, and I'm gonna keep it in so long, you're gonna leave here stewed, screwed, and tattooed!"

The things he said after that were filthy and the way he said them was worse. He used obscenities, savage indecencies, words, ideas—shock followed shock. All the people around her were weeping with laughter, while she sat unbelieving. The humor was not erotic or even, to Vivian, funny. It was about lust, mindless need. Vivian felt herself redden, then go cold, but throughout the long monologue, as everyone around her laughed, she was as lonely as she had been in her life. Soon she would have to get up and go to meet this man and try to talk to him about Daniel. It was impossible. It was what she had come here to do. What she could not understand, sitting in the rain of obscenity and coarseness, was that to this man, her brother Daniel had left an estate, and not only money, but the money of his honoring, symbolically at least, the money of his cause and calling.

Surreptitiously she looked at her watch. The act had begun promptly. If it ended on time there was still half an hour to go. She thought of escaping to the ladies' room, but getting up in the pack of tables and people and stumbling out in the dark was beyond her. Other forms of escape were not. She fell back on a childhood game they used to play during long trips. Any sentence ending, for example, in *ing* or in any proper name would have to be rhymed. She began to listen strictly for syntax. Content fell away. There was her *ing: eating*.

Jack Ripstein was eating
The new percale sheeting.

77

He said a place name. *Passaic.* She thought

> *The art in Passaic*
> *Is all of mosaic.*

She began to play in earnest, putting distance between her feelings and his vulgarity. Uncle Charley. Uh . . .

> *With Uncle Charley*
> *One does not parley.*

As content and meaning faded, there emerged for Vivian, to her surprise, a series of rhythms and counter-rhythms in Ripstein's delivery that was smooth as a dance. The rhythm was an art: long sentence, long sentence, short, then a kind of bridging sentence, and a very short one, like a snap, like a syncopated, dropped beat. The words themselves, the sounds of the words, devoid of their meaning, had also been very carefully chosen and artfully arranged. Years ago, this Ripstein must have evaluated himself, realized that he was not subtle or witty, that his humor was crude and cruel, a meat ax, not a scalpel. He must have sensed that he was, in truth, a ripper. Consciously, then, he must have begun to pare away all the subtlety, all the ambiguity and the conditioning words, flourishes that came, as it were, between the pie and the face. That the insult was not casually done but art, worked on, honed, perfected, somehow made it all the worse. To this man, who was now talking in the crudest words about the kind of sexual satisfaction each of the different world leaders would wish, Daniel had left his prize money, his honor money. *Why?* She wondered what questions she could use, what introduction to this gross man, that would elicit from him how he had come to know Daniel and where. He was so loud and the laughter was so loud she could barely think. As soon as the act was over she would have to think very quickly. If only she had planned before, made up her questions— She looked at her watch again. She wondered how he had the energy for all of it, because he didn't simply stand and talk. His body was in continuous motion, hands, arms, face. He turned and bounced. He simulated orgasms, minced and danced; he imitated a Jewish-American Princess. The worst Ku Klux Klan racist would never tell such things in open company, yet she was sure that there were other Jewish people sitting here and they were laughing at those slanders. She wondered why.

At endless long last, the act was over and people began to leave. As Vivian rose, a possibility occurred to her. It was the lawyer who had said that Jack the Ripper was Jack Ripstein. There could have been a mistake. Perhaps it was another Jack Ripstein entirely who had been Daniel's friend and beneficiary. There might even be an entertainer somewhere called Jack Ripstein because this man called himself Jack the Ripper. It would make her evening here a silly waste of time but it would be a great relief, well worth it, if she could learn this difference. That must be what had happened. Yes, two of them . . . a confusion of identities.

A waiter approached the table. "Ma'am, we're clearing the room—"

"I have to talk with Mr. Ripstein . . ."

"Oh, then you need to go around the back—out and then to your left," and he went away.

She got her things and went out, turning left. She saw a door there but was hesitant to knock in case the door opened directly on the dressing room. The casino was on her right and there was nowhere to sit and wait. People were moving past her to go in and out of the casino. She felt very much in the way.

At last the door opened and there he was, coming out. He was leading a group that arranged itself as a girl on each arm and two couples in tow. Vivian saw that offstage he was a little under medium height, but his place at the center of the group, and talking as loud and fast as he was, still made him seem larger. He talked to them all as they stood outside the casino. When there was a moment's pause, Vivian said, "Mr. Ripstein, I'd like to see you for a moment about a personal matter."

He stopped suddenly, dramatically. "Are you the press? Are you the mee-dee-ah?" They laughed. "Is the Ripper gonna be interviewed?"

Vivian came forward. "Mr. Ripstein—"

He stared at her in feigned shock for a tenth of a second too long and then cried, "My God, it's worse than I expected!" He turned to the group dramatically. "Who are they sending to catch the Ripper's golden words for posterity? Is it the fag from *Playboy* who rapes you with his eyes?" (He did a quick impression.) "No. Is it the bimbo from *Cosmo*? No. Who, then? Who? The Westchester Ladies Tuesday Garden Club *Newsletter*'s ace reporter, whose last article, 'The Place to Stick a Petunia,' won raves in Scarsdale!" The entourage laughed uproariously.

Vivian had not bargained for being part of an act put on for the benefit of Ripstein's fans. "This is personal, Mr. Ripstein, it will only take a moment." She looked at him straight on.

"Listen, honey," he said. "The Ripper's just been *on*! You get what I'm sayin'? I'm still so hot if I stuck my finger in a socket I could light up New Jersey. Give the Ripper a little time to re-lieve his in-can-descence!" He began to leer down the front of the dress of the woman on his left. The couple behind him asked for an autograph. They congratulated him again. He handled them with practiced ease. The other couple were staying too long, mesmerized. When Ripstein saw this, he turned to the larger of the girls and said, "Darling, get the Ripper a drink, a scotch and water. You go on. I want to stand here and look at your tushie." She walked away. "Look at that tushie! Is that peaches or is that peaches? Honey"—and he turned to the other girl—"with your boobs and her ass—"

It was all so old—why were they all laughing? Vivian was trying not to show how irritated she was. There was not an original thought, a new line or idea in the whole business—the old roué pose. This didn't even have the rhythm, the tempo of his act. And he wore two rings—pinkie rings with diamonds. Suddenly she wanted to laugh. It was everything she hated all rolled up into one loud package.

"The Ripper"—he was looking at her now, unsmiling—"the

Ripper is gonna give you two minutes." The girl came back with his drink. "Bottoms up!" he cried, and gave her a slap on the behind, and then with a deft move turned away, pulling Vivian along with him. "See you on the boardwalk!" he said, looking back at the group. "Watch out for loose nails!" They laughed. Ripstein guided Vivian away. "I don't know how much you know about the comedy business," he said, "but between shows we usually rest. I got two minutes for you, so get it said and then get going."

"Can't we go where it's quiet? I wanted to ask you about your relationship to Daniel Sanborn."

There was an immediate, gratifying change, some small revenge for the last hour she had endured. He stopped. "What is it? Who sent you?"

"Can we go somewhere to talk?"

He turned from her and walked away and she saw him go to a man who was standing near one of the doors. She saw him point to her and the other man nodded. Then Ripstein came back to her. "This'll be okay," he said, "in here." He led her down the hallway past the door from which he had come. There was a door marked STAFF which he opened with a key. There were a few chairs, a desk, a couch, all bland and impersonal. He ushered her in and was about to close the door when she said, "That's fine—you can leave that as is."

The time away from her had given him an opportunity to regain himself. He grinned.

"I'd be more comfortable."

They sat down. "Well," he said, "I got nothin' to hide, really. I was sixty my last birthday. I still got some of my teeth and some of my hair. I'm good at what I do. Damn good. Did you catch my act?" He looked tired in the fluorescent light and a little gray.

"Yes," she said.

"Great, huh? I was great. I had the people screaming."

She realized that he was fighting to keep away from her question, from mention of Daniel's name. She was no more eager now than he.

81

"Did you see that Benedetti? That guy stinks. I tried him out as a favor to someone, but he's going tomorrow right back to Hayseedsville."

"I liked him," Vivian said.

The Ripper did not like being argued with. He went red. "He's not for this room, this *city*. He tells you about his sister, the *nun*. You know where that act should go? Any place where the drug of choice is prune juice. Ask me, I know. I been getting laughs for thirty-five years and I know how. You name it, I done it. Most comics, they come into the business because they failed in their old man's shoe store." He was talking on and on, trying to stop her for some reason. His words were routine, smooth with use. "I been funny all my life. When I was a kid I was funny in school, in the neighborhood. Kids used to laugh at me, teachers, everyone. I figured why do this for free, so I went in the business. I like getting laughs—"

She took a breath and said over his voice, "Where did you meet Daniel?"

"Daniel?" It didn't work. His eyes had dropped, his voice had changed—not so badly as the first time, but visibly enough for Vivian to know that there had been no mistake. This was the Jack Ripstein to whom Daniel had given—

"Daniel Sanborn, the doctor . . ."

He seemed to cave in. He had been sitting on the couch. He lay back for a moment, his open jacket revealing a substantial paunch. He had not looked like a man of sixty before. Now he did.

"Wonderful," he said acidly. "Terrific. So who are you—a reporter?"

"No. I'm—I was Daniel's sister. I'm Vivian." If she thought that would change anything, she was mistaken. He got up and went to the door and slammed it shut.

"It's the money, isn't it? The goddamn money. That's why you're here."

"Well—"

"—and it's going to get out, isn't it, that I got Sanborn's

damn prize money. *You* tell; your brothers, the family, the kids. It's all over Mrs. Murphy's finishing school and half the bridge tables in New York City, and before you know it, media and every damn talk show in town!"

Vivian had not expected any such reaction. "What are you afraid of?" she said stonily. "Relatives, friends who might want a share?" She could not believe that this man could have had any relationship with Daniel. "Why you?" she asked. "Why you, of all people?"

"Search me," he said almost bitterly. "I'm damned if I can tell you why some philanthropic hero would bend down out of heaven and pick me. Yeah, everybody can use extra dough. But have you seen those *pictures*, those goddamn *posters* with the little kids and Sanborn looking like Death with bunions?"

"Why is that a problem?"

"Oh, God, how dumb can you get? Haven't you been listening? I been telling you about getting laughs and you didn't hear a damn word I said! *The Ripper*, that's who I am, and what I do is I get laughs, and how do I get laughs? I get laughs by saying what people think and are ashamed of thinking. I get laughs by saying what other people want to say but don't have the nerve."

"I don't believe people think those things. I don't believe anyone would want to say them."

"Believe what you want. I'm telling you what I do and what I have done, pardon my French, damn successfully for a hell of a long time in a racket that eats guys alive."

"And you never entertained the sick children—you never went to where they were, and gave shows—"

"Who, *me*?" He began to laugh. She wished he would die. It was the first time in her life that she wished someone dead. She said nothing. Her capacity for anger astonished her.

"Then you have no idea why my brother would have left you his money?"

"None. Maybe he saw my act and liked it, I don't know. Maybe he was one of those people who was ashamed to be thinking the things he thinks. Maybe he saw *my* picture and needed a laugh. Whatever it was, the word getting out ain't gonna do me one bit of good."

"I don't understand that," Vivian said.

Ripstein had put his hand to his head. "A dumb broad is all I need between shows—Daniel Sanborn, little kids, wars, faces, blood—*it ain't funny, lady!* Jerry Lewis, Danny Kaye—people start thinking they're nice guys, great guys, but they don't get laughs now—people ain't free with them. *They have stopped being funny.*" He said the words one at a time as though speaking to someone who was feebleminded.

"Perhaps you can give the money away," she said.

He snorted. "The money's not the problem. The publicity is the problem. You are the problem. People talk. That's the problem."

"Mr. Ripstein, if my brother's money is an embarrassment to you, it is as much to us. When I tell my family what you said . . . how it is, and if I may say so, what you are like, the last thing they will want would be to make his bequest public. You need have no fear."

"Great," Ripstein said acidly. "I know you can promise for your brothers' wives, their kids, their goddamn *maids*. Why did you come here in the first place?"

"I came—" She realized she couldn't confide in a man like Ripstein. Her quest was too personal to parade before this boor. "I came to see the man to whom Daniel left his prize money—money I thought better used in keeping on with his work."

"You gonna contest the will, you and your brothers?"

It occurred to Vivian that this was the third time Ripstein had mentioned brothers. "How well did you know Daniel?"

"I didn't know him at all. I never even met him."

"Then how did you know about his brothers?"

"The lawyer, what's-his-name, told me. So are you going to contest?"

"No," she said.

"Okay. So what else is there to talk about? I got another

show to do." By this time, Ripstein was pacing back and forth. She saw now that his body, which she had thought fat, was big but muscular. He must be very strong. One did not think of comedians as needing great strength. It made her nervous to watch him pace. Suddenly he stopped. "Wait a minute—just a secundo," he said. His face had brightened. "If it does come out, maybe I could get a handle on it—use it. It might even play. Daniel Sanborn meets the Ripper—so, uh—the great Daniel Sanborn has got to get *out*! It's mankind's darkest hour—evil is up, goodness is down, here's Daniel Sanborn and he's been working ten years—no jokes, no laughs, nothing but good deeds. This Sanborn is so good that the world is in danger of tipping over because of all that good concentrated in one place—" Vivian noticed that his accent had thickened, his grammar had changed, his gestures coarsened. He was working on his act, so busy with it that he looked through her as though she were no longer there. "Then one day Sanborn, the saintly healer, wakes up and he has got to hear one joke, have one good laugh. For one single day, he's gotta come down out of the jungle, down off the mountain, just to get to town for one single laugh in ten years of suffering and goodness. Of course, he wants a high-class laugh, something nice, polite, no toilet jokes, no blow-job jokes, no fag jokes. So he starts down—he fights tigers, charging elephants, the tsetse fly. At last, alone, exhausted, he stumbles off the desert. He's been away so long that the desert he started out on has turned into Las Vegas, and who's playing Vegas that night? The Ripper, and what kind of jokes does the Ripper tell? Toilet jokes, blow-job jokes, fag jokes. It's okay, it'll play. The money will play, too."

Vivian was suddenly very tired. He was pacing and didn't see her. She wanted to rise with dignity and leave. She got up heavily. All the tension and anger—

"What's wrong?"

"Nothing. I . . . I'm tired, that's all. It's been a long day."

"I got a show to do. Go home. This place ain't for you and neither is trying to figure out your brother. He was a big hero,

85

8

Kenji Koizumi had left a message and there were letters from some of the assistants. It was good to look over the mail, to read and be reinspired. Even after a night's sleep, or attempted sleep, and another nap at home, Vivian was unable to get Ripstein out of her mind. He clung there pervasive as mildew. Even though he had said he didn't know why Daniel had left money to him; even though he had said he didn't know Daniel—

Her letter of thanks to Koizumi had found him at New York University Hospital. He had come back from Africa with a parasitic disease. If she didn't mind visiting him there, he had said in his phone message, his enforced leisure would give them plenty of time to talk. Doris had copied him verbatim because, she said, "It sounded so nice."

A few of the assistants to whom she had written answered that they were busy with memoirs of their own and didn't want to be interviewed. Emma Banks's letter said: "I am now studying with a Yoga master. Our studies let us see that past, present, and future are one plane, and that events are strung along it as beads are on a string. To dwell on one bead is to lose the necklace. Your brother has not truly passed away, as life and death are two expressions of one mode of existence . . ."

There was a letter also from Cecelia Counselman. Vivian remembered Alston Fletcher mentioning her—what had he said: built like a barn, plain, but with a good bedside manner. Oh, yes, the Christmas cards—Rudolph among the Fra Angelicos. Cecelia had been with Mariella Marcantonio before Fletcher and after him with Mary Nell. Her envelope was bent and stained, and when Vivian opened it she saw that the letter was written in pencil on lined paper that had been torn out of a spiral notebook. There was some sort of stain or smear on the bottom of the letter—mustard, perhaps.

> I would sure like to talk about all the years I was with Dr.
> Daniel Sanborn. I was we were we worked together for
> almost eleven years. We were in about seventeen countries.
> It would sure be nice if you could come out here. If you
> can't, we could maybe talk on the phone. Where I am is
> right outside of Kansas City and easy if you have a car.
> It's a place called Horizon House. Let me know about
> coming. This time of year is the best for coming because
> it's not too hot yet. Here's the address and how you can
> get me by phone.

There was another piece of paper with written instructions, typed, on how to get there.

Vivian called to see when she could visit Koizumi at the hospital. Then, on an impulse, she called the number Cecelia Counselman had given her. A switchboard voice said, "Horizon House." Vivian asked for Miss Counselman. There was a long pause and then a background sound, the operator obviously asking someone else, and Vivian heard her saying off the line, "Oh, is that Cecelia?" and then, "Just a minute, I'll ring her floor." There was a ring and someone else answered, "Three-two, Cabot."

"Is Cecelia Counselman there?"

"Just a sec, I'll get her."

There was a long wait and a good deal of noise in the background and then a voice said uncertainly, "Hello . . ."

"Is this Miss Counselman?"

"Yes . . ."

"This is Vivian Eitzer . . . My brother was Daniel Sanborn."

At once the other voice went breathless. "Oh, gosh! Uh . . . oh."

"I got your letter and I wanted to ask you if I might come out there and see you . . ."

"Listen, it's daytime . . . I mean, if you want me to call back, it's real expensive calling from New York, like this, and I bet you didn't get me right away . . ."

"That's all right. When would it be best to see you?"

"If we met here, we could have all the time we needed. It's best on weekday afternoons."

"Is that a hospital?"

"It's a sort of nursing home, but it's also for disturbed and retarded people."

"Would there be a place where we could be alone?"

"Oh, sure. It'll be *so good* to meet you—Dan San's sister . . ."

"Dan San?"

"Oh, hell, I'm sorry. Daniel Sanborn. We—I—called him Dan San."

"Oh." They made their plans and said good-bye.

Dan San? Hardly the miracle-working saint Sister Mary described. Hardly like Fletcher's description of a cold, aloof . . . what word had he used? Jovian. "Dan San" did not sound Jovian. She had been so taken aback that she had failed to ask Cecelia whether she was a staff member or a patient at that nursing home. She got ready for her visit to Koizumi.

Koizumi was neither as small as she imagined him, nor as old. He sat in the fifth-floor solarium in a wheelchair, caught in an aureole of sunlight. At his side was a wheeled IV pole from which bottles and bags hung clear and gleaming, plastic tubes shining down from them like streets after rain.

"I love the light," he said, after he had shaken her hand and offered her a chair. "I always have. The sunlight. Suddenly we are told it is carcinogenic, like everything else," and he smiled. She wished him a rapid recovery. "Oh, I am on the way, only

89

somewhat weakened. It is a hazard of foreign travel. I must tell you that the first Sanborn I photographed was you. I was a student and it was at a museum display of porcelain in—1962. I might even have that picture. When I saw your brother in Peru I spoke of that."

"Did he say anything?"

"He was silent for a time, and then he said, 'The wish for this work comes from one place, the art from another. It was my sister who taught me to look at line and form, to see.' "

The man, his chair, and the light-shot IV bag were all suddenly swimming and tear-blurred. "Forgive me," Vivian said. "The pain is still very new."

"I was saddened to hear of your brother's death," Koizumi said. "He was a dedicated man, and they are few enough at any time. He also had an independent spirit one does not often see. I think that is very American, that spirit."

"How long were you with him in Peru?"

"I was there for a week. It rained almost the whole time; I did some nice things in that rain, I remember; mist-hung scenery. The camp had a breathtaking mountain view, although I wasn't there for that; it was an added opportunity. It was after the rain stopped that I took the pictures that became so famous, both of them on the same evening."

"Tell me about them—we've all seen them, and been moved, but I never heard what inspired them."

"On that particular day, they had been doing many small surgeries; their equipment was wet and fouled; everyone was cold. The rain stopped and I, knowing I had soon to leave, pleaded with them to let me have a little time after the last surgery for a picture or two. I took many pictures, one after another, and among them were those. Frankly, I did not know what I had taken until I developed them in the studio and I saw and was amazed."

"Do you have any more pictures—pictures the magazine didn't use?"

"I have the portfolio in my studio. If you wish, I can have my assistant bring it over. Then we can see them all. It's my practice to make one print. We can see everything quite comfortably."

"I would like that very much."

"Let me make the call."

He began to wheel himself to the nursing station. She offered to help. "No, it's simpler this way." When he came back he was smiling. "My assistant has located the portfolio and will bring it over now. I hope I am able to answer the questions you may have. The trip was years ago—much time has passed, but it was quite a memorable trip. I can still recall many incidents from it."

"I wonder—I think about Daniel, at his work. His work was his life and I knew almost nothing of it. How did he manage to do what he did for all those years—what was he *like?*"

Koizumi smiled in his sunlight. "Photography is always said to be the most objective, least artistic of all the arts, yet I am continually amazed at its subjectivity in the selection of angle, light, line, frame, and the distance at which one stands from the subject, not to mention one's selection of the subject itself. People are always sending me pictures to judge. These are pictures not of the subject but of themselves, though they do not know it. Because I am a professional photographer, I do know how subjective it is, the selection I make—what I see and how I see it."

"Are you telling me that those wonderful pictures were posed by you?"

"I am saying that my opinion of your brother is the man I see, and that is subjective surely. He will be characterized a hundred times, all trivializing, I think. If there are a thousand ways to photograph a cat playing with a ball of twine, how many would it take to describe a man, such a man as your brother?"

"I loved Daniel," Vivian said, "but since his death, I have begun to wonder if I knew him or understood him. People say he was formal, distant, one even said Jovian—I never found him distant, only reserved, a person who had suffered a great deal and who covered his vulnerability with reserve and silence."

91

"I did not know Dr. Sanborn at all, but I felt a conflicting need in him for solitude and for the near presence of many people. He ate and slept alone, but the rest of his day was almost overwhelmed with movement and noise when he was not concentrated on some person's teeth, lips, jaws, bones. He looked at *his* pictures, never at mine, by which I mean that he seldom got relief from the human face."

"I've seen some of those pictures," Vivian said. "Dr. Fletcher showed them to me."

"I saw them," Koizumi said. "I don't know how they stood it."

"We once talked about scar tissue—I always thought that scar tissue was tougher than normal tissue because one doesn't feel pain on a scar. He said it was far more fragile because though there is no feeling, the tissue is more easily reinjured. Daniel built defenses against feeling pain as a scarred arm feels no pain, but he didn't stop experiencing it, defending against it, being reburned, suffering whatever other injury burning is, besides the pain."

"It could be so," Koizumi said. He paused. "I think I will tell you a little of the famous picture, the one of Dr. Sanborn and the little child—I have told it to no one before. I use it only to illustrate what we are speaking of.

"I have said that everyone was tired and out of temper. It had rained for days, and living as we did, the rain had gotten to everything, the clothing in the day, the bedding at night, the hats we wore, and the shoes. People waited in the rain to be seen and the surgeries had gone on into the evening; the doctor and the assistants were hungry and tired, and there was cleaning up and drying out of everything to do. Then the rain stopped and everything hung sopping. I had been photographing surgery and I was moving my equipment. I, too, was tired, and in my clumsiness I bumped into the assistant and overturned a table of already used instruments. The doctor growled. I was mortified that I had been guilty of such clumsiness. They were finished with a last little patient and the doctor handed him over to the assistant. I had been picking up the instruments from the

92

dirt floor, mud then, and trying to wipe them off, and I was still bent low, and I saw a good angle and used the camera from there, a little bit low and off to one side. It was a deeply embarrassing moment for me; I got that picture and the one a moment later of the doctor sitting down, waiting for his assistant to come back with wash water and a towel. I was unsure of what I had gotten, which is unusual for me, and when I developed the pictures and worked in the darkroom, it took me a while to remember the circumstances."

"So Daniel was not *taking* the patient, but *giving* him to the assistant, and his expression was not sadness but irritation, tiredness, and hunger?"

"At that moment, perhaps."

Vivian began to laugh. Soon she and Koizumi were laughing together. "The expression is so complex," Koizumi said, and they laughed again.

"You mean that people were seeing what they thought they should see?"

"No, I don't think it's quite so deceptive as that, but one does make a leap of association—sick child, exhausted physician, surroundings darkened, lamplight instead of the lights of surgery, and the complex expression suggests itself easily enough. Add to that a somewhat strange camera angle that deepens the doctor's eyes and makes him larger."

"I never thought—"

"What they both are now is a cultural metaphor that goes far beyond the original study."

"Did you try for that?"

"Oh, no, and it makes me a bit uncomfortable. It has been used to raise money for causes both practical and harebrained." They laughed again.

"Why did you go into photography?"

"A feeling for order and composition. It's what makes us Japanese so visually oriented a people. One does not like racial stereotypes but I have observed that cultures vary in their outlooks. As for photography, it is truly a new thing in the world because before, one had only one image at a time, or, if one had a portrait, two. Only with Holbein's Henry VIIIs or Rembrandt's self-portraits were there more than that. Now, everyone has many images through life that can be shown together. One sees, if not reality, at least behind the scenes."

"I wanted to ask you about the assistants—"

"There were two of them when I was there; the young man—you will see him several times, and also an invisible woman, a fine strong woman, but overweight, and plain-looking. I wanted a special portfolio of her because she was a marvelous assistant and when she worked with patients she underwent a kind of transformation such as one reads of in fairy tales. This she never knew and so she was shy and when I approached her with the camera she wouldn't let me take pictures at all. She hid, she disappeared, or when the doctor needed her, appeared masked and completely covered, like a ghost." He laughed. "Like a family secret that all know and none acknowledge."

That would be Cecelia, Vivian thought, the woman in the nursing home. She was the assistant who had been longest with Daniel—almost eleven years. Fletcher had spoken highly of her; she of the Rudolph Christmas cards and the stained, wrinkled letter, and the flustered telephone manner. "Why did she hide?"

"She was embarrassed by her appearance, perhaps."

"One would surely have thought—in such circumstances, that personal vanity would be put aside—"

"And does one put aside one's ordinary individuality when one does service?" He smiled. "I think not." He took a breath. "I have a favor to ask of you."

"I think I know what it is," she said, "the pictures—"

"Yes. I own them now. They have reverted to me and I have been approached by a publisher. I would like to be free to act if there is an acceptable proposal, to publish the pictures. I will not do it if you are unwilling. I would like to show you what I have. If there are any pictures unacceptable to you, I will not include them. There is, for example, a picture of your brother bathing in a waterfall in the nude."

Vivian was surprised. "Daniel was physically modest to the point of prudishness. How did you ever get such a picture?"

"In camp, standards change. All the males of the community and the visitors bathed there."

Vivian said, "Visitors? What visitors were there?"

"During my stay two or three came and went. He was, by the time *I* visited, somewhat famous; his fame did increase because of the pictures. I have since had some pangs of conscience about the effects that came in my wake. To the doctor, I brought perhaps more fame than made him happy. Doubtless now, Mother Teresa has to feed and house tourists of various kinds, people studying her methods, others who would find some cachet in such a visit, pilgrims of faith and others who have none and wish they did. It is easier now, but even then there were visitors coming and going. You might see some of them in the pictures. He offered them nothing in the way of encouragement, yet they came."

"Was it always a feature of that life?"

"I think directly proportional to the scenic qualities of the location and the availability of access. He traveled quite a bit, yet such was his fame later on that I understand the camps were very busy places indeed."

Koizumi's assistant came to them from the elevator. He was pleasant looking, young, Caucasian, and not only did he bring the portfolio but also a carry-sack of Japanese food for Koizumi's lunch. Vivian declined their invitation and the two of them ate companionably as she looked through the pictures.

"At least you can take tea with us," Koizumi said, "to mask our rudeness for eating in your presence."

She accepted. He bowed courteously from his chair.

The landscapes were breathtaking. Peru's mountains a dramatic, spare terrain, great cliffs and long vistas, huge gorges, curtained by rain, mists in the valleys like inland seas, and in one of them, a sun commanding because the whole sky was given it to command. At that altitude the trees had receded; roads, rivers, men, even mountains took primordial places under heaven. Seamless and unbroken, the sky shattered the rocks beneath it with sudden lightning and slow rain. It was triumphant and almighty. And then here were the people, bowler-hatted, barefoot people, shy at the camera, girls hiding their faces, boys peering, rotund and stolid women, worn-away men. Then the lines of them, babies in arms, people with faces caved in or jaws so malformed that they couldn't eat; they waited to be seen, to go under the cruel stare of Daniel's camera—the assistant was posing them front view, side view, then surgery and the recovery house, a house they had built for Daniel in one day, all the men of two villages, for the patients to be watched while the anesthesia wore off.

There were scenes of camp, too: Daniel throwing his shaving water out a back flap and narrowly missing a passing villager, village men playing a game that looked like soccer, Daniel bathing in the waterfall, others there in a group spitting water at one another, children urinating at the side of the camp, a man serenely drunk beneath a bench. The assistant, the one who had appeared in the famous picture, was shown here and there about camp business. He was a dark, slim young man with an intense face, a large nose, eyes, and ears, so that he looked a little like a lemur. Of the other assistant, nothing—no, almost nothing. At the edges of some of the pictures, an arm, an end of dress, the blur of a motion and in among the lines a shape, someone at a tent flap here, and here again. In surgery there was the edge of a gowned, masked shape, more than a head shorter than Daniel. The pictures had not been cropped. "This leg here—"

"The assistant's, but who can tell. She tried to get away and I did not pursue her."

"Oh, and this one—"

"Yes?" Koizumi looked at her as she exclaimed. "Oh, yes, they almost used that as the cover picture because it was interesting photographically."

The picture had been taken at night. Through the doctor's tent wall one saw two people in silhouette, obviously talking intently. Their heads were close together and the viewer had a feeling of intensity that was almost confessional. The assistant? No, the young man she had seen was too slight in build. It was obviously an older man, heavy and round-headed. There was something non-Indian about the body posture—"Who is the man here? He doesn't look like a villager . . ."

"No, it was a visitor. There's a camp picture of him somewhere, although he was shy of the camera. I don't think he knew about that silhouette." Koizumi laughed. "Things were a lot easier in those days. I never needed releases from everyone as I do now."

She turned the page. There were the visitors—three of them, posed with Daniel. The heavy man wasn't among them. She looked at others, more village pictures, women, girls. Then, bending over a water tap on the mud street, there he was; it was the heavy man, the visitor. It was—she looked again, blinked in disbelief. It was, even to the ring caught in morning light—Ripstein; it was Jack the Ripper, his lips pursed to drink, and she hurriedly turned back to the tent picture. Yes, that was his silhouette, the sharer in the tent, the man leaning in as Daniel, his silhouette absolutely unmistakable, leaned forward in agreement. They were so close they were almost touching; it was what gave the picture its charm, that intimacy. For a moment, a feeling like nausea rose in Vivian. She had been lied to, fooled, sent away with an easy lie. The Ripper. He and Daniel had known each other well; the bequest wasn't a mistake or the result of some chance meeting or an evening of comedy that Daniel had appreciated after a long while away. Something in the shock was expected. She had a long moment of quiet rage and she had to work hard to recover. Koizumi and his assistant, busy with lunch, did not notice. When the photographer looked up from his meal, he said, "Here come the famous pictures, the ones that were used. The red mark you see there designates what went into the magazine." Vivian was familiar with the group of pictures—the views of the camp people, coming and going, surgery, eating, sleeping, playing.

And then the two of Daniel. That picture, so famous, so often used for so many causes over the years that it had become a cliché, and had even been parodied. The original was still commanding. Even though she now knew that the look of anguish on Daniel's face had been caused by hunger and annoyance and that he was giving, not taking, the child, and that the camera eye looking up slightly had been what was creating the sense of rise and exultation, the picture still moved her.

Koizumi was smiling. "You loved your brother very much, didn't you?"

"Yes, I did."

"I can see it in your face. It makes me want to take a picture of you, and by that I know I am recovering my health."

"You couldn't have simply been photographing a hungry and irritated man after a hard day."

"That is what I have said, that there must be much more, that the art is in the subjective, not the objective moment, and that the moment is many things."

"It's a marvelous moment. You've got the background all dark in this one, but here, where he's sitting and so tired, you got the instruments, and the light catches them, shining and— magical somehow."

"Those were the instruments I picked up," Koizumi said. "They used jar lighting a lot—you know, a kerosene lamp shining through a jar of water. That was what did that. I moved it a little, I remember, to pick up the tray near his hand. I was thinking of shared focus—light in two places—and I was getting something very nice so I was not looking at the doctor's face at all."

"Really?"

"I think I should tell you that seeing life as a photographic composition is the photographer's curse, his weakness and besetting sin."

She laughed. "Of the curses, not the worst."

"I don't know—we can end up looking at life instead of living it."

When it was time to go, Vivian asked Koizumi if there were anything she could bring him. He smiled and said he thought not. His smile was shy and a little sad.

When she left the hospital, she walked home to give herself time to think. What had Daniel, reserved, obsessed with his faces and the suffering of children, to do with that awful co-median? Of course, Daniel worked with children wronged by life; by birth and accident. He himself had been wronged in that way—secretly so; the wrongs had been hidden and were invis-ible. The saving of Daniel, however humane the motive, had caused him awful pain. Daniel was reserved, even secretive. Why was he so obviously sharing something important with that crude man in a remote mountain village? Why was Ripstein there? It didn't seem like his kind of place at all. Vivian had caught him as the camera had, bending over, pursing his lips. His presence to her in those two pictures was disturbing, like some ugly creature that surprises one in a garden—the caterpillar on the flower stalk, the snake among the leaves. Surprise and loathing. In all her life, Vivian had never had a reason to hate anyone. Because of this, she had considered herself incapable of it. She knew now that she had been very wrong.

She wrote Abner a letter.

> Welcome back to New York. Please try to stay longer. I won't be able to meet you on Wednesday, because I'm trying to solve a mystery and the trail leads to Kansas City. I'll call you from there. I have so much to tell you and we need a long afternoon alone. I'll be in Toronto for the exhibition. I can't wait.
>
> V.

9

During the flight to Kansas City, Vivian read copies of letters she had brought. They were from the assistants, and reading them over made her weep quietly. The attendant mistook the signs for flight nervousness and kept reassuring her of the safety of the plane and the competence of the crew. The plane landed in another time zone. Earlier. Into the past already, Vivian thought.

She didn't want to drive to an unknown destination in a strange city, so she had to get buses and a taxi. It wasn't until late afternoon that she was left standing in front of a large, neo-ugly, fifties-utilitarian building with HORIZON HOUSE lettered on the front. It looked starved, dry, even with a forgiving screen of trees. She felt new misgivings at what she had done. It was a depressing suburb and soon she would have to think about a place for the night. This Cecelia Counselman, whose crumpled and stained letter Vivian had in her purse, had not made clear whether she was staff or inmate here. Vivian felt foolish not having asked. Perhaps the woman went in and out of reason. She went up and into the main door, looking around for an office. Two women passed her—"I beg your pardon. Where would I find—" It had all seemed so simple in New York, the idea of a visit, a chat about Daniel with someone who had known and worked with him for eleven years—who was eager to tell the old stories and exchange reminiscences.

"Oh, I think Jesse's gone home—" The two women turned back courteously and led Vivian to a doorway, looking in. "Jesse?"

The receptionist was obviously getting ready to leave also. "My name is Vivian Eitzer. I'm here to see Miss Counselman."

The woman smiled then. "We were afraid something had happened to you. Cecelia's been calling down all day."

"The trip took longer than I expected."

"Oh—well, she's waiting for you. Why don't you just go up. It's on the third floor. You can check at their desk up there."

Now Vivian tried to think of a tactful way to ask about Cecelia, but the woman was gathering her things, putting a cover over the typewriter. "It's all right—just go on up. The elevator is to your left."

First, overheated air, then the smell: quintessential nursing home: urine, disinfectant, rubber sheets, stale air, floor wax, bedridden bodies, despair, fear of despair, and industrial deodorant—the floral, not the pine. Vivian had recently spent a good deal of time visiting in nursing homes. Two of her friends were there, one temporarily, she hoped. The odor brought a parade of associations. There were double doors here, leading back to where a ward must be. Vivian pushed through one of them. Past that was another, heavier door. It occurred to her that she was glad she had traveled light. The single small suitcase she carried was beginning to weigh. Perhaps she could leave it somewhere for a while— She pushed through the next door and was in the ward itself.

She stopped in horror. She was standing inside the door, gaping at what looked like a scene in hell—a hell well-lit and well-ventilated enough, although she suddenly felt she could not breathe at all. Her hands and feet went icy. She was loose in the knees. The sight of it—the sound—

Boys and boy-men, some large, some small, some children in football attire, knee pads, elbow pads, and helmets, were shuffling around the large room, dancing spastically, moaning, grunting, crying. The sounds weren't loud, but constant, a layer

101

of insistent, meaningless noise like the sounds in a rain forest, a background punctuated by louder cries now and then, from where one could not tell. They all looked withdrawn, vacant; not one of them was involved with another. Most were deformed in face and body; some were obviously blind. Yet she had been seen. As she huddled, or felt herself huddling, at the door, a young man came over, making a series of sounds unintelligible to her. He tried to take her hand, but she pulled away. "No!" she cried to him. To her horror, he began to howl with anguish, and he staggered away. His cries had brought others, a little group peering at her, one or two of them rudely close. She felt like bolting. To her surprise, the crying boy was soon back and with someone who was obviously staff, although not in uniform. "You must be Cecelia's friend—"

"Yes." She was too sick to say more.

"She's been waiting for you." Vivian could not speak; she was mute with terror and disgust. "She's in the back." The woman pointed. "You can just go on in. Here, give me that bag and I'll put it in the station." She seemed not to realize how fearful Vivian was. She was chatting. "Wait. Cecelia must have told you all about Mikey. Let's get *him*." She rang a bell.

Vivian wanted to tell her that she hadn't heard anything from Cecelia but the nurse had already left her. A cry arose from the inmates as the sound of the bell went out *bing, bing, bing*, the cry louder with each strike. A few of the helmeted and unhelmeted youths turned toward the source of the sound; some waved their arms and cried out, but Vivian noticed that others, most of them, seemed oblivious to it. After a moment or two the outcry was hushed, but not as she had ever heard a group sound stop, not as laughter slows to a stop at a theatre. Some of it kept on and on, even as those who were making it forgot why it was being made. From the hall a group was coming, moving toward them. One was in the center, two, bearing him along, pulling him faster than he seemed ready to move. "Here comes Mikey," the nurse cried across the space between them. "He'll guide you back." Vivian was on the point of protesting but the nurse had turned away again and was talking to the two who had pulled the middle one. Then she was patting them, then hugging them as they made unintelligible noises of pleasure. Vivian's sense of sick unreality grew. The nurse didn't seem to notice. She kept up a bright chatter to the two boys. Then she went to the young man, who had been making gestures, and began hitting him here and there, gently, on his chest and arms and then on his hands. At each blow he nodded violently. He put his feet together and she stepped lightly and quickly on one of them and he nodded again. Then he shambled toward Vivian. "No—" Vivian cried, quietly, half a whisper—"no—"

"Put your hand out," the nurse said.

In terror, Vivian complied. She thought it was to be a handshake. She was suddenly gripped by Mikey in a complete handhold and what happened then was executed so quickly that it was done before she knew what was happening. The other hand came down over her shoulder and she was turned, Mikey rotating her like pair skaters in a routine. She was now in front of him with her back to him and both hands in his. He had already begun to push her. With a cry of terror, Vivian fell forward, breaking his hold. He began to grope, uttering terrible, guttural cries. Vivian ran. She was in a panic she could no longer control. She bolted past the nursing station and through the doors the way she had come. The elevator wasn't there. She saw the stairway and ran down the stairs, her steps and her panting, coarse breathing all she could hear. It was a panic flight, and it ended at the downstairs front door. In sight of the ordinary afternoon of an ordinary suburban street, she was able to stop and rest. She was winded and cold, even though the day was warm, and then, suddenly, too warm as the blood poured back into her face and reddened it with shame. There was a small foyer here with a couch and some chairs. She sat down.

As the panic receded, Vivian tried to get her thoughts in order. Her purse and suitcase were in the nursing station upstairs. When she was calmer, she would have to go up and make apologies and get them and then she could leave. She would call Cecelia Counselman on the phone from the motel she would find when she had called a cab. They might talk; she could not face that awful ward again. Perhaps there might be someone to call up to the ward and have the things brought down to her here in the normal world. The thought calmed her. Her heart slowed, her breath came easier. She looked around for a phone— To her left she heard a sound, and looking up, saw the elevator door opening. A woman was coming out, a large woman. She was dressed in a pantsuit, vaguely white. Then, her face. It was a young face, pleasant, and so unwrinkled that it was difficult to tell her age. Her hair was a faded red-brown, scanty and not very well combed.

She looked around quickly and seeing Vivian, said, "Are you Dan San's sister—are you Vivian?"

"Yes . . ."

"Oh, thank God! I'm Cecelia. Please forgive us. Forgive me. It was all my fault." She came out to the couch where Vivian was sitting. "Can I sit here with you?"

"Yes, of course."

"*I* made this mess. I told them on the shift we were old friends. I did it because if I hadn't, they wouldn't have let you up after four. They thought you must work in a place like this, too, and wouldn't be scared of it, and that you'd heard about Mikey and all the others from me. I'd been hovering around the front of the ward all day but just then I had to go back and tend to someone, and you came and Dianne never had the best judgment. She *thought*, I guess, how happy I'd be to see Mikey doing his thing with someone new. So the whole thing ended in a mess and I'm so sorry!"

"It's all right," Vivian said.

"Can I do anything for you?"

"My suitcase, my purse . . ."

"Do you want me to go get them and bring them down?"

"Yes, I think that would be best—"

"Of course, this time, you'd be with me—there's not a speck of hate or meanness in Mikey. He thinks he hurt you."

"I'm not hurt. I'm all right. It's just that I—the way they look—I'm not used to—"

"But that's just the thing," Cecelia said. "It's only *strange*, that's all. Mikey is deaf and blind, but he's a wonderful man and he wants to serve, to have a place and a use in the world. All he did was to try to lead you to me."

"But those boys—those men—"

"Come on up with me, please. Stand at the door, and let me tell you about them one by one. You can go anytime. Please— let me make it up to you because I'll never forgive myself if you go now after I was so stupid and ruined this chance to see and be with you. I've waited so long. Please—"

"If we go to the door—if we just go to the door—"

Cecelia's face lit up. The laughter of her relief was so re- warding that Vivian felt singled out for praise, made courageous by it. "Honest, Vivian, I know you'll see it better this time. Let me show it to you." She had been sitting on the heavy couch beside Vivian, with a space between them. She clambered up, puffing. "I'd have met you in town, but I forgot—I forgot how special this place is—I know where we can talk all we want, though."

"A place we can be alone—"

"Of course."

"He grabbed me—" Vivian said.

"I know. It must have been awful. He can't see or hear and he has cerebral palsy, and everybody but me used to think he was retarded. Because he can't see you or hear you, he's got to feel you when he meets you, and when he guides. I forgot, Vivian—all of us forget after all these years, because we live with them and know them so well, we all forget how he . . . how they must look, all of them, to the outsider, so different and scary. If it bothers you, don't look at them, look at me. We do a lot of touching up there. I may have to hold your hand or some kiddo will grab it. Is that all right?"

Vivian nodded. She was listening to Cecelia's voice. The first impression, that Cecelia was big and dowdy, yielded to the second, something in her voice. Suddenly her size came to mean solidity, the disorganization and flutter, concern. "Alston Fletcher said you smoked. I could use a cigarette now."

Cecelia looked surprised, then she grinned. "I had to give it

105

up when I came to work here. It deadens the smelling power of the deaf-blind kids. We can get something upstairs."

"Never mind."

"You sure you're all right?"

"Yes."

"You look a little gray, still."

"I'm a bit winded, that's all."

"You're on overload. I've got the cure for that, too."

They went up in the elevator again. There were the doors. "Just stand in here with me," Cecelia said. Vivian kept her eyes riveted on Cecelia. She opened the door. They went in and stood in the clamor. Cecelia fended off the inmates in an easy, friendly way. Her touching seemed necessary to many of them but having been touched, they quieted and some of them drifted away aimlessly to the back of the ward. If Vivian's flight had alarmed or upset them, they seemed not to remember it. Cecelia kept up continuous talk as though to drown the sounds, the moans and teeth-snapping and attention-begging cries around them. "That's Jeremy. When he came here he had no control over any of his body and no recognition of other people. He's really come far. Here's Mikey waiting for us. I think—I *feel* he isn't retarded, I think he never had the right teaching. Let me just take a second to reassure him and try to tell him you're okay." She left Vivian's side. There was a moment of fear, but Cecelia's presence, ten steps away, gave confidence. Vivian watched, her fear giving way to fascination. Cecelia had gone to the boy who was standing staring vacantly, rubbing his face with his hand. She began to hit him gently the way the nurse had, first his hand. Expression woke magically in him, but not in his face—in his body. He writhed, his hands began to wave. Cecelia rubbed her hand over his face, then began the series of soft blows. At the first, he responded with excited twitches and sounds. She hit him, brushed, pushed, with the flat of her hand, her fingers very lightly jabbing, her palms rubbing up and then down on his shoulders. Mikey was crowing with delight. "I'm telling him what I can about what happened," Cecelia said, "and now I'm telling him to take over what I was doing so we can talk." A new series of touches, pushes, and pokes, and then she hugged the boy and gave him a pounding on the back. He clapped and hugged her back none too gently. "Mikey," she said to Vivian, "is worth meeting, but we'll save that." She came back to Vivian's side. "I'm so glad you came, and so glad you've forgiven us—" and suddenly Vivian was in Cecelia's arms, against her big breasts. She had never been hugged by anyone but a relative or a lifetime friend, but she had gone through terror and Koizumi had been right about Cecelia. Transformed into a beautiful woman, she was also transforming. Vivian was losing her fear. She hugged Cecelia back and they both laughed. All the laws here were different anyway. It was the custom of the country. Cecelia released her and stood back. "You weren't ready for that, were you—sorry—I couldn't help it—I've—it's been so long, and Dan San's sister—" and she laughed again, a big, loud, infectious laugh, all delight.

"We've got the time off till supper," she said. "We can go downstairs and sit in a waiting room or we can have two nice easy rockers in a room of our own." She looked Vivian up and down. "How are you now, okay?"

"Yes—it's just that some of them were so—big."

"Come on with me—" Vivian kept her eyes on Cecelia, and found that in that way action was easy. "There, that's my room."

"You *live* here?"

"I like it here and after being away so long with Dan, I didn't have much to come back to. The people here need someone who *is*, not comes and goes. There's quite a lot of turnover in help. We all decided I should stay here. Come on in."

The room was dim in the fading light, but the walls were papered in a flower print, the chair and bedcover in chintz— huge, lascivious roses. The total effect was overwhelming. Cecelia saw Vivian's look and laughed. "Kinda gets to you, doesn't it. The kids chose it. There's so little real color in this place, I can't blame them for going hog-wild."

Vivian could say nothing. She simply stood, tired and baffled, not guarding her look—Mikey, running, this room—

Cecelia laughed. "Lord, I wish I had a picture of your face!

Let it go, Vivian, you feel it—feel it; when you know these people, you'll see they're still themselves. Even the ones who don't have a *self*—have the beginning of one—like a map before the place-names get put on." She sat down in a rocker and motioned Vivian to another. "This room is getting to you, isn't it."

"Frankly, yes."

"Nothing quicker fixed. Why don't you draw the curtains?"

The flowered walls, bed, chairs were darkened into a mellow gloom as the curtains shut out the westering light. The two women rocked in the near dark without talking. Then Cecelia sighed. "How often I've wanted to sit and talk about Dan San and all those years." Silence; then, "Oh, listen, the people here don't know anything about that. It'd only make things tough for me if they knew. I have freedom to work with the kids and to act the way I want. I'd be glad if you didn't say anything."

"I won't if you don't want it, but Cecelia—you were unique, a phenomenon; you stayed *eleven* years in work that exhausted some people in less than two. Surely someone has come, or will come, to interview you. It's going to get out somehow."

"No one will come here for an interview and not with me," the easy voice said matter-of-factly, "and the staff people here don't read much."

"I have so many questions . . ."

The creak of the rocker moved in rhythm to the words. "We have all the time we need. Outside . . ." and Cecelia sighed, "in the world out there, time's in short supply, but in here, all that's changed. It's one reason I like it. It took me five years to invent a body code for Mikey and teach it to him. Now I'm campaigning to get the sign language people up here. I got a big ambition and that's to train all the walking people to exercise all the bed people."

They rocked companionably in the dark. In spite of the strangeness of the surroundings, the noise outside their door, which was only partly closed, Vivian found herself less and less frightened and no longer revolted. The eye holds grudges but the nose is more forgiving. The smell of the place no longer

108

seemed so offensive. She rocked on. "What was it like," she asked Cecelia, "working with my brother?"

It had all been done by letter, Cecelia told her—query, answer. The doctor himself hadn't accepted anything. He had only given her permission to come. It was 1961, and the team was in the highlands of East Pakistan, and when he saw her he could look one look and turn her away and there would be nothing then but the trip home . . .

Cecelia's life had been punctuated by people's disappointment. She had always been heavy and almost aggressively plain. By the time she was fifteen, ridicule from her schoolmates made her wretched and withdrawn. Only pictures now, those memories. Written on the girls' room wall at Deep Creek High.

> *Cecelia made*
> *A lot of shade*
>
> *Cecelia has a model's figure—*
> *A model-A truck*

Cecelia told Vivian how she went to work at a nursing home run by the Sisters of Saint Catherine, and how Mother Sylvester found her weeping in the linen room one afternoon. A month later, Cecelia was taken into the order as a novice. It was a pious fraud engineered by Mother Sylvester. Cecelia had no religious vocation, but as a novice and postulant, she had automatic entry into the school of nursing in Minneapolis run by the sisters for their hospitals. Her work there was so good, particularly in the operating room, that the fiction of her being a religious was slowly abandoned. As the other students took on more and more of the habit, she wore less and less.

A picture of the order's mental hospital in Barbados, geriatric section. Cecelia wrote glowing letters to her parents in Deep Creek about the tropics, and she grieved a constant, insistent grief. Her operating room skills were deteriorating. Those skills were the only excellence she felt she had. Three years.

A picture of a day in Bridgetown of a carriage ride with a tourist couple. Their daughter Mitzi was doing surgical nursing in East Pakistan with a doctor named Daniel Sanborn. In the end, they gave her Mitzi's last address. Cecelia wrote. Did the doctor need—could he use . . . "I am overweight. Would that make a difference?"

The surgeon traveled from the Chittagong hills to the marshy forests of the lowlands, bringing his surgery to road after road of remote villages strung in an endless web through that crowded country. The work was filthy, endless, and lonely.

Cecelia told Vivian how she stood like a novice again, knocking at a door for admission. It was the open door of a comfortable-looking bamboo house with a spacious veranda and thatch two feet deep covering the single large room. It was midmorning and all around her the village at her back and the road beyond it were alive with comings and goings. When she had knocked the novice's knock at the door in Minnesota, she knew that the people inside were, at least some of them, prepared for her appearance. These people might look, as others had, and look away.

It was humid and there was the smell of mold from the inside of the house. Barbados had conditioned her to such a climate. She had whispered, "Oh, God, let this become familiar." Insects buzzed and clicked everywhere. The grasses and forest growth were so high that only this large house and another nearby showed clearly above it. Yet on trails through it she heard people calling, moving here and there; animals were lowing as they moved to and from the cultivated fields beyond the screen of forest. She knocked again. A woman came and Cecelia said, "I read on the way over that the Bengal tiger comes from here." She said this quickly so as not to say, "For God's sake, see beyond my looks." She was trying to fend off the change, the familiar expression of distaste.

"Good God!" the woman said.

"Amen," Cecelia answered.

"Just a second," the woman said, "I'll go get him . . ."

"The tigers won't get me up here on the porch, will they?" Cecelia asked. She was afraid they already had.

And the doctor, barely seen in her anxiety. By the time she was relaxed enough to see him, he was past being seen objectively. He looked at her hard and said, "Our surgery takes a small field. We have to stand close. Could you do that and not get in the way?" Only that. No other judgment.

"I'll take up the room you leave," she said to him, eye straight into eye. "I'm short and I can fit in under your arms," and suddenly she wanted to work with Dr. Daniel Sanborn as much as anything she had ever wanted in her life.

He was looking at her with no change whatever in his face. "You like children?"

"And tigers, yes. I swim and ride a bicycle, and I've assisted in lots of eye surgery and Dr. Herrmann in Minneapolis used to ask for me because he said I was good in a crunch and I can stand for eight hours at a clip and my name is Cecelia and I'm here in answer to your ad."

"Well," said Dr. Daniel Sanborn, "let's get on with it."

It was good that she had not rigidified her surgical techniques. He had his own order of procedure; she learned quickly. The doctor was impatient and brusque but never capricious. The third day she was there, Mitzi said to her, "I thought you were a joke when you came, that you could never do this. I was wrong."

"I know," Cecelia said, and acknowledged a strength for the first time in her life.

They moved. Pictures of places. Cecelia ticked them off to Vivian. Assistants. She learned how to change encampments, how to train native help, to break down and set up for surgery and moving; above all, how to talk to the patients, calming, explaining, showing, telling, listening to fears, and explaining again and still again. Camp to camp. Village to village. Up the Ganges, across to the Brahmaputra, into the tribal places where there were native assistants who had to stand in pairs translating and retranslating before the English came drop by drop from the need-rigged pipeline of intermediate languages.

And nothing diminished the glowing truth which grew larger and clearer to Cecelia every day: that the job of surgical assistant, though necessary, was not the crucial part of what she did here. Everything she had endured, blundered through, become, had been an essential preparation for this present work. Her three wasted years in Barbados, the listening, the talking, the sudden welling laughter, the free access to tears had been, all her life long, preparation, novitiate for this work. Dan San, great as he was, could not give it; he was too shy, too guarded, too strongly pointed in the direction of his goal. For him, the patient behind the ruined face seemed irrelevant. This she did not tell Vivian. She described how the work reached out and took them as naturally as oxygen in the capillaries of the lung is taken for use, and with what must be, even on that cellular level, an eagerness of need. She told how they flowed upward into the work, breathing it in, expanding into it, making it theirs. They forgot everything in the work, old pictures, old fears, memories of past pain. They moved on to Iran after the earthquake there. They learned to ready the camp for moving in four hours flat from a standing start.

"And you called him Dan San—"

"Mary Nell got upset when Dan was too taken up to see something special she had done. It wasn't meanness; it was inattention. She asked me, dear old novice nun, if all the saints were like that. Was Saint Dominic like that? Was Saint Francis? So I started kidding about Saint Fran and Dan San and I made her laugh."

"Tell me more—all the stories—I don't care if they're complimentary or not. My brother was not an easy man to know; I realize that. I'm hungry for them all. I've been sheltered; you can see that, too. Now I want to know."

"There are so many memories—when I came here, I tried not to think about those days. Old wars—you know. But recently, sometimes . . . things come back, and I sit here and try to judge, to remember. Was I right in some decision? Was I wrong?"

"What decisions? Tell me. I'm eager to hear all about your old wars and what they were like."

"Once," Cecelia said, "we were near Cambodia. Dan wouldn't go to an island; did you know that? Someone once told him the continents were only big islands, but he said, 'The rivers are roads, but oceans surround an island.' Southeast Asia is like a series of islands. You cross lots of water. The patients had to travel quite a way to come to where we were, but Dan stayed on whatever seemed like a mainland to him. In one place we began to see people—men, women, kids even—whose faces had been ruined by trauma. It was as if whole villages had been hit in the face or been burned. Most were healed over. It took me two weeks to tumble to it."

"To what?"

"The numbers; the numbers did it. You get used to seeing grown people presenting with problems we fix in little babies, the burns and harelips and healed-over broken bones. This was different, the kind of burns, the kind of trauma."

"What was it?"

"It was from torture. They were coming miles to have their jaws rebroken and reset, their eyes put right again in the sockets after the upper palate and the bones on the sides, orbital bones, had been smashed and healed wrong, noses that were useless lumps, burns and burns and burns. What hit us first were the numbers, that and the fear. First I thought—we all thought—it was what I said—the collection of years. There are special kinds of accidents with special kinds of farming and sometimes there are traditions of fighting—eye-gouging, for example—but this was torture, and it bred a special kind of fear. They wouldn't have come at all except that we were days of travel from the capital, far even from the provincial towns. They weren't farmers, Viv; they spoke three or four languages, some of them. I could see Dan was angry. We'd be getting ready to leave and another bunch would come. We began to be scared ourselves; it was hanging in the air above us, the nightmares they all had, the terror everywhere. Assistants we got wouldn't stay. Dan never talked about the conditions of our work, but then

113

he said, 'I never thought I would end up being part of this animal's production line.' We were, you know, like servants of that tyrant. I think about things like that."

"What happened?"

"That was what I wanted to tell you. One day a little girl came into the camp. She was nine or ten—just an ordinary farm girl, but she had a letter. I took her to Dan. He read the letter and we struck camp right then. In three hours we were packed up, put away, and being poled upriver in a fleet of their pirogues—boats that will float on a heavy dew. Our patients disappeared into the forests; only those who were still recovering from the anesthesia came with us, and we met some later across the border. They said that two hours after we had left, a gang came and killed everyone caught within a mile of our empty camp."

"Why?"

"I don't know. I don't know who sent the little girl, either, or what was in the letter or why a government tortures its own people when it doesn't want information from them about anything. I sit here lately and the questions like that come back to me and I try to think about them, about the pride and the fear and the terrorism and sometimes I see things one way and sometimes another. It was on that trip upriver—"

"What?"

"That Dan said some things about you that I didn't understand then, but that I understand now."

"What did he say?"

"It was early in the morning . . . dawn. We had been traveling all night and listening for guns or people and being scared because we knew something was up and of course we didn't understand or speak the language or understand the people— we were like babies, dependent . . . and not *knowing*. Sometimes the riverbanks were close and sometimes they were far and the water was slow and then we breathed easier. When the dawn came there was a mist hanging over the river ahead of us. The boats with our equipment and one patient in each came and went out of the mist. When the sun came up, it was through

114

layers of fog, and we were in a gold haze lit up underneath, all the green kind of shimmery. It was like another world. I asked Dan if he thought it was beautiful. He said, 'I suppose so.' Then he said, 'My sister's world . . .' I didn't understand. I said, 'Does she live in a special place?' He said, 'No, but the beauty part is her specialty.' I didn't understand, but I think I do now. You have a special quality of . . . a kind of delicate way. I think he meant that."

"Maybe he only meant what I do. I appraise and authenticate porcelain, European porcelain of the eighteenth and nineteenth centuries. Years ago when I was just learning the various styles and methods . . . Daniel was in college then . . . during his vacations, I would nag him into going with me to the museums and galleries where there were good collections. He had a wonderful eye for detail and a real sense of form, but when I realized he was going as a kind of duty to me, I stopped asking him."

" 'The beauty part is her specialty.' It isn't true, you know. You may think this is funny, Viv, but there is a lot of artistry in fixing up a ruined face, in really elegant surgery. Surgery can be witty sometimes, too, the way something is picked up and incorporated into a facial line or plane. Maybe Dan San did faces the way you do your porcelain."

"It makes me happy that you would think so."

"Dan San seemed to mind heat and cold less than the rest of us. We'd be sweating, baking, itching with heat, we'd be shivering and blue with cold, and there he'd be, with the pictures or in surgery as though it were a day in May. I always thought his body shape helped—lots of evaporating surface—and, of course, I thought he was a wizard because of his bicycles."

"Bicycles?"

"Over the years, he had to make all of his equipment—sterilizers, suction, saws, respirators—usable in places where there were no electric lines. We had no power but human muscle. His compressed air power had to be generated by foot, and his electricity, too. It was funny, but sometimes it made us cry, seeing them. Most of those tribal people didn't fuss over their kids—you know, play with them. Sometimes they were indif-

ferent to them and sometimes they beat them, hard, for minor
things; they slapped or cuffed them and no one saw kids as
special, deserving to be free of everyone's daily miseries. But
whatever love was or wasn't, relays of them, fathers and uncles,
mothers, aunts, cousins, would walk Dan San's pedals or ride
his 'bicycles.' They were frames with pedals that turned the
generators that gave us our O.R. lights and hot air for sterilizing
and power for whatever else we needed. You'd see the people,
slow, no expression, and faithful as sand, walking hour after
hour, riding thousands of miles in place to charge our air cyl-
inders or to build the power that made us magicians. He invented
them all. When he wasn't doing surgery, he was inventing ways
of making better power independently.''

"I never knew that; he made model airplanes as a child.''

"I think he liked that inventing almost as much as—''

"As what?''

"He was happiest moving—funny. I didn't know that until
just now, seeing his face in my memory—'' Cecelia stopped
rocking. "What if I'm remembering wrong? I seem to know,
to have all those pictures in my mind, but it was a long time
ago. My feelings might have crept in and changed things—not
the facts, the truth.''

"Don't worry, I've talked to other assistants, too. It was
Alston Fletcher who taught me about the aesthetics of what you
did there—the beauty and the artistry.''

"Oh, that's right! You must have seen other people. Alston.
How is he? Who were the others?'' Cecelia's voice had risen;
Vivian could hear the delight and eagerness in it. She went down
the list, the letters and phone calls and the visit to Sister Mary,
and Alston Fletcher. "Oh!'' and Cecelia's voice in the dark was
as excited as a girl's. "How is Ramesh? How is Alston? What
did Stephanie and Richard say? I've thought of all of them so
much—I used to have such fantasies about all of us—''

"Dr. Fletcher said you wanted to get everyone together—''

"Yes! Yes! All of us, the old ones and the ones before me,
Mitzi and Anna and the ones before them, Dorothy and Pearl,
that could meet the ones who came after, that we could talk—

and then that we could help the ones who—the ones who maybe had a hard time fitting back into the world, or got sick, or lost jobs, or . . . well, just . . . Viv—the work was no cinch. God, they were wonderful people, those assistants. I had the feeling that if we'd ever come together, we would have been invincible—new projects, a network, like they talk about now." She sighed. "But it never happened. Ramesh got bitter and went to Europe. Mitzi says she's too busy. Anna Louis says she doesn't mind writing to people she knew, but she can't see what I see— a way to do so much more."

"Almost eleven years, Cecelia—that's longer—almost three times as long as anyone else. How did you do it?"

"Oh . . ." Rocking, the sound, the easy sound. "Oh, I loved it." Noise of the chair, noise of the floor, an easy *swish swish* on the hospital linoleum.

A sound, a gentle thumping from somewhere, and a cry. "It's the dinner cart already. I didn't know I talked so long."

"What do we have to do?" Vivian was afraid of having to venture out in the ward alone.

"Well, we're in a bit of a mess," Cecelia said. "I always invite the two best boys of the afternoon to eat with me here as my dinner guests. I'm trying to teach them what *future* means. The time between lunch and dinner is longer than any of them remembers. Would you—could you eat here with us? I'll choose neater kids if you want—"

Vivian's heart sank. Table manners . . . food. It was difficult enough to *look* at the inmates, much less eat with them. Then she thought that by one by one might perhaps be a little easier. This was, after all, their world and not hers. She was also aware that Cecelia gave their world an illusion of normality. She cast a spell that made the idea of dinner here not only possible but almost bearable with grace. Her room was protected, her bulk a kind of surety. "Can you arrange for dinner for me?"

"I told the kitchen I might want a staff meal for you. They're a little nicer."

"Then yes; yes, I'll stay."

The darkness rang with Cecelia's cry of delight. Vivian got

up and so did Cecelia, and she turned on the lights. The hideous walls sprang out at them. Cecelia looked at Vivian and laughed. "Viv, you should see your face. If Koizumi had his camera here—Koizumi—I haven't thought about him for years, but I remember those days in Peru . . ."

"I saw him in New York, just before I came out here. He was in the hospital."

"He's okay—?"

"A parasite—something from a trip. Men deny . . ."

"I know. And you talked about Dan—?"

"Yes, and about some of the pictures he had taken that didn't get into the magazine."

"I stayed out of his line of sight."

"I know, but he told me this: that you were beautiful to him as you worked, transformed, that it was miraculous to him but that you refused to be shown working. I think it was silly and a shame. Doesn't it make you sad now, that you were so vain and sensitive that you missed being 'there' the way the other assistants were?"

"No, but looking at those pictures makes me sad. My folks saved the magazine for me. They understood why I wasn't in them."

"Why did they make you sad?"

"Because Koizumi took them and they made us famous all over the world and yet he never saw—no one ever saw—"

"What?"

"How deep in trouble we were just then, how Douglas was falling apart, and how I, dumb and fat and miserable, couldn't help. I was scared for Douglas and I desperately wanted success for Dan San, which meant not being seen. I wanted like all hell to tell Dan what was happening, but with Koizumi there and the other people, I ended up doing nothing and then it was too late."

"What was it—what was happening—?"

But Cecelia had moved to the door and a roar went up when she was seen, those who could speak yelling to her as she stood in the doorway, blocking Vivian's view, "Me! Me!" and those who couldn't speak, howling. Vivian stayed back, safe in the room. Cecelia waited calmly in the clamor until it stilled. She spoke slowly but without the condescending glissando people use for children, the retarded, the old.

"Mikey fed all the wall-children for me when I was talking to my friend, so I want Mikey for my dinner partner. Arthur has not fought all day and has not banged his head, and today I saw him let another boy go through the door first. I will surely like a dinner partner like Arthur. Arthur, you are my second partner. Please go get Mikey and tell him to come. You know how to tell him." Before her stood two dozen grim-faced losers. Cecelia said, "Boys, this is my friend, Viv. It would be bad if she thought you were all angry. Tomorrow I will choose new dinner partners—two other boys."

There followed a cry, "Choose me tomorrow!" Vivian could see the other nurses behind the group, iron-faced with impatience. Cecelia turned and saw Vivian's eyes on them. She laughed. "That's what comes of living outside. They want routine for these kids, no risk and no excitement—lives they couldn't stand for one hour themselves. Hey, Mario—help Mikey. Arthur, come here and bring Mikey's tray for me."

It was another half an hour before they were, all four of them, sitting companionably and eating food long cold. "I'm used to cold grub," Cecelia said, "you're not. There's a microwave—"

"No need," Vivian said. "It's camping out."

"No nice dishes, either. Knowing what you do makes me shy; our ugly surroundings—these plates—"

"I'm the stranger," Vivian said. "Can't you see that? Nothing I know fits this trip of mine, these questions. When you came here to work, you brought a whole world with you. I'm in a place not my own, and I feel like a baby." Arthur laughed. Cecelia began to chat with Mikey, using the pats and pokes Vivian had seen before. Vivian's gingerly put questions to Arthur yielded the information that he was learning to use the toilet by himself and that Johnson was angry because there had been dogs on TV and he had wanted one and been refused.

"Our next battle," Cecelia said, "is going to be to get some animals in this place. Camels, giraffes, things like that."

Arthur got the joke and laughed. "Elephants!" he cried, and then he began to add the names of animals he knew.

"TV gives a lot to these kids," Cecelia said. "It's just the thing."

"Just the thing!" cried Arthur.

Mikey sat on Cecelia's bed because Vivian had the other chair. Now and then he would reach out to caress Cecelia or Arthur. He was still afraid of Vivian. He had been carefully taught how to eat, although he needed to use his fingers a lot. "Private language is so limited," Cecelia said, "we need teachers."

After dinner Vivian began to be worried about finding a place for the night.

"Why don't you just stay over?" Cecelia was grinning. "I'll get a cot and after the kids go to bed we can sit up and talk some more. And we'll turn out the light on this awful room, and I'll close the door if you're scared. *Please*, Viv—I've got so much I want to say—all those years, and you coming here has brought things back—"

"Well . . . would they allow—"

"Oh, sure, it's in my agreement with them: *my* room, *my* friends. Come on, you did so well at dinner with Mikey and Arthur. No one will bother you. You leave tomorrow anyway—"

Vivian had been looking forward to a hot bath and a soft bed, but inertia conquered her and she was comfortable now with Cecelia, whose magic seemed to have changed the place. "Well . . ."

"We'll give you anything you want—TV, a bath—"

"Oh, the bath!" Vivian cried.

"Well!" Cecelia grinned. "We've got *that* better than anyplace you've ever seen."

❧ 10 ❧

They lay steaming in two huge tubs in the tiled hydrotherapy room one flight up on the female ward. Vivian was stretched out full length, basking in easy heat, half asleep. Their voices were muffled in steam, drowsy and drawn out.

"These are the two floors where you live and work; is this enough?" she asked.

"Oh, yes. Some of the kids will leave here. We train some to go back to their families or to halfway houses, but most of them need to stay here. There aren't enough good folks who want to work with our people—the ones who will never leave but who need teaching and fun and groups and excitement and risk without malice. People say 'institution' with their faces pinched up, but Harvard is an institution, too. Sorry, it's a soapbox subject for me."

"Cecelia . . ." Vivian made an attempt at an easy tone. Cecelia was close to her but she couldn't see over the edge of the tub. Vivian was suddenly very shy, embarrassed. "Did you ever hear of a man named Jack Ripstein? A comedian—called Jack the Ripper."

A silence and then, in a changed tone, "Oh, *him*. He used to visit a lot. What about him?"

"So it *was* more than once. He *did* know Daniel well."

"Oh, yes; he was out two, three, sometimes four times a year."

"That often?"

"He'd come and stay for a day or two—never longer."

"Why?"

"To be with Dan. We used to say he came like stomach flu. He was a pincher. Mary Nell used to call him King Leer. I hated what he said to me so I stayed away from him. He had been coming before my time; because of that, I guess I never asked why. He came after, too. Stephanie said so. He was in lots of different countries with us. Will Rogers said he never met a man he didn't like—"

They laughed. "You have no idea why he was there—"

"No, but he wasn't like a regular visitor. He wasn't interested in the medicine or service to humanity; he hated bad food and bad weather. He couldn't stand to watch the surgeries or see the kids. The truth is, Viv, I used to pretend he wasn't there. He seemed to like hurting me, and that was awful. I don't mind anything the kids here say about me or my hair or my size. He'd call me blimpo and lardo and he'd make sex jokes about me that made me cringe. I was only an assistant. All I could do was get away when he was there. Yet he was the only visitor Dan would allow in his tent. Evenings he was there you'd hear that jackass laugh all over camp. And he was the only one Dan would interrupt his schedule for."

"So many times?" Vivian didn't know which emotion she felt more keenly: puzzlement, disgust, or anger. What could Daniel have in common with a man like Jack Ripstein, and why had Ripstein lied to her?

Cecelia said, "Oh, yes."

"Why?"

"I don't know. I don't think it was for the laughs. Whatever Dan had, it wasn't a sense of humor, even for jokes. Some people who don't see anything funny in life will tell jokes. Don't be hurt, Viv, but even the funny things that happened around the camp and had everybody else bent double went by him."

122

"And you have no idea why Ripstein visited?"

"No. Ripstein used to say that messed-up faces made him sick. Then he'd let go a shot or two at me."

Vivian remembered the awful night at the casino, and the kind of jokes Ripstein made to her. They were not made in humor; they were made to impress, to separate, to hide in, to gain time. Ripstein was a professional comedian. His humor served a purpose. She remembered how it had dropped away when they were alone. She said, "I wonder if he wasn't trying to keep you at a distance with those insult jokes. I saw him work; he doesn't waste his effects being funny for no good reason."

Cecelia was quiet in her tub. Vivian could almost feel her working on the idea. "I never thought about that. I've always been sensitive about my size. He must have known that. What was his reason for the jokes besides natural cruelty?"

"You're not that big. You're half the size you see yourself as being. Maybe you should think about why he wanted to get you out of the way. Then we might figure out what he was doing there with Daniel, who, by your own estimate, couldn't see a joke."

"Not if he fell over it. No offense."

"None taken."

They lay musing, unable to see each other over the high rims of their tubs. The anxiety and frustration of Vivian's day were untangling themselves and stretching out to relaxation. The foreign, fear-filled world into which she had come this afternoon had been changed for her in the space of four hours. She had, however squeamishly, dined with Cecelia's dinner guests and had touched Mikey good-night and had seen the residents dwindling off into dormitories to sleep. This was a part of the world she had sworn to look at for Daniel's sake. Under Cecelia's wise and powerful protection, she was relaxing and might, later, sleep. "This is a lovely bath," she murmured.

"Yes, it is. They used to use hydro back in the fifties," Cecelia said, "before the drugs came in. Lately in some quarters there's been a move back. You don't think, do you, Viv, that Dan's special treatment—special allowances for Ripstein—were because Ripstein saved his life?"

"Did he?" Vivian sat up and tried to look over the rim of the tub.

"Didn't you know about that? Twice, I heard. The first one happened before my time. I heard it from Mitzi who heard it from Pearl Gluysteen who heard it from God knows who. I thought it was only a rumor."

"The second one—?"

"The second one I saw. It was in Vietnam."

"What happened?"

"People sometimes misunderstood why Dan and his setup were there. I don't blame them. They were desperate; they heard the word *doctor* and they came. We would sometimes get bad medical cases. We had no drugs for them beyond antibiotics. Once a man brought his wife and mother, both dying of burns. We had nothing for the complicated care they needed. We put IVs in for fluid replacement, but they were too far gone and they died that night. The man went kind of crazy. He had a knife and he attacked Dan in his tent. Ripstein was there. We had followed the man and heard Ripstein yelling. We came in time to see him jump the man and deflect the blow. He got a slash on his arm but the man was off balance and the cut wasn't very deep. We found out later that the man and women were Vietcong and that the women had been burned trying to set fire to an army barracks. Ripstein bled like a slaughterhouse and howled like one when we were stitching him. Didn't Dan tell you that story?"

"No. Never about Jack Ripstein. Never about what happened in his work."

"Never about the assistants? About us?"

"No; I'm so sorry; no; and what a loss that was for me."

There was a sigh from the other tub. "That was Dan, though."

Later they sat up talking in Cecelia's room. "Sleeping over—I never thought someone would actually *do* it."

"I'm the first, then?"

"The first." Cecelia was quiet for a time. Then she said, "I've been thinking about what you said, that Ripstein used that ridicule to keep me out of the way. What was the reason?"

"What do you think?"

"I don't know, but I wonder why I never saw through it?"

"It's worth thinking about, but lifesaving or not, I don't like thinking about that man. I have something nice to show you. I brought letters from some patients and some of the assistants."

"Oh, yes, you were going to show me—" Cecelia bounced with eagerness. Her years on this ward had taken away her self-consciousness. Vivian smiled.

"I thought you might remember some of the patients and be able to fill in more places and people. Here's my list—one I'm making of Daniel's places of encampment and who he worked with at each place. Here's the list and here are the letters."

Cecelia took the sheaf and sat propped up in bed, reading. In a moment she was reading aloud to Vivian, punctuating what she read with exclamations: "Oh, isn't that wonderful!" "I wish I remembered this girl—there were so many, and she doesn't say exactly when . . ." "Here's a nice one, this is nice, yes." Then she gave a little cry. "Oh, this is from Stephanie and Richard! It's from their clinic. I hoped they'd write! I trained them, you know. Stephanie and I—and then Richard came. I left after that. They worked for a couple of years and came back and went to medical school. Now they have a clinic."

"I know," Vivian said.

"I always send them a card at Christmas, and Alston, and Peggy, and Mariella. I almost went down to Bolivia last year, but Mikey had that breakthrough, opening up our codes. I couldn't go then."

"No, I suppose not."

Cecelia read on. "And here's Alston—is he still so athletic? He used to play soccer with patients' families wherever there was a field."

Vivian told Cecelia about the interview.

"You ran around the park?" She was laughing, incredulous, spirited, and very beautiful. Vivian agreed with what Koizumi had said about her.

"He was wishing he could do his workout and talk to me at the same time. Later, he did a lot for me, showing me the pictures of the work you all did—I mean the faces."

"Was it hard, very hard to look at them?"

"I wasn't used to—people like me are sheltered from some kinds of ugliness and illness; Daniel—"

"Yes, Dan went out and looked for it in the places where it was the worst—"

"And these letters made me know, and Alston Fletcher showed me—"

Cecelia had picked up another letter, had begun to read it. Then she stopped. "Listen to this—" and she read aloud to Vivian: " 'I won't sign my name but I was one of the doctor's assistants. I didn't last very long. I failed him and myself and stole money—' Viv, this letter is from Douglas—I know it."

"Douglas Likens?"

"Douglas *Irons* is his name. I worked with him in Vietnam and then we went to Peru and worked there. He left when we were in Peru. I know this is from Douglas. Viv, when did you get it?"

"About a week after Daniel's death."

"I was going to tell you about what happened when Koizumi came to Peru and how Ripstein's awful jokes kept me away— I see now that I can't only blame Ripstein. It was *my* fault, that I listened to his insults and let them hurt when I should have been stronger. Bad things were happening there, and I was part of them. Poor Douglas. He's still hurting. Viv, turn out the light. I don't want you to see me cry."

"Cecelia—"

"No, please, please!"

Vivian reached up and switched off the light. In the near dark, there was no sound for a while, and then Vivian heard the sniffling of someone who has wept and is dealing with the results of it. Then there were half-sobs crushed into a handkerchief.

"So much pain," Cecelia said after a while, "and the money he talks about stealing wasn't stealing, really. He ran away. I begged him not to go. I begged him to wait, to talk to Dan, to let us get a replacement so he wouldn't have to go like that." She was caught by a sniffle and a hiccup. "Viv, you've got to keep the secret of what I say."

"It all happened years ago, surely now—"

"You've got to promise—"

"Yes, of course, but—"

"Douglas came while we were in Vietnam. He told us a story about being a war correspondent and quitting, but I think he deserted. We took him on because we were desperate. He worked his tail off with us. He was wonderful with the patients and tried so hard to be good in the O.R., learning how Dan liked things done." There was silence in the darkness; Cecelia blew her nose again. "I knew that half the time he'd have to go somewhere and throw up after surgery. I was always giving him milk because I was scared he'd get an ulcer."

"So you thought he wasn't fitted for the work—"

"Not for the O.R. part. We were in Vietnam for quite a while after he came to us. He must have gotten a passport somehow because he had one when we left. I thought he'd take off then, but he came to Peru with us and stayed there for almost two years. Douglas was a very moral person; maybe he was using us as a kind of punishment. I think now he would have stayed longer if it hadn't been for Koizumi coming and making us all so conscious of ourselves, suddenly, so aware of what we looked like to an outsider. We were caught in Koizumi's glass eye, and changed. It was part of the reason I hid and maybe why Douglas folded. Later, I thought the pictures might give him away to the army."

"Koizumi said he sensed a lot of tension, but he ascribed it to the weather, the constant cold and rain you were having, and to his own clumsiness and the demands he made on you."

Cecelia laughed. "How funny that is! I keep trying to make

our kiddos here realize that other people feel things, too, and now I've fallen into the same hole I want to lead all of them out of."

"Can I turn on the light now?"

"Yes, I want to see that letter again. I know it's his. When I think what he's been feeling all these years, a failure, a thief, a runaway—the kind of man he was—Viv, what was the return address?"

"There was none."

"A postmark?"

"I would have kept a record of it, at home."

Cecelia read the letter again. She turned out the light and they lay silent in the dark. Every now and then Vivian heard her blowing her nose and sighing. Vivian began to talk slowly and quietly about Sister Mary Binchois and Mother Tony and about Alston Fletcher and the nice things he had said about Cecelia. She left out his description of her appearance. There was silence from the other bed. Cecelia seemed to be in a kind of reverie. After a while, Vivian thought she might have drifted off to sleep, but now and then heard a sigh. "Cecelia?"

". . . thinking—I was just thinking . . ."

❧ 11 ❧

The earthquake had been in the mountains and they had gone
there, between the Andes' great ranges, where the earth seemed
to have been spilled in heaps as God had spun them in joy at
the world's creation. They stayed in rural settlements, some so
small they were without names and were a day's walk, two
days with the vans, on steep roads. The mists from the jungles
below did not rise to these heights, but often the camp would
wake to find itself as though islanded, their mountain rising
from a mysterious sea and all the lower slopes flooded during
the night. The stars, all new, and without the competition of
lights on earth, bloomed in their millions like fireworks frozen
at the heights of their trajectories.

Cecelia had seen beauty and poverty go hand in hand in other
places. Here there was even more of both. Sometimes she and
Douglas sat half asleep huddled in blankets on a village's stone
retaining wall after dinner, watching the night come down,
talking quietly. He never spoke directly about his past; she assumed it was part of his fear of being known too well, the self-
protection of a deserter, but there were clues in his language
and in what he knew. He had been raised near the water and
had sailed a lot. His height, or lack of it, had bothered him at

school. He often gave his food to hungry children and his clothing to cold ones, so that things passed through his hands and his wardrobe changed continually. She thought he must be from an upper-middle-class home because of this casual acceptance that he would always have food and clothing and because he was always working on schemes for cooperative ventures to make the villages strong and prosperous—food storage plans, ideas for new industries or arts. These ideas were the ideas of a person used to seeing the government as approving or at least unthreatening. He had blamed the war for all the shocking things he had seen in Vietnam. Caught in this anguish, he had been surprised by Peru. That poverty made him preach revolution. Cecelia kept saying, "I thought you hated war," but he saw no paradox and kept preaching, "Some people might have to die." Sometimes he berated her for what he said was her acceptance of the status quo. He saw her, she thought, as maternal but not very bright. When winter closed them in, they sat with the local workers who drank caña, a cane liquor, to keep warm, and Douglas tried to talk to them about politics over the fires they kept small to save labor.

It was early spring when Koizumi came. They had been wintering farther down in settlements near the big watercourses. All winter, snow and ice marooned the high villages so Dan had moved them from the places of stone to those of adobe and down again to stick and clay and thatch, still huddling the night away close to the warmth of braziers.

And rain. When the lower mountains opened, they went up to villages of woodcutters and orchard keepers, stopping at a crossroads town to work under what the people said was the best roof there, a quonset hut of corrugated metal it turned out, which magnified every sound and froze them at night. And the rain. It beat on that honored roof like an invasion of locusts. They were never warm or dry. Fuel smoked in the braziers and at times there was a rainbow in the operating room.

Ripstein had come through five times that year, like a prince on safari, bringing drugs and equipment, great laughter, and shouts for service. Couldn't they see he was cold? Didn't they know he was wet? Where was the bar—did they think this was food? The villagers took immediately to the oversized man and his demands and the power of him. A helicopter delivered him like a one-man feast day. Cecelia went small, dwindling away to disappearance.

Then Koizumi, the photographer, during the wettest, coldest week, became a presence at their backs, under their arms, seeing, or seeming to see, into the heart of their work and into them. When they looked up from the meal or the patient or the ruined face, there would be his wheel-eye, black and bottomless, drinking up the moment. He took picture after picture of the patient, poncho-clad people in line outside the examining station. He photographed the photographing of their deformed faces. He posed the mountains and the trees and the rocks and the families as they waited stoically for the explanations to be translated into a sound like birdsong. Dan San never acknowledged the presence of strangers in the camp except for Ripstein, but even he was put off by the presence of Koizumi squinting behind his Eye. Douglas and Cecelia guarded their separate fears and found themselves hiding from the camera and then drifting away from each other. Cecelia fled; Douglas left his body where it was and took his attention out of range of the viewfinder.

And the cold. And the rain. Leaks formed in the tent and equipment had to be resterilized. Dan reached for equipment that had been moved to avoid the leaks and took dirty water on his gloved hand and had to reglove in the middle of the surgery. Nothing stayed clean or dry. Their food grew rank. Their clothing stank with mildew. Douglas and Cecelia walked in a gray odor and woke up reeking and shivering morning after morning. Depression slowed Douglas. He got more and more torpid. He was slow and clumsy in surgery and Dan got critical, losing patience and once slinging the wrong instrument, delivered late, back on to the tray with a muttered word. Then the photo paper got damp and the pictures came out streaked, details lost, and Dan growled at the assistants. "Do them over," and they did, and had nothing better because the paper was wet.

When the sun came out at last, they found they had gone

131

beyond some point where a weather change would help. Cecelia went to Dan San. "We need to go."

"Not now," he said. "We can't."

"Maybe not move the camp—jump on burros and head . . ."

"We have to stay here now." His look was so intense she knew there was no changing him. As he turned away, he said, "We can shut down for a few days, that's all."

"With people still waiting out there?" He shrugged. She was as close to rage as she had ever been.

In anger blunted by knowledge, Cecelia turned self-blaming. She went walking the night camp muttering like a witch with spells. His refusal was inhuman. They were all unworthy of his energy. Who did he think he was? They weren't machines; they were human beings. She saw a light in the supply van, showing through a crack in the door. It looked like a flashlight beam coming and going and suddenly gone. Was Dan looking for something? Perhaps someone was trying to steal— She went closer and heard sounds. The camp was lit with the wet moon and still-dripping stars and there were cold disks of light in the puddles. There was the flashlight beam again and darkness. Then someone came out, furtively, so intent that he did not see her at the entrance, and when he went to climb down from the back, she put out a hand and a foot and tripped the intruder into a moon-mirror. The shock of the icy water drove a cry from him. It was Douglas. She forced him up, hissing questions at him. She made him go into her tent and strip, threatening to wake the camp. She wrapped him in a blanket and made tea on her little burner.

He had been planning to run away. He had taken the cash that was in the lockbox, the money they used for the payment of drivers and interpreters and camp assistants and the occasional bribe in times of trouble. It was also used sometimes when an assistant left, needing fare home. "Let me go, now."

"Not until you promise me you'll stay until we get someone else. Don't leave like this—not after the years you've been here. Wait a week—two." She was pleading for time.

His face was stiff. "I'm going now—I've got to. I'm taking

fare and the fifty dollars I brought with me that got spent for the blankets we made those kids' clothes out of. Don't try to stop me, just let things be. You'll get someone—use the local help—it's good enough—"

She tried everything she had—their friendship, Dan's need, the line of people that would be waiting in the morning. She saw that his exhaustion had roots deeper than hers. "It's something Koizumi did, isn't it? He'll be gone tomorrow."

"Tell Sanborn I'm sorry. That boy, Fernando, who hangs around—you can train him until you get someone. I'm leaving; it's almost day."

"Dan says we can't move now. I think it may be dangerous."

"He means for the group, not for one of us going alone."

"Please—"

He went to her and kissed her gently on both cheeks and then on the lips. They had worked together intensely for almost three years. They had moved from Vietnam's highlands down watercourses to farm villages and refugee camps. They had seen horror together, had moments of saving humor, incidents of triumph. Peru, Ecuador, Colombia, back and forward, following the earthquake and face after face of children whose loudest protest had been a murmur. The two of them had done these things as children of an exacting, distant father. Douglas had become closer to her than her own brothers. He slipped out, dressed in her blanket, carrying his sodden clothes with him. She lay on her cot and cried. The next day, Koizumi left without realizing that Douglas had gone before him.

"I begged him to write—to let me know; he never did. Once or twice I thought I would like to track him down. I never had the time or nerve."

"Was it awful for you after Douglas left?"

"That's the funny part. Good came out of his leaving. I know that if Douglas could be told that, he would stop hurting."

"What happened after he left?"

"We did have a hard time for a few months. People came and went. I wrote to the people I knew: Mother Sylvester, who had sent us Mariella—other people. Some of the ones who showed up couldn't take the isolation or the travel or were 'tourists' or got sick. Then we got Stephanie Plant and she stayed."

Cecelia's first impression had been of wispiness, fragility. This one will never make it, she thought. Stephanie's red hair resisted all forms of control. Her body was painfully thin; even her pale, freckled complexion had something labile about it. When she blushed, which she did suddenly and often, Cecelia waited for her to have a stroke. "She looks like traumatic asphyxia five times a day," Cecelia said to Dan. What was worse, she reminded Cecelia of Mary Nell; she had the same vulnerable look, the breastless chest, narrow as a child's. Don't beat me, the posture cried. With it all was Mary Nell's wide-eyed inattention, the core of her gone away to untouchability. In the midst of surgery, Stephanie might suddenly say, "I wonder why those purple flowers do so well up here—meadows of them, have you seen them? And the wind doesn't seem to destroy them, although it blows so hard . . ." smiling, while she suctioned or sutured, at a cause unseen and far inside her own secret borders. To the patients her fragility seemed sisterly where Cecelia's toughness was maternal. She could giggle with the local assistants and she wept at a death with no shame, sniffling and wiping her eyes with her arm, like a slapped child. When she was not in surgery, she was always hip-carrying someone's baby, her face dazed and dreamy in the iridescent light of the mountain afternoons. She fell asleep over her half-eaten dinner, and stuffed herself with bread and sugar drinks because she was too hungry to wait for something substantial. She wore gauzy dresses translucent against the equatorial sun and laughed when the older women chided her for showing herself. Among the mountain people where shyness and downcast eyes were a sign of modesty, she stared and laughed, frankly, into the eyes of the young men. They saw her as a little sister.

And everyone forgave. "All babies in the womb dream," an old woman said, "and if the mother has troubles, the baby wakes and it is born not having dreamed enough and it spends its whole life adream." So they named Stephanie "womb dreamer" in their dialect, and wherever they went, people said that unpronounceable name, "Here comes the womb dreamer."

Then one day a slim, bearded man with long hair, dressed in jeans and a once-white gauze shirt, appeared in the new camp. He looked to Cecelia as if he'd stepped out of the Nazareth tableau in the nuns' school play. "Are you Cecelia Counselman?" he asked.

"Yes."

Then he smiled and Cecelia became conscious that no tableau Jesus ever smiled. "My name is Richard," he said. "I came here to be with you."

He was the first of the ones who would come because of the pictures Koizumi had taken. He had run away from home at fourteen and been in jail for theft. He had tried marijuana and LSD before the rest of Cape Elizabeth, Maine, had ever heard of those things. He had been all over Europe. He told this to Cecelia matter-of-factly, in answer to the question, "Where are you from?" Somewhere he had spent time in college nursing courses, but he had never gotten certified or registered. "No degree; no proof," he said, and opened his hands to Cecelia. She thought he would tire of the work or the moving or something else would glimmer for him down the river.

And then, across the compound, Stephanie had come walking and Cecelia watched the thing happen she had never believed happened outside of movies. Richard saw Stephanie, who had stopped and was looking across at them. He said, "Oh!" as though he had been shot. He looked back at Cecelia and his face was suddenly full of pain. "Is it too late?" he asked. "I've been so many places; is it too late?"

Then Stephanie came on across the compound and went to where Richard was. She did not introduce herself but only put her hand in his and said simply, "Come and see the children."

That was the picture Cecelia had when she thought of them, the two of them hand in hand, moving silently across the compound. He did not call her from her womb dreaming; she took

135

him into it. They were in another element than the hard light of this present Peruvian day. Lovers. Cecelia just stood, suddenly cold and alone. Which of her garments had they taken to wrap up in together? A steady, pulsing sorrow tore at her. It wasn't envy but a pain as keen as any she had known in childhood when all emotions are newer.

The days went by. Stephanie and Richard were unfailingly courteous to Cecelia; they worked early and late, repacking unused equipment, remaking the inventory—all the things she hated doing. They walked wreathed in dreams.

Cecelia had thought to stay with Dan San forever, to roam the world with this life as her life. Suddenly, it was time to go. Room in the vans was for two. Surgery plans and food and mobility were for two. While she still took pleasure in the children and in patients' eyes that widened with joy to see her, something had changed. Her days of grace were over; she lay beached on Ararat, the voyage done. Miserably, she went to Dan San. "It's time for me to leave." She had prepared a little speech to give the reasons why, but he only looked at her and said, "Well." And that was all.

On a morning of no particular note, Cecelia packed her single suitcase, said good-bye to the native assistants and to Stephanie and Richard, who would not miss her, and left. Dan San was away in his tent. He had never, in all the years she had been with him, said good-bye to an assistant. Against all her experience, she hoped it would be different for her. They had been together for almost eleven years. The tent flap stayed closed.

"So when Richard came and he and Stephanie were such a good team, I knew it was time to go and I came home to Kansas. My cousin Mady had a friend with a retarded kid who was here. Things weren't so good here then. I took one look and joined up and had some successes and the people who ran things saw what I was doing and we made the deal I have now. They've been good with money and stuff for extras, much to my surprise."

136

"Do you miss the excitement, the new places, the feeling of doing so much good?"

"Maybe I got older, but after Koizumi we had people who wanted to come out and work and after—well, I saw it was my time to stop. I tried not to look back until I heard from you. I guess I didn't miss the traveling or I wouldn't have shut myself up in here so easy." She laughed.

Vivian felt suddenly tired. "It's almost one. I guess we should go to sleep." She listened to the sounds from the dormitory next door. There were soft moans and snores and the sound of plumbing and the house noises of a strange place but all together, like a sea.

"Good night, Viv. Sleep well."

Vivian was awakened in darkness to a series of shrieks which she had incorporated into a troubled dream about cats and mice. For the moment she had no sense of place and time, and the sound, coming from where she could not imagine, filled her with terror. She sat up in bed. Where could this be? Had something happened? Ah—Horizon House. She breathed easier. The cries stopped.

"Viv?"

"Yes, I . . ."

"This is terrible—I'm so sorry! Living here—we've learned to sleep through that. It's Charlie. We don't know what he dreams about, but he must have some pretty wild ones because every few nights he yells like that. I forgot, really."

"How come *you* weren't sleeping, then?"

"I was just too excited, I guess, going back in my mind—the places and the people, the old defenses, the old arguments. It seems like someone else's life now. I wonder how I could have done it, climbed all those mountains, ridden all those burros, run those rivers, especially the one in Korea on a raft, and being chased and shot at because they didn't believe we were who we said we were. It was such a different life. I did all of it and argued with Dan sometimes and felt awful about it. It's hard to let go—you keep on going over the old reasons, things

137

dead years ago. I was just lying here listening to the reasons again."

"We should get some sleep."

"I've been thinking about Douglas Irons, the man who wrote that letter. Stole, he said. Ran away. He's ashamed. He never forgave himself for doing what he did."

"Well—"

"I wish I could find him. You said you were going to look up the assistants—to talk to them—"

"Only those who want to—the young man is hiding."

"He wouldn't hide from me."

"But we wouldn't know where to begin—"

"If I concentrated, I think I could remember a lot of things about Douglas and his past—things he let slip, things he wasn't aware of having said." Her voice had risen with eagerness. "You said you were going to Montreal after this, to see an assistant. I could come with you to New York and on the way we could see Mariella and Peggy in Indiana and then I'd track Douglas while you went to Canada—"

"You'd do that—leave here, for the first time in eight years, to look for this man? It must be very important to you if you'd consider doing that."

"It would only be for a week or two."

"What did you say about assistants in Indiana?"

"I could call them tomorrow. They would love to see you."

"I suppose it's none of my business why you want to go—"

Cecelia's voice was soft with musing. "Douglas left in shame and I left in sorrow and *because* we left, there's a clinic in Bolivia today that wouldn't have been there. I've got to tell him that, that I was wrong, that we were wrong for feeling sad and ashamed of leaving. Our feelings were a little selfish and egotistical, or we would have seen . . ."

There was a long silence. Vivian didn't know what to answer. She thought again of what Cecelia had said early in the evening about Daniel. She saw a picture of the pirogue floating on the distant river and the sunrise and Daniel saying, "The beauty part is her specialty." It felt warming now. She would not weep

138

over it again. "He once broke a vase—" she said to Cecelia in the dark, "Meissen. It was at home when he was about nine years old. It was a good piece, but not a great one—a little too ornate. It was an accident, and the vase was top-heavy anyway, as some of them are, and it fell. I saw his face, the terror in it, that we would disown him—send him away. I don't know if he was ever easy around delicate and lovely things after that."

"Yet he did surgery on the most delicate muscles, he saved the tiniest bits of skin."

"Yes." What caused that choice? she wondered. "Cecelia—"

"Yes—"

"If going with me means so much to you, you should do it. Can you leave so quickly? I can change my reservations for whatever airlines go to Indiana—"

There was a long silence and then in the darkness, Cecelia's quiet voice. "Oh, yes, I want to go." Another silence, and then, "Oh, hell." And the darkness said again, "Oh, hell, here come my waterworks!"

❧ 12 ❧

Over Illinois, the pilot picked out features of the landscape and Vivian looked at them past the mountain villages Cecelia was describing in Iran and Afghanistan. As they crossed the Wabash, Cecelia opened Daniel's rivers: Brahmaputra, Shira, Gangra, Songwe, Nam Teng, Huallaga. They had left Horizon House with the memory of weeping and faces emptied of everything but sorrow. Even the brightest had no word for return. Mikey gaped in soundless misery. "Oh, God!" Cecelia had cried. "Let me talk about mountains three thousand miles away." So she did, and they flew away from the afternoon sun through snow-covered Peruvian and Iranian passes winding into wind-claimed mountainholds.

Evening in Indianapolis. Vivian called Paul.

"Why are you *there*?"

"I picked up a friend and there are two assistants on the way. It's wonderful; I've never seen this part of the country."

"And they actually want to talk to you?"

"Cecelia's calling them now. She assures me they do. It's been a very instructive trip, so far; I've seen a good deal."

"It seems such a waste of time, this assistant business. And *you* sound different, somehow."

"After passing over Terre Haute, everything sounds different. It's the French influence. We should be in by Saturday at the latest."

She called Abner. "I want you to be happy for me. I'm learning a little of Daniel's work, his assistants—"

"I want to be happy for you, too, but I miss you."

"I'll see you Saturday."

"Don't you remember? I go to Toronto with the exhibit—"

"Oh, Lord, I forgot . . ." She knew she had hurt him. The Toronto exhibit was one he had worked on for months, a combination of private collections and museum pieces. She had been planning to join him there. That she had forgotten was painful for both of them. "Please forgive me—I need to be here, to go where I'm going, to get to the bottom of Daniel's work—"

"I know as much as anyone how important your brother was to you. I wish—"

"What?"

"That it was over, that's all."

"It will be, and when it is, my life will be different, and we'll be freer, I hope. How I wish I could promise you . . ."

"But you can't. I know that."

"Be my friend and don't demand anything right now. We said when we were free . . . I'm not free yet. Give me the time I need—"

"Vivian—?"

"Yes, I'm listening—"

"You sound . . . different."

"Paul said that, too. It's been—I've been in a different world, that's all; worlds, really. Daniel's death and this pilgrimage of mine—"

"It'll be lonely, not seeing you. I've missed you. Please take care of yourself. I know it can't be a pilgrimage without the difficulty, but don't make it more difficult than it needs to be."

Vivian hung up, thinking that some of Daniel's thoughtlessness and single-mindedness was familial. She was doing no less than he had done when he called her from all those places, saying simply, "I'm coming in," or from the airports in New York, "I'm here."

Cecelia had finished her call. "Mariella and Peggy are dying to see you. They were so surprised—they never thought I'd climb out—Viv, the surprise alone is worth the trip."

"Just now I hurt someone I care for. It feels awful."

"Don't remind me," Cecelia said.

Vivian shook her head.

"I don't know how a person measures the pain he causes against the good he gets—" Cecelia looked at her steadily. "Otherwise," she said, "I wouldn't be here." Then she smiled.

"Tell *me* about Dan San, about his babyhood, his teething, his kindergarten girlfriend, his childhood."

"No," Vivian said, and took a breath. "I won't tell you any of those things or about his family. I won't because I don't know them," and she told Cecelia about Daniel's adoption.

Her tiredness helped. They were facing each other in the restaurant of a motel, too tired for tact or delicacy. Cecelia's mouth fell open. "Adopted? From an orphanage?"

"No, from his family in Jerusalem when he was six."

To Vivian's complete surprise, Cecelia began to laugh. "Aha! So *that* was it." She sat for a minute without speaking, her expression going slowly sad.

"Well?" Vivian said. "You seem to have the answer to something—" She had been watching the changes.

"Yes, to some of what I always thought of as Dan's puzzle."

"And what was that?"

"Please don't be angry about my comparison, about where I learned this. It was back at Horizon House, and it's about consent. There are foster kids there, and adopted ones, too, who never consented to the way their lives were changed. Dan San must have been a kid who never consented."

"I don't understand."

"Sometimes the kids say yes to the new arms around them and the new clothes and the lives they're given. Sometimes there's consent all around them but it never touches them. Sometimes the state consents, the parents consent, the Church consents, the welfare consents, the foster parents consent; everyone is consenting as hell. Bang goes the stamp and it's law. Everyone but the kid. How obvious it is now. Dan San could spot-weld with those eyes and he could say 'never' better than anyone I ever saw. Good God, eleven years and I never guessed."

"That reserve of his—"

"I don't know. What I do know is that we never ask *them*, the kids. Some of mine have just enough IQ to say 'Count me out.' "

The food came. It was nondescript, but Vivian was hungry.

"I wish I knew what that Jerusalem family was like. I think my father made inquiries, but that was before the Second World War."

"It's hard to think of Dan San as unconsenting. He was so powerful and decisive."

"But you don't dare drop the Meissen."

"No, I guess you don't."

"I have the picture that will prove it. You'll see."

The next morning they went to see Mariella and Peggy. It was a luminous, tender morning, sweater-warm, with a petal-blowing summer breeze. All along the highway, the backyards of houses and the waste places of old farmsteads were blooming with lilac and snowball bushes. The smell of them lay wistful in the air.

Cecelia told her that Mariella had come to the camp in 1964, because of a religious vow; that they had worked in Iran, Iraq, and Bangladesh. Peggy came later, when they were in Vietnam and the camp was moving up and down between the borders: Korea, North and South; Cambodia; China; back to Vietnam, North and South; Peggy came because of Mary Nell.

"*Poor* Mary Nell?" Vivian asked.

Cecelia looked at her. "Alston told you?"

"He only said 'poor dumb Mary Nell,' once or twice, and when you mentioned her there was a silence around her name."

"Alston thought she was scatterbrained. To me she was just someone for whom that work was all wrong. She wasn't meant to move so much, to be alone so much. We were in Vietnam and there was the war and she had a kind of guilt about it that I never did. Everything must have overcome her. One day we found her hanging on a net-drying frame near the river—not the Mekong, but a sludgy, smelly river whose name I don't even remember anymore, and in no more time than it took to ship her body home, we had to move again. I wrote a letter; I know Dan was sad about it."

"How did you know Daniel was *sad*?"

"A brother of hers came out, wondering what had happened. He said things to Dan—told him he was cold and uncaring. We had patients to see and all the things there always were to do— it sounds cold, but that's because we're sitting here where everything is easy and you can use the telephone and the mail and there's no crisis on—"

They sat in silence. There had been twenty-seven assistants on Vivian's list, but who knew how many others who worked a week or a month, or who looked and left? Cecelia was defending Daniel, and felt the defense sounding hollow. Consent. This, too, was about consent.

Because all through the years when Vivian lived with her parents, widowed, the years when she had dropped everything to nurse Daniel in his vital rest times, the years when she helped nurse her father after his stroke and her mother during her long dying, she had done those things by choice, consenting. Her friends had praised her with what seemed like half blame: "don't you feel your life is passing you by?" She had felt foolish defending the care of her parents and Daniel when people called it martyrdom. It was a matter of consent.

"After Mary Nell we thought we would have the usual trouble trying to get someone. I knew she had been writing to her friends. I found the address and wrote and asked for help. I didn't know she'd been lying right up to the day she died."

144

"Lying?"

"Concealing, telling about the beauty of the work and not about her loneliness—about her excitements, not about her fears. She was playing to the house. Apparently she hooked Peggy with those letters. Peggy came. The work wasn't right for Peggy, either, even though she was a game girl; she stayed for almost a year. After she left we had two or three who didn't stay, and then Douglas."

"It seems each of you came for a different reason, and each left for the same reason . . ."

"That the job got to us? Hell, Viv, humanity can fall on you like a safe off a roof. You know, after I left, some psychologist went out to study Dan and the assistants."

"Really? What did he find?"

"It was all in a scholarly article. Alston sent it to me, and I've still got it somewhere. I'll show it to you."

"What were the conclusions?"

"About what you'd expect if you thought about it for half an hour: that the assistants had mixed reasons for being with Dan. I got the feeling that the psychologist was having a good time getting even—the way you feel when you find out your local minister is fooling around. The ones whose reasons were completely high-minded and virtuous—they were the ones who didn't stay long, or who cracked up like Mary Nell. I want to find Douglas and see him because that Koizumi picture must have been hurting like hell all these years."

"You mean the famous one?"

"Yes—Douglas helping, Douglas holding, caught that way forever. How it must have hurt to know that the pictures were a kind of lie."

"And you really think you can help?" As she spoke, Vivian became aware that Cecelia had changed the subject. She had been asking—but the words eluded her, the precise framing of the thought toward which she had been reaching . . .

"The assistants should have kept a line on one another, for the help they could give . . . I shouldn't have listened to Dan on that."

"Daniel discouraged reunions?"

"He didn't want any more contact than was necessary. You felt it in everything he did."

"But why?"

"I don't know. I'm sure there was a reason."

"Psychological or practical?"

"I don't know."

"And when you did keep contact?"

"Sometimes it helped. It helped Alston, for one. He had a kind of breakdown when he got back. Did he tell you?"

"He hinted at something."

"Well, it was pretty bad. He was in the hospital and they couldn't figure out what was wrong. It was something like combat fatigue."

"Good God, Cecelia, all I'm hearing—suicides, breakdowns —what does that say about Daniel's work?"

"That it was long and hard and uncomfortable, an isolating job in foreign places."

"But he knew, surely. Did he take steps to *help*?"

Cecelia did not answer.

It was almost noon when they arrived in front of an old house in a wide-lawned suburb. Vivian, standing back, watched the embraces. She knew right away which one was Mariella, the small, dark one, elfin and sparkling. Alston Fletcher had mentioned her beauty. Fortunately, considering his chauvinism, he had not seen her with Peggy. The two women were obviously lovers. It showed in their postures and positions: the eye that sought the eye, readable as words.

Peggy was the shier of the two, a leggy, honey-blond woman, somewhat heavy-faced. Her hair was long and hung in a single thick braid down her back. As soon as Vivian was introduced, Peggy led them back to where the women were painting rain gutters they had obviously taken from the front of the house. "Y'got two more brushes?" Cecelia asked.

Soon they were all busy priming the gutters. Talk was easier when they were working.

"So you're Dr. Dan's sister—"

"Yes . . ."

"And you're taking Cecelia to New York to look for someone?"

"That's right."

"I never thought *anyone* would dig Cecelia out of that place."

"Viv wants to hear about the things we did, war stories from the days in dear old Iran and Bangladesh."

"It was Korea for me," Peggy said, "and Cambodia."

"Never mind the silly details, tell the lady the stories." They laughed.

"Remember the ball games we had in Iran—those ball-crazy kids and that game they taught us?"

"Remember that picnic where the rain was mud—?" "Remember that river trip when we thought we lost the other boat and the chasm—how it got dark and we were hearing all those noises we thought were alligators and how everyone was laughing at us—?"

"Viv—" (They were all calling her Viv now, the way Cecelia did. It was a name she had never been called and had, indeed, never liked. She found she liked it now.) "Did you know that Dr. Dan hated cold water? He really hated it, and when we were in Korea we had to travel a lot by river. He'd bundle up against that and he had all kinds of ideas about keeping dry and warm. He never complained, but when he did, it was about being cold—wet. He drove us all crazy."

"I forgot that, but it was true. Once it got so bad, rivers in winter and getting so wet, he took to trying to follow us on land, and that didn't work, so he'd just grumble and sulk. We all loved the rivers. They made us feel free and adventurous, riding on those low-going rafts."

"—And do you remember that time when suddenly, in what seemed like pretty calm water, their boat hit something and he flipped out of the boat just as neat as a seed from a pod? We saw him in the air and then, of course, in the water, splash. The rowers jammed poles deep into the bottom to stop us, and everyone was yelling to everyone else and then Dr. Dan stood

147

up and we saw that the river was only knee-deep there. He stood there for a second or two and then put his head back and laughed and laughed. I never saw him do that before or after. He got back on the raft with a very dignified look that broke us all up so we could hardly stand it."

"And after that—"

"Well, he still hated getting cold-wet, but he did ride rivers after that."

"—And he was very fussy about washing up. He always washed up two, maybe three times a day, even when he wasn't doing it for surgery, but he hated getting rained on or being wet by spray."

Jerusalem, Vivian thought, and Jewish laws of dirty and clean. Water. Customs and admonitions so old he never knew where he had gotten them. How much did Jerusalem stay with him, after language and laws and perhaps the family itself had been forgotten? They talked on—stories of the camps and patients and the differences between the places they had been, the places no one knew they had been.

"Yes, it's true that Dr. Dan didn't encourage . . ." ". . . They were in awe of him . . ." ". . . It was the people of the smaller tribes who were most aware of dignity and manners . . ." ". . . Special language they used for him and us that separated us from them."

"How did you know it was time to leave a place?"

"Dan San would know when it was time to move. He would say, 'There's a guide coming at noon. Pack up.' " ". . . And we would go upriver or down." ". . . On burros or in the vans, if there were roads." ". . . Two miles or ten or fifty into a new country or over a pass, to a village or a town." ". . . And there they'd be, all waiting, camped out, the new patients."

"Sometimes there'd be allies on one side of a compound and enemies on the other." "Oh, yes, the tight jaws and only their eyes moving here and there."

"We had a dozen almost-wars, hand-to-knife, but never a real one. Good God! Look at Viv's face, all screwed up," Cecelia cried. "That Sister Mary and Alston told you it was always too

148

hot or too cold or raining, didn't they? But it wasn't, not always. Some of the days, most of them, seems to me now, were good weather, and some were wonderful. And we did laugh, didn't we? And when things got tough, we had one another, and sometimes even a nice visitor or two."

"About the visitors," Vivian said, remembering. "There's someone else I need to learn about—Jack Ripstein. Jack the Ripper."

There was the silence that follows obscenity in public. The two women stopped and stood with their brushes dripping on the grass.

"Our big argument," Peggy said, "has come to sicken the day."

"Our big argument," Mariella said, "needs to be ventilated."

"Our big argument," Peggy said, turning to Vivian, "has concerned whether or not we bring the awful, the ugly, the destructive parts of our pasts here to this house. Mariella says yes, that we should share it all, deal with it all, understand it all. I want to keep this place free of filth and ugliness. Mariella says that that . . . person . . . because I don't want to mention his name, is a buffo, a clown. I think he's evil and I don't want to bring that evil to our home." Her face was stiff. She was near tears. "I'll tell you why I think he's evil and then no more. He tried to rape me."

They were in Thailand, in a boat-village. They had come after the rainy season, an adventure to Peggy, who was from Nebraska and had never seen any more water than was in the town reservoir. They camped on a small peninsula and boats tied up at it pushed close like feeding livestock until there were so many they made a dry land, boat to boat, two acres deep on its three sides, rising and falling with the tides that commanded a distant sea. They were a noise like a hundred trees full of a thousand monkeys, a smell compounded of stale water, sewage, rancid fat, cloves and cinnamon, sweaty feet, pepper, and flowering trees. On the shore, because Dr. Dan stayed clear of islands, were the tents of the doctor's camp, and a few huts. Sometimes the rain made the ground so spongy that all of them had to sleep separately aboard one of the two hundred or three hundred boats, hospitality of laughing people, cracking, chewing, cooking, and eating, handing food and children in and handing out the day's waste to other boats that carried it away. The noise of the boat people rose and fell like the tides, day and night, but it never stopped. Their talk was high-pitched and loud, their colors sharp and loud, and they bought and sold, their boats moving away and coming back to reposition themselves in the solid phalanx on which one walked dry-shod to and from the boat of one's host or his friends.

Peggy and Cecelia took turns assisting the doctor. They also did minor procedures on their own, mostly on burns and scalds—here children often fell into or against cooking vessels. There were also wounds from the bite of a particularly savage rodent that could chew a baby's face half away. They saw cleft palates, cleft lips, yaws, on which there had to be extreme care taken to assure a sterile environment. They used huge amounts of penicillin which came monthly from a source Peggy never questioned.

Cecelia loved laughing with the mothers of the little patients; Peggy was shy and reserved. Cecelia's weight shamed Peggy; the boat people were tiny and delicately made, but they considered Cecelia lucky. Peggy felt embarrassed to be a burden to those who had so little. She couldn't mime her wants or use the gestures Cecelia found easy. It was three months before she discovered how the local women dealt with their menstrual problems.

When the summer came, she found the heat enervating and the boats claustrophobic. Dampness rotted her shoes and she walked around in the haze of Clorox she used to keep down the various fungi and body parasites. She saw Ripstein now and then. He stayed with the doctor when he came and never went near either the patients or the operating tent. She was conscious of his presence, demanding, complaining, and of his coarse humor, which she hated. The local people seemed to enjoy him. His complaints amused them and proved his need to be tended assiduously. He was regal; therefore, he must be treated as a king. They loved his grand entrances, once from a helicopter, once in an enormous boat with a carved and painted prow. They gave him garlands of water flowers when he came.

The boat visit happened when Peggy was sick of mosquitoes, Clorox, nausea, and the bobbing motion of the boats, of rats and heat, of rain, noise, and the lack of privacy. His arrival precipitated a festival and to the sound of five hundred noisy people living their lives in one another's kitchens were added firecrackers and a kind of cannon that was set off at odd intervals. Even the adaptable Cecelia seemed rattled. "In California, there's a Carmelite convent. They don't talk. They don't make any noise at all except to sing. Loud belching is forbidden. There is no Ripstein. Ever."

But he had brought more penicillin and sulfa and IVs in plastic, not glass, and there was a new fungicide. That evening he gave a big party on his boat. It was for the favored: the doctor, local helpers, assistants, and the heads of families of the boat people. Cecelia elected to stay with the post-op patients. The Ripper had made jokes about her swamping the boat. There was a real bathroom on his boat, and a real shower with hot water. After dinner, she thought, she might ask—

The dinner was grand. Peggy smelled none of the pervasive odor of rancidity she had never gotten used to and which the local people seemed to like. She was the only woman at the long table. To satisfy custom, she did not sit side by side with the men but at the end, at a place somewhat in shadow. With her, in a little bag, were her shower things and a towel. She had told Cecelia she would scout the boat for possibilities. There might be a washing machine, and before Ripstein left . . .

There was a local drink of some kind and Ripstein had brought champagne. Ripstein used to joke that it didn't matter to Danny whether he was eating the hamburger, the bun, or the paper they were wrapped in. Peggy noticed that he did not offer the doctor anything to drink, but the native helpers drank, and having eaten well, fell back on the cushions behind them, lulled by the slapping of the water on the boat and its slow rocking, like a cradle, up and back. The doctor, too, had let himself doze off. Peggy dozed; the meal had been heavy; the champagne—and before she realized it she was away into the cushions that had been piled against the wall behind them.

She came awake to Ripstein, fumbling at her clothes. Her blouse was open and half off, her skirt open, her bra unsnapped under the blouse. He was trying to undress her. He was a little drunk. She started, fully awake. "Don't make any noise—" and then a whisper: "what a sweet little ass you have. You're going to be just the right dessert."

There were lights but they were few and dim. Ripstein was busy at her. Men had never interested Peggy but her feeling for Ripstein was active repulsion. It was almost dark. Quickly she looked around for ways out, weapons, pulling away and trying to get her blouse back on. He was whispering urgently to her, holding her with one hand while he kept at her clothes with the other. For a moment she went limp, and when he moved to change his hold on her she pulled away and dove in among the cushions, causing a groan to go up among some of the sleepers, and amid arms and legs and the stir she made among them, came free of him, stood up, her clothes falling around her. She let the skirt go and stepped out of it. She saw the open hatch and, jumping the low table, bounded away and out. He came lumbering after her, laughing. The deck was open. She ran to the rail and saw that the boat was tied up to a kind of piling in the water, and that she would surely fall if she tried to climb onto it. She looked around and saw a boat hook in some rigging, and there was a fishnet, big and heavy, draped over the rail. She had seen the men throwing it. She went for it and tried to pull it free. It was heavier than she thought. He was coming toward her, laughing, saying things about her, a kind of constant joking cajolery. His advance gave her a strength in panic she didn't know she had. With a cry, she wrenched the heavy net from the rail and threw it. It went over him as neatly as though she had been doing it all her life. She was amazed at how well it worked. It fell around him and he became entangled in it, roped a hundred ways as he tried to find an edge and throw it back

152

over himself. She undid the boat hook and told him over his muttered cursing that if he tried to follow her she would kill him with it. She held it while she buttoned her blouse with one hand, and then went quickly back to the large cabin and got her skirt and the things she had brought with her. When she came out on deck again she saw he had moved, still in the net, to the forepart of the boat where he was unlikely to be seen among the ropes and supplies. Hidden by the covered wheelhouse, he could work away at his entanglement. She walked around the boat, looking over the rail, and saw to port the small pirogue tied up beneath, waiting for the revelers to wake. Its owner was sleeping. She let herself down by a rope from the rail, walking down the side of the boat as she had seen the native men do. Waiting for the others in the little pirogue, she fell into a dreamless sleep. She said nothing to anyone until she told Mariella one evening at an amusement park, years later. Ripstein left the next day without seeing her.

❧ 13 ❧

"Why didn't you tell me?" Cecelia cried.

"I don't want to say any more. Mariella made me tell her, but I took her away. I don't want those memories *here*. We don't talk about ugliness here," and Peggy left them and went toward the house. "It's time we ate. It's time we put up coffee at least," she said, without looking back.

"Not *rapist*, really," Mariella said, "or at least I didn't feel he was that kind of menace."

Cecelia was all but hopping up and down with frustrated rage. "That no-good bastard! Oh, that— Why didn't she tell me?"

"What would you have done?"

"Done? I would have told Dan, I would have put Ripstein on notice. I would have been there guarding Peggy and all the others. Who else did he use, and how badly, and who didn't wiggle away, and who didn't have a near thing, or figure it out in time to escape? Don't you know what he did with those damn jokes of his? He separated me from *you*, from all of you, and I was so busy thinking of myself, my stupid self, that I let him do it."

"I never thought about that—that there might have been others—"

"Oh, God, Viv, what if Mary Nell—what if Sister Jennifer—?"

"It wasn't your fault, Cecelia—" and Mariella began gathering up the paints and brushes. "I had my little encounters with him, too— We could have told you but we were cowards. I didn't want to make a fuss. To me they were only passes. My vow meant a lot to me. If I went to Dr. Dan, I thought he might ask if I had led Ripstein on. Then he might tell *me* to go."

Cecelia shook her head. "All these years I've been so proud of being in the background, taking care of things, the patients, 'my' people. I was the one who wanted us to meet again, because I was so proud of what I had done, how I looked out for everyone for almost eleven years. Longer than anyone. That damn Ripstein got me twice, once when he made me hide and be ashamed, and once when he tricked me out of my relationship with my friends. I thought I was done hating him. I'm not."

Vivian said, "I hate him, too, but he was Daniel's friend. What do we do with that? There are marks on Ripstein's arm where he fended off a knife meant for Daniel. Everything you say is true about his crassness and his boorishness. But Daniel wanted him there, wanted and maybe needed him. What are we to make of that?" She didn't mention the bequest, but they must eventually find out about it. During the trip she had almost given it away more than once to Cecelia.

"I still say he's a clown," Mariella said.

Cecelia shook her head. "There are different kinds of laughter. What do you think, Viv—you've seen the Ripper's act."

"I saw a comedy act, which I thought was pretty awful, and afterward, another act, Ripstein playing his Jack-the-Ripper role, pretending he'd never known Daniel."

"The Ripper is no fool," Cecelia said. "He saw me hating my size and my looks and he used that against me. He saw Viv's shyness and used it against her. I think he's smart that way. He

155

knows why people laugh and I don't think he asks any of the questions we do about whether it's good or it's bad. I hate him for having pulled us away from one another when we most needed to be together, and I'm scared about Mary Nell, that something *he* did to her was the reason she killed herself. What if he did get to her and I was too busy being safe and you and the others were too busy protecting yourselves from shame? Then we all have some part of that awful thing.''

"I still don't see why you didn't tell Daniel," Vivian insisted. "He was the one who could have stopped it."

The two of them looked at Vivian. "Cowards," Mariella said.

Vivian thought, Not cowards. They were mothering Daniel, arranging his reality, protecting, protecting, as she had done when she was ten.

Peggy called them. She was standing inside the screen door but they could tell by her voice that she had been crying and was now trying to get control of herself. "This brunch is so late it's almost too late to eat lunch." They went into the house.

Over the food, they bantered, comforting one another. Vivian said, "Alston Fletcher mentioned that Daniel had pictures to mark, that he had sets of pictures and written things on each patient, lots of records. Now they seem to be missing—disappeared. Do you know where they were sent after he was finished with them?"

Mariella said, "There were boxes—crates made by local people."

"Yes, and when they were full, we took them—he took them and . . . then, I don't know. It's funny, because he never let us handle them after they were put away. They were put in the boxes, all those pictures, and then he'd seal them himself and he'd be fussy about taking them somewhere else. It was one of those things we took for granted because it was routine, that there were boxes and yet we traveled very light."

After the meal, Vivian took out her copies of the letters, the smudged, travel-worn mail from distant places. Mariella wiped her hands carefully, taking hers. "This one—it's from—I think

I know this girl—the garbage girl. I think she was the one. Do you remember?"

"Garbage girl?"

"Oh, God, I forgot!" Cecelia cried. "How could I have forgotten that? It was in Indonesia, Viv, in the highlands this time, and we had been traveling almost constantly so we weren't sure where we were or over what borders we might have crossed. It was morning and a nonsurgery day, by good luck. I was taking photographs and we were numbering the people and the photographs—names, too, for verification. You tell this, Mariella."

"I was walking rounds with Dr. Dan—later there would be a clinic for the people we had seen six or eight weeks before and who were ready to have jaw wires taken out or stitches pulled. The rounds were to check for infection or disease. Some of those groups would be very resistant to surgical infection but would be knocked flat by communicable diseases. We had to be very careful about that. Anyway, the camp was noisy and lively and we were working away. It was about eleven in the morning. Suddenly there were gunshots and everyone ran. It was amazing. In thirty seconds there were only the very sickest people and the three of us. It was as though the people had been trained and were all dancers or acrobats and the shots had announced the show and they suddenly went into their act—clear the area.

"It was the army. God knows whose; they never told us. They walked from place to place rooting in this and overturning that. They dumped the sick off the mats and pulled things apart. Our suitcases. My curlers. They thought my curlers were radio parts—"

"They hit her," Cecelia said, "yelling things we couldn't understand, and I thought they were going to kill us all. First they hit her because she had radio parts and the captain or whoever he was wanted to make her tell where they were sending messages and when we showed him there were no wires and no electricity at all, but curlers, he hit her because of his own loss of face."

157

"They were going to shoot us, I was sure of it," Mariella said. "I remember thinking, 'Look at them; they're slum kids in the country.' I looked at the sleazy uniforms, the sandals made of old tires. I knew if we showed them whatever documents we had it wouldn't matter because they were illiterate and they had the illiterate's suspicion of writing—"

"And Daniel—"

"He got very cold, very strong and angry, which they were used to and made them comfortable. It was the best thing to do, but I didn't think it would work. Then, providentially, someone came, a higher-up of some kind, and he ordered the other soldiers away. They went into Dan's tent, which was a shambles, and there was some sort of message exchanged, but we were given twelve hours to leave. As we were packing up to go, people began to reappear. Some had been hiding in trees, some were behind boats on the river, and they came back full of leeches and stinking like the swamps. I was standing near the garbage mound—not the medical garbage—*that* we burned every few hours. There was a midden where all the patients dumped fruit rinds and all kinds of waste. It was a mound, knee-high. They would take it away with them when they left, to use on the fields or garden plots. By then it had become well rotted. As I stood there—I was checking off a list I used to keep—I saw the mound move. Sometimes a mound like that will heave with maggots—I'm sorry, Viv, but—"

"I can take it," Vivian said. "Go ahead."

"The mound was moving. Then I saw—I thought it must be some kind of animal in there, and then arms came out, a leg, and the mound broke open on one side and a girl came out, a girl of about ten or eleven—they are very small people and their children are like the smallest of ours at their ages. Still, it was a miracle that she could have done it. We cleaned her off. Her name—I remembered her name because, as you see here in the letter, it rhymes and has a meaning in English. The time she describes is right. A delicate child; by the writing, a delicate woman. Thank God she doesn't know we called her the garbage girl."

"Why should they have menaced you? Who was behind it?" Vivian asked. "Who would interfere with poor people's treatment like that?"

The three women looked at one another. "You answer," Cecelia said to Mariella.

Mariella shrugged. "Countries are jealous and proud, just like people, and the poorer the prouder. People say power corrupts. Well, Viv, so does weakness. Borders are all some of those tribal strongmen have. They may not care about their people but they care a lot about their sovereignty. Daniel's scorn for borders mocked their sovereignty."

Vivian looked through the open window. In the small yard and in the yards of their neighbors, pear trees were in flower; their white blossoms glowed and shimmered in the afternoon light. "It's hard to look out at a day like this and know that people do such things."

Peggy said, "It's enough to know about all of it without trying to bring it here—"

And suddenly Vivian's mind went to Sister Mary, sitting stiffly in the drab convent dayroom, which someone had tried to brighten. What had she said about "them," "they," governments, soldiers. What was the other thing—"they dared interrogate him," "they went into our boxes, our things—" "What did they say to you, those soldiers? What did the other man say?"

"I suspect," Cecelia said, "but I could never be sure—the languages were foreign to us, remember."

"What do you think, then?"

"I'm almost sure they thought we were spies. Mariella was right about the borders. Sometimes it seemed to me that Dan went back and forth so much just to annoy those bozos. Our freedom angered them but they must have suspected us of carrying drugs or information or both."

"Do you know who the other man was, the one who stopped the soldiers?"

"No, and what they said among themselves our interpreters were too frightened to tell us. Remember, they had to stay on after we left, and often they were just people we picked up whose relatives were being helped by us. They were never smooth or comfortable in English, not enough for more than simple messages to patients."

Vivian was silent. They thought she had been puzzled or saddened by what they had said. They were embarrassed and dove back into the letters they were holding. Vivian said, "Peggy, I heard that Mary Nell had written to you—"

Peggy nodded and looked up from the letter in her hand. "Yes, she had written to me and I was eager to come, to—to—oh, the lies—"

"What lies?"

"The lies you tell when you are doing something supposed to be heroic and exciting and you are ashamed of how human and lonely you are. I thought she was the luckiest person in the world. Here I was in Indianapolis doing shift work in a second-rate hospital, and she was all over East Asia, a heroine. We'd been nursing-school buddies. I got a letter every month, letters all spotted with rain and greasy with fingerprints. How I treasured those letters! She lied to the very last one, or if they weren't outright lies, at least they denied anything dark or painful. The last letter I got was about how they'd had a harelip day in this place and one mother brought in all four of her kids with it, and how the villagers held light for them on into the night and how they made recovery rooms out of their own bodies."

Cecelia cried, "I'd forgotten about that, too. It's true, Viv; when we'd do the quick operations, there might be nine or ten patients in post-op. The villagers would make instant rooms by holding mats or netting, one person at each end, and they'd stand there for hours at a time, absolutely still, just holding their mat ends up, and there'd be somebody in each of those mat-sized rooms with each patient, watching him."

"I read that letter to the nurses on the shift. We all sat around green with envy and the next letter I got was from Cecelia telling me that Mary Nell had died, and did I know someone who would come. I quit my job that afternoon. The first month I was out there, I knew it wasn't for me, but guilt and wishing kept me on. After Ripstein, I lost the wishing. Ripstein made me feel dirty and used. I was feeling both anyway. I started writing back to Indianapolis to get someone the way Mary Nell and Cecelia had gotten me."

"Then came—"

"Uh, Martha—"

"What was her last name?" Vivian had her chart out.

"I don't remember; she took one look and left— Three days."

"We went through three, four, five people, and then we got Douglas Irons, and he stayed for almost three years. This is his letter. Maybe it's too personal to show. I want to tell him what happened after he left. I want to find him and tell him about me, too, about Horizon House. He's felt bad for years for all the wrong reasons. Besides, he left owing me two dollars and fifty cents, and a pair of wool socks."

"Do you have any idea where he is?"

"No."

"How will you find him?"

"I don't know, but over the years I learned this—" Cecelia began to comb her memory.

. . . That Douglas had appeared one day, sick and hungry; that he used good English and had a slight southern sound in his speech, the *ah* sound instead of *r*; that he had been in civil rights marches in Virginia and Georgia; that he had a younger sister. Family money—black servants. These bits were the unconsciously dropped words or half-made confidences of almost three years of daily contact. It amazed Vivian. Around them were the muffled Saturday sounds of neighbors in backyards. Now and then dogs barked, kids shouted. Someone was mowing a lawn . . . That Douglas liked neatness and order, but hated liking them because he thought those habits bourgeois. That he had a beautiful handwriting. That he kept giving his clothes away to patients or their families so he lived in a series of old hats and shirts. That he was smart about numbers and organizing things . . .

"—and what you are will come out sooner or later," Peggy

161

said, "so maybe you had better not look for him in migrant camps or mental hospitals . . ."

Clouds had come up; the day had gone cool. "It's going to rain, soon."

"Fair weather friends," Cecelia said, "we should be leaving."

"It's too late," Mariella said.

They were suddenly beset. Lightning, thunder, and rain came all at once. Water in sheets, layers, curtains, pounded on the roof, drummed and hissed on the walls. They stood under the eaves on the protected side, not wanting to go in. After the worst of the storm passed, Vivian was able to ask, "What are your lives like now?" They talked easily. They were O.R. nurses at a large hospital. Most people didn't know they lived together. It was a quiet life. Mariella's big Italian family was close by.

The rain went easy, and then the storm was gone, its delicately pungent after-aroma hanging in a tremulous, weeping sunshine.

It was time to go. Vivian gathered the letters and put them back in the suitcase. They called a cab.

"We hope you find him," Peggy said.

"And tell Jack the Ripper he's a good argument for lesbianism." And Vivian, who would have been shocked a week ago, laughed.

"Tell him—tell him . . ."

"We'll let you know what happens . . ." The ozone-laden atmosphere gave their words the removed quality of sounds under a dome.

"We are going to see one another again," Cecelia called. "We are going to be a group with reunions and newsletters and T-shirts and special words and a secret handshake. We were wonderful, you know. We still are . . ."

But on their way to New York, Vivian and Cecelia argued.

❧ 14 ❧

They argued about money. Vivian had insisted on paying Cecelia's plane fare. Cecelia realized that with trips here and there, meals away, and motels, the trip would cost more money than she had. It made her feel helpless, and ashamed. For over a decade she had traveled free in a moneyless economy; for another eight years she had lived in a place where the money was spent only occasionally, on outings.

"I get paid a regular wage—I've been sending it to my folks, that's all," she cried helplessly. "Lend it to me; I'll pay you back whatever it is."

The argument went back and forth until Vivian cried, "Which is more important, that we do what we came to do or use the time and energy being careful about whose money is financing it?" Then, unable to stop, she had gone on, "Good Lord, Cecelia, if I contributed a thousand dollars to Horizon House, you'd take the kids out with it and think I was a godsend."

Cecelia, wounded twice, gave in. It had been years since Vivian had had to remember that for many people, money was the conditioning factor in what they did or did not do. She had been suddenly, uncomfortably reminded.

Cecelia had never been to New York. She had had no idea

there was a park in the middle of it. When they pulled up at the Sanborn house, her eyes widened in awe.

Whatever surprise Doris felt was lost in Cecelia's wonder at the U-shaped staircase and carved banisters, front stairs and back stairs, and a butler's pantry the size of her room at Horizon House. They went up to the second floor while Cecelia marveled. "Dan San grew up here—this was his house, and when he thought of home, he had this picture in his mind."

"I hope so—" Vivian said, but he might have thought of a hovel in an old quarter of Jerusalem.

"Later—could we look at those albums you made? I'll try to pick out the parts I know, pictures and people, to get them straight."

"—and I want to call my brothers. They are practical and they know how to get things done. They might have some suggestions as to how you should go about tracing Douglas; things that could save time."

"I never knew Dan San had brothers."

Vivian paused and then said quietly, "Yes, two. Paul and Steven."

"Older?"

"Yes."

Cecelia saw that she had caused Vivian pain. "Dan wasn't a talker; you know that."

"What did he say when he left to come here? Would he say, 'I'm going home?' "

"I don't think so. He'd say, 'I'm leaving now; I'll be back in ten days.' "

"Oh. I see," Vivian said.

Since her mother's death, Vivian had begun to eat with Doris in the tiled kitchen. The dining room had seemed too big and cold. Now, with a guest to serve, Doris had set two places there. Because of the size of the house and the ornateness of the room, Cecelia was subdued and shy. They had coffee served in the antique blue Bavarian. "These *are* old," Vivian said. "A fine factory. It went out of business in 1820."

164

Cecelia would not use the set. She said she was afraid of breaking something. Vivian laughed. "They're my compliment to you, not my challenge. Besides, from what I hear, there are sets like this being made all over the Far East."

After dinner they went upstairs into Daniel's old room where the letters and books were laid out and organized. Vivian handed Cecelia the list noting Douglas's letter. "I wrote down return addresses if there were any—postmarks if not." There was only the note: *Assistant, unsigned, postmark obl. No return.*

Cecelia sighed. "Where is he? Where can he be?"

They opened the second book first, the one Vivian had made of Daniel's life. Cecelia saw the postcards he had sent her to announce his moves: "Flood in India, we leave tomorrow. Typhoon in Honshu. Trouble leaving. Tibet. We are in Iran now, earthquake."

"Oh, God! I remember those!" Cecelia cried. "He used to cadge postcards from us all the time, the 'makins' because he never thought before—I didn't mean that . . . that he didn't care . . ."

"I know," Vivian said. "It's all right."

Cecelia went back to the beginning of the book—Daniel's first trip with the relief organization in India. She read the early articles and looked at the pictures, fame begetting fame. She came to her own years. "Oh, I had forgotten this—and this—"

"—and in none of them are *you* there."

"Viv, *they* didn't want me in the pictures any more than I wanted to be there, don't you understand that?"

"You're not that fat."

"But I'm plain. Big and plain."

"So—"

"People have ideas about how they want life to be, and expect it to be, and they try to make what *is* fit that idea. That's why our little kiddos at the House have so much trouble visiting the 'real world.' " She turned the pages. "Look, *here*'s Douglas—see—oh, you have *these* in the wrong order—"

"That's Alston Fletcher, isn't it?"

"Yes."

"Looking younger, really much younger."

"And here's Mary Nell—see, here with these people."

They looked at pictures of other assistants, and at the end, the pictures at Benegalbon and the pictures of the two assistants who had died with Daniel, and the car, and the funeral, and the Archbishop.

"Over twenty-five years—what a thing it was—"

"Now," Vivian said, "here's the family book."

Cecelia opened it eagerly. She didn't skip through the early years as Vivian thought she might, the years before Daniel came to them. She went slowly, steadily, through all the pictures of grandparents, parents, and the early family days, the summers in Lenox, Paul and Steven, and then Vivian. Suddenly, in mid-smile at the turn of a page, was Daniel—the picture taken by that boat passenger, the stark, haunted eyes in the thin face that seemed to have no other purpose but to hold those eyes; the rough clothes, the tag.

"Oh, Viv—!" Cecelia began to breathe quickly as though to outrun tears.

"You said once . . . you used the word 'unconsenting.' "

"Yes."

They both looked at the picture for a long time, at the world-shocked face. Then, slowly, Cecelia turned the page. "I didn't recognize," Vivian said, "not until I looked at all the pictures together after Daniel's death, how unconsenting he had been all those years."

"You mean, standing away from all of you—but he's growing up. See, here—he's beginning to have his own way of doing things. Look at this one—see his hands—he's decided something."

Vivian looked again at the pictures. With Cecelia's patience and enthusiasm, she began to look carefully at the frozen gestures, the attitudes of faces and heads, the postures of bodies. Daniel had changed somehow, toughened in his teenage years. "I wonder what could have brought that change about," she said. "I don't remember anything specific, but now that you

166

point it out, yes, there is a difference. He's still standing apart from the family, but—"

"As if he's not a part of it, it's like he's visiting."

"Oh, yes, visiting. He's fourteen here."

"He looks more relaxed."

"Why not? Visitors go back home. I guess he must have decided then, this early, to go back to Jerusalem."

"Or else to belong somewhere else."

Vivian turned the page. "Here are the high school pictures. Here are the college, and here's Daniel in medical school. He never knew I had these. Here's medical school graduation. How dignified they look. They *were*, as I remember. Pick Daniel out in this one. It's not easy because they all look so—"

Cecelia had already started moving across the rows of faces. "Viv, *look*."

"What? No, that's not Daniel."

"No, *look!*"

"Where?"

"Here, *here!*" Cecelia was jabbing at a face in the second row, middle left.

It was Ripstein. It was Jack Ripstein. "It's not. It can't be."

"It is. It's *him*."

"Wait. Turn the picture up. There's a list underneath."

The paper was getting brittle. The fold line had begun to separate at the edges. They opened it down and began to count front row, left to right, second row. "He's second row. He's fifth from the left."

" 'Ripstein. Jacob Ripstein,' " Cecelia read, " 'Brooklyn, New York.' Jack Ripstein was a doctor! He never—not even a medical term, not a hint."

"They knew each other *before* Daniel's trips. They knew each other in medical school. They've known each other for thirty years at least and never once did Daniel mention—never once—"

"They used to go into Dan's tent," Cecelia said, "and they'd be there talking, and I'd hear Ripstein laugh that awful laugh of his, and I'd wonder what they talked about, but Ripstein *knew*,

knew the surgeon's moves and the medicine, he knew what Dan was doing all the time. And how smart he was about it all. There were other doctors coming through now and then to see how things worked, how we did the number of surgeries we did in a day. Ripstein would fade out, gone before they came. I always thought he was ashamed. I put my own feelings on him."

"Maybe he was ashamed."

"He did it to keep from being found out."

"Look again; are you sure?"

"It's him, Viv, good old Doc Ripstein."

"We are going to see him again," said Vivian. "We are going to tell him we know about his attempt on Peggy and that he lied and lied to me, to both of us."

"After Canada?"

"We're going to ask Jennifer about him—all the assistants."

"We could go where he works, and this time he won't be able to fatso me off the track. That man owes me. He owes me for Peggy and maybe for others."

"I hate to see him again; it was so awful the first time."

"You'll have me now. I'll be there."

Vivian lay in bed that night, thinking about Daniel and Jack Ripstein—all those years—and in her dream for a moment, they seemed to be dancing together, and then she moved closer and saw they were joined to each other, like Siamese twins, and they were not dancing but struggling with each other, the expressions on their faces rictuses of effort and not smiles, as they had seemed from farther off.

The next morning, she read the mail that had come while she was away. There were answers to two letters she had sent weeks ago. An assistant who had been with Daniel in Italy and Greece in 1958 added names. Marie Gluysteen from the Bahamas added names. There were a few other letters. Now that the tide of condolence had slowed, a different kind of letter began to appear. People were beginning to ask for favors—children wrote to get information for school reports; people wrote wanting money or advice or information. She read the letters quickly so that she could put them into the piles she had arranged in Daniel's room.

Cecelia had been making calls to people named Irons in Virginia, Maryland, and the District of Columbia.

"Let's talk to Paul and Steven about finding Douglas. They can think of things that would not occur to us."

Cecelia made a great effort to look nice for the meeting with Paul and Steven Sanborn. She had seen the pictures in the albums, the formidable poses with tennis rackets and golf clubs. She bathed carefully and powdered with scented powder. She had changed into her nicest clothes. She had forgotten that when she had last worn these for a trip with the children, one of them had spilled his drink on her, and there was a stain on the front which the cleaner had been unable to remove. One of the mothers had made this outfit, and it did not hang properly. None of this had mattered on Horizon House trips. She was horrified when she looked in Vivian's mirror, saw the stain, and realized that the fabric of the bodice was stretched tight across her breasts. The stain: she went downstairs and for half an hour, she and Doris put various things on it—vinegar, ammonia. The result was that a peculiar odor emanated from the cloth and seemed to hang in clouds around her, and she had to go back upstairs and put cologne on her hands and then rub them carefully over the stain to mask the odor. By that time she was perspiring with tension and anguish, and the cologne reacted against the odors of her stress. The brothers were due any moment. She called Vivian.

"I can't meet anyone. You tell them the problem—about Douglas. I'll stay here—"

"Cecelia, you are altogether too nervous."

"They're Dan's brothers. They're men. They won't see me—can't see *me* through all this . . ."

"Cecelia, you are overweight, not communicably diseased. Be reasonable. I could never explain the need to find Douglas. Only you can talk about what it means to you to find him—"

"Oh, God, Viv—"

169

"The stain is hardly visible and you do not smell bad. Paul and Steven are a little stiff, but when they know what you have done—where you have been, they can't help but admire and respect . . ." They went down, still arguing, to the parlor where Doris had pulled the shades against the westering light.

As Cecelia had forgotten that the young people at Horizon House were profoundly unusual, Vivian had forgotten Cecelia's unusual looks. Paul and Steven had had none of her preparation, and none of Cecelia's biography. The realization of this came immediately, meeting in the front hall: "Steven, Paul, this is my friend, Cecelia."

The men drew back. The introductions were done in slow motion as they strained to surmount their discomfort. Handshakes. Chairs in the library; it was a room Vivian had thought of as being intimate and which was now only small and too close for people in states of surprise and incredulity. Cecelia began to sweat with embarrassment. Paul and Steven couldn't imagine or believe Vivian's description of Cecelia's work with Daniel. The words "my friend" made them gape. Cecelia began to state the problem of finding Douglas. She was aware of her strangeness and became self-conscious and halting. She had planned this talk during her bath, trying for brevity and precision, but she only sounded ignorant. She thought a big word or two might help. "You can readily apprehend our predicament." Hoping to gain their approval by including their sister, she added, "Viv needs to find out more about Ripstein. I need to find Douglas." Anger was added to their displeasure.

Vivian tried to help. "We have no way of tracing Douglas Irons. We thought you would know . . ." When Vivian finished, they sat in dead silence for what seemed quite a while. Then Paul spoke.

"I think this is ill-advised. You are not detectives. The man obviously does not want to be found. As for you, Vivian, I thought we had all decided that the will was legally made. The process has begun to get it probated. Your contact with Jack Ripstein should be over. Why are you concerned with him? What do you hope to accomplish?"

170

Vivian drew in her breath. She had not told Cecelia about Daniel's will. She thought if she spoke quickly she could get past it. "I hope to accomplish knowing Daniel and where Ripstein fit into his life. If you knew him you would know how strange it all is."

"Daniel is dead now," Steven said. "His former assistants have lives of their own . . . uh . . . work to do."

"Yes, as you say, Daniel is dead, but where are his medical papers, his records and pictures and field notes? The Archbishop's secretary said they would be found. Have they been? Where have twenty-five years of medical photographs gone?"

"What does it matter?" Paul said, trying for mildness in his tone. "They might be of value to another facial surgeon but no one else would have any use for them."

"Not true," Vivian blurted. "The villagers used to cut them up for talismans."

Cecelia laughed. "True! That's true. I forgot that!" She became aware of Paul's look and stopped dead.

"We also want to find Douglas Irons," Vivian said. "We need help, and we came to you. Maybe it's not the wisdom of acceptance. Maybe it's not wise at all, or useful or practical, but it's what we want to do. Can't you help us?"

"The best advice I can give, especially about this . . . your friend's quest, is to drop it. If the man wishes to remain hidden, as he seems to from the letter you describe, he will not welcome your intrusion. If he is hiding, it is probably for good reason, and your meddling may result in trouble for you or for him, the last thing in the world you wanted. Remember that this is a selfish quest on your part—parts. Vivian, you know the assistants to whom you can send Daniel's awards. It's a very simple matter. He didn't ask you to trace anyone. It's to everyone's advantage that you stay away from Ripstein because someone might accuse you of self-interest. This matter should be handled quickly and impersonally. It is not as though you are trying to find Daniel's heirs." Paul added acidly, "We already know who the heir is."

For a moment, Vivian thought Cecelia must have understood

what had just been said, but she saw that Cecelia was so self-aware and miserable that the words might not have been absorbed. She watched Cecelia rise, sighing. "Well, I want to thank you. Dan San—I mean Daniel Sanborn—was a big part of my life. It's a real great treat for me to come here to his house and meet his family." She went over and shook hands with Paul and Steven, wringing a little hard to break the stiffness in their arms. "I thank you for your advice, too," Cecelia was saying, "from a lawyer's point of view. I want to think it all out," and she left them.

"What in God's name has happened to you? That woman and you—"

"She wasn't at ease here—"

"It doesn't matter. What does matter is that the whole idea is ridiculous, looking up all those people—making contact with Ripstein. Did it never occur to you that he might think you had plans to stop his bequest?" Paul was drumming again, the familiar sign of his familiar irritation. Familiar. Of the family. The weight of it was suddenly very heavy.

Steven began. "I . . . we're worried about *you*, Vivian. You've always been preoccupied—obsessed with Daniel all the years . . ."

"I *served*. Don't you understand? I had a purpose in the world beyond anything I could have accomplished alone. I gave Daniel a home. The respites he had made the work possible."

"Yes, and when Daniel died and that sense of service was taken away—you see what has resulted. That *woman*? Someone you *found* in an *institution*? What are you going to do, play Pied Piper to Daniel's ex-nurses?"

"Cecelia wants to find Douglas Irons because he needs to know certain things. To be told . . ."

It suddenly seemed so idiotic a quest: to Canada to visit an emotionally enhausted stranger, to look over letters written almost a decade ago about things that happened in encampments long since gone back to desert or jungle— She tried to remember how she had felt about it all yesterday, or the day before, painting rain gutters in the yard in Indianapolis talking about a past

172

its sharers both wanted and did not want to examine and clarify. Her brothers were facing her, their faces stiff with righteousness. "Did you ever think how memory changes?" she asked them. "When I worked at the ceramics laboratory during the war, most of what I did was incredibly boring, but over the years the memory of it began to change in my mind. It keeps changing. Different parts come forward, retreat, blur. The people, too, come and go like a dance. It makes the past as mysterious as the future."

"What has all that got to do with what we're saying, that this running around you are doing is dangerous, silly, undignified, unseemly—?"

"We are both very dignified," Vivian said. "We are very seemly. We are involved only with people who were in the work with Daniel, except—mainly except—for Ripstein—only with people who want to see us."

"And Ripstein—"

"Perpetrated fraud on Cecelia and on the assistants and should be answerable for it."

"Good God, Vivian, *Cecelia!*"

"You don't really see her," Vivian said.

"Don't see her? When you look at her it's all you *can* see!"

"Well, Mother Antonia *asked* me to go to Canada. Cecelia promised them at Horizon House that she'd be back in two weeks. If we haven't found out what we need to know by then, I'll stop."

"There's been a great change in you since Daniel's death," Paul said. "I blame myself, because I was busy—I didn't visit as much as I should have."

Vivian shook her head. "Cecelia says her children are kept from growing when they are allowed no risk. I think half the delight in the world comes from challenges met. Admit it—you and Paul love that part of your lives. We've just been looking at your pictures so the truth of them is very fresh. That tennis, that boating, now that business deal, that case— Wars are fought for it. Give us your blessing."

"You and that woman are making yourselves ridiculous."

"Yes." Vivian smiled a little. "I suppose we are."

Later, the two of them sat in the window seat in Vivian's room. "So they pulled an Uncle Bucky on you."

"What's an 'Uncle Bucky'?" Vivian was numbed, chilled. Paul and Steven saw her as a dithering, frantic adolescent, mooning over a lost brother. Looking through their eyes at herself, she, too, had seen those things.

Cecelia knew. She tried to smile and be easy, but her face was sad and her body slumped. "Uncle Bucky was my mother's brother. He had a way of seeing what the 'real reasons' for everything were. Remember when people used to say 'Tell it like it is'? That was Uncle Bucky, and 'like it is' hung stinking from the back porch. Religion, politics, personal lives—friends. Nothing was safe. When somebody'd have the blues at home we used to say, 'Has Uncle Bucky been here?' "

"I thought . . . I used Daniel as a model for what was good in the world and in people. These trips—meeting his assistants— I seem to be seeing him more and more as cold and failed."

"Viv, if you want to end things here—I'll find a way myself—"

"Did a talk with Uncle Bucky stop you from going to nursing school?"

"No, it only took all the lovely glow away from it. Uncle Bucky made things poor. The whole world was one big sour dishrag when he got through with it."

"Well, glow or no glow, we're going to Montreal." Vivian sighed. Abner was in Toronto by now. He would be at the museum, arranging, fussing, working. It was a picture that suddenly seemed homelike and cozy. "Paul and Steven make our trip—seem so *silly*."

"They thought they knew you. It's a kind of comfort people can get to depend on. They sounded—no offense, but I thought, when I got over the hurt of it, that they sounded like my kids. Remember how Rupert Lee kept saying, 'Why are you going away?' He didn't want to know *why*. He wanted to know why

174

he couldn't depend on me. Your brothers are smarter than Rupert Lee, and they make better reasons for the way they want to feel, but—"

"They're the ones who should be helping us."

"Why can't you stay the way you were?"

They laughed.

Dear Miss Sanborn:

I am writing this by the nurse, Betty-Joe Davis, and pardon me, you don't know me, but I wanted to write years ago when I came to America and never got the time. I was living in Jerusalem then, it was Palestine in the fifties, and I was there in the quarter when your brother came to look for his people. Maybe it's too long ago, but it seems like yesterday to me. So if you want to call me or come and see me, it's Harry Ganz and I'm at the Home for the Pious of Israel, 19 Wickson Street, Brooklyn. If you want to come it's better because I don't walk so good and it's hard for me to come by the phone. It bothered me because later we remembered something he wanted to know. If you come you should call before.

Mr. Harry Ganz

He was a fragile old man in a skullcap. His hands were knotted with arthritis and lay on the arms of the wheelchair so deformed they might have been the sculpting of a child.

"It's from the meat," he said, "because I was a butcher." He looked sane enough; many of the people around him were not;

their faces had absent, withdrawn looks. Some of them babbled. "Let's go where we can talk," he said. He directed her to a back porch. The day was warm; it was uncomfortable inside. "It's not fancy, back here," he said, "but at least we can be alone."

Vivian was glad Cecelia had not come; in the small space they would have seemed to overwhelm him. The porch overlooked a bare backyard littered with blown papers and gridded with washlines. "So you're his sister?"

"Yes."

"He was famous, the doctor. All over the world."

"Yes."

"Me, no one ever heard of. I was a butcher."

"You wrote that you met my brother in Jerusalem."

Mr. Ganz smiled then, showing Chiclet-square dentures. "He was lost." He gave a little laugh. "He came into the quarter one afternoon. In spring it was, sometime in the early fifties. Tall, skinny he was, something around the eyes—but a stranger. He couldn't speak; no Yiddish, no Hebrew, no ladino, no Polish. He said, 'Sanbenito,' and English words. The kids came to me because they knew I was American. The family: a mother, no father, aunt, grandfather, three cousins. They all lived way in back, the end of the quarter. Poor. The rains drained down there and gathered because the road was low. People dumped things in the little field behind the house." Vivian wanted to interrupt. There had been no mother. It was the aunt who had sent Daniel to America. Ganz kept on. Vivian began to wonder if he had really known Daniel. "They had goats, two goats. They had no floor in the house. You can be poor—we were all poor there, but they were not *balabatisch*. You know the word?"

"Something like 'self-respecting.' "

"When you respect your own life. 'Sanbenito,' he said. So I asked him, 'Who are you?' 'I'm the son,' he said. 'Daniel.'

"I couldn't believe it. He was too tall, too well-dressed, too dignified. 'Do they know you're coming?' 'I wasn't sure they were alive. I couldn't remember how to get here.' I was, well, embarrassed.

"Soon there's a bunch following us. The quarter never saw

177

anything like him before. 'So you are living in America now?'
'Yes,' he says, 'I'm a doctor.' I couldn't believe it.

"We get to the house. The old man is in back. The mother comes out. I think he took her for a servant; she was drying her hands on a rag. She thought he was an official—a suit like that, a face like that, up in the air. 'Sanbenito,' he says. She says, 'So what?' and puts her hands on her hips and gives him back look for look. 'It's Daniel,' I say, 'your son.' She stops dead and stares. Then she grabs his hand and holds it up, looking for a mark, I guess, because then she goes down on her knees and picks up his pants leg and rolls down one sock. All the time he just stands there, stiff like a statue. I guess she finds what she's looking for because she grabs hold of both his legs and holding on, climbs up him, hugging him. She's sobbing, laughing, yelling, making the sounds you make to a baby. Him—he doesn't move. Not a muscle. His mother—"

"Mother? I thought—"

"She lied, the mother. They never would have taken him if he wasn't an orphan."

"Oh."

"The gawkers can't get over her. By now there's a crowd. Suddenly she notices. She stops and steps back from him. She's saying, 'Come with me,' in Yiddish, but he doesn't understand, not even that. Suddenly, she stops. She looks him up and down, walks around him looking, and then she nods and says, 'That's good.' And before he can stop her, she grabs his suitcase and takes it in the house. I go in to translate, kicking the door closed in the gawkers' faces.

"I got to tell you this: that family was not respected much. Because of that, she has a hard time getting. You know what I mean: a couple of plums to stew for dessert, a piece of chicken— she sends out one of the kids. Nobody wants to give. At last someone comes with some day-old cake, poppy seed, I remember. While the meal is cooking, they sit. She's staring at his face like she's waiting *hard* for something to happen. The aunt comes in, the cousins, the old man. None of them speaks English. The doctor asks about some white birds. 'I want to be in the room that opens up,' he says, 'that opens on top, like a skylight, so you can see into the sky,' and he is sure, he says. We look at one another and shrug. He forgot how poor they were, and forgot or never knew that even their poor neighbors think they're trash, people without pride.

"As soon as the sun goes low, they eat. Fried bread, lentils, tomatoes, oil, and the cake with tea. He eats, too, but you can see he has no taste for the food. The aunt gets mad, but the mother laughs and says, 'Why should he like this stuff? He's used to better than this. *I* did that for him.' "

Ganz stopped talking. Vivian waited for a while, thinking he was collecting his thoughts and then that he might be asleep. As suddenly, he was back at the same place he had left as though moving back and forth through a doorway.

"They get ready to sleep. He says he wants the room with the door in the roof, and they show him there are only two rooms in the house and the back one for storage, airless. The night was peaceful, the weather was good, so they sleep on the roof. I sleep home so I don't know what happens in the night, if she stays up looking at him, or if he sleeps or not."

Vivian wanted to ask some questions, but she was afraid to stem the flow. She was too intent to be horrified at what she was hearing, first to be sure that the stranger had been Daniel and then, when she was sure, to hear the details of his family.

"The next day him and the grandfather, they go here, there. I got to translate because he still has no memory for any of the languages. We go to the synagogue, the *cheder*, the shops, the field, and every place the grandfather asks if the doctor remembers and there is nothing, not one sight, and he doesn't remember a word, not one word of Yiddish.

"But there are three things he says he remembers. One is the smell of the oil lamp and one is the goats' smell and one is that room open to the sky, a door in the roof held open by a stick, and those white birds. Nobody knows what he is talking about. The women, his mother and aunt, worked from the house. They and most of the quarter made things to sell for the religious market all over the world. They wove *lulav* branches for *succos*, cut Chanukah candles, stamped letters on dreidels—all for a few cents, and by all that they made a little living. They were ignorant, small-minded women. He made me ask them later and they shrugged when he argued about the room, the white birds. It seemed important to him because he kept trying, describing and asking me was I saying it right, 'There were white birds that came—' showing with his hands how they fluttered. When he tried to show them, they shook their heads and finally to keep the peace I said maybe it was on the ship."

Again he was still. Vivian let him rest. She wished she had brought a tape machine or taken notes.

"Did I tell you about the cousins?"

"No."

"Three cousins, all much younger. One of the cousins was burned in a raid years before and afterwards he was never right in the head. He sees those cousins clear for the first time the next day. The oldest, the burned one, is about eighteen then. One side of his face is gone and one arm useless because of the burns. It was a raid the Arabs made before I came, and the quarter had been shot up and the fires started and all the rest, rapes, you name it. The kid had gotten used to standing near walls, hiding his bad side. The two men, the uncle and Sanborn's father, had been killed in raids like that." He launched into a discussion of the raids and the shortness of the world's memory.

Finally, Vivian said, "About Daniel—"

He looked at her for a moment, helplessly. "We were . . . It was . . ."

"About the cousins, Daniel's cousins—"

"Oh, yes, about the burned one. He asks me to talk to that one. 'Tell him,' he says, 'tell him he should come to America, that there are hospitals where they fix burned faces.' So I did. I told him. Listen, I was no good interpreter, what the hell did I know how to say things nice, to pick careful what word to use? The kid, Ikki, listens and then, then he starts to cry. Just like that, he stands and cries, cries like an ox would cry if it could, without turning away, head on, without making a sound. Sanborn and I, we stand there; we don't know what to do. Then

180

Sanborn says, 'Will he come? I'll take him to a hospital in New York.' I tell Ikki. Ikki shakes his head, half of it good-looking and half of it ugly, going back and forth. No. No. 'Why?' Ikki understands the question without me, but he walks away out of the house and up the street. I know the doctor wants to run after him. I can see him clench his hands and his face gets all tight. This doctor is a modern man with modern ideas. He can't understand any of these people and how it is when you never went a mile in any direction all your life. The doctor looks at me and says, 'What should I do?' I'm no philosopher; I'm a butcher who speaks English. I say, 'Search me.' The other cousins come. They want to know how much money he has. They want to go to America and have wristwatches and rings. The doctor has a school ring from medical school. The little *momzers* stole it that night. The mother comes and yells at the kids they shouldn't bother the doctor. She takes him to sit outside in front of the house even though it's at the end of the quarter. Still, it can be seen—a woman and two men and me not even a relative, sitting out there. She acts like she's having tea with the king, bold as brass. She's sitting there with us, picking over lentils or something. *She* has questions. Does he have a car? Does he go to the movies? Does he live in a skyscraper? Every question shows her up as an ignorant, common woman. Every question you could see hitting him harder and harder. Finally he stops answering, a long time, and then he says to me, 'Ask her why she did it, why she gave me away.' 'It's done,' I tell him, 'it's all over.' 'Ask her,' he says. I ask her."

Vivian was leaning forward. Suddenly a woman came through the door. She was carrying a tray with paper cups. "What are you two doing out here? You're not supposed to be out here. We have a perfectly good dayroom or the porch . . ." Vivian got up. Maneuvering around the wheelchair in the small space, she approached the nurse and leaned close. She said in a low voice, "I'm working for Paul Sanborn, the lawyer. A case. Confidential. Millions of dollars are involved. It's international litigation. He was a witness. 1950s. You can see why any word of it getting out . . ."

181

"Oh, well, yes—" The woman backed away.

Harry Ganz had not heard. "She left? She went away?"

"Yes."

"How did you do it?"

"By being Daniel's sister for a minute. We were—you were telling me about Daniel and his mother."

"What about them?"

"That Daniel had asked his mother why she gave him away . . ."

"I don't know what the hell answer *he* expected, but she surprised *me*. She gives a big snort like you give when you're embarrassed at a compliment. She says, 'Oh, you were the best one, the smartest one. You I chose and you I saved out of this. No pain will touch *you*, no ugliness. I lied for you and I would lie again.' She gives a kind of smile and she says, 'I told them you were an orphan, that I was the aunt, not the mother. I told them your family was dead. I made them put you on the list to send away. *I* did this, on my own. Let the neighbors look their looks and say their ugliness. None of them could do what I did.' And she goes back picking little stones and dead insects out of the beans, proud, you know, and we both sit there dumb like death."

"And Daniel?"

"I don't know what he thought. He didn't jump up and down or nothing. I guess it was hard on him, hearing that."

"Yes," Vivian said, "I guess it was."

"So, while we're all sitting there, the aunt comes out. The aunt has an idea. The doctor should stay in Jerusalem, she says, and be a doctor and they're all going to move in with him because it's his duty, they're family after all, etc., etc. The mother lets out a yell and pretty soon they're at it like two seven-year-olds over a doll. The words were awful, not even fit for the war. In the beginning he has me translate but after a while *I* couldn't even say the words they used and I stopped."

"My God," Vivian said, almost in a whisper.

"That was all there was. The next day he leaves, just up and goes."

"When was that? What month?"

"It was June, I think, late springtime."

"Do you know where he went afterward?"

"No, but a month after he left, Ikki came and told me he figured out about that room with the roof that opened, and about the white birds. It was from stories they told him about the times back in the twenties. It was like this: They all used to go during the autumn to a kibbutz to help with the harvest. Everyone felt good then because there was enough to eat. They would all be laughing and full of talk. It was a barley field, they told Ikki, and they sickled it off by hand, like the people did in Bible times. Then the birds, doves and pigeons, would come and fly down for the fallen grain. The doctor was—must have been—only a little kid then, three or four. They told Ikki they used to put Daniel in an empty grain bin, on a blanket, and they opened the top of the bin and propped it up with a stick, and Ikki thought maybe *that* was the dark room and *that* was the ceiling open to the sky. Daniel forgot, see, that he was so small and he forgot they put him in there to keep him out of the way of the sickles. So there *was* a room and white birds in one way, and in another way there wasn't. Ikki wanted me to write Daniel and ask him, because Ikki had only heard of that in family stories and had figured it out himself. Years later, back here, I read the doctor's name in the papers when he won some big prize, and I saw his picture and recognized it was the same person who had been those few days in the quarter. I meant to send him a letter about it, because it seemed like it was so important to him—that room, those birds flying . . ."

The old man was quiet for a time. Then he said, "Listen, they're kosher here. *Glatt*. Pure as snow; and that's what the flavor's like. Down the block there's a Chinese place. Could you sneak me in an order of fried shrimp? They could put it in a bag so no one can see . . ."

"Viv, you look awful."

"I came home by instinct, I think."

"Then that guy in the nursing home was really what he claimed to be; he really knew Dan in Jerusalem the summer he disappeared?"

"Yes." Vivian opened her mouth to speak, to tell Cecelia everything Harry Ganz had said, the terrible family, the white birds, the ugliness of the quarter, the triumph of the mother, all the pride and blindness and ambition and the realities of lives so foreign to her that she could barely comprehend them. The telling was beyond her. She sat on the couch waiting to be able to say the words until Cecelia said, "Not now, Viv. Don't force this. Let it come out when it comes," and went away to get Doris to make some tea.

"We're supposed to go to Canada tomorrow. I feel like someone swimming at night in filthy water. What must *Daniel* have felt? We never knew and he could never tell us because when even the description was hard to deal with, what must the experience have been!"

"What can I do for you besides give you the added shock of a sixty-dollar phone bill trying to find Douglas Irons?"

"Turn on the TV. Let's watch the most inane show we can get."

But the colored shadows flickered and in all of them were only Daniel's gaunt body and haunted face.

❧ 16 ❧

The grounds of the Canadian convent were gridded with grav-eled walks and formally marked like the Stations of the Cross, with low shrubs whose branches were cut into geometric shapes. To the right was the convent, to the left the small hospital. Over both entrances stood a statue of Mary, an older, sadder Mary than the young mother usually portrayed. She was carved in the same gray stone as the buildings. The paths were lined with carefully trained flowers lying close and neat on the edges of the gravel. No daisies blew or morning glories trailed. At the entrance were two circular stands of white lilies, rigidly upright as kneeling nuns. Vivian and Cecelia went up the steps and into the convent building.

A habited sister directed them to the parlor. A row of high-backed chairs stood on one side of the room and a row facing it on the other. The room smelled of floor wax and lilies. Cecelia giggled. "I'm sorry, Viv; places like this bring out the worst in me. It's so much like the convent I went to for nursing school."

"Goodness," Vivian whispered. "I can't take you anywhere!"

"I guess I'm a little scared, too. I don't know any of these people; I wasn't in Africa with them and the way you tell it,

185

that Sister Mary sounds like she dreamed up a Dan San *I* never knew."

"Mother Tony sent the letter; they know why we're here."

"You would have made a good assistant, Viv."

"Too squeamish."

"Squeam doesn't matter. Stay does. You've got that."

Vivian was moved. The silence of the parlor hung in the golden morning, dozing. On the plane up, she had told Cecelia all she could about Harry Ganz's account: Daniel's two and one half days in his mother's house. The telling had been very difficult. Vivian was making an effort to clear her mind in the consciously disciplined order and quiet of this place. After a while, a sister came to guide them to the Mother Superior. "I thought they were out of the clothes," Cecelia murmured to Vivian. The sister heard her and smiled a routine smile. "We have permission inside the convent to wear our habit. It has great significance to us."

Mother Elizabeth was very different from Mother Tony, about whom she asked in a carefully neutral way. "Mother Antonia has written that she feels a visit to Jennifer Keene might be helpful. Our convent records are also to be open to you. We are deeply grateful to have been associated with your brother, Miss Sanborn, and we are proud that our sisters played a small part in his work of mercy." Cecelia opened her mouth to say something, then thought better of it. "Our guest house has been readied; Sisters Marguerite and Veronica have also been alerted. They were involved at that time in the placement of our sisters. Perhaps you would like to refresh yourselves before you begin—"

The formality of Mother Elizabeth's manner struck Vivian in a surprising way. She had often deplored the disappearance of grace and stillness in modern life, but in this world, the manners spoke of a disengagement at which she stopped, startled. Nothing in her own tradition echoed it, but she realized that the nuns' way was a little bit the way she had been living. She had their light step, light touch, soft voice. Years among displays of priceless porcelains, some thinner than eggshell, had

186

given her that delicacy and had led her to value deliberateness, consistency, patience, little novelty, and no risk. A life—good heavens, like Cecelia's retarded children. She had a sudden picture of the grimy woman in Jerusalem, Daniel's mother, and her daring, her action, her lies, and the risk of lifelong shame to save the son she loved. Had she never weighed right and wrong? Was that the secret—to *do*—courage without thought, without imagination, without a sense of future in it? Daniel's life—Vivian reached out for something but the inner words eluded her. They went with Mother Elizabeth to lunch.

"The community goes to bed at ten in the summer," Mother Elizabeth said over the dessert fruit. "We had planned your visit to Jennifer this afternoon before compline and the sisters' recreation—we thought forty-five minutes would be sufficient."

At her side, Vivian felt Cecelia's immediate physical resistance. Both the women had almost cried out, "Oh no—" They both took a breath and Cecelia said, "She'll need time to get to know us a little." Vivian nodded. "What we have to ask Jennifer is personal—very personal; there has to be some trust first—"

Mother Elizabeth's smiling refusal was bland and total. "We have our schedule to consider but there has been adequate time allotted. Jennifer has been told the purpose of your visit and she has been told she may be perfectly frank." Cecelia's mouth opened but Mother Elizabeth went on smoothly. "We thought you might look at the records in the early evening. The hospital's rules are less stringent than those at the convent. There is also something more, something I think will please you. Dr. Forestier is one of our physicians at the hospital. He heard you were coming and wishes to meet with you. It seems that he and your brother were students together in medical school. We were unaware of this; perhaps it is not part of your inquiry . . ." She saw the eagerness in Vivian's expression. "I see it does please you."

"Very much," Vivian said.

"Well, then, let me call over to the hospital and see when he will be free. His needs might also affect when you go to Jennifer and the records."

She was back in five minutes. "The doctor will meet us in the convent parlor. I think he has chosen a place where he is less likely to be called away." Vivian began to say, "Thank you, Mother Elizabeth . . ." but the nun had already turned smoothly to lead them to the parlor.

The morning sun had left the waxed floorboards. The refectory was now empty. Daniel's mother . . . what was her action, her courage, without the consent . . . perhaps there had been no time for eliciting it, no words to state the case to a small child. Yet the woman's *pride* in what she had done . . . Vivian sighed and turned, and they walked from the refectory back to the parlor, smelling of lilies.

Dr. Forestier was a short, wide man, bald as a baby. When Vivian introduced Cecelia as an assistant, he bowed and kissed her hand. "None of you have had the honor you deserve." When Mother Elizabeth left them, they pulled the heavy chairs around in a circle so that when they sat down their knees almost touched.

"The years go," he said, and then he smiled. His English was heavily accented Canadian French. It lilted like a brogue and was pleasantly mellow. "Daniel Sanborn and I were in school together. One should say I was in school with him. He has been doing miracles all over the world, and I'm back in the little town I grew up in, fixing ski injuries and doctoring at the convent hospital." Vivian and Cecelia found themselves smiling also; his manner was merry, even childlike. "I heard you were coming to see the 'poor failed one.' A pity, really. A lush. Sorry. I call them alcoholic when they're sober for a while. That one drinks all the time and she's usually drunk as hell. Not now, though. No, the sisters have been fixing her up for your visit. She has been nailed to the wall to keep her back straight."

"But—"

"Not the way to do it? Tell that to them. I argue, but they have their way."

"You were in medical school with Daniel?"

"Surprises you?"

"No—I meant . . ."

"Surprises *me*. One of those ski accidents when I was a doc-

188

tor's assistant, years ago. I was sponsored through college and medical school and with loans by two American families. I was older than the others—" He looked from Vivian to Cecelia. "I love to talk. Just interrupt. I don't mind."

"What was it like for Dan in medical school?" Cecelia asked.

Forestier's look was searching and they saw him pause and fumble. Then he took a breath. "Dear Lord, I have waited for this moment so long, and now that it has come, what do I say? It was a shame, what we did. The shame waits to be forgiven. 'Someday I will beg that man's pardon,' we say. Then one day we read that he is dead. Too late the words. Too late."

"What was it?" Vivian asked.

"Your brother was a very quiet, very stiff young man—no offense." Vivian shook her head. "And because of that, he was a natural one to play jokes on. I am not excusing us, any of us—we sometimes hid his equipment for dissections, put sawdust in his stethoscope, spilled things on his papers so he had to do them over. When we found out, for instance, that beyond the forbidden foods of his religion he would eat anything, we tried to prove it. He seemed to have no idea of what foods people do not eat in combination. Sugared meat? Salted ice cream? Peppered cake? Vanilla fish? We fed him all those things, and sat and watched while he ate them reading, oblivious to our snickers, our wonder, and the food alike."

"Well—" Cecelia said, "those are only silly pranks."

"Please—I haven't told you yet. I'm wishing something could come and call us all away, but this time it will not. That is how childish I am. We got him drunk once. What happened was so bad that we never made jokes on him after."

"What did happen?"

"It seemed only a funny trick at that time in medical school when students badly need some fun. In a way, he brought the class together, all the jokes and the plans. Forgive me, I am still making the excuse that will not save me the shame I feel. We made him drunk. We made the trick of challenging a run across the quadrangle. It was June and very hot. He ran well. We let him win. The winner was naturally hot and thirsty. We had put a stiff shot in a glass of grapefruit juice and he drank it quickly, then another and another. Victory drinks, we said, and after two it was easy to make him take more. It took four or five before there was any effect. We thought the alcohol would make him loose, easy, that he would laugh and be jovial. Medical students are among the world's greatest *naïfs*. Most of them have little life experience and they have spent their days listening to authorities. We were surprised, then horrified, at what happened. There was nothing to do in the end, but let it play itself out."

"And . . . ?"

"First, he began to cry. Then louder, stronger. At last, he lay on the floor in one of the school buildings shrieking, sobbing like a lost soul. He said no words, but the sounds echoed through the whole building, at least it seemed so to us, as though someone were being kept there and tortured. We were desperate by that time that some passerby would hear and think it was a woman being misused by us and that we would be arrested. We begged him, we tried to stop him, to muffle his cries. He was uncontrollable. I'll never forget that afternoon. He lay thrashing in the pain of some sorrow beyond our power to control or even to conceive of—beyond our control and worse, beyond his own. He was howling with an awful anguish. We thought he might die, madame. Then, that he might be permanently . . . impaired. Thank God, it was not so. He was cold with us afterward and never took our apologies, for which I can hardly blame him. He ate alone then, things he bought and kept with him. It must have been hideously lonely. We did apologize, even the instigator apologized, but it was no use. Medical school is hard enough without fellows like us as companions, and the loneliness. The instigator was a fat fellow, one of those clownish men—"

"Ripstein!" both women said at once. "Jack Ripstein."

"Jack Ripstein? Oh, no. Jack Ripstein was his friend; to my shame, his only friend. All that we did we had to do behind Ripstein's back." The two women stared at each other. Forestier went on. "I had forgotten about Ripstein, but by your knowing

190

him I see your brother has told you something of those hard times. It was Ripstein who came in on us there, desperate as we were in our selfish fear, and took your brother up wrapped in a bedsheet and with three of us carried him to his room. I stayed some hours with them, until your brother had quieted. Ripstein was three days nursing him."

Vivian spoke sadly. "We learned what we know from other people. My brother was no more open with me than he was with you. So please, tell us more, tell us all you know."

"Well, your brother was, as you say, a taciturn person and Ripstein was jovial in a rather crude way. Some of us wondered aloud why Ripstein defended your brother. Forgive me, madame. It is the besetting sin of youth, to slight substance for shadow, to love the wrong people and value the wrong things—"

"That friendship—"

"I don't know if it was a *friendship*. They were not often together; their tastes were different, habits, interests. Your brother studied all the time, but Ripstein played. He had a room in the hospital, in an unused attic. He lived there rent-free, being very poor, but he always had girls up there. I don't know how he had time for them all. We used to envy him, and by some strange chance that envy found outlets against your brother. I think now that was one reason we deviled him."

"He never told us about any of it."

"Men are stupidly vain, perhaps even great men like your brother. What saddens me most is that I did not see—none of us saw the greatness in him except Jack Ripstein. All the world knows what happened to Daniel Sanborn—he became a great healer and a hero. Now, I wonder what happened to that other."

"I don't know if he ever practiced medicine, but I know that he's now a nightclub comedian. His agent says he travels to Montreal sometimes. He's called Jack the Ripper."

"Amazing," the doctor murmured, "amazing."

Cecelia had been listening without comment. She said, "Do you have any other memories of Dan San?"

"You were his assistant . . ."

"Yes."

"Where?"

"Bangladesh, Iran, Vietnam, Korea, Peru—other places."

Forestier shook his head and gave a little whistle. "I would like very much to invite you to my home and to sit and hear all of the adventures, the excitements, the different ways you have lived. Can you come to us tomorrow evening?"

"I'm sorry; we have to leave tomorrow—to go back."

"I see. A pity. We would have been greatly honored. You ask about other memories—there is another on which I have thought a great deal. The picture stays the same but the meaning changes over the years. I will give you the picture and spare you my ruminations . . ."

"Did it happen before or after the other thing?"

"Oh, after— It was during our third year. In those days students never saw patients until that year, and by then, their notion of the human body was of a collection of chemical fluids and physiological responses. We were all shocked to some degree by our first clinical experiences. The X-ray of a tubercular lung is interesting in its differences. The patient whose interesting X-ray it is—he is strangling to death. We hid from the patients—yes, and we got professional and brisk and we'd give our orders and leave—we couldn't bear their eyes, you see, their pain, their fear.

"One day I was on the ward we hated most—the charity ward. There we were always sure to have lots of very sick children. On a certain day there was a child burned in a fire. He had been taking lunch to his father at a factory and there had been an explosion. The father and several others had been killed, and the child—all along one side—burned, and an arm broken. He was six or so, immigrants—Mediterranean, I remember; the mother all in shawls, a heavy, peasant woman. She sat by the child as it lay, covered almost head to toe in bandages. Now and then she would give it small sips of water, wipe what of its face she could with a cloth, and all the time whispering a kind of song to it. They were screened off from

192

the others for fear of his being contaminated—burned flesh infects so easily—there were two screens—one on each side. I was passing, and I looked in quickly through the opening between and turned away, and then I saw the shadow of someone sitting between those screens where they overlapped—a small space where one could be almost unseen, and yet could see. He had brought a chair there and was watching. It was your brother. I was going to greet him—you know, the hearty talk doctors use with each other—we were just learning it then, to be breezy over the bed of the patient. As soon as I opened my mouth to speak and came close enough to see his face, I knew I was no fellow doctor conferring, but an intruder breaking in on the most intimate of moments. Your brother was watching them. He was giving his complete attention, the kind of perfect attention one sees on the faces of lovers, and now and then on the faces of our young sisterlings here when they are new to religious life. He seemed so close as to be part of them, every gesture, every sound. I said before there was nothing beautiful in the scene itself—the mother was heavy and harried, not lovely in feature or body. The child was mostly hidden; its hair was lank and covered with sweat; its face, even that part not bandaged, singed; the eyebrows gone. There was the stink of medicines, his burns, and the sense of his pain. Your brother was not looking at that, at any of that, I think. He was seeing something else, her touching, her crooning, her constant, endless, patient presence. I felt the embarrassment the man feels who blunders in on a lovemaking. I went away and came again in an hour through the ward and he was still there, sitting in that hidden foot of space, caught in that scene, watching the mother wipe the child, still it, and wrap it in her sound. Of course, I never mentioned it to him that I had seen him. I never told anyone until now, but it remains for me as intense as it was then."

"And he never *spoke* to the mother or the child—"

"Not that I know of. I don't think they knew he was there."

The two women looked at each other. "Unconsenting does

17

They walked on the aggressively directed path, metaphor, Vivian thought, for the directed prayer.

"We have never found a tactful way to thank you for all you have done," Dr. Forestier said.

"I don't understand."

"It's not that they wouldn't care for her," Forestier continued, "it's only that it would have to be at great sacrifice to others and the sisters, too."

"I beg your pardon?"

"Madame, there is no need for this delicacy. The money you send. It does so much for her and for us. Mother Elizabeth cannot thank you because the money comes anonymously and because of some nunnish nonsense. I'm not a nun, and 'Thank you' is all right with me."

"I'm sorry," Vivian said, "but I have no idea what you are talking about."

He gave her a long stare. "We assumed," he said, "we have all assumed that it was you who were sending the money each month—the money that comes each month for Miss Keene for her medical care—we had always thought it was your brother who sent it. The sisters assumed so, and when the doctor passed on, they wondered, with some pious circumlocutions, if the money would stop. This month the money order arrived as usual. I thought to thank you for it. When you see Miss Keene, you will know how necessary it is."

"Doctor, if there is money being sent, I don't think it was from my brother. He was always away and sometimes miles from even a tiny village. Where do the checks come from?"

"They were—are—postal money orders, I believe. We had thought that you—acting at his request—"

"I didn't know about Jennifer until I talked to Mother Tony—Mother Antonia at the convent in New York last week." (It had only been last week . . .)

The doctor looked nonplussed. Then he laughed. "Why do we imagine we are so important that everyone knows all about us and plans for us so much? We saw ourselves blessed, and so we are, but by whom?"

"I wish it had been by us," Vivian said.

The doctor laughed again. "You have enough to do where you are."

"No, I don't," Vivian said. "I have been seeing that."

"From where exactly does the money come?" Cecelia asked.

The doctor appeared to be thinking. "From the United States, which made us think it was you. Let me ask the bookkeeper what she knows—ah, our time must be up—here comes Sister Margaret Mary."

"Now we're to talk to the sisters who set up the program with Daniel."

"While you are there, I will work on our mystery. I'll see you later with what I learn." He was grinning like a boy.

"It couldn't have been Jack Ripstein, could it?" Cecelia asked.

"How? You know the kind of man he is!" Even with what Forestier had told them, it was still difficult for Vivian to think of Daniel sitting with Ripstein, walking, talking with him. She could imagine them together only if there were some need involved, some force or compulsion. Ripstein had befriended Daniel during his lonely years in medical school. He had taken many risks for Daniel—deflected a weapon, who knew what else? So there was, of course a loyalty there, and Ripstein had, for some reason of hero worship or neurotic attachment, followed Daniel to this place and that and so— "It must have been Daniel working through someone, and not Jack Ripstein. Daniel would have done it in secret because his modesty would compel it." Cecelia nodded and then sighed. Vivian could tell she was less certain.

The two sisters were of no help. They were defensive and had forgotten the facts about the order's involvement in Daniel's work. It was a relief when the meeting ended.

The order kept a special room on the third floor of the hospital as its infirmary. Sister Margaret Mary explained that when she was able, Jennifer Keene had nominal jobs around the convent. When Jennifer was "ill" or "recovering" or suffering from any of the illnesses exacerbated by her problem, she stayed in the infirmary, where she was now. "We have done our best with her, but she is quite ill spiritually as well as physically . . . our best efforts . . ."

They went up the stairs and came to the infirmary door and knocked. A sister opened it and smiled professionally at them. It was still early, a little after four. The light was just beginning to mellow. The woman was in a bathrobe, sitting by the window. She looked up. Her eyes passed over both of them without stopping and back to her clasped hands, from which a rosary hung unmoving. Vivian introduced herself and Cecelia, trying for the simple friendliness that would put Jennifer at ease. Cecelia went forward in the slow but steady way she used with new people at Horizon House. "Hello. We're from America. Mother Antonia told us to come." She went close and put her hand on Jennifer's fists. "I'm real pleased to meet you." There was dead silence. Vivian had the sinking sense of failure. The woman looked rooted there, unwilling or unable to respond to them. After what seemed a long time, Cecelia said, "Viv, here, is Dan San's sister—I mean Dr. Sanborn's sister. I was an assistant, like you were." Jennifer Keene continued to stare but made no move to speak. Her expression did not change. It seemed useless to go on, but Cecelia did. "We came to talk to you about your years—your time with him."

"Why?" The voice was flat.

Cecelia persevered. "I guess because since he died, his sister and I got to remembering him, thinking about him." The infirmarian brought chairs.

"I don't know anything," Jennifer said in the same flat voice.

"You know what Africa was like, what the work was like after I left."

"I don't know anything." She was round-faced, fatter than Vivian had expected, but there was an unhealthy quality to her skin and the roundness seemed puffy.

"I guess we don't know much either," Vivian said, more to help Cecelia, "but we wanted to meet you, to hear anything you had to say. We—I—feel so much about Daniel, and you have experienced so much—"

Vivian sighed. Jennifer was hurting herself through them. Making them press, declare before the normal social comforts and limits had been established, she was using their conversation, Cecelia's eagerness, as a way of wounding herself. Cecelia saw it happening. She stepped back to give Jennifer some room. She didn't notice how wide the legs were that braced the old-fashioned chair. Vivian didn't see her backwards lurch and trip, but there was a sound of Cecelia's indrawn breath and then the sound of the chair's backward friction against the floor as Cecelia fell. Cecelia had put her arms out to shield herself and had fallen, the chair sliding out from under. By the time she had turned, Cecelia was on the floor.

"Are you all right?"

"I tripped—"

"Are you hurt?"

"I don't know; let me rest here awhile."

"Do you feel anything broken?"

"No, I'm just winded."

Vivian looked over at Jennifer, still in her chair, her hands still knotted around the rosary. "Can you come and help us? If we each take a hand—"

"I'm the patient," Jennifer said. "I don't work. I get worked on."

"I'm all right," Cecelia murmured. "It's more embarrassment than pain, but my foot's twisted under me."

From the floor beside Cecelia, Vivian was looking up at Jennifer. Jennifer was half smiling and the dullness had gone out of her eyes. In the secret, perverse way of punished children, she was enjoying, behind her guarded face, the discomfiture of her elders.

"Should I get someone?"

"Oh, God, no! I can get up—"

But the infirmarian must have heard the noise because she came in. Officiously she lifted Cecelia onto her feet. Now and then Vivian looked at Jennifer sitting in her chair. Jennifer's face was working with unuttered laughter. Vivian wanted to slap her. Cecelia grimaced. "I can stand on it—I think it's okay. It's my fault; I didn't look. I was so busy trying to say what I wanted to say to Jennifer—trying to show her—I didn't look."

The infirmarian turned a red face on her. "I'm so sorry. I've tripped on that thing myself a dozen times—I didn't think—"

"Could I use this bed here—just for a while—"

"Of course." They helped Cecelia limp to the bed next to Jennifer's. She sat gingerly.

Jennifer spoke naturally for the first time. "What do you have to ask me, what do you want to hear from me that's worth all this?"

"Oh, hell," Cecelia said, rubbing her ankle. "We wanted to see you—we didn't want you 'prepared' for us, 'fixed up.'"

"You worked with my brother," Vivian said. "I met Sister Mary at the convent in New York. I met Mother Tony and she told me you had memories to share, thoughts, ideas about your experience with Daniel in Africa. There are things about Daniel's work that puzzle me. One of the puzzles is why working with Daniel was so hard on you sisters, so hard, in fact, that your order gave up its plans to send more assistants out to him."

"We thought—" Cecelia said, "we thought that maybe it had something to do with Jack the Ripper."

In the carefully dead face, the skin blanched and then suffused. At the outposts of the drugged and medicated body, alarms went off. Jennifer began to tremble, her hands driven apart and now bouncing on the arms of her chair. The rosary fell and lay unnoticed on the floor. She whispered vehemently at her visitors: "What do you know about that! Who blabbed about that!"

"No one blabbed," Cecelia said. "My friends told me their experiences, that was all."

"What do you know?" Jennifer shouted suddenly. From the door they could hear the infirmarian moving to listen, in case there should be a need— "What do you *know*!" Jennifer whispered.

"What will you tell us?" Vivian asked.

"Nothing. Not a goddamn thing. Not a lousy, stinking thing!" This she said in a hate-filled hiss, lest the infirmarian come with a pill.

"Let's make peace," Cecelia said, "because we don't want to hurt you or have you hurt us. We all know the Ripper, and what he did to our friends, but we don't know what he did to you or the other sisters—"

"I don't know why he was *there*," Vivian said, "what purpose he served there, why my brother wanted him, permitted him there. People protected my brother because of his . . . well, his work, his dedication, his personality. Some of it must have dawned on him, some of what Jack Ripstein did or said, must have become apparent to him. Tell us. Help us."

"Why me?"

"Because of what's happened to you, to the other sisters. The toll it took."

"Oh, you mean because I'm a mess now, an alcoholic with a liver like a brick? Rest easy, girls, I was an alcoholic years

200

before I went to Africa. People suspected, maybe, but no one knew it. I drank secretly *here*, all during my novitiate. They suspected two gardeners whose whiskey bottles and hiding places were really mine. I had stuff stored all over the house. I went through Africa in a haze. I worked with Sister Mary, the biggest hysteric there is. I worked with Louise Goldman, who wanted to be loved by the whole world, and Peter Hulme, who wanted to computerize facial surgery so he could have robots do it. *They* didn't drive me to drink; I'd already made the trip."

A bell rang. Jennifer began to laugh. "The convent day sweeps you away."

"What is that?"

"Never mind, it's a bell, a change; drop the old thing, pick up the new. Like chimps. Like trained apes. *Nunc Dimwittis.*"

They were walking to the guest house. Cecelia moved slowly, limping.

"How bad is that ankle?"

"I'll be okay. This limp is a ploy to get your pity."

"It was awful, Jennifer smiling like that."

"At least it got her talking, it broke that frozen surface of hers. I was trying too hard to see her, to get past those defenses. It was all too fast. Oh, Viv. Pain, where *I* come from, is common run, but there's no surface to crack, none at all."

Dr. Forestier met them at the guest-house door. "I heard you had an accident—that you had fallen," he said.

"Not exactly."

"You're limping."

"I'm all right, really."

"And how was your meeting with Jennifer?"

"It was disappointing," Vivian said.

"It was awful," Cecelia said.

Vivian shook her head. "Not that bad—Jennifer told us she had been an alcoholic for years before Africa, so at least I don't feel that my brother caused her problem. Her condition puts new light on Sister Mary's comments, too, about how the sisters

201

were selected." Forestier didn't answer. "It makes me wonder why she went into the order in the first place," Vivian continued. Forestier and Cecelia looked at each other and began to laugh. "What?"

"People go into religious life for lots of reasons. Maybe she thought she could be cured through prayer, or at least that she could find peace. We were laughing because we know that nuns are no different from anyone else; no weaker, no stronger." Cecelia looked at Forestier again. "What did *you* find out?"

"I spoke to the bookkeeper," Forestier said. "The money for Jennifer is always a postal order. The postal orders always come from three places: Coeur d'Alene, Idaho; Augusta, Maine; and Del Norte, Colorado. There was twice a confusion and the sisters received a money order meant for someone else."

"For whom?" both women asked at once.

"For a clinic in Bolivia, the Daniel Sanborn Clinic. We sent their order to them, they to us. You can see why our assumptions about you and your brother—how we could make such an error—"

"And no return address?"

"No, just the postmark."

"Viv—"

"I know. Someone is doing what *you* always wanted to do. Someone is helping the assistants."

"Do you know anyone in those places?"

"No one," Vivian said.

Cecelia shook her head. "I don't either; no one."

"Well, here is the most recent money order. You see how it's made out, with no name except the recipient."

"There's no return address," Vivian said. Out of courtesy she handed the envelope to Cecelia.

Cecelia took the envelope and looked at it for a moment. "I know who sent this," she said quietly. "Are all the envelopes like this?"

"Yes—"

"Look at this writing—like printing, like lovely printing—it's from Douglas."

"What?"

"Douglas, it's Douglas Irons like an eight-by-ten front-view photo. Look at that writing! What did I tell you, isn't that beautiful?"

Vivian looked. The writing was perfectly formed, a printlike manuscript, pleasant to read. She was, for a moment, simply and deeply grateful that Ripstein was not a part of it, Ripstein, the loyal; Ripstein, the befriender—how Vivian hated him. How she envied him.

"And you said"—Cecelia was speaking to the doctor—"that there had been a check sent here by mistake that was made out to the clinic in Bolivia—"

"Yes, the same printing. When the sisters sent back the clinic's check they wrote a letter. As the sisters had always assumed it was from Dr. Sanborn, apparently so also did the clinic. Quite a large amount the check was for; the bookkeeper had the feeling it was sent each month, like Jennifer's. Please forgive me; I'm due back in town now. Sleep well. If I do not see you again, please know what a pleasure it was to meet both of you."

They thanked him and went into the guest house. "I don't think I could face dinner tonight," Cecelia said. "I'm too full of questions and confusions."

Convent discretion saved them. Promptly at six, two sisters arrived with trays and came again at seven to pick them up. Cecelia and Vivian spent the evening quietly. Cecelia wrote postcards to the kids. She and Vivian spoke little; Vivian was seeing pictures of Daniel: a shadow behind a bedscreen watching a mother comfort a suffering child; Daniel, drunk and howling, held down by frightened students; Daniel in Jerusalem at his mother's door, unable to understand his own first language; later, standing horrified as his mother and aunt screamed obscenities at each other; Daniel looking at his cousin's burned face. The pictures were wordless, unexamined, but words were forming, meanings moving toward identity, if only she could give them room and time.

Cecelia was thinking about Douglas and the printing on the envelope. By nine o'clock they were ready to let the nuns' bell end the day.

The next morning they went to the convent library to look at the records. Vivian wasn't prepared for seeing Daniel's long, spidery handwriting. She found herself tear-blinded, and Cecelia had to read to her. "All this is valuable now," the librarian said, "to collectors. The signature itself has value, but in a letter and about his work—you can see that this would triple its worth. I suppose we should keep it specially. We have quite a few valuable signatures, you know. I think I should ask Mother about a special airtight case."

But there was little to be learned in the records. They saw the inquiry, first, second, letters back and forth, letters from the sisters in the field, pious and equivocal. Daniel's answers were short, more like the notes for a letter. In regard to the first two sisters, he used the word *neurasthenic*. The sisters, he said, were neurasthenic, high-strung, nervous with the travel and stress of camp life. Their dedication was admirable but they seemed unable to adapt easily to change. Perhaps the mother house was selecting for sensitivity rather than strength. His last letters were even more abrupt; the convent's answer, dignified and chilly. The nuns' interviews, letters, and statements were full of stylized self-criticism. Sister Mary Binchois's was a pathetic mea culpa. Cecelia snorted. "It's as bad as the stuff you hear from the psych students at Horizon House. Every language has its code, I guess. We're getting nothing here."

Before they left, the sister took them to the bequest room to see what Mother Elizabeth believed to be a chocolate set of Sèvres, made for Napoleon in 1812, which was neither 1812 nor Sèvres, but looked like a familiar Boston copy from a factory that was counterfeiting them in 1906. "Mother told us you were an expert in porcelain," the librarian said, "so we knew you would appreciate this."

"I appreciate Sèvres very much," Vivian said.

They received Jennifer's refusal of further talk. "I've already seen her trick," Jennifer had said, "the one with the chair." Dr.

Forestier was at the hospital in town. Mother Elizabeth said a formal good-bye.

The day was muggy and there was the promise of rain. They had tickets for the flight back to New York, and they stood waiting for the bus to Montreal feeling strangely raw-spirited.

"We got more than we planned to get. I don't know why I feel so sad. I keep thinking about Daniel, sitting there in secret watching that mother and child. It was the Daniel I loved and recognized, the memory of him I've come so far and waited so long to find. It was the boy I knew when we were children, still and watching, always watching. Daniel watched that peasant mother in the hospital. Then he went to Jerusalem, to his own peasant mother, with whom he couldn't speak either. He spent the rest of his life with poor people with whom he didn't or couldn't speak. Was any of it a conscious choice, I wonder."

"It must be Jennifer's pain that's making us feel so blue."

"I suppose it is."

They stood waiting. They were silent. Cecelia found a bench and Vivian walked around the depot outside. The mugginess was oppressive, but restlessness kept her moving. When she came back to the bench, Cecelia was gone. She waited for fifteen or twenty minutes, pacing up and down, when Cecelia appeared from the ticket office.

"Viv, I made a few calls. I started to think about Douglas sending that money to Jennifer, and to the clinic in Bolivia. Something went off in my brain. On a hunch, I called Horizon House. I called Marcia Spring in the office. My hunch was right. They had them, too, Viv, money orders, from Maine, Colorado, Idaho. Years of them, Viv, and I never knew. Marcia and the other girls had a whole fantasy about one of our kiddos being the secret child of some celebrity. But it was Douglas. It's been Douglas all along."

"How smart of you to think it out!"

"That's not all. I called Sam Firey. He's head of a bank in Kansas City. They gave me an award a few years ago because of his nephew. I asked him about those places, those three places—

'Sam, what do you think of when you hear the names Augusta, Maine; Del Norte, Colorado; and Coeur d'Alene, Idaho?' "

"What did he say?"

"He said . . . he laughed and then he said, 'Maybe not a grower, but a broker.' "

"What?"

"Then he said, 'Potatoes.' "

❧ 18 ❧

"Are we wise to do this? Your Mr. Irons has shown he wants to be anonymous. Look how badly it all went with Jennifer Keene because we intruded."

"That wasn't our fault, Viv. Mother Elizabeth got nervous and turned her into an exhibit. Besides, neither of us knew her. I worked with Douglas. He knows me."

"But time has passed and what my brothers said . . ."

"We'll let him decide." Cecelia got up again and left.

"I got him, Viv. I told him about you. He says he'll pick us up at the airport in Augusta."

"We'll have to change all our flight plans. How did he sound?"

"Quiet. Sad. He's done the time, Viv."

"What do you mean?"

"He's been in jail; the desertion thing. Don't ask me how I know. I knew it when he recognized my voice."

Douglas Irons was a small man, neatly articulated. Vivian could see that Cecelia wanted to lift him, to hug him to her, crying out in greeting, but she was stopped by his look. He had made himself come. He was holding himself as stiffly as a fracture patient. "Here," he said, "let me take these suitcases. The car is this way."

They followed him quietly. At the car, he stowed the suitcases in the trunk, and then he turned to them, shaking hands with Cecelia and allowing himself to be introduced to Vivian. "How do you do, Miss Sanborn; I hope you had a nice trip." His voice was a mellow baritone, surprising in a man his size; a soft voice but with ragged edges, tearing slightly at the ends of his words. At last Vivian was able to say, "It's Mrs. Eitzer, really—"

"I beg your pardon."

"Douglas—" Cecelia started.

"Let me take you to my office first. I have to make a call from there. Afterward there's a restaurant I like—it's a fish place—a shame to be here and not have fresh fish."

"Douglas, we're not here to eat. I wanted to see you again—"

"I know," he said.

"And there's the money, the two dollars you owe me and the pair of socks."

Then he did smile, a slow, shy smile. "I thought I returned those socks."

"Oh, well, yes, with the toes gone through, and stretched beyond fixing."

"And the money?"

"In Lima; the first day we landed in Peru. How soon they forget."

His laughter was mellow. "If I buy you lunch—"

"Well . . ."

On the way, Cecelia asked him about his work. He spoke of it with enthusiasm. "It's a wonderful food, the potato. Potatoes can grow in land that grows little else and in the most inhospitable climates. I belong to a group that experiments with their cultivation in less arable parts of the world and we've found—" and then he laughed. "Remember those missionaries we met in Chile? Do I sound like them?"

"Yes, you do. And still out to feed the hungry."

208

"Yes, I guess I am."

Something was weighing heavily on him; there was something in his face . . . After the stop at the office they walked to a small restaurant.

"How did you find me?" he asked. They were seated in a booth at the back of a long room. It was late for lunch and they were the only diners.

"Your goodness caught up with you the way some people's evil catches up with them," Cecelia said. "We'd been to Canada, to the convent. Your writing was on an envelope. They told me about a mix-up with Bolivia. I called Horizon House. Who else do you give money to? Where else could I have found you?"

"It's nothing," he said. "I've got money. It's a tax break for me to spend a little of it here and there."

"Potatoes!" Cecelia cried.

He smiled. "Please don't use that word as a term of reproach."

"Mr. Irons," Vivian said gently, "we've just come from hurting someone in Canada, of causing pain without giving any significant help to compensate for it. If you wish, we can finish our lunch and leave. Cecelia has found you; I've met you. The mystery is solved and we can all go on as we were."

"No," he said, "that's one thing we can't do. Something has happened to me, and I . . . maybe if you knew, it would help . . ."

"You did time, didn't you?" Cecelia said.

"Yes, I did time, but that's not the problem now."

"We're only here to thank you," Cecelia said, "to tell you what your help does at Horizon House, about the trips we take and the extras we get—the Christmas parties, the picnics."

Douglas's eyes filled with tears. He sat in silence while the tears rolled one after the other down his cheeks. He did not try to wipe them away. After long moments, he said, "It's *this*. *This* is what's been happening to me since Sanborn's death. Morning and night, anytime throughout the day, without any suggestion of a reason. Say any one of a dozen words, evoke any one of a dozen pictures, and this is what happens, tears—

209

When I see any of the Sanborn pictures or hear his name, I cry. I've told people it's an allergy, that it's being treated. I've been on the brink of it with you since you came. I cried for forty-five minutes before I picked you up and I almost broke down when I saw you. I want to tell you . . . to tell you . . ." and suddenly he rose and bolted for the men's room at the back of the restaurant, his hands before his face.

They waited. The food came. In ten minutes he returned and sat down. He inhaled something from a small squeeze bottle. "This helps; shrinks the glands so I don't swell shut."

They ate in silence for a while. Then he said, "Maybe if I go slow, with time out for visits to the men's room to sob my heart out, I can say something."

"Okay by me," Cecelia said.

"When I came back home, I turned myself in. Because I had been in combat, I did only two years. It was hard but not impossible."

"You shouldn't have had to do anything at all."

"I'd *deserted*, CeeCee. You knew that. Everyone knew it. It was lying there stinking in the middle of the camp and everyone had to walk around it. By the time I left, I was sick of the smell, the stench of it. In jail I started to think. I stopped being ashamed of what I was good at. When I got out, I got a job with a broker and started learning commodities. I got married, got a house, had a daughter. I thought I was catching up to the classmates who had once seemed so far ahead of me. I was even doing a little to pay back—sorry." His tears had come again. He held his handkerchief up to his face and was silent for some time, then coughed, used the little spray, and went on. "I was paying back in a way that pleased me. I loved the idea of the Van Zandts in Bolivia, of you in Kansas, of—well, never mind. Even Jennifer. I was happy, growing, working things out, and then—two months or so ago, I was in Colorado—in Del Norte—and I heard about Daniel Sanborn's death on the late news. I spent the next days in a kind of shock and then there was the funeral and I watched that little girl putting the wreath on his coffin. I fell apart, tears, weeping, for hours. It happened so suddenly it took me by complete surprise. Maybe it was the power of it, the suddenness of his death, or the way he died. I suppose I had always hoped I would see him again, that someday I would get a chance to explain why I did what I did, that *he* would explain, that we would—that somehow there'd be a healing, an end, something to be said about those years. It was a fantasy of mine, one I often dreamed about. The regret—that I wasn't equal to . . ."

Vivian watched the tears build again and spill over. He let them go. "Cecelia told me the first day I met her that you were the most idealistic of all the assistants, the gentlest."

"Yes," he said, "and I ran away on a single rash judgment and left her with the mess, which is a thing gentle idealists often do when they find out the world isn't the way they want it to be."

"But you'd paid—prison—"

"A man is jailed by other people than the ones he has injured. I did time for desertion from the army, not for desertion of Daniel Sanborn or for the judgment I had made of him. For whatever reason—I lie in bed, crying, night after night and I can't stop. During the day it hits me at odd times, suddenly, like a storm blowing in, tears and sobbing. I've been to Pennsylvania to see a therapist I'd had in prison. She encouraged me to write the letter I sent to you. I don't even remember what I said, but I did it sobbing like a beaten child. No one here knows about my desertion, my working with you and Sanborn, about prison. I'd put it all behind me, or thought I had, and now it's all back and not under my control—frightening, sudden. I've canceled meetings scared of it, worn glasses inside, concocted stories about allergies, more lies and more desertion. I'm sick to death of desertion."

No one spoke; they sat waiting. The plates were cleared away, the bones and the shells; Douglas had eaten next to nothing. Coffee. Did they want dessert? No, thank you.

"I watched the funeral, too," Vivian said, "watched it when I should have been there. I suddenly felt too old to venture the trip. Old age has to do with the number of people one loves who are dead. It doesn't seem to matter that the terrorists meant to kill the Archbishop and killed Daniel instead. Our family has been caught in that truth. Ask Cecelia what it's done to my brothers, how frightened they are. When you get old, your eyes get dim and you can't see things as they are. I felt old when Daniel was killed and tracing him, learning his life, has made me older. My brother Daniel, whom I thought I knew so well and whom I loved so much, was a man I didn't know at all. You saw how secret he was, how private—I always thought I could feel him beneath all the secrets. It wasn't so. My brother Daniel saw his assistants in desperate loneliness and did nothing; he refused them the simple friendships with patients that might have given them strength. He took his pain alone, giving none of it to me to share or to know—not even the facts of it, any of it, and his single friend was a man I despise. My brother left all his prize money to Jack Ripstein."

They stared. Cecelia's mouth went forward like someone blowing out a candle. Douglas shook his head and then he whispered, "Yes; yes, but still—"

"What is it?"

"You're grieving now and it makes you angry. I guess everyone wished Sanborn were different. If he had been different, he couldn't have done what he did. None of us liked Ripstein but there was no proof . . ."

"Proof of what?"

"I thought—I used to think Ripstein might be blackmailing Sanborn, using something against him."

"But what could that be—and why after his death? How could Daniel be blackmailed after he was dead?" They stared at her. "You mean a secret about himself—his reputation—something he didn't want—"

Douglas sighed. "I don't want to talk about that," he said, "but I need to talk about Ripstein, now, because everyone always avoided that part of it. He'd come and everyone would pretend he wasn't there. Except when we needed him."

"You needed Ripstein?"

"Yes."

"Why?"

"I don't know why others needed him; I'm sure they did. I know why I needed him. Sanborn told us we were leaving Vietnam. I was so grateful. I hated the heat, the rot, the stench, the guilt I felt—I thought *that* would be over when I left. The things I'd done were going to be buried "

"You mean deserting—"

"Deserting and all the lies connected with it. Then I realized I wouldn't ever be able to leave; I had no passport—I'd come over with the army. My parents didn't know and I couldn't bring myself to tell them or ask for their help in a thing like that. I had no way of getting out of the country. I went to Sanborn. He didn't seem angry. National borders never meant much to him; passports and permissions were always official nonsense, something to be circumvented if possible. He only said, 'Give that to Jack,' and the next time Ripstein came he called me in to his tent and asked me for my driver's license, which I had, and the next time he came he brought me a passport with my name and dates, picture, everything. I was grateful. I thanked him and he laughed the way he did—the way he always did. They passed me through. Ripstein was much more than a fussy guest, a pal. He brought medical supplies, but he did other things, too, lots of them. Ripstein was necessary there. Ripstein was essential."

❧ 19 ❧

Peru's mountains were high and clean. The air vibrated; the light cut like a scalpel. Released from Vietnam's wet hazes, Douglas felt he had been forgiven. The surgery part of the work still sickened him. There were times when the look of cut flesh and the smell of blood and burned bodies made him ill enough to vomit and he had to go outside and be sick behind the tent. He always drank large amounts of water on surgery days so he wouldn't get dehydrated with vomiting. He could feel the water reaching and sloshing inside him during the morning.

The guilt would only subside under a new challenge: body lice, head lice, an unplanned move, the training of difficult people, problems with interpreters. He dove into these challenges with a desperate headlong tenacity, and for a while he could forget that none of the things he did were things he would have chosen had he been free to make a choice.

His answer to the affronts of Sanborn's coldness and their isolation from the people they dealt with was tactics, order, and structure. In these mountainhold villages, he made a series of plans that got their camp quickly organized in any new place it found itself, able to see people as soon as the supplies stopped moving. He created details for all kinds of work that he instituted

214

among the local helpers. He taught and scolded and cajoled to convince all of them of the good of his plans and he tried to stifle his anguish when they didn't follow them and inefficiency resulted. He hated himself for being angry; they were so poor and so ragged, so bedeviled by fatalism and inertia.

As he came to know the problems of the Peruvian mountain people, he began to see various ways out of the poverty in which they lived. He began to write up these insights when he had a minute or two. They covered intermediate kinds of mechanization, irrigation, and storage of water and food.

At first, he thought he might show his ideas to the people themselves, to headmen, leaders in the villages, but he soon saw that the plans he was making required a capital outlay that was beyond them. There had been regional planning set up. In the larger towns there were government agencies charged with making such plans. He thought he might go to one or more of these agencies and discuss his plans with the people there. He wrote out the most complete of his ideas as well as his observations of all the groups they had seen and a description of the climate problem and took it to Sanborn.

The doctor was sitting in his tent, eating; he always ate alone, or tried to. Socializing village elders made him curse softly and viciously under his breath. "What is this?" Sanborn said, taking the paper.

"It's a plan, a study of the places we've been, the people we've seen—"

The doctor ran his eye over the papers cursorily. "I have no use for this," he said. "I'm not an agronomist."

Douglas sighed. "We fix their faces and go on and they starve and get nutritional diseases and how much good are we doing after all? How much closer to a good life are they after we've been here?"

"I didn't know I was responsible for giving them good lives," Sanborn said acidly.

"Would you let me take this to the regional agency, or when we go to Lima?"

"Definitely not."

"But why not?"

"Because we told them coming in that we were here to change faces, not lives. They don't want people's lives changed."

"Then the government is corrupt and should be gotten rid of."

"Good. Let them do it. We don't do governments; we do faces."

"Can I take this to one of their agronomists, when we go to Lima?"

"Jack sees people. You can give it to him when he comes. To no one else," and Sanborn turned away, muttering, to his meal.

So Douglas waited for three months, perfecting his ideas. By the time Ripstein arrived, Douglas's observations had filled the two school notebooks he had purchased from a peddler. It had been raining on and off for days, a cold, clinging rain; the camp was an icy mire. A photographer had come into the freezing slop to photograph Sanborn and the work. Everyone was angry and on edge, cold, wet, and slow in movements, clumsy with fatigue, and hating the water that found its way through ponchos and sweaters, down, all the body down, next to the skin. Sanborn had yelled at him twice in the common misery and exhaustion; Douglas was angry and tired and low in spirit.

Ripstein was being unloaded like an emperor on safari. Like an emperor, he dispatched people everywhere, and the life of the camp came to a halt while he ordered his orders and made disposition of his plenty—his tent, his tea, the medical supplies. Cecelia had disappeared into the farthest house. Ripstein being a guest and unphotogenic, the photographer went off to do misty mountain scenes and Douglas and the locals were left to do his bidding. He had seen Ripstein many times in Vietnam, but it had always been in passing; Douglas had been ill or busy or had slept through the arrival or had been with the river boats or nursing dying children. He had sought out Ripstein only twice—once when he had asked for, and once when he had been given, his passport. This was going to be more involved and would take the right timing.

216

Douglas waited all day while Ripstein and Sanborn conferred in Sanborn's tent and interpreters scurried out with the visitor's demands. They had stayed over the dinner hour, and afterwards Sanborn left for night rounds and Douglas went to the tent and asked if he might show his plan. "Come on in," in that heavy, too-loud voice. Douglas handed his book to Ripstein. Ripstein looked over it quickly as Sanborn had, and then said, "What is this, some kind of social plan? I thought it was about the camp, about moving or something—"

"I do the plans for moving—these are other ideas I had, ideas about poverty—" Ripstein stared at him. He went on, "—about helping the people to do better agriculture, to increase crop yields and end starvation."

Ripstein was still staring. When he finished, Ripstein shrugged. "What does that mean to us?"

"With better—"

"We don't give a rat's ass about any of this," and he flipped the book back to Douglas.

It had been a long wait. Douglas persevered. "I wanted to know if you would take the book back with you to Lima and take it to an agency—to agronomists, maybe."

"They wouldn't care," Ripstein said. "Trust me."

"But these ideas, they're—"

"You think no one ever thought about this stuff before? Grow up. No one wants it and that's why it isn't being used right now."

"But the people . . ."

"Forget it," Ripstein said. "Use it for wiping their ass."

Dismissed, Douglas left the tent with his notebook. His face was red with shame and anger. Evening meals were being made in the stone houses of the villagers nearby. Others who had been days walking to the camp with their rat-bitten children were eating at the sides of houses under the eaves. Some few who could not be accommodated had set up their stoves with a small supply of dry wood at the openings of tents. The rain had eased a little and the mist of it hung below them, raveling off the lower mountain peaks and making this place seem like a tiny

217

island in a boiling sea. Sounds were muffled, but from his small tent where he had gone to be alone, Douglas saw the light lit in Sanborn's bigger tent and heard the sound of Ripstein's coarse laughter. They were probably laughing at him.

He looked back across the space and he saw the shadows on the tent wall closing. The two of them were face to face, a closeness Sanborn permitted only in surgery. Douglas thought: faces of lovers are that close. He knew that the angles of shadows are often deceptive, that the flatness of them made them change. He knew this, yet he had already said the words in his mind. Faces of lovers are that close. And all of a sudden he was ill at what he had thought.

He had gone with Sanborn into villages, through Vietnam, Cambodia, Korea, then Ecuador, Chile, and Peru. With Sanborn—as much as Sanborn, he had suffered heat and cold, rain and snow, mist, mosquitoes, parasites, agues, and poverty, hunger, and loneliness, and the smell of blood and burns and putrefaction, but suddenly at that word, a word that had not yet been said aloud, he knew he would not stay another night as Sanborn's assistant. He also knew he could not face the man with the word. He would take fare home, take it out of the cashbox they kept in the van. He would leave a note with Cecelia, apology, not explanation. Down the mountain. Gone away.

It was too late to get his things together, now. He would need warm clothing for the trip. He would have to sleep out at night on the way down and the journey might take days. They had traveled to so many places he didn't even know where Lima was, or how far away.

He spent the night planning, his mind spinning with possibilities. The next day he got a pack together, trying to trade for something more serviceable than what he had. The rain stopped in the morning and the sun came out. They were having a surgery day and Douglas's eagerness to be gone made him clumsy. Everyone else was angry, the camp disordered. By noon, Ripstein was gone. He had left as always, without good-bye, as suddenly as he came. Cecelia, who was always out of sorts and irritable during Ripstein's visits, was even worse this time, as though she had sensed what was in Douglas's mind.

Later in the day, exhaustion overwhelmed him and he dropped things and got in the way of that photographer, Koizumi, who was trying to do pictures of the surgeries. And then he and Koizumi overturned a tray and Sanborn, who rarely spoke during surgeries, cursed and said something withering to Douglas. Koizumi began to pick up the fouled instruments. Sanborn took his mask off and barked, "This is the last one," and lifted the little patient up angrily, and handed him to Douglas muttering, "Don't drop him."

It had been a long day. Douglas went white and said nothing, but thought, "Ripstein's gone. His lover is gone and that's why he's snapping,"and he remembered a couple of GIs he knew in Vietnam who had been like that and pouted and pined in each other's absence. He took the patient and handed him on to the others and began to clean up as Sanborn sat by exhausted and depressed. Douglas was conscious of touching all these instruments, of making all these moves for the last time. A tremendous relief engulfed him. No more. No more nerving himself; no more vomiting. He thought: the next time I vomit it will be because I'm drunk, and he began to laugh and Sanborn looked at him, hawklike, and Koizumi snapped a picture.

That night he broke into the van and got the cashbox and took what he thought was fare home and enough extra to get to Lima. Cecelia caught him and tried to talk him out of what she said was another desertion. Half of what she said he didn't hear. His way had been made by two shadows on a tent wall. All he saw he had seen already. He wondered while she talked and talked, thinking that it was not his hatred of Sanborn as a homosexual that had decided this but a kind of betrayal of him with Ripstein and not in a sexual way at all. The betrayal was of all the days and the months he had worked with no encouragement, praise, or support. Cecelia had said that Sanborn didn't have it to give. Well, he was giving it to someone, wasn't he— to Ripstein, to that miserable excuse for a man. Douglas, not a homosexual, knew male jealousy for the first time. He was gone before the light woke and stretched its benediction on the places where nothing grew.

"Are you saying that Ripstein had something criminal to do with Daniel?—that he did other things for him, like getting passports and using influence to go in and out of countries easily?"

"I don't know," Douglas said, "but I know that they used to confer for hours together, that when Ripstein came, the camp, whatever phase we were in, closed down for the time Ripstein was there. There were girls for Ripstein, and he had little things for them, scarves and hats and parasols and stuffed bears, but the girls were . . . I had the feeling they were an extra. The valuable time, the real time, was the time they spent together."

It was as far as he would go. The three of them sat and stared at their empty cups. Cecelia said, "I always wondered why Ripstein was there. He hated the life, the cold, the heat, the rain. Why did he go three, four, sometimes five times a year to places he hated? I hated *him* so much I stayed away and didn't ask myself if he could have been necessary to Dan—vital to him."

"—a man like that . . ." Vivian felt the heaviness again, at the thought of the two of them.

Douglas called for more coffee and then paid the check. "I'll have to go back to the office soon," he said, "but if you are staying over, maybe we could meet again for dinner—we live here—my wife—"

"We have to watch our time," Vivian said. "Cecelia has only a few more days before she needs to be back at Horizon House, and we want to find out where Jack Ripstein is now appearing. I think we both have scores to settle."

Douglas looked troubled. "Don't," he said, "there's no need. I have a feeling he's not safe to see, that there is danger in getting too close to him."

"He owes me," Cecelia said. "I'm going to get back from him what he owes me."

"Can I talk you out of it?"

"Nope."

"Then can I do anything else for you?"

"You can take us to the airport."

His eyes filled again. "I'm sorry . . . this . . ."

"It's all right," Cecelia said. "I came here for me, not for Daniel, to thank you for Vietnam and Peru and to tell you about Stephanie and Richard, which you knew already, and about Horizon House, which you knew also, and to tell you that your decision to leave opened all these things for us. You were right to go and I was wrong to try to keep you. Cry for whatever you need to cry for, but not for any of us. Promise me."

"I'm glad you came," he said.

Vivian was calling Abner. "*Maine?* I thought it was Canada. I thought you might come . . ."

"It was Canada and I'm yearning to end this and be home and seeing you and talking about problems that don't make me doubt everything I've ever lived for and thought was real."

"You do sound tired. I want to ask you something. The kids have taken a place on Nantucket for the summer. I'll be going back to New York on Friday and then up there for a couple of weeks. I know you have work to catch up on, but what do you think about taking just one more week off or part of one anyway and coming up?"

"Won't it be difficult with your children there?"

"That's the point. I want them to meet you. We won't have to spend all our time with them, but suddenly the old plan of keeping our relationship separate from everything else in our lives seems awfully empty and hollow to me. What do you say?"

"Let me see how things are when I get home. That depends on one more thing but it won't be longer than a few days."

"Take care of yourself."

"Thanks for not calling me crazy for what I'm doing."

"Have your brothers been . . ."

"Yes."

She called Doris. "When are you coming back?" The voice sounded defensive. "Your brothers call every day and Mr. Pellegrino wants to know which color you finally chose for the new drapes. Mrs. Felder called. There are more letters."

"Anything special?"

"Yes, Father Keith—that priest who came—he wants you to call him. He says it's important."

"I will when I get back. Tell my brothers I'm fine and should be coming home in two days or three. Tell Mrs. Felder I'll be at the museum on Thursday. Tell Mr. Pellegrino the champagne color. I want you to look up a number for me. It's a number that's on the pad by the phone, not in my book. It says Jack Ripstein's agent, Sam . . . I forget the last name."

Doris put the phone down. Time went by. "Is it 'J. Rip. Agt'?"

"Yes."

"His name is Seymour Feig?"

"Yes."

"Here it is. You're sure about the champagne color? I thought you decided the dusty rose."

"Champagne."

"So I'll let him know if he calls again?"

"Yes, and thank you, Doris. I know this trip has put some pressure on you."

With the number of the agent in her hand, Vivian waited while Cecelia made the call. Feig was in. Ripstein was playing Boston.

❧ 20 ❧

They were waiting for the flight to Boston.

"Are you okay?" Cecelia's look of concern, open and with no dissembling, made Vivian want to weep. She knew she was looking worn and sad.

"I'm all right. Cecelia, your friend Douglas was saying that my brother was homosexual."

"Do you think Dan was?"

"I don't know. I never knew his friends. Maybe the ones he had were all like Ripstein and he was ashamed; maybe his tastes were so low that he couldn't bear them in the daylight himself—" The words were slow and full of exhaustion and heartsickness.

"Want some water?"

"Oh, God, Cecelia. I'm losing him! I've been here and there, finding you and all the others to find Daniel, but I'm losing *him*. Why are all those assistants wounded by the work they did, anguished and defensive and fragile, fighting old battles, or too mute with grief to fight at all? Did you see Jennifer's *face*?—and Douglas, crying like a child? That's what I'm getting, and the knowledge that Daniel might have been Ripstein's—*lover*—"

"You have no evidence of that."

"—the closeness, the fact that Ripstein was the only one

Daniel allowed in his tent, the hours they spent together, canceling everything else—"

"All true. It still doesn't prove they were lovers. Now I'm going to hurt you some more. What if Dan *was* gay? Does that change what he was as a person or what he did?"

"Don't you see how that's a betrayal by silence? It means that everything was hidden from me. It means I knew *nothing* about the only person besides my parents I thought I knew at all. It makes me feel like a dupe and a fool." She began to weep, spasms of sobbing, that worst of all social breaches: display of sorrow in public. She pushed her handkerchief into her mouth, bit down on the sobs; nothing would stop her short of strangulation. When the worst of the weeping passed, Cecelia left her and came back with coffee for both of them and they sat quietly. It was almost time to leave.

"I wasn't wounded by the work we did," Cecelia said, "and I don't think Dan San was homosexual."

Vivian drank the coffee listlessly, sighed, and then said, "Ever since Indianapolis, I've been armed for this confrontation. Now the anger's all gone and here I am without any weapon at all."

"Viv, I've got anger enough for both of us and for a passing battalion."

"If he was—if Daniel had him as a kind of lover—"

"I know Ripstein wanted to get rid of me, but it was so he could chase the girls. I know that someone like Ripstein could have both male and female lovers, but if he and Daniel had been lovers, I would have seen it in the way they looked and moved. You miss very little, living as close as we did. I would have felt it, known it somehow. Ripstein generally came only three or four times a year, and he never stayed longer than two days. They did spend hours together in Dan's tent, but it was almost always during the day, and Ripstein was always giving orders— bring me drinks, hot this and cold that—if they had been lovers, that time would have been spent more . . . privately. Ripstein would probably have gotten his women somewhere else, not spent time with Daniel chasing them. He always arrived with a big production, but his leaving—I've told you about that—

his tent and his special chair would be gone in the morning and we would know he had left. It's funny, now that I think of it, to be so loud coming and so soft going, before everyone was up. If they were lovers, Viv, they would have gone off together somewhere, which they never did. A lot more is forgiven great men in the places where we were. They could have done anything or gone anywhere and been honored all the same because they weren't breaking local laws or interfering with local society and because most of the time Daniel *was* really loved and honored where he was."

"I don't want to forget that—I'm in danger of forgetting—"

"Viv, he remade thousands of ruined faces, burned, deformed, harelips, anomalies—people whose deformities made you sick to look at them are walking around with *faces* because of Dan and what he did. Please, please don't forget that. Maybe he couldn't love individual people. His love came out in another way, to all those people. I can't think of any greater heroism in life than turning a weakness into a strength, a hole into a well. Maybe everyone wanted more from Dan than he could give. Your brothers wanted someone who would be like them, Sister Mary wanted a saint to worship, Jennifer might have wanted a loving brother, I wanted—yes, me, too, I wanted his approval, and Douglas wanted his forgiveness. Whose fault was that? How awful he must have felt, being asked all the time for things he didn't feel and couldn't give. Look what he did with what he *did* have to give—"

The plane landed, and they got a cab to a small hotel downtown. Vivian stared disconsolately out the window as the cab went through neighborhood streets, past backyards strung with washlines, and, here and there, people in fragments. The blue-gray glow of TV showed through windows. It was time for the evening news. Troops marching. Women crying at gravesides. Famine. Fire. She was aware that since Daniel's death, the noise of nations had all but faded from her consciousness.

"Are we at war somewhere in the world?" she asked Cecelia.

Cecelia laughed. "You know, half the places we stayed in were at war while we were there, and we didn't know it because we were not experiencing it ourselves and didn't have the news to tell us. The rural world has some special kinds of happiness. I don't think we're at war, but I know we're not at peace."

They were tired when they got to the hotel, but they called Ripstein's club to see if they could go that night. "Sold out," the woman said.

"What about tomorrow? The second show?" Vivian remembered her discomfort at Atlantic City. She asked the woman to hold. "Why should we subject ourselves to what that awful man sells for wit? Why don't we just come in afterward?"

"They might not let us see him," Cecelia said, "and if we wait for him outside, we may miss him." Vivian went ahead and booked the seats.

Cecelia came to her side and patted her arm. "This time I'll be with you. I want to tell him I know about every fat joke that slid me off into the convalescent tent so he could go stalking my friends. 'Hey, Cecelia, you must have gone swimming in the Bay of Bengal, Bangladesh is flooded.' 'Save the whales, hell—' "

"Stop it. That's enough."

"It's not enough. *Me! How dare he?* Instead of hitting him, I let it make me sad. Why didn't I get angry like I should have? Damn it, Viv, I've stood up operating for twenty-six hours. I've gone three days straight with only four hours' sleep. I've done without more meals in a year than most people do in their lifetimes. *This body* did those things—this body that he made fun of. And I believed him. I let him do it."

"Let's get him, then. Fact by fact."

"With that and everything else."

"Then, let's check the things we know."

"One of those things is that Ripstein saved Dan's life in the field and protected him—tried to in medical school."

"Why not? Daniel was wealthy and lonely and Ripstein might have seen a way toward that wealth."

"And the visits—? Mountains, forests—isolated villages east of nowhere—?"

"A cover, a front. Smuggling, maybe, drugs, jewelry, women—"

Outside, the sentry streetlights blazed; all the line lights of their encampment. In their room, they paced, going over everything they knew about Jack Ripstein, facts, lies, motives. Smuggling, smuggling drugs. It made sense—cocaine in South America, opium in the Far East, hashish in the Near East. And his weapons, also—ridicule of Cecelia to keep her away. Daniel couldn't have known, because to Daniel, Ripstein had brought medicine and medical supplies, coming with fanfare and leaving almost in secret. Why not in secret, having been met in the camp by a drug dealer and given the drugs or told where they were, and having paid the money?

She didn't sleep well. It was a toiling night, treading the sheets, waking and drowsing, dreaming scraps. Daniel's burned cousin and the white birds and an argument with the Archbishop in full attire. There was Douglas in Peru, but that was awake, tossing, trying to crawl back between the minefields of dreams. When she found a way again, half-dreams exploded here and there in fragments through the night. She heard Cecelia in the other bed groaning like a prisoner in her struggle to find a way through her own unlit geography.

As the dawn broke, Vivian lay trying to count Ripstein's lies—even the first one, that he did not know Daniel, when they had been students together in medical school. That he had hidden that school experience and spent his life as a saloon comic making ugly jokes that wounded people, when he should have been curing . . . and down again through the shadows into the minefield.

They woke at noon. During the night, the weather had changed. The skies were low and spat rain. Vivian had thought to take Cecelia sightseeing in Boston, but by the time they had eaten, heavy drops were pounding on the streets and raising a steam that made the world invisible. They read and watched TV and slept again.

"I wanted to see the Liberty Bell."

"That's in Philadelphia."

"Oh, dear."

By evening the rain slowed and by nine it stopped and the streets gleamed under the lights. Cecelia and Vivian got a city map and decided to walk to the club, killing time and getting in shape for the evening. "Oxygen to the brain," Cecelia said.

The streets through which they walked had a festive air even at this hour, a Saturday night in late spring. From the Common the rain smell came leafy and pungent, a smell of water-beaten flower beds and the matted layers of white webs from which mushrooms grow; a secret smell, a dank ripe smell: heaped earth in late spring.

Cecelia walked entranced. "Look at all the people! Back home they close everything down at night and the only people allowed out are drunks and safecrackers. Even the stores are open here!"

Vivian was annoyed. "Don't get happy. We don't want to let down. Think of where we're going."

"Good God, Viv, you're a pistol. Dan San must have been proud of you!"

"It was a part of me he never saw, because I never knew I had it."

The club was a room in a remodeled factory in what had been a basement. A descent. Cecelia expressed surprise that the room was so small. Vivian explained that the act needed many people at very close quarters. She had learned this at the casino in Atlantic City, where they could have had a bigger room and didn't. Understanding what was going on made her feel competent and in control. They ordered drinks. Cecelia protested the price.

"It's how the house makes its money, being small as it is."

"European porcelain isn't all you know," Cecelia said.

"Two weeks ago it was," Vivian said. They laughed.

"Close quarters. I can hardly breathe."

"You should have seen the crowd when they auctioned the La Fehr collection."

"This is no place for a claustrophobic."

"You taught me about consenting. Here it is."

The drinks came, watered. The serving stopped; the show began.

"That's not—"

"That's his warm-up." Vivian grinned at Cecelia, then leaned in and whispered into her ear. "He can be risqué but not as filthy as Ripstein. He can be funny, too, but not as funny as Ripstein."

"Where did you learn all this?"

"Oh, casinos."

Gone, as Vivian knew he would be, was the gentle Italian boy she had seen in Atlantic City. This one was a blurred copy of Ripstein, but the jokes were not delivered with Ripstein's rhythm and the manner was a little strained. Some of it was funny, though, and not all was filthy. Beside her, Cecelia was shaking with laughter. Vivian relaxed, and now and then laughed, too.

And then it was Ripstein, and both the women gaped when he bounded onto the stage with a cry of triumph for the applause and the whistles.

"Good God," Cecelia shouted into Vivian's ear, "I expected a giant, a . . . tidal wave. This is only a fat guy, not *even* as fat as I am. Why didn't I ever see that? He's not as big as the smallest of my nightmares."

Vivian nodded. Her own fear at the idea of Ripstein had diminished at the sight of him. He had once been very important to Daniel. And he had truths to tell.

"Has he gotten the money yet, I wonder?" Cecelia mused in the din.

Vivian shook her head. "Probate."

"Too bad." They giggled.

Vivian began to listen to the jokes. Most were the same but some were new and the timing very slightly different, a shade less frenetic, she thought, unless it was a difference in the audience's response, the very tiniest holding back before the laugh.

With Ripstein's power to shock diminished, Vivian was able to let go of the thread of what he was saying; her mind was on what she would first say, how they would get to see him. Now and then, she would come back on the inbound wave of the audience's laughter, to where he waited, dancing, spinning, gesturing on its shore. She thought he might tell the story he had begun to concoct for her in Atlantic City, the one featuring his relationship with Daniel, a Daniel coming out of the wilderness to see a "decent comedian" and finding the Ripper instead. There was no word of it; perhaps he had discarded the idea. Was there any idea he discarded? She sighed. He made some filthy but topical jokes about Boston, and some more about people in the state and local government, things she wondered how he knew. They were funny enough to be laughed at and applauded very vigorously. She shot a look at Cecelia, who shrugged.

At last the act was over and people began to file out. Cecelia said, "Viv, you know nightclubs, I know how to get where I want to go. Let me handle this—" She took Vivian by the arm and corraled a waiter. "Listen, we're Ripstein's cousins. We told our mom we'd say hello."

"Let me get the manager."

"Hell, you don't need to do that," she cried and, with a kind of tanklike wide assault, moved against him. He backed; she advanced, overpowering him with her body, pulling Vivian along and beginning to shout, "Cousin Jack—where are you?"

"Wait—wait—I'll take you."

She didn't slow her impetus but crowded him, moving on him as he led her. He began to try to get away more than he was trying to lead them to Ripstein's dressing room. Vivian followed, amazed, trying hard to suppress laughter. Over her shoulder Cecelia gave a quick head turn and winked. Vivian bit her lip. They came to the door. Cecelia pounded and then opened it, not waiting for anything but her own noise.

They burst in, Cecelia pulling Vivian behind her, and crying,

"Cousin Jack! Cousin Jack!" The waiter turned and fled. The dressing room was small and very crowded with the three of them and Ripstein's corpulent body. Ripstein was half-dressed, standing in his undershirt. The smell of him was heavy in the tiny room. For an instant he stood there, wide open, before recognition came, in what Vivian saw clearly was fear.

❧ 21 ❧

For the moment before recognition, everything stopped, and then they were only certain of Ripstein's look of fright. His face went dead white, his hands came up to shield—until he recognized Cecelia, so far out of context and nearly a decade older. Anger came, but it was too late to hide what they both had seen.

"What the hell are *you* doing here?" And then another pause, collecting himself, covering the fear with bluster. "I thought *you* were in a nuthouse in K.C. And *you*. What kind of idiot trick is this?" Then, to their surprise, he stopped and shook his head. "Don't you stupid dames know how dangerous this is? How long do you think I can protect you if you keep doing stupid things?"

They were stilled. They looked at him. What was this, more deception? Another lie? Ripstein was a good actor but there was something here too raw and clumsy to be acted.

"What do you mean, protect us?"

"Who in hell do you think we've been dealing with, teddy bears?"

"Wait a minute—" Cecelia cried.

"No, *you* wait. Are you so damn fat that a bullet won't go

232

through you? *She* may be dumb, but you're unbelievable. Why would you let her come within a mile of me?"

"I don't understand. I don't understand a word you're saying."

He stared at both of them. "My God, you don't, do you? Oh, Jesus," he said, "Jesus H. Christ." The words hung in the air with the smell of his body. "We have to go somewhere, then, somewhere we can talk. I couldn't get you to leave, could I, to go away, get lost and forget all this? No, I guess not. Then we'll have to talk about it, maybe figure a way to save everybody's hide."

"What kind of danger . . . *if* we're in danger . . ."

"In danger? You're damn right you're in danger."

"You mean here, now—?"

"Maybe not here, unless people knew you were coming. How many people knew?"

"No one—only your Mr. Feig—but he doesn't know it's us, I mean by name."

"Well, it's too late, anyway. You might have fixed me good and yourselves, too. We'll go out front and sit for a while. It's better than going somewhere else. They'll be cleaning up for another hour. Tell them I said it was okay. I have a drink and a sandwich here after I clean up. We'll talk. Just beat it while I wash up."

Vivian made a move to leave but Cecelia stopped her. "Do you believe him, Viv?" Vivian looked wide-eyed. "Well, don't. He's playing with us."

"I don't think so. Did you see his face when we came in?"

"He'll send us out there and then get away—"

"Are you through?" Ripstein asked. "What am I, a statue standing here sweating, waiting to get creamed while Dumb and Dumber argue about it?"

"We're not going out front while you slip out the back. We'll wait outside your door. I see there are no windows."

"Have it your own way. Just get out of here."

"Cecelia, are you sure he—"

"I'll *come* if only to tell you why you should have given me what I needed—room to operate, to do what I could—and you, Danny's big sister—didn't those Church bozos tell you that there *is* no Black Thirteen, or Black Poodle, or Black anything else? Do you still—did they let you think those bullets were for the Archbishop?"

"What do you mean?"

"I mean Danny got it because people wanted him dead. The Archbishop was a ringer. *He*'s the guy with the kick coming."

"What?"

"So they didn't tell you. Wonderful. Terrific. You dumb old broads are making a dangerous mess."

"Then *tell* us."

"Then wait outside."

"Who is after us? Just tell us that."

"That's the whole point. I don't know. I know you have to be careful and I do, too." He all but shoved them out of the tiny room.

"Do you believe him?" Cecelia asked.

"I don't know. Did you see his face? That didn't lie."

"I guess not. I guess I didn't want any more time jammed in there with him."

"I wonder how many times people say yes just to get rid of a moment they can't stand anymore."

"I'm so tired all of a sudden," Cecelia said, "and so blue. Whatever life at Horizon House was like—it seems like paradise now. I don't like this part of the country, Viv—the trees are too close together; it's unnatural. Things and people close in on you and after you've walked through, everything closes up after you. I want to go back where the craziness isn't catching, where—"

"Wait!" Vivian said.

Something had come back, memories of past conversations— details Vivian had not thoroughly assimilated. Sister Mary had spoken about soldiers rifling her possessions, Mariella about the confrontation at the camp, Cecelia about enemy groups facing one another and about the hostile governments, and suddenly there was an arc across some memory track snapping a picture in place almost with the sound of the snapping.

"Cecelia—I'll bet Ripstein has Daniel's records, Daniel's medical files. All those boxes and bundles you said he kept—the special food, the special things he took with him—" She saw the pre-dawn loading in her mind, and one or two more boxes, maybe covered with burlap or a plastic sheet—who would notice that among all his other possessions? And a pre-dawn departure—it was a strange leave-taking for someone so flamboyant. "*He* took them away with him. He gave Daniel some kind of safety by taking those records. Daniel did not send them to me. Why not? Jack Ripstein was out there and he left quietly each time, without fanfare, with all his equipment—"

"We thought that was because he was smuggling dope."

"Maybe it was; maybe *that*'s the reason for the danger we're in now, but how he kept his contact with Daniel, his entrée into places all over the world, was by protecting Daniel; medical supplies in, medical records out."

Cecelia stood in the half-light of the club room that was now closing. At a table in the back, Ripstein's drink and sandwich had been set out. Young men went about their work, putting chairs up on the tables, sweeping the floor of spilled food and drinks and wadded napkins. From the kitchen came a sound of voices and the clatter of dishes. It gave a normal homelike atmosphere to the place. A T-shirted boy came through the doors with a rack of glasses for the water bar and began setting them up. It was hard to believe it was two-thirty in the morning. Vivian watched Cecelia trying to comb her memory about the boxes of records. Where had the boxes been taken? Had she seen them carried somewhere, and when were they gone? What else was in them besides harmless medical records that could be of interest to no one, pictures of children's faces—

Ripstein came. He had washed and changed into casual clothes—a blue sportshirt and dark blue slacks. Vivian realized she had not seen him dressed casually before; he looked more vulnerable somehow, and more approachable. He sat down and began to eat the sandwich. "I don't eat between acts. I don't eat for a couple of hours before, either, so I get hungry." The boy brought a Danish and a cup of coffee. "It's hard to get good food on the road," Ripstein said.

Vivian spoke bluntly, without preamble. "You have Daniel's medical records, don't you?"

"No, not anymore."

"But you know where they are—"

"That's right."

"I want them."

"Nothing doing."

"Where are they?"

"Burned. I burned them."

"You couldn't have—the waste—"

"I did."

"But those records belonged in Daniel's room with his things, or at a medical school—Alston Fletcher said other doctors could read—"

"You still don't get it, do you? People could have been killed because of what's in those boxes and what those pictures show—"

"What are you talking about?" Cecelia's tone was scornful. "I know what was in those pictures—people's faces, front views, side views. There might be the occasional camp scene, but most of them were tight shots of people's faces."

"Torture victims, maybe? Proof of some clown's secret police methods? Tortured kids turning up when some chicken-chasing pisspot king puts in for foreign aid to a touchy country like America? City people you have documented in the villages, village people in towns? Poverty in places where our government's money was supposed to have been spent, starvation in places where there was supposed to have been food?"

"But they were for medical—"

"Who knows that? Who *knows* what those faces show, what was in the background? Tyrants get scared. They worry. When they get rich and powerful enough, they want relief from those worries. Gun-barrel relief. Where have you been—it's the history of the last forty years in Danny's part of the world."

"But Daniel is dead . . ."

"We're not. You and you and I could get killed for having them. Right now, my problem is that I don't know who killed Danny and I don't know how I could convince the killer and his buddies that the records are gone, ashes. No copies. Luckily when Danny got it, I'd just been out to see him and the last few things he had with him didn't amount to anything."

"How can you be so cold?"

"Cold?" Ripstein stopped eating. His face changed from annoyance to incredulity and then to an anger that frightened Vivian until he spoke. "Danny and I worked together for twenty-two years, and he couldn't have done *any* of it without me. I brought him out of depressions they write medical books about. I went to places God doesn't know. I got infections and fevers and parasitic diseases from being out there in the damn bushes with him. We worked the world together, the whole world. Cold? My ass!"

"Why were you there?"

"That's my business."

"There were drugs there, and women—" Cecelia said, "—all those ripe assistants . . ."

Ripstein stared at her for a long minute and then put his head back and laughed. Vivian realized that although he was a comedian, she had never heard him laugh in his performances. His laugh was engaging, an open laugh, nothing hidden. There was a boyish quality—Vivian remembered hearing about that laugh; Douglas had spoken of it ringing around the camp. To Cecelia, it had been something hateful. He was wet-eyed now; he forced himself to stop. "Oh—"and he took a drink of the coffee that was by his hand. "Honey, I could have stayed safe and gotten better nooky on Forty-second Street at three A.M. in the pouring rain."

They were quiet. Vivian could see that Cecelia was having trouble staying calm. She said, "You were in medical school with Daniel. Did you and he plan all this together then?"

Ripstein's head turned toward her. His eyes widened. Then he smiled. "So Danny blabbed."

"No. You were in the graduation picture."

"I forgot about that. I'd been careful coming and going, when and where I was seen. The people who knew about me and Danny had lots of reasons to keep quiet."

"What is all this about?" Cecelia asked. "This danger business?"

"It's about the *work*—I thought you of all people would know that. About the work."

"And what did you have to do with that? You never even saw the patients. I remember I once asked you to help with a stretcher when you were the only one around and you vanished like . . ."

". . . like the bloom of youth."

". . . like all the smutty talk, I notice, and the fat jokes. Where are they?" Cecelia was following him down with the questions they had formulated. Vivian sat silently and listened.

"There when I need them. I don't need them now. You're not the audience now."

"You sonofabitch."

"Not so fast, lady. Didn't you ever wonder how you got to be where you were, in all those places? Didn't it ever dawn on you that most people have to take national borders a little more seriously than you did, that in 1961 when you went skipping through South Asia like a pudgy Red Ridinghood, most of those poor sweet little people were at deadly war with one another? That in a war they might take a dim view of people sauntering back and forth across disputed borders? Combine your IQs for a minute and try for something higher than room temperature. You sailed back and forth down rivers between Laos and Cambodia like Cleopatra down the Nile. You've been in most of the big-time tyrannical dictatorships in the world and half the small ones. How? Did that never occur to you? No visas, no stopping off at the capitals? *Think*."

"You did that?"

"Modesty forbids," he said sarcastically.

"How did you do it?" Cecelia asked. Vivian saw she would not be balked.

"Any way I could."

"How?"

"My business, again."

"I don't believe you. You're lying."

He sighed. "What would that get me? What big reason would I have? Listen, ladies, you're in danger. I'm telling you what you need to know to get the hell out of here and go home and never see me again except for a laugh on Saturday night."

Vivian said, "Then tell us about you and Daniel; about why you were with him when you hated it so; about what *you* did in his work. You didn't operate or assist; you brought medicine and supplies but anyone could have done that; what did you do?"

"I did the people, Viv; Danny did the faces and I did the people."

"How?"

"Approaches. I got Danny into those places and out again without getting killed. I did it any way I could. I'd try the humanitarian approach first. It seldom worked. As you say, I'm a pretty gross type—not the wonderful figure of a man your brother was. My next line worked better. I made them offers—something they didn't have or couldn't get easily. We never had the money for big bribes. If we had, things might have worked out differently. Some of them wanted an enemy taken care of. We would oblige—oh, nothing physical. Let's say we compromised people, even some people who were guarded pretty closely."

"Who were these people?"

"Village headmen, chiefs of police, kahunas and local chiefs, provincial leaders, any of the bozos who get things done on the local level where influence is personal and day by day, cash and carry. Provincial people have room to get around whatever the people at the capital impose if they're careful and it's in their interest to do it. Their needs are more modest; they are used to the sweatier practical stuff, the daily stuff. We understood one another. When that failed to please, as they say, I did the other thing."

"What other thing?"

"Blackmail, extortion. It wasn't hard. The fellow in the next province usually knew where the bodies were buried, literally and figuratively. I bought information, I bribed the people who bribed the secretaries, the underlings. I wasn't any more in most cases than an evener of scores." He laughed. "I evened scores all over the world and I got Danny in wherever he wanted to go." His face had lightened. "Sometimes he was in and out before the big boys even heard about it. Why do you think we tried to keep you and the other assistants from talking to people or getting friendly? It was too dangerous. Didn't you ever wonder why you never went to the cities and especially never to capitals?"

"We were too busy to wonder."

"You were too stupid. People talk. People remember. Gifts are given. Oh, yes, and some of those dear little natives you gave trinkets to must have eaten gravel later for having had them, gravel or worse. When a hostile government gets wise and sends its goons down, there should be nothing showing; no gifts or Hershey bars from the good old U.S.A., no funny stories about how Big Cecelia taught them all the rhumba. Stories like that are sweated from some people hard, very hard."

They sat in silence for a long time. Vivian said, "You saved Daniel's life. More than once."

"Let's not get overdramatic. I did what was necessary."

"For drugs?"

"I dealt drugs, but as bribes, not as business."

"Wait," Cecelia said. "About the patients, about not giving them things, about no socializing—that was the hardest part of it all, the harshest order. It was soul-destroying. Why didn't you tell us the reasons for it?"

"Oh, that was Danny. He overestimated you. Danny knew everything about faces and nothing about people. He said he wanted you relaxed and easy and not afraid. I thought if we'd told you, you'd only have blabbed somewhere and gotten us all killed."

Vivian listened to Jack the Ripper talk about Danny. Not her

240

Daniel, or Cecelia's Dan San, not Sister Mary's Dr. Sanborn, or the Archbishop's Beloved Healer. Another Daniel; still another. Koizumi had been right. The real Daniel had died with Daniel. "Who is after you?" she asked him quietly. "Who are you afraid of?"

"I don't know, I really don't. We dealt with dozens, maybe hundreds of those clowns. A few of them might have gotten big enough to be worried about what was in those records of Danny's you were so interested in showing off. I think it's one of them. When you're powerful you want to stay that way. You get nervous. You think of what's out there to hurt you—a past, records in a box, old bribes, old blackmails. Just the fact that they once had me do a job on one of their enemies gets dangerous. I think it's someone whose stupid little deal I forgot years ago, and whose stupid little province Danny forgot years ago."

"You really think they killed Daniel, that they meant to—"

"Yes, I do, and it was stupid. Danny had no interest in politics. None at all. He didn't *care*. I wonder if that not-caring doesn't make tyrants madder than anything else."

"You said something like that to Douglas when he tried to tell you—to show you his plans—"

"What plans? Who's Douglas?"

"Douglas Irons, in Peru—the assistant who tried to—"

"Oh—" His face lit with recognition. "The deserter. That was a scream. I wanted to write that one up, it was so funny."

"You treated him cruelly."

"Oh? I got a passport for him. That other business? His plan for reforming peasant society?" Ripstein shook his head. "We had gotten walking papers three times there, death threats twice. We had a photographer nosing around taking pictures of poverty and starvation in an area that was supposed to be a model of land reform. A coup was in the works and Danny had been denounced as a spy. In the middle of this comes a turkey with a land plan to save the peasantry. The local administration, which had to be bought out *three separate times*, was already bent double trying to look the other way. They were swearing to the front

241

office we had gone already. Then the turkey *leaves*! Did he check with me when, how? He did not, and he very nearly got us all killed in that one."

"Why didn't you tell us?"

"Dumb was safe, then. Then as now. Dumb is safe. Be dumb and be safe."

"And Dan's death—"

"It caught up."

They looked at him. He was tired; it was late. Then they saw the sorrow, the grief he was too tired to hide.

❧ 22 ❧

If only he had followed his instincts, Danny might still be alive. His instincts had said no to North Africa when Danny first started. There had been bad vibes enough, warnings enough. People knew he was there who shouldn't have known. Danny had listened too late and told Jack too late and much too little, and the bribes weren't working. Danny never saw anything but what he wanted; his goal: the euphoria of moving, of surprising everyone, of the movement *he* initiated, chances *he* took, pitting himself against probability, losing himself in strangers' faces. He would say, "Make me some trouble, Jack; make me some fun," and they would go into the tent and laugh. In North Africa, they had gotten bogged down in endless desert encampments and lost their surprise and mobility.

Who had it been? Terrorism has gone international. The client could have been someone from years ago waiting for such an organization, but Danny must have been betrayed by local bullies gotten up as chiefs on the single good horse in a hundred miles. False hope. False comfort when Jack's contact's call to the Archbishop had gotten Danny away and to Málaga. Jack had been utterly unprepared for what had happened. He had never believed the story about Basque separatists. He still did not know who the killers were, or who was behind them. The target had not been the Archbishop; the target had been Danny. Danny. He still dreamed sometimes about the car they had shown on TV, the road, the mountains, about the guns and the white heat of the bullets. He kept hoping that in these dreams there would be a clue, something in memory surfacing to help him, a threat deciphered, a face seen and seen again. The faces remained covered, the dreams revealing nothing but their terror. And how badly he was missing Danny. None of the faces he would ever see again would be Danny's face, none of the welcomings, Danny's welcoming.

Jack was the son of the Wrangling Ripsteins, a wing-walking act. They staged family fights on barnstorming airplanes; they yelled and threw punches in carefully choreographed donnybrooks with flying plates and thrown pies for county fairs, movie shorts, and air shows. They died, both of them, on their way to a date in Perth Amboy, New Jersey, in a car that was hit by another car in a fog. He was seven. First his mother's sisters and brothers and then his father's, one by one, took him in. All of them were thin as soup, poor, tired, and defeated. He was a year here, a year there.

He was too big for his cousins' cast-off clothes, too loud for their small, airless rooms. In nightmares he kicked through their threadbare sheets. But he was bright and he could be funny; he made them laugh. He made the neighborhood laugh. Because he was always hungry, he stole food, and every time he was caught, he made such jokes, such tumults out of it that no one had the heart to beat him for what he had done. Finally, the grocers and bakers and the man at the candy store came out to him with what they had: "Better I should give than you should take. You make up such things, you turn my paying customers against me." By the summer he was eleven, Jackie and his cousins were roaming the city. He learned where he could go and where he could not. He perfected his effrontery. He learned to pass for Greek and Italian and Iranian; to adopt a walk, a gesture here and there, to use the demarcation phrases of each group, and he ate hugely at Greek weddings and Polish funerals and at church basements and the bar mitzvahs of strangers. He passed through school on his wits.

When he was in high school, his cousin Lenny was struck with polio. The doctor, a quiet man, came twice a day. Everyone hung on his word, his examining "*Hmmm,*" his sigh or small "Yes, yes" when he palpated, listened, tapped. Jackie was drawn to the man, the scene, the drama, in a powerful way. He was not drawn to the patient; he was frightened and embarrassed by Lenny's twisted face, his pain, the sudden deformity of his body. It was the presence of the doctor, the eyes that went toward him, the hands reaching, the whispered words, the importance of his every nod and sigh, and his frightening tools that fascinated Jackie. How gleaming were the chrome and steel that lay heavy with importance in the medical bag. The hypodermic syringe slipped so slickly into its steel casing. All eyes were on it and the hands that knew its use. Even the single piece of cotton made them rapt as lovers, watching as it rubbed the place where the needle would penetrate. They stared as at an eclipse.

Lenny's fever broke and drew away and the paralysis that had pulled him up like a marionette faded, leaving only a single muscle affected. There was only the slightest limp when he was tired. Of course they gave the credit to the doctor. Didn't the Lepinski boy downstairs have the same, exactly the same symptoms, and wasn't he right now in an iron lung, praying for death? Jack Ripstein decided to become a doctor.

The family was agog. Having been no one's child, the possibility of so marvelous a thing suddenly made him everybody's. They saved; his aunts, his uncles. They bought shares in him, made a bank account, and began to plan. Suddenly they saw that their thin blood could beat through a stronger heart than all their combined hearts and could, in some way, redeem them.

They were so completely absorbed in the struggle for survival and the struggle for Jackie's success, they paid no attention to the Nazis in Europe. There had always been pogroms back there, persecutions, roundings up. When one of the cousins suggested that money be taken from Jackie's college account to go to a refugee fund, he was waved away with scorn. "What do you think, if you get polio like Lenny did, those refugees will help you?"

Finally, in the fall of 1940, he was able to start college. But it wasn't the Nazis, it was the Japanese who, for no reason, attacked Jackie and the family's dream on December 7, 1941.

The army took him on December 20. They reached out to Brooklyn for him with the sureness of complete confidence, as though he were anyone else, as though the whole family had never had another wish for him. He was sent to Camp Croft, South Carolina, a place of which none of them had ever heard. A month later they had word that he was in the hospital, seriously injured. The army had been vague on the details. During training, the letter said, a gun had gone off. The bullet had gone into Jack's left kidney and up into the spleen. He had lost a good deal of blood. Jack never told about the barracks fights, the name-calling. Jew-boy. He lived. The family's war with life had been entered in higher books than the U.S. Army's. He returned to college in the fall of 1942.

Jack liked college; he did well. He liked medical school. For the first time in his life, he was challenged intellectually, given games he could play only by using his full mind. He liked studying the organization of the body, the cause and effect of its sufficiency, its elegant mechanics, the exchanges of its chemistry.

During the first semester of medical school, Jack was seated next to Daniel Sanborn in one of his classes. Something about Sanborn's look, gesture, hesitations of speech, something so subtle and pervasive that it could cling all the way from a forgotten childhood, told Jack that this Sanborn was a Jew. It gave his patrician airs, as Jack saw them, the quality of a joke, a *shtik*, a scam. Jack could sit and watch with amusement as Sanborn looked down over the invisible barricade of privilege. During the second semester, they were assigned with two other students to a cadaver for dissection and study. Jack was amazed at his partner's fastidiousness and delicacy. During a lung dissection, he leaned over and whispered, "So what was it before it was

Sanborn? Segal? Solomon?" He was gratified by the suddenness of Sanborn's movement, a blaze of widened eyes as Sanborn paled and then as suddenly went back to his work. "Don't worry," Jack said, in a barely heard murmur over the shining pleura that was leaving a wake behind the deft scalpel. "Your secret is my secret."

Jack liked Sanborn's pride; there were other Jews in the class—three of them besides Jack and Sanborn, and there would have been more had there not been quotas set up to contain them. The three kept their heads down and practiced what Jack had been taught but never learned: To endure, be obscure. He thought they were spineless. They accused him in his crassness, loudness, blaze, and libido of supplying validation to the other students' stereotypes of the Jew. He laughed in their faces.

At the beginning of the second year, the class found out that Sanborn was Jewish. In medical school, where teaching methods used ridicule and provocation, Sanborn never gave a wrong answer or exposed a weakness. Jack laughed back at the gibes; the others despised him, but they hated and envied Sanborn. The envy, harder to bear, exploded in near-savage ways.

When they found that he would eat anything, they gave him anything to eat, including samples from the laboratory. They fouled his work, hid it, changed it. Silently, expertly, he redid it. They replaced his dissecting equipment with dull and rusty pieces. His dissections were done anyway, perfectly. He became more cautious but never acknowledged them. Jack's pride in Sanborn grew. He began to help him actively, intercepting the plots when he could. "Jews stick together," the class said, ignoring the three others who would gladly have done without both Ripstein and Sanborn.

Slowly, Sanborn began to accept Jack's friendship, very slowly, to open up to him. In Jack's crassness was a freedom Daniel had never known. "Danny, I'm gonna flunk out. My lab work stinks." "I'll help you." They broke into the lab for three nights and worked on another cadaver and the slides until Jack could turn in a passable dissection. Neither Jack nor Danny had known friendship before. Jack's cousins and acquaintances envied him at the same time they wanted his protection and his privilege. During vacations, he still lived in the streets, eating at ethnic celebrations throughout the city, sleeping on relatives' couches, bathing in public bathhouses or train stations. At school, only Danny knew that Jack did not live in ordinary lodgings. He had found a room in the school itself, in a disused storage place in the attic. He ate from the patients' trays at the hospital and continued to live as he did even after Danny offered to share his spacious rooms with him. "I have a bedroom and a study. We can both—" "I want to be free. Besides, the girls know where I live—" Jack and Danny were too different to befriend on interest or politics. Their relationship was single and absolute, a bond made of complete acceptance and knowledge. As time went on, they came to know more about each other than anyone else ever had.

By the end of the second year, the other students knew that any trick they planned on Sanborn would have to include Ripstein as victim or exclude him as carefully from all knowledge of it. In May, two weeks before final examinations, someone got the idea of getting Sanborn drunk, and to do this by having a race which he would win. On the day of the "race," Jack was kept in the lab by what seemed like a series of coincidences, but by two o'clock Jack began to realize that something was wrong. A female student told him that something was going on in the study room in Lattner Hall. Jack went to see. As he came to the building, he heard a scream, high, piercing, and cut off in the middle. It was late Friday afternoon; the campus was nearly deserted. He ran upstairs, floor by floor.

Danny was on the floor near the stairs, being held by four frightened students. His screams were echoing through the building. What the students had done as an embarrassing joke had caused a madness they could not control. Besides, he was being heard outside and someone was sure to call the police.

Jack leaped on them and fought until he saw that Danny was beyond reason. For six hours, Jack wrestled with Danny, turning him quickly to let him vomit, being careful to position him so that he would not breathe vomit into his lungs, talking endlessly to try to get him back. When Danny was a little quieter, Jack and the Canadian, Forestier, took him to his room and tried to shower him. He had fouled himself and was unable to see or walk. No one had expected any more than the sight of the withdrawn and chilly Sanborn singing or shambling drunk or weeping over a trifle. For six more hours, Jack stood by Danny's bed while he lay shivering and gray. Jack showered him again to warm him; he worried about blindness or brain damage. Slowly, Danny quieted.

Jack stayed the weekend, sitting by Danny's bed, studying. After one of the sleeps, Danny woke with his vision and balance returned. By Sunday afternoon, he was able to eat and drink some of what Jack brought him. They never spoke of the incident or made any reference to it.

After that, the others left Sanborn in an almost complete isolation, but the friendship between Danny and Jack deepened. Danny told Jack, in his guarded, almost wordless way, about his past, his adoption, his rearing, his choice of career, his ambition to go back and find his parents and family in Jerusalem. Jack told about cousin Lenny and the decision to become a doctor. He was, he admitted, completely unfit for the profession. At the same time, he was loyal, and he hated the idea of telling this to the family for whom he and his success were the single overwhelming hope. He admitted that he had few of the compunctions other people seemed to have about lying to strangers or sex. His appetite was prodigious. He never forced anyone, but he was avid enough to begin with few preliminaries. There were girls like that, he said, and it was his mission to find as many of them as he could.

Danny told Jack, "Something is missing in me. Something was left out."

"You don't get enough loving. They say use it or lose it."

"Something else, something more."

"You're not queer, are you?"

"No, at least I don't think so. The truth is, I don't care either way. I've never been hungry the way you are. I don't burn; I never have."

"Never?"

"No; and when I need it—I take care of myself. It's simpler. Then, it's over. What I'm talking about is something more than that."

Jack was the only man Danny ever met who did not judge; he had no expectations whatever. Danny told him about the white birds and the room that opened to the sky. He told Jack that when he was fourteen he had tried to take his own life by hanging himself. He did it in the coat closet, from the bar, on a weekend he had engineered to be at home alone. "Never try that."

"And—?"

"The rope broke. I thought I would study the human body so I could control my next attempt better. The next time, I thought, I'd know a way that didn't hurt as much or fail so shamefully."

He told Jack how the study led to an interest in the workings of the body. By the time he was fifteen, he was reading anatomy and physiology books. One of his teachers said offhandedly, "You might make a good surgeon." The remark captured his imagination. It was a goal that spoke of mastery and control. And the people he dealt with would be asleep. What elemental thing that was missing, that he knew to be missing even then, would not be seen in him. "Then I decided that when I was a man I would find my way home to my own people, that I thought I could live for that, and it helped."

"Once," Danny said to Jack, "I watched them, on the wards, the families. I know I should understand why they cry, why they care. I used to think people were only acting, showing what they had been told was the right thing to show, but I've watched them secretly; I've come in on them when no one was there, and they didn't know I was watching, and they *care*. They *love;* what holds them so close to one another?"

Jack shrugged. Years on the street had made him good at figuring motives but he was not an introspective man. He didn't answer for a long time. He said, "Let's go into research, both

250

of us. Draining boils doesn't thrill me. Feeling where it hurts—
I hate all that. The smell alone . . . !"

"You like the ideas."

"I love the ideas. Who am I kidding? Research is one idea
followed by one hundred years of proving it. Six months of
that and I'd be ready for a rubber bed."

Sometimes they would take long walks together. Jack remembered one of the November evenings in Boston when they
stirred the powdering of dry leaves. The air was cold and still,
giving nothing. "Lorenz has asked me to think about his specialty," Danny said. "I could do eye surgery very well, and I
know he'd help me. I like the specialty; I've always been good
at small, intricate work."

"It gives me the jitters," Jack said. "I'd rather cut bowels if
I had to."

"What bothers me about it is that Lorenz has to *talk* to them,
to understand them . . . Lorenz *knows*."

"Knows what, for Chrissake?"

"The . . . the love business—what I've been trying to tell
you—about the love."

Jack sighed. He had gone home to Brooklyn for the Thanks-
giving weekend. He and a crowd had gone out drinking. He
had gotten up in one of the clubs, half bombed, and had begun
to talk about what it was like being in medical school. For half
an hour he had kept people laughing, clapping, wanting more,
and all the time as he was talking he was listening to himself
from some place quiet and detached and happy. That part was
saying, even as he heard them laugh, "You can do it even better.
There is a rhythm, a pace. They're all drunk and wanting to
laugh because it's free. You could make them pay to laugh. You
could take them anywhere, willingly. You could make them
go . . ."

"So, are you going to work with Lorenz?"

"I don't know; would I be able to do it the way I am, or
would I have to find out . . ."

"What?"

251

"What's missing."

Jack got through medical school by the narrowest of margins. Danny made honors in every area. Jack went to residency at Brooklyn Jewish, Danny stayed in Massachusetts. They didn't see each other, although Jack knew where Danny's house was. After a lackluster residency, Jack began, halfheartedly, to practice in Brooklyn. Except for his relatives and their few friends, his days were spent in despondent idleness in the office the family had bought and furnished. His nights were becoming his only relief. He had begun visiting clubs and variety shows, working with comedians as a paid heckler, and soon supplying acts with remarks and repartee. He began to write an act himself; then another. In this he worked easily, happily. He began to write material and practice it in the office, hoping no one would come for medical care. It seemed as though his frail family, all the stringy, phthisic men and the huge, varicosed women, had been holding their dying bodies together only until he had finished school, hanging on the moments until collapse. They were almost the only ones in his practice. They came to him groaning to lay their burdens down, their hands burled with arthritis, their hacking coughs preceding them up the stairs, their bellies tidal with the fluids of ascites. All the chronic incurable griefs: here, take this, cure it. When he told them he could do no miracles, their faces fell. They began to hate him because after all those years of school, all that knowledge for which they had paid so much money, he was willfully denying them.

His nights were nights of glowing faces, of mouths that opened to laugh, not to display disease. Arthritic hands applauded, eyes shone. And the rhythm began to beat inside him. His stroke got surer. He heard it in his own work and soon he was getting calls to do shows out of town. He got an agent.

His training in medical school had coarsened him but no more than he wished it to; his was not a gentle humor. In 1955 he played clubs in Washington, D.C., Philadelphia, and New York. That summer he went on the vacation circuit, to the mountains, the shore. He got the clap. Before he was cured of it he was using it in the act.

By 1957 he was headlining. He made a series of party records. He made $150,000. He quit medicine.

In January 1958 he was playing a club in Pacific Grove. Feig called. "There's a man here who says he needs to see you. He says he knew you in school. His name is Sanborn."

"Is he there with you?"

"He's in New York. I told him you would be in California until March."

"What did he say?"

"He said it was important; that if you fixed a date he would come out there."

"I don't have to do a date until Friday. Tell him I'll see him in front of the New York Public Library day after tomorrow—"

"What the hell's happened to you—you look like Gunga Din!"

"I've been in Tibet."

It was cold in front of the library; a hard wind was whipping people through the streets, stopping to whirl sand into their faces. Danny was even skinnier than he had been in school and his olive skin was many shades darker than Ripstein had ever seen it.

"I need your help," he said simply.

Jack grinned. This directness, at least, was not new. "To do what?"

"I want to go to Greece. I need someone who knows—what you know."

"What's that?"

"How to fix things, how to move in strange places, how to be Greek to Greeks and Italian to Italians. Someone who knows how to come and when to leave."

"You mean how to lie and cheat."

The dark face flickered with its rare smile. "I need help for what I want to do."

"What's that?"

"To be invisible, to be there and gone, to change shapes, to deal things." He laughed. It was a laugh without smiling.

"Something's happened to you. Something bad—you haven't cracked up—"

"No," and Danny told Jack how he had gone back to Jerusalem, looking for parents, home, familiar people and places. There had been nothing but poverty and misunderstanding in the filthy quarter. He had remembered no word or person. The disfigured cousin had refused his help, and his single shining memory of the white birds had been a lie. These things he said in three or four sentences.

"What happened then? You didn't try to bump yourself off again, did you?"

"No."

Jack grinned. "You always hated waste."

"Yes."

"So where did you go?"

"—to Syria, Lebanon, places I don't remember. I saw there were people in those places just like my family, poor and ignorant and burned. It helped."

Jack laughed outright. "And people who wouldn't try to shove you around because of your family." Again Danny smiled.

By this time they had walked to Grand Central Terminal and the Oyster Bar where Jack ordered a fish plate for Danny and said, "Eat that." Danny told Jack about reconstructive surgery and how he had spent two years with a group that went to various countries following wars. He had been the face man.

Jack laughed. "Couldn't take it, could you, the group."

Danny's "No" was said without either arrogance or shame. "I know what I am."

"Well, what now?"

"Working with that group—a traveling group—I saw how I could do the work—not emergency surgery, reconstructive. I could get by with two assistants, paying them minimally for the experience, and using local help, families as orderlies—I've seen it done and it works."

"Where do I fit in?"

"I want to go to Greece again; we'd been there after the quake. I want to go again and to do reconstructive."

254

"So—"

"This time I won't have any UN clout to get me in, to take me where I want to go. And of course I don't speak the language—"

"You need an interpreter—you need more than an interpreter. You need a wise guy—someone who knows who to see and what to say, somebody streetwise, scamwise—" Danny was nodding. Jack could see he was relieved and happy to have been understood. "And you think I can help you get one—"

"Can you?"

"I know someone from the old neighborhood—a Greek. He won't work for nothing, though."

"I can pay him."

"You won't need to pay him much—not if we can offer him the right kind of deal. Let me work on it a little."

The Greek trip. The first trip. Jack had found Taki easily enough. They didn't even need to pay him much more than airfare and keep. He was streetwise and spoke Greek. He had wanted to go back to Greece and see family. He also liked what Danny did. They worked for a while in Greece, moving away from trouble when necessary.

Then, Honshu, Japan, after the typhoon. The Japanese were used to an American presence. By the time Danny went to Pakistan, India, and Bangladesh, Jack knew what to do. He hired the wise guys. The wise guys told him who and how. Sometimes it was a gentle persuasion for the second-level provincial people, sometimes a delicate bribe. Jack found out who the key people were and how they could be gotten to. When Danny went to Vietnam and Korea, Jack used the drug connections that supplied both armies there. He did Iran through the Iranian students' drug contacts in the United States. That was in the sixties. By that time Jack had friends in the CIA whom he had made by doing favors when he traveled with shows in certain cities. They had contacts abroad. Three or four times a year he came out to where Danny was with news and to see how things felt.

He never understood how Danny endured it; in the rain for

days, eating local mushes and drinking rust-tasting tea. And the faces, and the endless lines of waiting people. Diarrhea, above all, and insects, itches, heat, heat cramps, cold, and chilblains. Jack always laughed when he saw Danny and the assistants. "What is it this time, red bumps? Army ants? The shivers? The shakes?" and Danny would flicker with his secret-keeper smile. "I'm doing good surgery," he would say, "new things; I'm learning all the time. Did you know that Dinaric faces have different architecture from Oriental ones and that the jaw rests differently?"

"So?"

"So let's go somewhere else."

And they kept secrets and they exulted and they laughed at the bullies and the bureaucrats for their national vanity, their flags, their borders. The prouder the chief, the more Danny wanted to get it past him. Micropolitics, precinct stuff was fun for Jack, who had no interest at all in political science or international relations. He got all the guides and interpreters. His own street wisdom had sharpened his instincts and his choices were brilliant. True, some of them stole, lied, wanted too many women. Danny found out and complained.

"So what?" Jack would say, and laugh. "Some food, some money, some skirt—it's only enough to justify their being here to themselves." Sometimes the interpreters tried to extort money from the patients. "Keep it down to the equivalent of a meal," Jack said. "They expect that. Watch them. If they get any worse, tell them you'll shame them publicly. Don't fire anyone without letting me know. Some of these *boychiklech* make very good friends but very bad enemies."

Danny couldn't understand other people's motives. The usual ones—sex, greed, power, except the power to travel freely and work as he wished—were beyond him. He was unable to look into anyone else's mind and understand what was there. Jack took nothing for granted. He told Danny about each guide and interpreter. Often he had women. He liked young girls with old husbands. Vietnam had been full of them. He had always found it easy to get them, even at home. Twice he had married, twice divorced. This was the only thing he kept from Danny, whether out of pride or to spare his friend he did not know; Danny never asked about his domestic arrangements, which was a good thing because both women testified that Jack's sudden, demanding departures were a main source of their discontent. His breakups gave Jack so much pain that he decided he would stay single and develop relationships with women like himself. He had women in all the cities he was accustomed to work. None of them knew where he went when he disappeared, as his wives had not known. The only person who knew was Mancuso, an old drug contact who helped Jack get the medical supplies he brought with him when he went to Danny. "Why do you do it?" Mancuso asked once, when Jack had come home with a parasitic problem. "What's in this for you?"

"Who knows?" Jack had said and shrugged. "The guy's a friend is one reason." He couldn't speak of the others; he didn't examine them. No one knew that after each trip, Jack went to a cemetery near Perth Amboy, New Jersey, to a mausoleum he had purchased with his first big money. There he would sit, sometimes for two hours, and give a complete report, aloud, of his trip, its details and conditions. Beneath the mausoleum were buried his parents and a baby born dead to his second wife, Louise; a daughter.

In the 1970s, Jack discovered his niche in comedy. In addition to his club act, he began performing at medical conventions, where he used his knowledge of the field in special acts. Throughout the year he did a circuit: Los Angeles, Denver, Chicago, New York, Miami to medical or forensic conventions, and smaller cities with specialties of these professions, of which there were dozens. He read and kept up easily in medicine and had then added forensics so that his humor, scatological as it was, was intimate, almost arcane. The surprise of shared recognition gave an edge to all his work; he was immensely popular in the male world of the profession, and also moderately in club circles. This made it easier for him to schedule time between gigs when he might disappear for a week, two, three weeks at a time, often returning for the next gig tired and occasionally ill. No one associated these disappearances with travel abroad, no less with pest-ridden riverbanks or isolated villages. His agent, Feig, thought he had some secret kind of problem, drinking or pills, something that made him have to regain himself for his performance dates. As long as he showed up, Feig didn't care. They made good, steady money, and with Jack's work and persona, a reputation for girl-chasing or even drinking wasn't always bad. Jack had exotic fevers twice, one almost fatal. He was in the hospital with it for three months. He told people it was two kinds of VD.

Jack tried to fix his trips when the camps would have no other visitors; if he ran into them, he played an act about dropping in between foreign bookings. He liked to appear noisily. When he left, he took all of Danny's records with him, because all of them were dangerous for Danny, recording as they did where Danny had been and whom he had seen. There was constant danger of reprisals. It was best to have as little evidence as possible. They left behind only small eddies of cut photographs and X-rays whose lines and arrows summoned strange spirits, a sprinkling of surgical equipment, wisps of wire stolen from garbage middens, and pain pills, jealously guarded and never used.

And between the fevers and the pestilential encampments, between the arguments about venal interpreters and the danger of fraternization between assistants and patients, they laughed in the richest and deepest laughter they had ever known. "What a circus!" Jack would cry at Danny's tent flap. "What a Chinese fire drill!" And he would sit down and tell the new story of how he had gotten to the man who would run the scam, and what was the planning, and who got bribed, and who got black-mailed, and where were the promises, payoffs, threats. They made it work. They danced between countries and wound around wars and when Danny got more famous the stakes went up and it got both easier and harder, with higher payoffs and visitors to protect and media people to steer away from questions.

They would sit up late in Danny's tent, and Danny would soak his feet or pick his lice or smoke the single cigarette he allowed himself a day, and they would laugh, Danny sometimes even out loud, in his oddly high whinny, at all of the upstarts and clowns, at how each one reacted, at who had fawned and who had wheedled and who had been stymied and at who had had the knife out for a friend and who had had it in his back. Mostly they laughed that the poorest of the chiefs, the most wretched of the headmen, were the most grandiose. Authority of any kind amused Danny. Sometimes he didn't laugh, but stood and shook with suppressed merriment. Jack was the only one on earth who had ever witnessed the tremors of Danny's mirth, who had ever heard his laughter.

❧ 23 ❧

And finally North Africa; Algeria, Tunisia. The trip was not occasioned, as the others had been, by wars or natural disaster. Jack had suggested they leave India and go east to the Pacific and the Philippines. Danny had said no. Islands made him nervous. North Africa had been his way of working westward. He said he was thinking about the lower part of South America, or about Central America and Mexico, where they had not yet been.

Jack had hated it from the beginning. None of the vibes were good. He got the interpreter, Modi, by luck, spotting him by his way of advancing his grandchild in the line. Modi had been a jewel, a find. He had been all across these areas as a driver, and knew everybody. The rest was a nightmare. The assistants, all of them, were kids with no street smarts and no sense about keeping away from the locals. They were as dumb and friendly as Irish setters. The camps seemed always to be bogged down, moving so slowly that second thoughts were all too easy for each little sheik in each little wadi.

Jack had increased his visits; he was uneasy, frightened even; he reached out for control as far as he could, using contacts at the State Department, underworld doctors, and influential visitors who could be trusted. Nothing worked. He heard rumors of an organizing force on the left and one on the right. Threats came from mysterious places. People who should not have known of their movements did. Jack warned Danny. Danny didn't see how dangerous it was; he kept saying, "We're moving. We're slower than I want, but this is the desert. Remember how bad it was in Bhutan? Remember those soldiers in Central Africa? Remember Prince Tuga? Ban-Pé? Remember San Agneda? Dofo?"

But this was different and Danny, blind and willful, didn't see it. Jack wasn't a worrier, or had never been before. His work was going well; there were medical conventions to which he had been coming for twenty years with a new act each time. He was free and well paid. He had the life and the women he wanted. Sylvia, with whom he was very comfortable, didn't seem to resent his need for others. Even she had begun to ask him what the trouble was, why he seemed so unsettled, starting at a sound, then lost in worry. Since the beginning of the trip— now almost two years—anxiety had risen into fear, fear into anguish. It was all wrong, and there was no one in whom he could really confide. Then one of his State Department contacts told him that his visits were causing talk. "I've got to see, to feel what's going on out there," Jack protested. "It's too dangerous," the man said. "His fame has made him a target."

"Who's doing it?"

"We don't know. These terrorist groups are pooling information now, identifying enemies. They probably think you and Sanborn are spies."

After an orthopedic convention in Salt Lake City, he met Mancuso, who had helped him before. "You're really worried," Mancuso said, "and I owe you one, which you know. Leave this to me." The Archbishop's invitation had come four days later.

Jack had breathed easier. Then it happened, and not in Africa at all, but near Málaga, safe and happy, in the Archbishop's company. He saw it on TV as he lay resting in a hotel in Denver before a show for a convention of pediatricians. He did the show afterward, cursing himself for having watched the TV before he had to go on. Afterward, he lay in bed smoking. He had sent his woman of the evening home. He wanted to cry and be rid of the awful lump in his throat, the weight in his chest. He said to the empty room, "At least I won't have to go back to those damn places. The deserts, the jungles. Ever again." Quietly, under his breath, he cursed Danny, trying to make himself cry. It didn't work. Nothing worked. Day and night for weeks, weeks of shows and women and travel, the choking sadness moved under his skin, a constant sliding, like something tidal. Only once in all that time did anyone mention Danny. A man stopped him on his way to his dressing room after the show in St. Louis. "Sorry about your friend," he said. "A nice thing, those little kids." Before Jack could see who had spoken, the man was gone. His grief was now polluted by fear and both were as secret as the triumph had been. Then the sister, Vivian, came to Atlantic City, and there was a moment he had thought he might cry—that they might cry together, but it had not been safe. The casino people had contacts God knew where. She was naive and wide open, with no idea of Danny's danger or that his murder had been no mistake. Shut her up. Send her away. Be careful. And the cry was trapped in his throat.

"One of the assistants intimated that Daniel was gay. Were you his lover?" Vivian spoke the words very softly. The club was closing; only one waiter moved in the near darkness, sweeping up.

Cecelia's mouth dropped open. Ripstein gave a tiny gasp of surprise, then put his head back and laughed. "You girls are getting sophisticated so fast I can't believe it. I'll tell you this: I don't know about Danny. I know *I'm* not. I never slept with him; I guess that's what you wanted to hear. Danny was my friend. Best friend. I got lots of buddies—drinking buddies, show biz buddies. One friend: Danny. Danny was a hero. Do you really understand what that means? Everyone wants heroes to have lots of urges—food and sex and excitement, and to have all that under control. *Just* under. What do the shrinks call it—sublimation? He stays good but he's always tempted. No hero turns anything down because it doesn't interest him. Jesus, don't they know the energy that takes?" He sighed. "You're his sister and he loved you. Besides me, you were the only person on earth he gave a damn about, so I guess if you want to know what I think, you have the right."

"Go ahead," Vivian said.

"It worried Danny a lot because he had so little feeling for people. He didn't understand what made other people tick—not the so-called bad urges, money, power, sex, revenge, hate, and not the good ones, either—love, family, honor, altruism. I loved him because he had no fake about himself; what he was or what he did."

"And what was he? What kind of man did you think he was?"

"I think Danny had almost no sex drive at all. He didn't need the control because he didn't have the urge. Did you ever think what a hell of a secret that is in a sex-driven country which, let's face it, we are. I need it. I always needed it. Danny never understood why. When he was away in the villages, he was more comfortable, less different. Danny was scared of what was missing in him, but he couldn't fix it. I liked him in school for his pride and his classiness. Afterwards, I admired him. And the laughs—God, the laughs we had! Danny used everything he was. Oh, I'm tired. It's not the company—" He called out to the man sweeping. "Yo, Luis—get me some more of this poison, will you?"

Luis shrugged, "Hey, man, the bar's closed. Have a heart—I got a home to go to."

"We have some more questions," Vivian said, "and you promised you would answer them—"

"Shoot."

"About Mary Nell . . ."

"The one who killed herself? What about her?"

"Did you—were you involved with her?"

"Involved? No. I think I asked her once. She said no. That was that. Before she bumped herself off—maybe a month, two months, she asked me to take her with me when I left. I couldn't; it would have been too dangerous. That was all."

Cecelia said, "What about Jennifer Keene—"

"Who?"

"Sister Jennifer—"

"Oh, that nun?"

"Yes, that nun."

"What about her? I kept her supplied with booze until I was trucking more booze than morphine. I told her she'd have to cut down. She made me an offer that would have been insulting if it hadn't been so ridiculous."

"Sister Mary said—"

"Oh *that* dingbat. She thought Danny was a saint. You call it schizophrenia when someone sees things that aren't there. She was phrenoschitsic—she didn't see anything that *was* there."

"You were there all right," Cecelia said, "with your fat jokes and your big orders and you weren't above rape, or attempted rape—"

"What!!"

"Peggy—"

"Don't tell me *who*, tell me *where*."

"Indonesia."

"Oh, *her*. Well, I'd had a bit to drink and I thought she'd like it, too. I was never deaf to a forceful no."

"She had to throw a net over you."

"I remember that. It would have worked with less, but I admit I might have come on a little strong. I wasn't very subtle in those days."

"Show me your arm," Vivian said, "where you got the knife wound meant for Daniel." Ripstein raised his arm. Even in the dim light, it was easy to see the long red weal running almost from elbow to wrist.

"Let me see that!" Cecelia sounded incredulous. She took Ripstein's arm and turned it into what light there was. "This isn't the thing we stitched. That was one-third the size this is!"

"I know. They think something was on the knife. It infected and reinfected. They had to go in and clean out the bone."

"How long did it take to heal?"

264

"Look, I didn't want to suffer. I don't dig suffering at all. Besides, there's worse pain than a sore arm."

Luis came to the table. "Take it home, man, we gotta close."

Ripstein yawned and stretched. "Give us five more minutes, okay? My cousins gotta leave and they came all the way from Pennsylvania to see me."

"Hurry up, then, okay?"

He looked back at them and his voice dropped. "Think what you want to think but do it at home. There's been one murder already. You"—to Cecelia—"were safe in the nuthouse. Go back there. Don't dig anybody else up. I don't know who these bozos are who killed Danny. I don't know who's following me. I got a feeling, that's all."

"You said before that Daniel was a hero to you. Why? What made him that?"

"Who knows? Who wants to talk about it, anyway. It's romantic shit. Danny never hid anything from me. The hero part? He took his yard of cloth and made a dress suit out of it and he did it with class." He shrugged, said "Hero," and gave an uneven laugh. "A hero is supposed to do what he does and hate it, to do it because he *has* to. The secret is that the ones who do it best are the ones who in some way like the risk of it, the joy of it—who do it dancing the way Danny danced on borders and played tricks on tyrants and gave people faces out of bone shreds and thin air. God, how good those good laughs were! I've been making people laugh all my life. Danny made *me* laugh. His jokes were the best there are."

Ripstein got up. He looked tired and old. He moved heavily. "It's time to go. You go ahead. I'll think of something that'll keep me here for ten, fifteen minutes."

"But . . ."

"Go," he said, "go home and cry for Danny. Commission a statue, fund a scholarship; leave everything else alone." He got up. "Hey, Luis—" he said, "is there a way to cut down the damn ventilator noises while I'm doing my act?"

❧ 24 ❧

"We've made it. Tomorrow I'll fly to K.C. and Mikey's uncle is sending someone to meet me and drive me back to Horizon House."

Vivian nodded. "I'll miss you, Cecelia."

"Two weeks," Cecelia said, "and it will take me a year before I figure all the ways I've changed."

"All of them good."

"I don't think so." They were looking at the pictures a last time together, the medical school picture. There was young Daniel and Jack Ripstein and they had just found Forestier, second row middle. Shyness gave him a truculent look, like a convict. His first name was Achille.

"Cecelia—do you really think Jack Ripstein is in danger?"

"I'm not sure, and I'm not sure whether Dan was supposed to be the victim or not. Ripstein is a liar, remember. He lied to you about not knowing Dan at first. He kept me out of his way with something like a lie. Still—some of those people in some of those places were like what he described. We did see torture victims, lots of them, and people who had moved or were moved from other places. And when he talked this time he didn't sound like the old Ripstein."

"I don't know how to take any of what he said. We should try to figure it out before you leave. I want to make some calls."

Abner said, "You sound worried. I'm glad you called now—I was just leaving."

"I *am* worried. Things have changed here, or the reality of them has changed. Doris tells me Father Keith wants to see us."

"Do you want me to postpone my trip for a day or so?"

"I'd be so grateful if you would."

"Call me when you've seen the priest."

Vivian had forgotten which of the two priests was Father Keith. He was the younger one, alert, intelligent, but less polished than the other man. "We've been trying to get in touch with you for the last week."

"I've been finding Daniel's assistants, talking to them."

"You must be worn out with all the traveling you've done."

"That's true," Vivian said, "but I've learned a great deal."

"I came to tell you what you may already know. From Málaga . . . there are rumors about . . . danger. We have already notified the police."

"Then what he—what we heard was true? Is it true that the people who attacked the Archbishop's car near Málaga might have meant to kill Daniel all along?"

The young man looked surprised, then uncomfortable. "Yes. I hesitated telling you because I—"

"Now you don't need to worry about telling me; and now I suppose it is we who owe the apology. Two of your men were killed; your Archbishop and another priest seriously injured because of my brother. The comfort should be coming the other way."

"Who told you this?"

"Jack Ripstein."

"You've seen him, then."

"Yes, twice."

"What's he like?"

267

"Like his act. He says we're in danger, but that he didn't know who was behind it."

"We've been worried for some time. There had been rumors that your brother was in difficulty. The Archbishop in Málaga had been alerted."

"And when you came here, you knew how dangerous it was; that Daniel and Jack Ripstein had bribed and blackmailed their way into some of the places they went—" He nodded. "—and you said nothing."

"We wanted to spare—there seemed no need—"

She sighed, but realized with relief that her rage was gone. "I think you were sparing yourselves."

He dropped his eyes. She thought Father Keith was like her brothers in their relationship to her. Sparing others was a euphemism for keeping control.

"Neither you nor my brothers like loose ends, do you?"

"I suppose not."

"They say they are throwing me a rescue line but a rope without a loose end can be a noose."

"It might be wise to make no more inquiries . . ."

"I'm—*we're* ready to go on with our lives. Cecelia is going back to her work. I'll be at the museums and with my clients as I was before—"

Father Keith looked relieved. "You see, there are only rumors; no one knows who these people are . . ."

"I think I have the answers I wanted. Come and meet Cecelia. Let us give you some tea and cake and tell you a little about the man my brother was, now that I know something about him."

Father Keith smiled. "So you did see to the heart of his heroism—you did trace the steps he took . . ."

"Yes and no. He was heroic and a flawed man who went to the edges of the world because he didn't belong in familiar places. He was a man to whom ordinary give-and-take and ordinary relationships were unintelligible. Most of what he was, I'll never know. Koizumi, the photographer, was right; Daniel was everyone's version of him, and a version I cannot have because he took it with him."

"You're glad you went, though . . ."

"Oh, yes! I knew that Daniel was a hero, wonderfully courageous. I didn't know that among many other things, he was a man at play, at risk, a man who loved the risk. I never dreamed I would think of Daniel with the phrase 'for the fun of it.' "

Father Keith was shaking his head as he left.

Cecelia and Vivian spent the rest of the afternoon assigning and packing Daniel's tributes to be sent to the assistants who had worked longest with him. They sent medals to the Spragues and the Jamisons, the families of the young people who had died with Daniel; to the Van Zandts in Bolivia; to Sister Mary; to Douglas. They sent plaques and scrolls to many others.

"Take this medal," Vivian said to Cecelia. It was a small medal but solid gold.

"Well—"

"You don't have to show it to anyone. Take it for my sake."

"If you'll take this one—the last one."

"I won't be able to wear it either."

"For one night we'll both wear them. Tonight we'll wear them."

"You've changed," Abner said, "but I can see how tired you are—all that traveling . . ."

"There's one more trip in us," and Vivian smiled at Cecelia. "Cecelia is going home tomorrow morning. It's a shame to be in New York and not see anything. Where can we take her? Statue of Liberty? Chinatown? The Plaza?"

Cecelia had been anxious about her meeting with Abner, but he was a courtly man, and having been told of some of her background and work, he admired her. Cecelia opened happily in his warmth. "I don't want to go touring—I guess there is something, though."

"Let us know what it is."

"Viv told me a little about what you both do—the porcelain—old and beautiful things. Could we go somewhere and look at it, and you and Viv could tell me what I'm seeing . . ."

"Sudermann!" they both cried at once.

269

"There's been quite a stir since your evaluation," Abner told Vivian, "a stir you missed. Jospe and Ranier have come out *for*, Hiller *against*. The museum has done quite well by it all. They've moved the collection to Acquisitions' main gallery and it's all been arranged to show what various authorities think."

So they went to the Metropolitan and looked at the Sudermann dinner service, Cecelia staring in delighted awe at Vivian's name and evaluation on a card which also listed the pieces she felt had been made at a later time. Abner had a more conservative view, but the disagreement was friendly and given in a bantering way. Then they walked among the other displays and collections, pointing out styles and details to Cecelia, talking and laughing, at ease. Then Abner took them to dinner at an old and quiet place, and in those calm surroundings Vivian and Cecelia summed up as they told him about Douglas, Mariella and Peggy, Jennifer Keene and Dr. Forestier, and about Jack Ripstein. Vivian described her visit to Alston Fletcher and to Sister Mary, and her stay at Horizon House.

"I'll admit I was puzzled," Abner said, "when you kept calling me from places all over the landscape, telling me we couldn't get together. It was quite a tour."

"Pilgrimage, Mother Tony called it."

"She was right."

"I don't think I could have done it without Cecelia," Vivian said, and Abner gave Cecelia a grin. Cecelia blushed. For an instant Vivian saw the girl who had gone to Deep Creek High.

"We talked a lot about Daniel," Vivian said, "and about consent, and I remembered the pictures of him, years of them, showing that unconsenting face to eyes that wouldn't see. When the priests came I was rude; I shocked my brothers by talking about the Sanbenito . . . You've never met my brothers," she said to Abner, "all these years—I guess I didn't want to show you the person they think I am. Mother and Father—well, there was a reason for that—convention, but Paul and Steven are . . . formidable."

"And has that changed because of this trip?"

"Yes, it has," Vivian said.

"And they have not seen those medals?"

"No. I don't think they ever will."

"No more trying to convince them of Daniel's worth or yours?"

"No."

Because they were tired, Abner brought them home by nine. Vivian spent some time in the parlor, reading. Across the hall in the living room, Cecelia and Doris were watching television and while they had the set turned low, every now and then a dramatic voice would rise. There was even an occasional scream. At ten-thirty Vivian went up to bed, leaving them still watching. She took a leisurely bath and began her preparations for the night. She was just settling herself in bed when the ugly-sounding upstairs buzzer went off. The sound confused her at first. The system had been put in during her father's illness, and it had not been used since. For a long moment she lay listening to it, feeling only the anxiety she had once had at that sound. Suddenly she realized they were calling her and she got up and went to the speaker by the door. "Doris?"

"It's on the news—you better get down here quick."

Hurrying was not something Vivian did well. By the time she had her robe and slippers on and her other glasses and had gotten downstairs, Doris and Cecelia were calling to her.

"They gave the headline. It means there'll be more."

"What is it?"

"It's about Ripstein, at least I think it is," Cecelia said. "These commercials will be over in a minute."

The reader of news can scan with his eye; the hearer must wait. Vivian all but trembled with frustration. Problems in the Mideast, criticism of our policy by both sides, a senator questioned. Damage by tornado in parts of the Midwest. Groups of citizens criticizing U.S. actions in Central America. An economist expressing dismay at the U.S. export-import ratio. Vivian wanted to pound the wall. Commercials. Commercials. Then it was there.

Jack Ripstein, whose comedic career included nightclub acts and convention appearances along with the popular sixties series *In Stir*, where he played the role of Cueball, was the victim of a pedestrian-automobile accident as he left the Boston nightclub where he had been performing. A witness said the 1970 blue Lincoln left the scene without stopping. Ripstein was taken to Massachusetts General Hospital, where he died late this afternoon.

A fire this morning swept a trailer park in—

They stared at each other across the space; the news flow had moved on. Vivian went and turned it off. Cecelia said, "I didn't really believe what he said about people wanting to kill Dan. I know there were deals made to get us in and get us out of those places, but Dan was a doctor, not a spy or a smuggler . . ."

"Ripstein must have been run over right after we saw him."

"I've hated him for so long I don't know what I feel."

"We were with him, Cecelia, and there were those rumors—we'll probably have to make a statement to the police."

"Should we be scared, Viv?"

"I think so. Jack Ripstein knew things and we were with him. Maybe someone was after Daniel's records. No one knows they were burned. Maybe they thought he told us something."

Cecelia said, "If they—someone suspected *that*, why kill Ripstein? Why not kill us?"

"I don't know."

Father Keith came back the next morning. "We think there may be danger, and I feel somewhat responsible because in the act of protecting you, we kept things from you. I did, your brothers did, Dr. Sanborn did, even Jack Ripstein did. Then we all wondered why you poor protected women went blundering around upsetting everything." He looked levelly at Vivian. "Is there anything you want to ask me?"

"Was Jack Ripstein's death an accident?"

"We don't know, really. The witness said that the car was a fairly old model, and that there were two or three men in it, and that it was weaving in the street. Perhaps the driver was drunk. Perhaps they only wanted to make it seem so."

"Will the police want to see us?"

"Maybe later. Did you learn where Dr. Sanborn's medical records were?"

"Burned," Vivian said. "They were dangerous."

Father Keith looked at Cecelia. "You know something about this, don't you."

Cecelia nodded and then looked down. "How did you know?"

"I guessed. It was to be expected, really."

Cecelia turned to Vivian. "We were supposed to take pictures of the patients' faces only, very tight. Front and both profiles. Pre-op, immediately post-op, and then after. But sometimes there *were* other things I took—scenes, people. I thought of us years later going over them all. I thought that some day all the assistants would have a big party. I took pictures of the lines of people, of the headmen, of the goons. I took body pictures, too, of people who came to us to get their torture injuries fixed up. Some of the time I posed people who had come in secret, standing to the side of people I was supposed to be photographing and I moved the camera to get both of them in. I was mad about the torture and in case people doubted later, I wanted to be able to have it again, and I wanted to remember the people and places later when we met years after, when Dan and all the assistants . . ."

"Got together for a big reunion?" Father Keith said.

Cecelia laughed. "Yes, at the Nobel Peace place, that's where. Where they were going to give Dan San his prize. And we would be there, all of us."

For a moment they all stared at one another and then Cecelia and Vivian began to laugh. "God bless the brain cells it takes to dream!" Cecelia said. Then she sobered. "I didn't start any of this, did I? I mean, they didn't know I was taking other pictures . . ."

"Probably not. This is more likely about what the terrorists, whoever they are, *think* is in those files rather than what actually is or isn't. Guilt breeds fear. We're not certain of a plot at all,

273

although Ripstein had apparently been worried for quite some time. I don't share your brothers' anxieties. I think your trip could have done little harm."

"I owe you an apology," Vivian said.

"Oh?"

"I was rude to you when you came after Daniel's death. I was angry at the Archbishop, I suppose, and I spoke about the Sanbenito and the Inquisition. Sorrow and anger made me rude, and I apologize."

Father Keith shook his head. He seemed embarrassed.

"What's going to happen to Jack Ripstein's body?" Cecelia asked. "Has it been claimed? Does he have any family?"

"He has family," Father Keith said. "There are cousins in Brooklyn, nieces and nephews. Actually, there are ex-wives, also. Two of them."

"Where is the funeral to be?"

"Fox's—it's in Brooklyn. Tomorrow. You should not involve yourself—we don't really know if it would be dangerous."

"And the police?"

"Let them come to you."

Vivian and Abner saw Cecelia off. The women cried a little. "I'm no good at writing," Cecelia said.

"Maybe we'll talk on the phone, then, or I'll send you a questionnaire to fill out."

"If we smudged those pictures of Dan for you—"

"I wouldn't have missed Dan San for anything."

"Take care of yourself. The world has gotten scarier than it used to be."

"Well," Abner said, "where to now? Do you want to go back home and pack and come up to Nantucket with me?"

"Yes, I do, but I can't, not for one more day. I want to go to Jack Ripstein's funeral. I didn't go to Daniel's and I want to honor the part of Ripstein that planned and plotted so that Daniel could go where he wanted."

"From what you told me that might be dangerous."

"Will you come with me?"

"Yes. Then can we go? The kids are waiting."

"It's a deal."

She looked at him. "You've changed, too," she said. "Why after all these years do you want me to meet them?"

Abner shrugged. "It's time. Time for me and, at last, time for you. I always knew your loyalties were divided. You'd get a card or a phone call or a telegram and you'd drop everything and run to your brother. It was more than that, though, because I did that when Elaine had a medical crisis or the kids, when they were younger. I thought—you seemed—too fragile. Your fragility was what attracted me at first, and then—you were too . . . I thought . . . unworldly. I was afraid you wouldn't be able to take what ordinary living dishes out. Then this quest of yours—and I couldn't help admiring your courage and tenacity. I once compared you to that Capodimante set we saw in the museum at Basel. It was so fragile, so elegant. Now I know that fine porcelain has to be tough enough to endure or we wouldn't have antiques."

"Are you calling me antique?"

"Well . . . classic."

Vivian was shocked but not surprised at the funeral's lack of decorum. Everyone talked through the prayers, but nowhere was there a hint of the energy, the loudmouthed arrogance she had heard from the Ripper. At this distance his energy seemed more bearable than it had face to face. Here, the relatives resembled the Ripper only in feature. Arthritic old female cousins sighed in their corsets, the men bleated querulously from unaccustomed collars. People walked in and out during the service coughing antiphonally, and later at the cemetery, balancing on aching limbs, they bracketed the prayers with mumbled comparisons of illness. An old man came to where Vivian and Abner stood at the edge of the group. "You didn't used to be one of the wives?" he said to her.

"An acquaintance."

"The wives didn't come. Feig, he didn't come, and from the

clubs they didn't come. Family. In the end it's family that re-members."

"I suppose that's true," Vivian said.

"I think he was in some kind of trouble, Jackie," the old man said. Vivian did not reply. The old man went on. "Detectives came. Jackie always kept secrets. A doctor, he was; did you know that?"

"Yes, I did."

"So if a doctor, why not a doctor? Why a comedian? And if a comedian, why a picture collector? And if a picture collector, why did he burn them all?"

"I think I know why. He . . ."

The old man had not heard and he went on in wonder. "Down the incinerator, boxes and boxes of them. The stink! All those chemicals on the paper. I was sick all day. You were to the apartment?"

"No," Vivian said, "I never saw him there."

"The whole wall was stacked with them, floor to ceiling, in boxes even after he had gone over them and thrown half of the stuff away."

"So he burned everything?"

"Like I'm saying—down the incinerator and everyone had to go three flights to the furnace room, me with my leg, Evy with her arm, all of us. One whole day it took, burning that stuff. I'm coughing still from it."

"I'm glad you told me; I was wondering what was going to happen to his things."

"You're not a creditor—"

"Oh, no! We were even, all paid up."

The old man looked sheepish. "The funny thing is, now we took those goddamn boxes away, we hear all the noises from the next apartment. Fights, lovemaking, you wouldn't be-lieve it."

"The boxes were a kind of insulation, then?"

"That's right. Evy used to complain all the time, the room those boxes took. Still, they protected us—"

"I guess they did," Vivian said.

"Jackie was a good nephew, really. Loyal."

"Consenting," Vivian said.

"You know him from his work?"

"Not his comedy. Your nephew and my brother were best friends. Those boxes of pictures belonged to my brother."

The old man moved back a step. "You can't sue us," he said. "We didn't know whose they were!"

Abner said, "Has anyone come asking about them?"

"A couple of men—"

"You said they had been burned?"

"Sure—"

"Good. They served their purpose; they're gone."

"Up in smoke. Best friends, you said?"

"Yes."

"And your brother's name?"

"Daniel—Danny."

"No—he never spoke about him."

They were reciting Kaddish at the graveside. The old man turned from them into the prayer.